# the rerun of dracula

## a novel by
## ben ohmart

BearManor
Media

Albany, Georgia

Published in the USA by:
BearManor Media
PO Box 1129
Duncan, OK 73534-1129
www.BearManorMedia.com

ISBN 1-59393-381-9

Printed in the United States of America

Design and Layout by Allan T. Duffin.

# the rerun of dracula

*For Lance Hendriksen,*
*My choice to play Vlad*

# chapter 1

He had this long, wide brown cigar under his nose that was hair. Weirdest stash I've ever seen. You want to roll it for crispness between your fingers. I seriously thought he was a comedian, with those bulging eyes, something out of Jerry Colonna, and I immediately looked around the room, counting up my windows. Wondering which one the camera was filming through. I mean, he was too *serious* to be real.

Intense.

Like he was going to have his own earthquake, any moment.

A tinge of pity dripped out of me for a second. I felt really sorry for the guy who was so obviously walking around funny yet clearly had no clue.

On his head, a flat, soft brown hat folded over into itself, the kind you'd see young Brits drive off in, in the 1930s. A half-cape that a moment later you realize is just a fan of long, beautiful (again) brown hair weeding over those straight, broad shoulders. And a Dracula cape under that. Black eyes. Bell-bottom Levi's. An orange-tinted, short-sleeve t-shirt on which was written, "Destiny," and no potbelly to pull it over. In pretty good shape, actually. Maybe 56. 57. He glowed what I can only describe as a surreal complexion. And wore high David Bowie shoes left over from the 1970s. These I stared at. Just the extra second.

"Gath Wein," I said, standing, shaking his power grip.

His eyes smiled back as he regally intoned, "Call me Vlad." No accent. Maybe a native Floridian.

Damn controlled.

"Please. Sit." He sat in my short leather chair, taking his superhuman posture to the next level. "What can I do for you?" I checked Celia's note. "You're having some trouble with identity theft, I believe?"

His lips *could* smile. "Yes." That was it for the moment.

I smiled and said, "What can I do you for?"

With that, his face just broke out into a big grin. His cheeks curved in, I could see his teeth—no black or gold fillings—and it turned him downright handsome. Like I was the wedding photographer, he stared at me.

It was *hard* not to laugh at that face. At that moment. With that stash.

Very hard.

"I want to come home with you," he said.

That did it. And I was *laughing*. And he was smiling, so that was good. The trouble with working for yourself and not having the budget for a bigtime office is that you don't have your own screener like a lot of these Something & Something & Something Jr.'s have, so you have to take whatever comes in off the street and hope it doesn't plug you one.

"How's tonight?" he asked.

I was skidding to a halt in my laugh, getting ready to park on a high condescending note, when he upped and plunked more than my house was worth, in cash, down on my desk, between the daily planner and the keyboard. My condescension turned to a giddy, girly laugh. Not crisp bundles, just loose fifties, mostly. A *lot* of fifties. Various degrees of freshness, all sparklingly real, I thought. But what did I know of fifties?

"Please," and he spread his hand out as if to say *you may touch*.

I touched.

Felt real. Smelled—well, I didn't know what real smelled like. *Seemed* real. Different dates and serial numbers and everything. So then of course my mind went to—

"I assure you," he said, reading my mind, "they are not stolen."

I offered him a, I hoped, winning smile, and said, "You mind if I…" and I let it hang there, and picked up the phone.

Celia came in, already half laughing, I guessed from the thought of *that face* in my office. To her credit, she never laughed in the room. Thank god.

"Celia, would you mind taking a couple of these..."

"I'll take 'em all!" she said, impersonating my own giddiness. Contagious.

I smiled at Vlad, and said to the other, "Do a quick check on a couple of these bills, please. Celia. Thanks."

It was hard getting her out of the room. With just a couple bills, I mean. She went, smiling wider than normal. Ready to laugh, holding it, again. A professional.

I just noticed that the weird guy was standing, facing the one window in the room which looked out into Tallahassee's main thoroughfare. Just tourists or deadbeats now. Too early in the day for students and government cars.

I got up, joined him looking out. Looked at my watch. 4:37, afternoon. I didn't feel like pressuring him—that would be like trying to strong arm boiling water, I figured—but...

That's when he looked at me. Straight in the eyes. Like he was reading the *fine print* behind my skull, on the wall.

It seemed to take forever.

Or,

it was like a dream, really.

I felt myself hazy or thirsty or sleepy, I couldn't tell which. Really *strange*. And I said so.

"Come on," he said and put his arm around me. And led me out. Somehow, it got to be after 5:30. Celia must've seeped into the inching traffic that would soon greet *us*. I was too sleepy to be bored. Or behind the wheel.

"Come on," I heard him say again, and somehow, there we were. In the food court of the Tallahassee Mall, which is as far away from the gov't section as you can be and still be in Tallahassee, and I had *no* memory of any of this.

We were sitting down in front of a six-inch Subway Club. He was drinking from a cup of something clear and sparkling, staring at me again. But his eyes weren't extra *wide* eyes this time.

I looked at my sandwich. "What is this?"

"A Club sub," he said. "Bacon, too. No cheese. Cheese sucks."

*Cheese sucks*? Two words I never would have guessed could come out of that mouth.

All right. Now I was getting scared. Blow the money. Blow the client. This was unreal.

As if sensing my panicking thoughts, he said slowly, softly, "You need your nourishment if we are to get you home. You needn't eat all or part of the pizza. Merely say—"

"What pizza?"

His mouth formed an O, like some bushy fish. And for the first time in this whole elongated day, I was glad to be with someone who was walking around funny. It suddenly put me at ease.

A bit.

"You ordered a large pepperoni from Hungry Howie's which we shall pick up on the way," he explained.

"Did I?" The mall was in a fog.

He nodded. "The good thing about children and pizza is that left to themselves, there will be no pizza."

Whatever *that* meant. I started chowing down on the Club. I *was* famished. Of course. It was almost 6. But I forced myself to eat slowly. Stalling—

*Children.*

I looked at him as I ate. With a lawyer eye this time. Forgetting the money or the magic. I ate and thought.

He looked at the FSU girls and the fat Florida grandmas forever in shorts and unnecessary visors.

Near the end of settling my stomach, and saving room for a piece of pizza myself, I said, carefully, "You know I can't take you home with me."

"Oh, I know," he said vaguely. He stared at boys and girls alike.

"It was a joke, right?"

He looked at me, and smiled at me, and went back to watching a group of hot stuff.

I prodded, "You want to tell me a little more about it?" and still finished my club.

"We have time," he said, still not looking at me.

"Look." I turned his chair to face me. *Getting tired of this.* "Look. I've got a really full schedule this week. I need to know more about what you expect me to do for you. I need to know if I can *help* you."

His eyes grew cloudy. "Oh, you can."

Somehow we ended up at my house. I was frantic. It was like I was sleepwalking and woke myself up with a knock at the door. My door. *My* knock.

I was almost *screaming* at him—but silently, so I wouldn't worry anyone—like, nearly jumping up and down frantic. I could not *believe* this situation!

Medge opened quickly. Perky from starvation, she really just grabbed the pizza from me and rushed back in the house, down the hall. It was all I could do to conceal my intense desperation from her when that door bolted open; not that she would've noticed. I could hear her and Doll already screaming with delight and hunger pains, plates scrapping, yelling for the knife, and last on the list, "Hi, Daddy!"

I still wasn't sure if I wanted to cross the threshold of my own life, with this... this man who was somehow here. That I brought?

"I don't know you!" I scream-whispered.

He just looked at me.

I *so* expected him to roll his crazy eyes. And he didn't.

"What took you so *long*?" Medge yelled. Delighted. Saliva going strong.

I was pointing at Vlad's chest. I had to say something, so I screamed back, "Traffic!" Then quietly I told him, "You just watch yourself! Some things money can't buy!" And I poked him.

"You have that right," he said, following me in.

*I have that right*, I scoffed to myself. *Cheese sucks*. God.

Moving into the hall was like being surrounded with quicksand and snakes. I must have looked like a criminal. God, I felt so...wary. Because I didn't know *why* I was leading him in.

Vlad slapped my back once and said, "Come on, Gath. I am really not going to kill them. Ever." And he led the way into the living room like he owned the joint.

There they were. My happy family, in the throws of pizza. Heaven was ours. Medge had that you're forgiven face, and Doll did nothing but chomp and watch Hanna Montana take her wig off. The TV was loud, so I had to say it twice: "Darling, this is Vlad. We've got some very important work to discuss. I'll see you soon, okay?"

I grabbed a piece that had more pepperoni than the others and tried to usher Vlad into the next room. It was like moving a tree. He wanted a piece of pizza. So he got one.

Then he walked. If I was pushing it did no good. But I wanted to *feel* I had some control. We got into my dinky office, which no one but me ever goes in. Until today. Of course Doll can interrupt me anytime, and Medge gives the best hand massages right in this chair. But today, I didn't care. Vlad could have the chair. I just needed the answers.

"Okay." Dead serious. "This doesn't go further. Not a step further. Nothing." He was trying to eat. "Okay." I let him eat half. "Not a step further until I get some answers."

He nodded, like I'd caught him at the end of a mystery.

"I understand your point of view."

"Great."

"Your concern for your family is touching."

"Wonderful."

"It is part of why I wanted to be here." He finished the piece, and just like me, he wasn't a crust eater.

"Who are you?" I asked, with nearly my whole being. It gushed out like an upturned bathtub.

There was a pause. A twinkle in his eye? I could rarely get past the mustache.

"Before I tell you that, I'd like the benefit of your doubt."

That was good. I laughed. "Okay."

He was always serious. "It's *important*."

I sat back against my tallest bookcase and put on my attorney-client privilege face. "I promise to listen without prejudice."

"Well," he smirked, "I hardly expect that. But without too many interruptions."

"Just to say your name?"

"Like that."

Scolded. "Okay."

"Let me preface my statement by saying that I know you will not believe me. Do you mind if I smoke?"

I did mind. But figured it would get to the meat quicker. I nodded.

He did smoke. He just didn't use a cigarette or a pipe or a match or anything.

I admit, his words were lost on me as he said something like, "I am Count Dracula. Actually, I am Vlad Tepes. Vlad the Impaler, as you might say. I was born in 1430, though most current texts have it amiss. To be fair, most of the best sources indicate that there is an approximation on my birthdate, and those I applaud."

Anyone who has ever been in a car accident or... rushed at the cement wall right below you as you bungee or come close to a shark, you will understand shock. It is more than paralyzing. It is like an out of body experience where only 1% of your brain works. Like that part of a dream that's most vivid, at the same time that someone is trying to wake you up.

*The shock.*

Of being in the same room, for the first time in my life—never mind all the criminals I've passed on or tried to defend—of someone truly *crazy*. Or dangerous. It didn't matter. To me, they were both the same. And here was one of them right here before me. So *close*. So close to the people I love. A crazy with a smoke machine up his t-shirt. Somehow.

He snapped his fingers.

"Mmm?"

A soft knock on the office door. I looked at it dumbly.

I looked back at him. "I think I heard some of that," I told him, like I was speaking like a child.

A soft knock again.

Removing my intertwining legs from beneath me, I took my confused time getting to my feet. Then I ran like a firehose to the door.

Medge whispered, "I'm sorry, honey, but that show's on and you're being paged." Paged by Doll wanting me to watch it with her, I knew. I could only look at Medge's petite nose. Thinking that I really didn't know *who* she was, but she was kind of attractive. Shock. "Doll wants to know if you'll—"

"I don't know," and I shut the door on her, slowly, but rudely, I knew. But there was nothing else to do.

Slowly I turned... He was still sitting there. No smoke in the room. *At all.*

He glowered. Like someone who's just read a will to a group of people. No self-satisfaction there.

"Did...you—?"

I tried to point, but had nowhere to point, really.

He raised his eyebrows and said, "I realize I cannot buy your belief. That's fine. I could control you, but that limits creativity. Actually, it demolishes it. But that's okay. Come into the bathroom, Gath."

And somehow we were in the bathroom. I remember walking. But it was like through a wall or a cloud. Something. We were just... there.

He pointed at the mirror. The stereotype was right. He wasn't there at all. Don't let them tell you stereotypes don't work.

I guess I must've fainted.

First time in my life.

There was sunlight, and there was music—the Henry Mancini I always put on repeat play in Windows Media Player. All night. Every night. It always steams through my house eloquently, bouncing up from the hardwood floors. You've never gone to sleep until "It Had Better Be Tonight" sambas through a crack in the door. Medge had long since accepted my personal quirk of finding quiet *deafly* loud. So I was always, always playing tunes. I guess it was growing up in a city that makes total silence just too…there's this buzz of fuzz I get in my ear. *Loud.* They say knowing you're weird is half the fight.

I heard a couple clicks and quietly Ratt came through the computer speakers. *Dancing Undercover.* As usual.

It took me a minute to calm. Okay, minutes. Eventually I got my heart rate down to where it should be. I picked a point on the wall and I stared at it. A doctor testified for me once that if you want your witness calm, you have him focus on something mundane until that focus is the only thing in his mind. Then, and only then, could you move on. There was nothing more mundane than staring at my FSU degree.

Safe. Dreams already fading. Not a care in the world. *Dreams?*

A caress of my stubbly jaw, a thumb in my tiny bald spot and a blender toss of my hair, a kiss on the tip of my pointed nose, and she was gone, without a word. Early for her.

It was surreal. *Had I been home last night? Was that Medge, in my memory, kissing the tip of my nose?*

No. It had just happened.

I was home. In my home office. Medge had just come in and left.

Ten more minutes. Staring at the wall. So fuzzy, still.

Then it all drained back, and my eyes popped open.

Dracula.

*Dracula?!*

My eyes finished boiling, and I laughed. And laughed and laughed and laughed until I coughed. It was *funny.*

I don't know why the image of Dracula popped into my head, and stayed there. He didn't *look* like Dracula. He didn't sound like him.

It was funny in the shower. It was funny over scrambled eggs. But they were crude because I can't fix scrambled eggs. They always get hard and old before they're even out the pan.

Quiet in the house for a change. Me being last in. Unusually. Quiet. Except for me laughing.

It was funny in the car. Even all the red lights had a charm that morning, and traffic was quite separate from me even though I was thigh deep in it.

And it was funny when I said, "Hi, Celia."

"What's wrong with you?" she said, computer typing, catching my smile, like a yawn.

"An experience!" I yelled, going in.

That's what it had been. An *experience*.

I slapped a file down on the desk and went right to the window, wondering what bird was going to sing first. Blue jay? It was the first one yesterday.

A knock on the door. I like a sec who waits to hear "come in."

"Come in."

In she came, laying down transcriptions for the D'lak case. Putting the terminal dispute in front of me to sign; an impossible case: a lady of 17 and wealth was taking on her bank for stiffing her on twenty bucks at the cash machine. I signed. And like it was the best and last thing, Celia said, "Oh, and those fifties yesterday? Were *real*."

Shock.

When I awoke I was in a movie theatre. The $3 one next to the hair cut place. The whole strip mall, if people still call them that, was about 20 years old and still next to godliness. They make their money on the popcorn—I know, because I looked into it, curious, after some student fool had come in, all heated, wanting to know if she could sue the Carmike in Tifton, GA for not letting her bring in chocolate covered raisins. "Drinks are fine," she said, "because a friend of mine has to take pills for migraines, so they can't stop you from doing that. But suppose I have diabetes, and I *need* chocolate and can't afford *their* prices?"

What was playing? It was hard to tell. My eyes were sleepy like fuzzy, and there was hardly anyone in the place. Except Vlad. Right next to me. I could smell butter on him. He was smiling.

Long ago I'd learned to roll with everything. You never know when whoever is going to blast crazy, so don't confront anyone, don't complain against the weather, there's *nothing* you can do.

I grabbed a fist full of the oily stuff in his lap. Stuffed my mouth and said, "What are we watching?"

"*Final Destination 4*," he said, laughing at fate catching up with someone young and toned.

It was more interesting to watch him watch. His eyes were alive. The intensity that permeates his whole being, usually, was out like a light. Or flickering. He got actually *excited* at seeing the deaths—which *were* clever.

"You needed a day off anyway," he said softly, never moving his eyes off the escalator victims.

"How long have I been here?"

"It's half over, sorry."

"You brought me here."

He nodded. "You like movies?"

"Who doesn't?"

I went for more popcorn, but he pulled away. Pointed. Seems like I had my own. Cold and greasy and delicious. I chomped and tried escapism. I tried not to worry.

"This is supposed to be in 3-D," he said, crunching his teeth together. "Does this theatre suck?"

I think it was an honest question, not rhetorical. Mostly I was just watching him. His stash was getting quite yellow. His cape was draped over the empty chair next to him, he had his feet up on the seat in front, like a teen. There was laughter from the back. I turned to look. About 5 witnesses in this place—if I needed them—none of them witnessing me.

"The younger you are, the further back you want to sit," he said wistfully. There was a lull in the action that I didn't catch, so he looked at me finally. "Rested?"

Confused, definitely. But I had to admit, "Yeah."

"I love movies. I did not used to. It took me about 12 years of them for me to appreciate what they do for you. Then I saw *Girl Shy*, and I could not stop laughing."

"What's that?"

"Harold Lloyd at his best. There was nothing much doing that night, so I followed this lovely throat into a Seattle all-night cinema. She was dour. She was really lonely looking. Perhaps she had had a bad date or a breakup, anyway, she was hardly interested in the picture, and we were the only ones there. Perfect. I ate. I drank. I stayed for the show and I was hooked."

He went back to watching, and I went back to my puzzle. Seems…like I'd heard of that Lloyd name before. What I was really working on was the eating and drinking, something about that…

"Throat—"

He shushed me through some action scene, so I fixed my eyes ahead and *tried* to enjoy the spectacle of blood and screaming. It was—

He was talking to me. He snapped his fingers. "Gath." He smiled when my eyes came back to him. "This is all I need to see. I've seen it before. We can talk."

"Huh?"

"Time to get down to it."

"Yeah?"

"You think Dracula is a literary figure," he said. "That's fine. Read the book. I'll answer any questions. Throw me any test, that's fine. I'll do so in court, too."

"Do what in court?"

He took a small mirror out of his jeans pocket and shinned it dimly into his face. I could hardly see anything, so dark in here.

"See that? Nothing!" He had a face like he'd just scored the winning goal.

"I can't see a thing."

Out of his back pocket he brought out a gun. *Damn.* My knuckles went white, the hair on my chest started to sweat. It always started there when I got nervous. *Really* nervous now.

And he handed to me. "You can shoot me anytime you want."

I stared at the weapon.

Until the credits came.

I had to laugh.

# chapter 2

Somehow, we were out back? In an alley? Could've been the theatre's alley. It was dripping with night. Couldn't see a thing when my fuzzies opened, and then I felt the weight of the gun in my butter slick hands. Eventually I saw the heaviness, the gun, and I tried to cat my eyes to pick out the dumpster. The other dumpster. The wall of bricks. The nothing and no one around.

"Whenever you're ready," the voice said.

I spun around. I was on fire. Mind racing. Scared to death, past death, beyond anything I'd ever experienced, even the time that midget hooker set me up. This was *crazy*.

I threw the gun away and stalked off.

Suddenly…

He was there at my side, like he flew to me, walking along, keeping the pace easy. My anger was compelling. And driving me.

And the next thing I knew, we were back at it. Me with the gun in my hand. Him on the other side against the dark wall. Waiting for something. I could just make him out this time.

I stalked off.

About the fourth time I awoke from the haze, I just fell to my knees and whined. "What do you want from me?"

"Oh, Gath," he said, a great impression of being concerned! "I'm just trying to prove myself to you. You don't have to shoot me."

"Thanks." I was out of breath.

He was bored or something. "You could just contemplate how this is happening over and over again instead."

That was a point. And I woke me up.

The *fourth time*? How was this—

Suddenly I straightened up, suddenly terrified. I searched around for the gun. Couldn't find the bloody—

"I think it's by the Filet-o-Fish," he helped.

So it was. Tartar sauce from the wrapper was on it. I tried to clean off the trigger with my shirt.

"Woah, woah," and he was suddenly there beside me. Careful, his thoughts seemed to say, eyes boring in me.

He put the gun right up to his chest, and smiled at me.

I didn't know what to do. My face must've been blanked.

He looked at me like I'd insulted him. "Do you want to look at the mirror again?"

"Look," I said, exhausted. "What do you *want* from me? Just leave me alone."

"I could I suppose," he said thoughtfully. "But I figured you could use a couple million."

"Million what?"

"Dollars of course." That woke me up a second time. "More than that, of course." And stupidly, more to himself: "Obviously."

My eyes shriveled down like Celia said they do when I'm being bullshat. "From where?"

He sighed up, and let it go. "Okay, here's the pitch, like they do selling screenplays."

He took the gun from my hand and shot himself in the head. It exploded out of the other side of him, him still standing there, talking to me, whatever he was saying about copyrights.

I was probably jumping up and down, going absurdly crazy, hearing the dogs in the nearby backyards reacting, then suddenly, I was intensely calm. No more raised heartbeat thumped through my spliced, killing-me-mind. No dogs barking.

A blip in time. That was happening more and too much more lately. I struggled. I struggled just to keep from crying, shouting.

And he was talking again, maybe the same talk as before, I don't know, but I found myself catching bits of it.

"I know *The Deer Hunter* did that quite well, but come look at the hole in my head."

I did, and he stuck a long thin guitar player's finger through where his brains should've been, and

there was that blip in time again. He'd somehow stolen my reaction to that… yucking… horrifying thing that was already a stored memory. I didn't need to scream, didn't *want* to scream. It was just, somehow, *over*. Like a dream gone in your morning shower.

He was talking, "…as many times as it takes…that's okay." I only caught glimpses of his speech, which was doing a good impression of avuncular empathy. Like he wanted me to understand. Like I was a victim.

and that blip again, and he was saying, "…only recently for me, of course. But I love them. I sat with Keaton on the set of *Our Hospitality*, and he laughed and laughed, with a full open mouth! They took a picture of it." My stomach rumbled, and somehow I knew it was later, even later than I *thought* it was a moment ago. "…anywhere. Not in any book you'll see. I am miffed at what's left. Even a small percentage of silents themselves remain. Not that it matters if they found the photo!" He was suddenly angry, kicking up a clump of dust-clay that had been happily on its way to being mud.

Trying to slow the words, just for a moment, to capture them, I just held up my limp hand and said, "What is happening here?"

I caught him in the middle of a story, so he blinked. "What's what?"

"What's *happening* to me?" Serious. "Where is the time going?"

He understood. He came as close to a smirk as he was ever going to get without actually *moving* any part of his face.

"It is one more loop of proof," he said. "I am guiding you out of your haze. Read your Stoker. You'll see I can do this. I can furnish you a hundred proofs of—that is a figure of speech—I can answer questions of history from which I was personally involved, though it will have to be more in the general realm of personality and scope, that is, the *tone* of the era. I haven't not met Napoleon, and while I think Mel Brooks as the 2,000-year-old is quite mirthful, he could not meet everyone. It would require a car."

"What are you *talking* about?"

"I want to make it clear," he said in his usual serious tone, high-pitched though it was, "that I am not a history professor or John Jakes, whatever I may say."

As if I was calling into a fog: "Who is John Jakes?"

"He wrote *North and South*, and several other things that became TV mini-series. How I despise television, the cheapness and shakiness of its camera."

He was going on and on like that until I discovered we were in a car, and I was driving. I didn't know how this was happening, how I could concentrate on the oncoming lights blaring at my weak eyes, so I only caught bits of some of his ranting. His favorite films were *After the Thin Man* and *The Gay Falcon* and that Wallace and Gromit flick I'd taken Doll to see at the $3 place back when it was $2.50. Really, it was all just a blur, audio and all, splurging into a nasty headache and squinting eyes and fatigue and stiff shoulders and impatience and the need for intrigue being so low on the scale.

"What do you want?" I interrupted somewhere.

After a pause, he said, "Have you ever see *The Verdict*?"

"Which verdict?" I asked wearily.

He seemed surprised. "Was it remade?"

"Vlad, what are you *talking* about?"

"*The Verdict* did star Paul Neuman. This man was down on his luck. Hired for a big case. It's what gave me the idea. High powered vs. high powered does not mean anything. It is always what keeps fantasy in the mainstream these days, with Harry Potter, so ordinary and boring, everyone telling him *he's* the only one who can defeat the greatest evil in the world—"

"Wait." I tried to focus. The car was driving itself, I'm sure of it. "You're hiring me because my waiting room looks like crap?"

"You leap to poetic license," he said with a millimeter more bulging eyes, "I like that. I like you. I've been watching you a few years now."

"*Years?*"

"Off and on."

I made a conscious decision to pull over. It was hard. The car did not want to Stop. Skid, or rest from its destination. But, I *made* it.

I looked him in the eyes. "You've been watching me for years?"

He nodded. I had a semi-good shit detector, and could usually—50% of the time—tell if a witness was lying, or what foot they were standing on and what they were leaning away from. True, now that I type it down, 50% does suck.

"You're honest," he said. "You care about things. You see some movies. Not enough, but the more than one a month average. Though your choices are dictated mainly by those with you, such as your child, but that's oke."

"Oke?"

"Watch your Dead End Kids, Gath."

"Who? What are you talking about?"

He looked at me. Closely. "I can trust you. You are boring and you do not cheat on your wife, nor do you frequent addictions that take you further from home than you need to be after five o'clock. You do not take payoffs and mostly work with people you believe to be honest. That does not matter much to me.

"But when you find yourself nearing 500 years, you see that *Groundhog Day* is indeed correct. I've heard reviewers who question why Bill Murray would suddenly turn to a life of good when confronted with the same choices day after day, year after year, why wouldn't he just rape and shit and do it all? I am living proof to say that, yes, there *does* come a change in life, when boredom overrules, and there must be something greater than yourself."

I closed my eyes, struggling with the words. I wanted to ask a question. The question that wouldn't come. His insanity was making me tired. So tired.

He continued, "I am at that time in my life. Call it my mid-life crisis in immortality. I want the record to be clear. And I like Florida. And I like you. So I am going to trust you."

"Well…"

"Or I'm going to kill you."

He smiled, so I smiled back.

"You don't need to trust me," I said.

"I am of course joking. You do not kill good people. They are the ones who don't interfere and make like better than it should be."

"What…"

"You will be paid well. To extract the truth."

I shook my head. "You've been talking a lot about movies. I really don't *remember Groundhog Day*—"

Like an excited child, he suddenly said, "Oh, you need to watch it again."

I nodded. "Yes. Definitely." I nodded, more to myself—stock taking time. "I'm honest. You like me. What is the point?"

"We're going to shake up the studios. And Midnight Marquee and Cemetery Dance, and Random House is going to be *great*. It is my image. Based on *me*. You're going to get my life back from the films, from the literature. We're going to sue the *world*!"

It was a nice idea.

I felt bemused.

That was the word. Bemused.

"So… all those Dracula movies…"

"I want to *fuck* with Universal!" he blew like an umpire. "Miramax, Fox, made-for-TV, made-for-video though there isn't video anymore, only DVD, they've all done it! Paramount, fucking *Tru Blood*. They will all *pay*!"

Trying to remain cool or to disguise my complacency in close proximity to a costumed closet Tourette's put me somewhere constant between terror and wanting to laugh my fool head off. My gameplan was just to keep things moving.

"You said *you* do not kill good people. You mean, *I* don't or—"

"'One' does not. I will not. I shan't kill anyone you know."

"Thanks."

He held out his hand for a shake, so I laughed at it and shook it.

"Okay, so we're going to sue the world. You're Dracula!"

He was beaming.

And we were at Whataburger. I must admit, crazy though he was, these brief spasms of void time were creeping me out, but yeah, somehow, when the freaky is all around you, you start getting used to it. I had no idea what was happening to me. Stress? I always thought that was stiff shoulders and no time warps.

I figured, we were here, so we went in. He ordered a couple large combos and I got a regular with lettuce and mayo. Been a long time. Pretty good, I thought, as I chowed in. The hamburger was real and in my hand, so it was easy to concentrate on eating.

All he did was talk about how great William Powell and Warren William were and John Williams' music for the 1979 *Dracula*, and how he could kick himself for not knowing about Universal in the 1930s because he was roaming around Spain and New Zealand, just living for the blood and the moment, and he so wished he could go back in time and kick Tod Browning's ass for directing the *famous Dracula*, which conflicted with his compulsive need to be Browning's technical adviser and really getting it right, but the burger was gone and delicious.

Truth be told—crazy as he *was*—I liked him, too. I mean. He just didn't look like a killer. Just an aging film fan who ran away to the circus and it ran over him, elephants and all.

It was just a pleasure watching him foam at the mind. I smiled and asked, "So how many guys you killed?"

"I never counted," he said, a might haughtily.

I shrugged. "Any difference in the taste between a woman's blood and a man's blood?"

"None. –But rats are different, as are animals. It is the outsideness, I would say. Like…" It was a thought he'd thought before, I could tell. "Like a cowboy's hands compared to the dish washer who also works with her hands, but works a different sort, roughing up their hands differently, so it is with the blood of insiders and outsiders."

I nodded, nodded, "I'm still starving." I got up, he grabbed my arm. Stuck a $50 bill in my hand. I got myself two full meals, too. He was right to get himself a couple. After all, the fifties were real, weren't they?

I chomped and chewed. One of the best meals. Ever. I didn't know why.

"So you prefer human blood."

"Oh yes. It's more pure."

"How long does a throat last you?" I'd always wondered that. Well, not always, but I wondered it once when I was a teen watching something. "You know, are you like a gas tank, and you have to refill…"

He acted like he wasn't paying attention. Weird man.

Eventually, after he'd eaten everything and was looking at the four-lane out the window, he said, "Did you know that there is a sequel to *Dracula* out written by the Bram Stoker estate, for the Stokers of this world receive shit all for their part in history. This will not happen to my man Vlad." He looked me in the eyes. "Me." Back at the window, "I care not for Lucas and his Kenner doll empire. I merely want what is mine."

"What's that?"

His fiery eyes came back at me. "*Everything.*"

I nodded. I said, "But if you prove the story is true, based on your life, you've got the O.J. Simpson syndrome going—you're going to be in nothing but constant litigation with all those families of all those victims of yours. There's no statutory limit on murder."

"Nor internationally."

"You've killed people all over the world," I questioned as statement, in that soft, non-judgmental way I'd learned made things less confrontational, more commiserating.

He nodded. "I have never been arrested nor questioned. Well." He thought. "'Never' is relative."

"To what?"

"Lifetimes."

I said nothing. My stomach spoke.

"Not that anyone would remember…" he whined. Strange. Usually he had this lower, passive voice. It went back to normal: "That would be hearsay. From a long way off."

"What are you talking about?"

"No one is alive who can—"

"You've killed people!"

"—who can put the figure on me, as gangsters have said. Of families, of police. The only thing that exists from my crimes are on paper."

"Yeah?" in my best sez you voice.

"Even so—when the truth be known—I'm magical. I can't be held by any of your mortal bonds."

I thought. "Okay," I said. "Using your rules. Suppose all the CIA, all the FBI and Interpol, and everyone just ganged up on you and—and put a stake through your heart or something."

"As if that's likely to happen."

"Okay. So that's a stupid scenario?"

"I shall run away to Italy. Cream sauces…"

"If you're dead, how can you taste anything?"

"I am 'un-dead'—how can I speak?"

What a logician. How can you win?

"I cannot be killed," he said.

"Is that true?"

"If it were true, would I confess it?"

There was something missing. "Come on, we're off the subject."

"As if."

He was smiling, waiting for me. I was sort of disgusted, for some reason. "'As if…' What are you, a 14-year-old girl? 'As if'—"

"Language is utterly and ultimately fascinating. I have picked up a lot. I have been in California since the Gold Rush, consequently I have lost my Translyvanian accent." Suddenly, angrily, "Which sounded nothing like Bela Lugosi! *Ever!*"

He pounded his huge fists on the table and intensified, "God, how I hate that man!"

While people were still looking at us, I took this outside. Into the car. Vlad got his cape caught in the door again and tried to look cool about opening the door, closing it again. I don't know. Do you laugh or do you cry? Or do you just think of Doll and college and the money that's going to take?

He sulked. Whether it was about the cape or the day, I didn't know. He didn't give me much to go on at all. I just drove us to the nearest park. It was a weekday day so there were plenty of parking spots. I had plenty of gas, so I just left the engine and the A/C run.

We sat there.

Thinking about it, *now*. It was foolish of me. There. With a killer. No one else around.

*Then*, it didn't seem like it. Or I couldn't see it. Somehow, I trusted this lunatic. He was just so over the top, so *ridiculous* with what he was and what he wanted, there didn't seem any danger. If you can believe that.

At last he spoke up, and blue, all he said was, "*The Brides of Dracula…*" Then, as quick as he was manic, he snapped out of it and was all business. "If Hammer still exists, we must go after them and break their bones. Fuck the British!"

"Well." I tried clearing my throat.

"*Fuck them!!*"

"Yes. We can fuck them. True. It's going to be *expensive*," I enunciated *clearly*.

"$1500 a day for your services. And whatever expenses you wish. I have all the money in the world. Literally. I could take it out of your pocket and hand it back to you, you wouldn't know. Unless you then checked. It means nothing to me."

My hand had moved to my wallet without even being aware of it for the first five seconds. Then I was embarrassed. He patted my shoulder nearest to him.

"You can mark your bills if you want," he offered. "I won't be offended."

"—Thanks." I thought, for a long time. "What are you trying to achieve? You know you can't win, right? That this is just… an absurd situation, right? Even if you're…" I waved my hand up and down at him from a distance as if that was going to say "Dracula" for me.

"It doesn't matter if I lose," he said calmly. "Winning is winning."

I nodded. I got it. At long last, I got it. "You're looking for *nuisance money*. Who's your target?"

"Well…there are many."

"Just one. Pharmaceutical company?"

He looked startled a moment. "Is there a Dracula pill out there?"

"Drug companies are the top target."

He shook his head.

"Come on, don't make me guess. The payoff is out of court, and that's the important thing, right?" I wanted to say something about suing his mustache maker, but there were two good reasons not to.

"It is more about knowledge," he admitted, vaguely.

After a thought, I ventured, "You've got a secret for the world, and you can't figure out how to log in to a newsgroup. Is that it?"

"You're getting colder."

It felt like it. The more I thought and sized him up, the more I wanted nothing to do with this *character*. What a perfect word. Character. He couldn't be… Just couldn't *be*. I was gonna go out and buy the vamp book *tonight*.

I drove us into Krystal's drive-thru. Had to get a sweet tea. Had to. This was getting *silly*. But thinking about all those fifties on my desk, I figured it owed him *one* consultation at least.

"I'll take a bag," he said.

"A bag?"

"A bag of Krystals." He handed me another fifty.

We sat in the pretty full parking lot, me sipping, nibbling on the one Krystal he "loaned" me, he said. Me, getting worried to death, him, dull eyed, not much to look at. He was facing the dollar store next door.

I watched him eat. Suddenly curious: "I thought you just drink blood."

"No." He shook his head as if it didn't matter. But it did matter: "That's exactly why this is so important. One reason. People don't understand. They don't *get* it."

"Get it? *Get it?*" I felt rage now. "Dracula saying 'get it'?" I rolled my eyes to think. "What was the other one…" I mouthed to myself, but the thought wouldn't come.

"I am Vlad the Impaler, not Dracula!"

"Right!"

"It would be the same as if a black man—"

I remembered. "Cheese sucks! That's it!"

"The last black man on earth sees a film about his kind, and it's all—"

"Ooo," I prodded, "that's racist." Sorry, but I couldn't help seeing it as all a joke. It was all so unreal, the "undead."

He sat back in silence. Royalty. Polite. But not used to or willing to be interrupted. My fault really.

"I'm sorry."

I started the car. All the tiny little hamburgers had been dealt with.

I felt a whisper in my ear. Somewhere in my brain I could hear, *Put your case together.*

And I looked. And I was alone in the moving car.

# chapter 3

A lot of reading. Not just Bram Stoker, but Vlad III the Impaler. Briefs and techno-jargon is fine, but it requires some sturdy nerve and lots of Mr. Pibb to keep me awake through biographies. God, these are the most boring creations devised by men. Or perhaps I'd picked up the wrong ones. Trouble was, when dealing with a 15th-century Wallachian voivode, amazon.com doesn't stock a lot.

Of course, this was all for my own benefit. Well, maybe not. Dealing with character background and study. But this wasn't the jist of the crux. The past didn't matter right *now*. What I really needed was a competent copyright lawyer on my side, and I didn't know any.

One with a really good sense of humor.

Jo, the runner who often moonlights as gopher (the two are *very* different) on side, etc. projects, I thought would be best to get out and about trying to match me an intellectual property ambulance chaser with the type of mind I was seeking. Creative, sexy, knowledgably confident. I just threw the sexy in there to keep her interested until she found someone. She's the get up and go type anyway, naturally magnetic with her short stature and blondeness and boldness and without emotional scars, so usually what she's looking for comes to her. A good ally in the search for what is essentially a science fiction matter.

I didn't know. I didn't know what I was getting myself in for, or if it would be worth it. Those fifties were sure enticing. But I didn't know. Why I was doing it, I didn't know.

Then, *suddenly*. Suddenly, right there in the library, I had to check. I bolted to the bathroom like I was on fire. I threw off my shirt and stared at myself from every which way, in the bathroom mirror. Looking for those two telling little marks on my neck or arms or shoulder or hell, even nipple.

I was clean.

I was also out in daylight. Well, it was morning and it was coming through the window. So that counted for something.

And it was then I *knew*. Knew the answer I didn't know.

I think I felt—deep down within me somehow—past the money and the novelty of the situation and the delight I'd "have" in soon everyone thinking I'm crazy—I think—no, I *know* I felt that…being near him. Being in the middle of the situation was the safest place to be.

Mark Clock was just a terrible name for anyone, even a lawyer. But he kept it. And like me, he had no partners, so it was just a simple Mark Clock ATL on the door. A door that rattled a bit as you closed it. No secretary even. Just a one-room office that I know Vlad would approve of. Even more *The Verdict* than me. I'd watched the movie the other night. Pretty good.

Too bad Mark wasn't a Paul Newman drunk, but after he heard what I had to say… maybe he'd start. He had curly grey hair and stooped over at 6 foot 2, and having caught the movie bug from my favorite vamp, I'd have to describe him as closer to Stan Freberg than anyone else on earth.

"What can I do you for?" he asked with a trace of mouthwash and southern drip.

I smiled. "My usual greeting." I shifted into the offered seat. A Kermit-green slip cover over a wobbly metal chair. Kermit. I was thinking in movie stars now.

"Mark, I'm looking for specialty counsel on a copyright infringement case."

"Why doesn't he just come to me?" And we laughed at that, like you're supposed to.

"It's very…it's not complex. Actually, it's pretty simple. My client is crazy. And rich. He thinks he's out of a public domain horror novel. And he and I want to know if that makes *him* public domain."

Swear to god, he fell backwards in his chair. Swear to god.

I helped him up, as we laughed, like you're supposed to. And once we got back to where we figuratively were, he said, "Is he Frankenstein's Monster?"

I shook my head.

"He can't be killed, you know." He chuckled.

"So say the movies," I said. "In that, that's part of it. He says the films misrepresent him badly. Terribly. Even if he loses, he wants to set the record straight. With Universal and all that."

"*Universal Studios*? Would you like a drink?"

"Whatcha got?"

"Just water."

I shook my head.

"Is it worth it?"

"I told you, the man's wealthy. So, you lay me the groundwork on how we can *prove*, or as close as we can, that a man, even 500 years old, can claim his own life back. I've got others prying into the identity theft lead, so just concentrate on intellectual property and image licensing. I don't know how much show business you do, but there are some agent companies that handle deceased stars—there's one that represents Buckwheat and Telly Savalas. You can promise them cash to talk with them, see how they tie up rights. You don't need to secure them as witnesses, yet, just a talking to."

He was nodding.

"I won't tell you how to do it, but I need everything as you get it. Don't bother waiting or writing reports."

He stopped nodding and asked, "Foreign or domestic? I shrugged. "My client was born in another country. But our case is only here."

"Where—was he born?"

I hesitated. I used the pause to its max. effect "The leak factor is great on this one. I can't

hear about the press getting wind of any of this, before the fact."

He nodded again. "I'll sign a disclosure. I don't care about my name in the paper."

"That's good. Don't make me sue a lawyer." And we laughed, you know.

"Can you give me some immediate ammunition, though? At least, a guess what I can expect."

He sighed and said, "I can tell you about what I know, not people walking around. Copyright

exists from the moment of creation, when it is in tangible form. You don't have to send it to the Library of Congress once you've written your lyric, it's yours, it's part of you. Send it to LOC if you a time and a post office date stamped on it. A picture, a film, the photograph of a face, belongs both to the owner of the photo and the owner of the face. *You're* talking about a sp—"

"Don't guess before you look into it," I said, "just give me a gut summation based on previous cases."

"The Copyright Act of 1976 states that works are the property of their respective author for the life of the author plus 50 years. After he split up from Cher, Sonny Bono started CTEA, effectively extending the time that 'public domain' begins, so it's really 70 years after the author dies, or 95 years after publication, whichever is earliest. That's for works created before 1978. If your man is Dr. Jekyll, that's *considerably* before."

Had to smile at that.

"Different rules and dates for unpublished works of art. I guess your guy is unpublished."

I laughed out loud. "This is going to be fun!"

I don't like cell phones, they just bind you to constant questioning, so I stopped at Texaco and called up Holly and Fred and the bunch to get them started on background history, everything on the historic Dracula, vamps in general, and Vlad himself, of course. College students work harder for credit than 50-year-olds for cash. Besides, this is cult. "No, you don't need to watch the movies," I told them. Kind of dashed their excitement. But their heat was still smoldering, and they'd watch them anyway.

I turned off Queen's *The Miracle* album and just sat at my home desk thinking about what the Clock said as he was shaking my hand, and the door in my mind half opened: "If you can prove this guy's birthdate. I mean prove it. Then 70 years after the author's *death*—is going to *get* us to court. Maybe on the novelty of it alone."

There'd been sparkles in his eyes.

He wanted to believe. It was obvious. Sad. And obvious. And sweet.

*Dracula* by Bram Stoker, written in 1897, placename to a very prestigious literary award (The Stoker) for horror fiction these days, is actually a blatantly very boring book. It's all diaries and journals. Not the quaint or juicy stuff a Twilight girl would write these days of "oh, Jas kissed me when he kicked the ball closer, I love him!" No, before you get to anything even smelling of murder or gothic streets in *Dracula*, you start out with: "3 May. Bistritz.—Left Munich at 8:35 P.M. on 1st May, arriving at Vienna early next morning; should have arrived at 6:46, but train was an hour late. Buda-Pesth seems a wonderful place, from the glimpse which I got of it from the train and the little I could walk through the streets." It goes on and on and on like that.

Now, I know I was reading for background, but even at the time—it was so late, most of TV was stocking bed, blender and L. Ron Hubbard ads—I was reading, I could care less about what time Jonathan Harker should have arrived by train. Luckily I'm a lawyer and tedium in text is the way of things. I mean, think about it: "the truth, the whole truth, and nothing but the truth" has rhythm in a completely unnecessary way, just because Americans like trilogies. ("The truth" is enough, right?) So be it. I would read. I told Vlad to read it again, too. Tomorrow we'd start on his background.

I read. Nice hardback published by Barnes & Noble. Since it's in public domain, the bookstore cuts down costs by publishing it themselves and keeps a greater profit for them. No author to pay either.

Printed and bound in China. Copyright 2006 by Barnes & Noble Publishing, Inc. Even the introduction by S. T. Joshi was copyrighted to them. And the usual disclaimer, which gave me no clue to anything, on their copyright page: "All rights reserved. No part of this publication may be reproduced, stored in a retrieval system, or transmitted, in any form or by any means, electronic, mechanical, photocopying, recording, or otherwise, without prior written permission from the publisher." Straight forward stuff.

I grunted to get up and put my hand on first thing from Medge's beach reading collection I could. My knuckles slipped quickly over some used thing with cartoon flames and a picture of a real girl holding a doll, on the cover of *Ghost Light* by Clare McNally, "author of *Ghost House*." It was the Bantam Book. On the inside copyright page, just the All Rights Reserved thing. Copyright the author 1982, and "This book may not be reproduced in whole or in part, by mimeograph or any other means, without permission." And the publisher address.

Curious. And a nice way of my putting off reading a boring book.

I've sat to the very end of movies—just enjoying the tunes—and I remember the disclaimer at the end, which books didn't seem to care about. Something about "this film is a work of fiction. If there's someone real walking about who lived this story, it's not our fault."

Reminded me of that.

So I got up, yawning. Pulled the first thing off the shelf there was. Didn't matter that it was *The Man with Two Brains*. Which reminded me again—I need to get that *Dracula* DVD collection off amazon for $24.95. Probably the *Frankenstein Legacy* or collection or whatever it was called, too, just to be thorough.

Popping the DVD player open, I didn't think I was going to get through it that night. I was right. There's no scene selection to get you to the *end* of the credits of *Brains*. I was falling…

Looked at my watch. 1 digit something and some minutes. I was falling

asleep…

Into the weirdest dream imaginable. And all, like, uneven around the edges, like viewing through a cut cereal box, and hazy. Dreamy, and fuzzy and clear.

There were women all around me, in a big room, women wearing something like red buttons, but they flashed. So, more like slot machines, and not dancing, more like moving around. They were either dangerous or friendly to keep the guys with their drinks happy and mobile.

Strange. Because I was coming down upon them. Like I was on a movie crane, a terrific point of view shot that put me into the inaction, right into their smiles that didn't light up but remained steady for me.

And I moved around, and there was a drink in my hand. Caramel colored and cold and clinking with ice though I always asked for no ice wherever I went. That's my habit. So I remember thinking at the time—and I know that's hard to control in a dream, the self-awareness—that this isn't right. Yet I was smiling. Like I was a chin on the cover of *Internet Retailer* or *Internet Life*, something like that. Happily drunk or dreamy or both.

And I walked around the other side of the slots, now machines, not ladies, and every other seat had an ass in it, all reading books. Eyes down like they all had eye glasses but they'd all gambled their glasses away (somehow I knew this). A cross section of intense interest and waiting room patience. They read mostly thick books. With a dealer standing in his semi-circular table trying to and yes dealing cards, but he had to slip them under all their books. It wasn't boring. Somehow there was a lot of chatter and winning sounds and even the readers would look up now and then to chat and sip a drink, but had their eyes attracted back like books were TV or something.

So I climbed the three stairs to the upper tier which was just slot machines. Really, I never thought they were this popular. They were, but the people here were more bored than the readers. Actually the readers were pretty content. As was my friend Vlad who was standing against one of the slots that was somehow rolling and playing without him playing it. He was reading a book on the TV show *Quincy* and laughing.

He looked up at me and said, like Bela Lugosi, "Gath! I'm so glad you come make it."

I wanted to speak, but water just fell out of my mouth. Then an ice cube. And a trickle of just a little more brown water.

He chuckled. There was actually a dimple on his right cheek when he laughed. "You're drinking too much."

I laughed like a chicken—just high and forced by the situation, not actually *like* a chicken. Then I managed to calm. And I threw the drink in my hand away. And then, there was another drink in my hand. I did it again. And again, like a magic trick.

Vlad closed his book, using a little red strip attached to the glue binding, and put it under his armpit, and applauded me.

"Is this a dream?"

"Sure looks like one," he said, glancing around.

"No, come on. I need to know."

He got serious again. Came up real close to me. "You'll ask me this tomorrow. I just want you to learn tonight."

And he pushed me away. I felt like I'd been on an airplane too long, still on it, not *quite* being able to shift my balance to my two feet. So I was going down the three steps again, like I was top heavy, not wanting to spill my drink and not wanting the drink. No one was in my way, I didn't hit anything or anyone. They just looked at me a bit, until I stopped. So then I was in the center of a dining room, all in brown, so far away from the table, but so close to it, with however many hard empty seats.

The walls were lined with glass cases which held drinking glasses and figures made of glass and more and more stuff the more I looked, until I'd made an entire circle of once overing the place, and suddenly all the chairs in the dining room were full.

And I woke up with a sweat and a scream. A drink in my hand.

I was freaked for most of the next day. How do you process something like that? *The drink?*

Had I made myself a drink? Unconsciously?

Medge hadn't woken up. I'm not a sleep walker.

Creeped, I read to take my mind off it. I can block out anything if concentrate long enough on *trying* to read. I read up on Abraham (Bram) Stoker because I thought it would give me a few clues as to his friends—not that I believed Vlad was anything like 500+ years old. It seems that the Irish author of *Dracula* had most of his life monopolized by writing half a million letters (no joke) on behalf of his idol, the famed British actor, Henry Irving. He functioned as Irving's secretary, business manager and slave for most of his life, causing Stoker to construct his only famous novel in an expansive seven years, off and on. Of course it also gave him the opp of meeting lit bigs like Oscar Wilde and an aging Walt Whitman. Looks like Oscar even had a fling with Florence, Bram's wife, before she was Bram's wife.

Too bad *Dracula* was a dud that caused Abraham to think he'd wasted all those years writing it. It even fell out of print for a bit, according to one source. Others claim it's never been out of print. Some call the book highly autobiographical, so that was good. But the "real" presence of Dracula was—depending on who you listened to—Irving again, impressing Abraham with his larger than life presence from portrayals of egghead characters like Hamlet and Macbeth.

According to a Les Daniels book (I was reading all the cults, dear god), it was Bram who first shot the vampire character, via Drac, into the role of a bat, a mist, a wolf and a dallier of female victims. He also might've been responsible for the stake thru the heart, the fright at the cross, and that the vamp's condition from a bite on the neck is contagious.

Irving died in 1905, leaving Abraham seven more years to be alive. He needed cash, and completed lots of non-fiction and some novels like *The Lair of the White Worm*, a Roger Corman flick if ever I heard one, and the fitting *Personal Memories of Henry Irving*, the year after the master actor died.

Abraham sounded a little like that character that eats spiders—I need to watch the movie again—I keep putting off reading the *D* book, it's just too thick—because he was always subservient, always bowing and walking behind the vamp and not good enough. Of course Dracula would have real presence compared to that.

I sipped some peach tea and read more of the research notes Holly, one of the first-years at FSU, made for me. Every webpage print out cut off at the bottom, but a good try. Medge snored softly beside me, and I smiled. Always admired her superpower of sleeping with the light on. I can't do it.

Wasn't really what I was *looking* for at this point, these pages. Mainly she brought me the origin of the Romanian word Drac, meaning "dragon," and Balkan history shit, but I'd call a mapping session in the next couple days and see where we were.

I had to take time off. If I lost $1500, so what? The Fun Park mini-golf was pleasant and it just wasn't too hot yet. I *love* weekday days when everyone's at work or home. Doll was thrilled to death with her hole-in-one on #14, and I told her if she did it again, I'd bankroll a half hour in the game room for her, and of course she didn't win, but we just moved to the bowling alley where Medge beat the pants off me, and we ate chili dogs while waiting for the balls to return.

Fun. Just *fun* being with your family. The only time I thought of my rich crazy Vlad was when I stared down at what I call the clown shoes they rent you for bowling. Something about the absurdity of them just…

While Doll was contemplating the very lightest ball she could pick up, the wife and I moved over to the snack bar for some microwave pizza pieces and no ice Coke Zero for me and maybe one apple fritter that looked like a corndog, I can't recall.

She was smiling at me like I didn't have to *ask* if she was happy. I love that kind of non-talk. She squeezed my hand, and gave me a wink. I gave her her wink back.

And then the obvious question came. "How did you manage it?"

"Working on a big case," I said, stuffing my mouth with boiling pepperoni-cheese, and I looked, and Doll was standing, hands on chubby thighs, giving us the evil eye for holding her pizza.

We moved back to business as I said, "Important case, lots of lolly, long hours. But I *had* to take a break."

She accepted that broken code for what it was: enjoy today, who knows when it'll clone.

We rounded things off with a catered picnic at Mock's Gardens off I-10. Yeah, apparently you can call up Publix and they'll throw together whatever weight of sandwiches, potato salad and deviled eggs and even the Double Stuff Golden Oreos or whatever off the shelf into the same basket, if you don't mind the $40 service charge and a degradable wicker basket that says Publix on it. I didn't mind a bit.

We laughed and watched the flowers grow and sweltered slightly and swatted unnamed bugs and generally tried to eat everything packed for a family of five.

**Fun**.

Medge and I made love that night. Falling to a satisfied sleep, my hand slipping down to my favorite place on her, the heaven for hands, if it could die there…that bit of hair only I get to touch, palm on her very flat stomach, which I never failed to appreciate her for out loud.

We did it in silence, like parents do. But it lasted longer, and I was complimented for that. I smiled, and her lovely face, with the soft, almost nonexistent eyebrows, and petite brown mole between her nose and mouth, as my last waking sight.

# CHAPTER

Few have the soul to understand that the red of blood is more vivid at night. It is the difference between the white rind of a watermelon and the deep juice of its seedless heart. A woman of just over 40 has been the best I have ever tasted, as it was now. Her beautiful throat ripped open like thick burned plastic, exposing tendons and bone gristle, inviting me...

I feasted.

How I loved to bathe in the strong moonlight, so wanting to scream up to the sky that I was at last at peace with my fill. The stench of teeming garbage cans doing nothing against me. My eyes, bulging with the red that was slowly filling me, creeping to my head, a rush that I swear I could feel and hear crinkling the very follicles of this ageless head.

It is like being bathed in lightning, jumpy at the possibilities that you can do anything. An eternal teenager who merely has to turn on his want and use his imagination.

This supreme ecstatic glory of being was only marred by the time. The time to collect up cats. For the evening was at hand when alleys turned vacant and midnight snacks walked in groups.

# chapter 4

I asked Mark Clock—I love saying his full name—to sit in with us on this. It was important for everyone to get uniform on direction.

It was 6. After work and classes for everyone. There was Red Elephant pizza, two huge kinds (mushroom & cheese vs. the meat eaters) on the table Celia slides out and assembles for group sessions.

"You know the germ of this," I told them. "Our wealthy client, Vladimir Tepes, thinks he's the embodiment of Dracula and wants this proven in a court of law. If not proven, I expect, in his words, he just wants 'to fuck with Universal.' It could be his expenses are limited and he's going after a major out of court cash pocket, or he wants to be a rock star and this is going to get him in the papers. As it is, and as it's the off season, I say we assume he's not crazy and go to town while his money holds out. Who's with me?"

"Why doesn't he file in California?" Holly asked.

I shrugged at her. "He likes me. I'm Paul Neuman."

"Who's that?"

"In *The Verdict*. An honest lawyer. He wants this on his own turf. He wants them to come to us. Mark Clock informs me that copyright is national, so we're going from here. What do we have already?"

Holly had the minor in history, so I'd given her the boring stuff. "Mr. Tepes I'm going to call him," she said, "is personally credited with killing between 40 and 100 thousand people." Whistles all around the room. "In the mid-15ᵗʰ century Vlad Tepes, or Vlad the 3ʳᵈ, or Vlad Dracula, or—"

"Alias," someone said.

"—or Vlad the Impaler ruled Wallachia, which is an area of the Balkans, which is today southern Romania, and our man was documented to have personally punished his victims by impaling them on stakes, hence the Impaler, naturally. Tepes the name even means or has come to mean 'impaler,' though I don't know which came first. Like Xerox stands for 'copy' now."

"What is impaling?" Jo asked.

No one.

Holly whipped out her ever-online personal organizer, probably pointed to Merriam-Webster, and came up with, "To pierce with something pointed. Or—" She paused. "This is good, to torture or kill with a sharp stake."

That quieted the room down.

"To put in an inescapable or helpless position." She paused again. "That's it."

"Okay," I said, and went for the white remote I always keep handy. Some Ace of Base was called for, I thought. It's positive music. It boomed for a few minutes from my secret speakers, but as we went on I had to shut it to concentrate.

"Is he dangerous?" Jo asked.

"He's not dangerous," I spoke, softly, the confidential tone with confidence. "He's just rich and delusional, and probably lonely. A loner, obviously, and he might be just looking for attention. But his money's real, that's the thing."

Everyone laughed on low.

"You're not Paul Neuberg," Fred said. I could never tell if he was serious or not.

"A little more, Holly."

She nodded at me and read from her notes, "The impaling was to frighten his enemies and warn any upcomers of his morality—"

"Any luck on the birth cert, Fred?"

"1430, Gath!"

"I know, I know."

"1430!"

"I know."

He was excitable, but I'd known Fred since high school. Ace case prepper and usually as stolid as stone. The man never drank or ate red meat, I mean not even a hamburger bun, and always seemed to answer the phone *whenever* you call. No wife, kids, sweetheart, but a sweetheart himself, already whiting and balding. The two of us had our own language—a sort of gibberish to the rest of humanity who wouldn't know where all our sounds and sound bytes came from. I only knew about 70% of the origins of our secret language myself by this point.

"Beside, you should give this to Holly, she's—"

"She'll take it if you can't get anywhere, but this is more about permissions and finding where to go," I said. "You're the most organized person I've—"

"Charm offensive," he said and waved, and only I got the joke. "He looks great for his age. Aren't we worried when we appear in court, that all the kiddies are going to start drinking blood to look as good as him?"

"But he isn't *even* Dracula, or claiming to be," Mark Clock said, getting rather angry as he went on. "Say he's Vlad, 500-year-old Vlad, upon whom was based this character, Dracula. The films are not *claiming* he is Vlad. These are stories and films about *Dracula*, prince…of wherever."

"Transylvania."

"Right! So, worse case, you've got a 500-year-old case for defamation which should have been filed with some rights attorney at the time, so he's neglected timely rights. It's a ridiculous situation."

"I think we should all get used to that phrase," I said. "We're going to hear it a *lot*. Let's say it together, shall we?"

We all said "it's a ridiculous situation" and I think that weeded some of the farce out of the room. I hoped so. I know no one was 100% serious about this. Me, too. But. If they'd seen what I'd seen…

Mark Clock held up his coffee mug half way. "Can I get some more?"

I buzzed and held up my brown cup for Celia to see, did my little dance around the table to mean *more for everyone, please*, then thought, before she closed the door, "Oh, and another two large supremes?" Red Elephant had the greatest pizza pie in the world. And we were all out.

"So, you think this is a defamation case?" I asked.

"What does your client want it to be?" Mark Clock asked back. I don't have to keep using his full name, but it is a great name.

I shrugged. "He just wants to cause trouble?"

Jo said, with a smile, "Is that your Jewish accent, or was that a question?"

"Defamation is the poor man's friend," our copyright friend said, growing a bit calmer now. "It's up there with getting rear ended, but really a far second. But still… anyway…I don't see how he's seeking vilification if he's going to admit to all the killings, as you say."

"I didn't say he was going to admit to anything. I haven't advised him on any statement yet."

Mark Clock continued, "And it's a money milker, that's all. A direct-to-out-of-court settlement monkey that requires no court time. Yet you say that's what he's set on? Court time?"

I put my hands flat on the table, just for no reason.

"So where are we?" I asked the room. "First, I need direction. Assuming it's trouble he wants—and every major and indie studio has a vampire film, whether or not it's Dracula brand or not, if our client has clear proof of…"

I wasn't going into a daze or suddenly waking up somewhere, but I was thinking of that dream I had of him shooting himself in the head, and trying to show himself in the mirror, and all the tricks he promised—promised when I was awake, I was sure of it—and it slowed me. Was it too early to give the Night Gallery stuff to my Trusted Few? I knew they wouldn't leak it. It was them thinking I was crazy without the *real* crazy being here, that's what I was concerned about.

Jo said, "Gath?" She was quite attractive. My thoughts always filled with Medge when the stirrings started, but beauty is a painting and you just can't not appreciate the good ones.

"Yes," but I didn't mean it. Whatever I was thinking. Then I woke. And said, "Yes. Mark. What's your bottom line about the sitch in general?"

He sighed. "Does he have proof?"

"Proof, or documentation?" I was hedging it.

"What's the difference?" Fred asked.

"Let me think on it." And I mused.

We tossed some theories here and there, and got into a whole conversation about *Love at First Bite* and that George Hamilton was planning a sequel (Jo had looked it up) and how Fred really liked the Wolfman series, and he would hate to come down hard on Universal, until the coffee came. The second wave of Red Elephant only came in as we were wrapping it up.

"Take them with you," I said, grabbing some slices for myself.

Butts unclenched from seats, I gave homework as the good people stretched.

"Holly, try to get that documentation. Even if we can't prove anything, at least we have our years straight. Try to establish a relationship between Bram Stoker and Vlad—" There were laughs. "You know, if they *knew* each other. Or knew *of*, that's fine.

"Mark Clock, just ride the—"

"You can just call me Mark, Gath."

Smiling, I said, "Ride the open window of a man, any man, who was or is alive at the time of a major story or film, and is the subject of that film and is portrayed as a villain—"

"It's called vilification. Rated to hate crimes. We can even get into 'racial villification' but I don't how strong this—"

"No, no, I want Fred on that, he's strong on political-emotion. No, I mean you—" meaning Mark Clock, and I pointed at him so I wouldn't have to say his sweet full name—"you take today or case histories about someone trademarking himself or getting money out of anyone for a fictional character based on himself. After the fact is good. It's *best*. Estates suing. But someone walking around living is fine."

Fred suddenly asked, "Could Hitler have sued Hollywood in 1942?" If there'd be crickets in the room, you would've heard them rubbing. "There were anti-anti-semetic films being made all the time over and over..."

Mark Clock was waving, the idea pouring seawater down his head. "Give me *one* problem to think about."

"It's a good analogy," Holly said.

A little lite laughter, as everyone made their way to the door.

I was curious now. "Could Hitler?"

"He was born in Germany," Holly said. "Arrested for crimes against humanity as soon as he set foot on the Walk of Fame."

"So's our guy," Fred quickly reminded her. "I mean, Vlad's a foreign import."

She asked, "Hitler banned films from being shown, didn't he? Even Charlie Chaplin, I…" She was thinking.

"So where does that leave us?" Fred asked.

"A headache," I said. "Just make the answers good enough to make the nuisance suit good, and time consuming. That's as far as we're going to get." I took a good full mouth of grease and chewed. "Verbal injury. Intentional infliction of emotional distress. Cast your nets. I'll get us some proof from the source." They left, laughing.

It was salty in my mouth. I felt good too.

I closed the door, but Mark Clock popped his head back in a second, all serious. "Get a deposition."

I nodded, and closed it on him in a friendly way.


It had been first on my to do. Legal Video Services did depositions, Paul Rapp being an old friend of mine. Besides, he'd done things with a Michael Jackson case and celebrities before, having himself a Hollywood address.

A deposition is for discovery purposes—taking testimony outside of court, before and sometimes during a case. It helps litigants assemble information. This time, it would be to get ourselves ready to rule out the crackpot theory immediately (if we could) and not get thrown out of court in the first two minutes for reasons of incompetency—our biggest hurdle to get our foot inside the vault. Fred set the time and place for a rehearsal, setting down questions based on my prelim sketches of where to concentrate: the loopholes. Usually, the trick to being a shyster is not thinking about your case, but considering what the *other* guy is going to do

This was a different animal. Fred had a deep deposit of killer instinct that would earn him a high living someday, all from logic, so I could trust him to plug up the holes before the opposition—who still knew nothing about anything—could hole us.

The dep rehearsal went a couple hours at Paul's place, to get Vlad used to formality and a setting he'd either laugh at or—well, I couldn't see my friend Vlad Drac get nervous, so let's say, I wanted to remove his abnormality to the proceedings. Relax him.


F: Relax.

D: I am always of relaxation.

F: This is an affidavit, a simple sworn statement of fact for the purposes of verifying your intent and that the things you say are true and correct under oath.

D: I do.

F: State your full name please.

D: Vladimir Tepes is my most common name, as it states on my driver's license.

F: Wow, you have a driver's license?

D: I do.

F: Where were you born?

D: Sighisoara, Translyvania, now Romania, a beautifully gothic city back when that meant something. Born to Vlad Dracul, the second, mother, Cneajna of Moldavia, a lovely princess of the region, now, sadly, dead.

F: In what year were you born?

D: 1430. Not 1431.

F: You claim to be over 500 years old.

D: Closer to six.

F: Six hundred years old.

D: That is correct. I shall go on a cruise that year. I have never been on one.

F: Really?

D: I'd thought of doing it when I turned 400, but I thought—no. Wait.

(Pause)

F: You have documentation of your birth nearing 600 years ago?

D: I am ready for any test, physical or mental.

F: You have documentation of your birth?

D: I am sure it is somewhere. But just how would you connect me to your piece of paper?

F: That's my question to *you*.

D: There is no photograph. They did not think to fingerprint in my day.

F: So, we are just going to take your word for it, your age?

D: I believe there are physical tests to determine the age of bones. I have read books on dinosaurs. And Quincy once used a femur, I believe, to reconstruct an entire man. Then, there the dentists, they may prove who is who, and when.

F: Suppose you just had all your teeth taken out, and complete false bottoms and tops put in, to confuse the issue?

D: That's really rather good. That shows dedication! No, but there are x-rays, showing extractions and manipulations. I put it to the offense that—

F: The prosecution.

D: The prosecution may hire whomever they prefer. Examine me. Let my body speak for papers.


It wasn't the first time I'd pressed pause. In fact, there was blood on little button with the arrow on it. Blood had squirted out from between my nail and thumb, that's how hard I must've pressed while watching the recorded rehearsal.

Or listening to it.

It was a full evening's entertainment with Fred's off-camera voice asking questions of Vlad's on-camera voice, and *no Vlad. Just the chair.*

*Where the hell was he??*

*Fred was talking to* someone.

This was ridiculous. And unbelievable.

I sat with my head down, my head in my hands, for the longest time… It was like I was asleep. No thoughts came. I wouldn't let them. For the *longest* time…

Then. Eventually. To have something to do, something that didn't involve me looking at the screen, I pulled out a couple case books, trying to find the admissibility of vocal depositions. 1973, Tadem, Wisconsin, Mrs. Adelair, 43 and suffering from severe bee stings that kept her wrapped up.

So, we wrap Vlad up, say he's disfigured? Severe stress, tried to kill himself after watching Leslie Neilsen in *Dead, and Loving It?* Then we'd be repping Claude Rains vs. the Invisible Man, wouldn't we?

My head hurt and it pounded. Nothing made sense. So this makes the camera the mirror? He's *Dracula*?

No.

I didn't get it. Unless Fred was having me on. But he didn't have a sense a humor when I last saw him. He was doing a good job, though. The awe in his voice—how would it have been if he'd been sitting in front of Claude Rains here?—was unprofessional, but he knew it was a rehearsal shot.

I fasted a little and pushed *Play*.


F: --anyone that the rest of us might relate to?

D: (Pause) No one.

F: Did you know Bram Stoker?

D: His book—I know, he wrote others—wasn't successful upon its first printing, so I had no reason to seek him out at the time.

F: Quickly, where were you in 1890.

D: (No response)

F: Okay, that's a tough one. (Pause) Do you understand the concept of time?

D: What do you mean?

F: What is the length of a minute?

D: What do you mean?

F: How long is an hour?

D: What are you talking about?

F: I want to make sure that your concept of time matches my own. For instance, if you are a being from the future, or you have deluded yourself into thinking that yesterday was 1920—

D: Sixty minutes. Twenty-four hours in a day.

F: Thank you. Getting back to Mr. Bram Stoker, the author of the book you claim—

D: You know, actually. I've seen more leap years than you will be alive.

F: (Pause) No, that's not right. Don't confuse the issue, Mr. Impaler.

D: Sorry.

F: We just want to keep to the germane—

*Pause.*

It was the second Tuesday of September and it was all Fall. Just the kind of windy, moderate day that makes the dying season the most popular with everyone I knew. I loved all the orange. Doll loved it. Right then she was running up and down our steep backyard that overlooked the pond or largish lake that usually had snakes lurking somewhere. But since we got the Yorkie, I hadn't seen a slither, and no one reported anything. Let her run.

Besides, she loved it, and we could watch her fine from the great wooden deck overlooking the dual pecan trees that towered around us.

"Why are you doing it?" a voice said. It was Medge, through the headphones.

I took them off. I'd had Celia make me an mp3 of the dep. "Just catching up."

"I don't mean *what*," she said. "Why are doing this *case*?"

"Oh. You know. Off season."

"That's all?"

I nodded. So she went to grill buns and keep an eye on the hamburg that I needed well-done. Don't you hate that pinkness in the center?

But it was a good question. Maybe it was always in the back of my mind. I thought projected to her: "You know I like magicians." Mix that with infinite curiosity, fearing for my life, the money, the novelty factor, the dreams he'd given me; it was such a complex answer.

Great smell. The dogs and burgers would be ready soon. "This guy is the greatest… something I've ever seen. I mean. He's intense. I think…it's…I think it's his true…" I couldn't think of the word, so my unconscious waited for it.

"Doll!"

That lovely golden head turned with a splash of hair and looked at us. Then she went back to playing. Medge had a three-call system, only good between the two of them, and this was just Stage 1.

"*Energy!*" I said when the word came. "He's so *passionate* about this stuff, babe. You wouldn't believe it."

"Passionate, but not dangerous?" She looked at me. Worried? No, she was just giving me the eye to respect or reject the round glob of meat on the end of her long fork. I nodded. Doll's steak was the last to go on. She liked it, for some reason, so rare you'd think there're maggots inside.

*That* made me think, watching her climb the stairs with a puff. "Now there's a vamp!"

Doll put her hand flat on the top of the post and purpled and wheezed, really going overboard and bulging her eyes, then she laughed at me. Her way of showing me she *wasn't* out of shape. She was kind of porky though.

Medge laughed. "Where's a vamp?"

"Vampire!" I yelled and pulled Doll's hair until she laughed. I did my usual thing of pretending her dirty yellow hair was stringy cheese, like I was pulling a hot piece out of the middle of the pizza and couldn't get the moz off my fingers, stretching and stretching.

We ate our steaks and burgers and Doll fell asleep in the tiny three-seater swing we kept at an angle so that we were out of the sun and all we saw was the neighbor's deck. Luckily the neighbors never liked weekends and never came out during grill time. Medge doubled over and brought out the dreaded brown box I didn't even see was there until it was too late.

"Don't groan," she said.

"I didn't!" I shout-whispered, but she opened it up anyway.

The bill box. Too cool an evening. Too nice a day to do this, and I said.

"Some of these are coming really close, Gath."

"I've got the money now."

"For what?"

"*From* what? This." I waggled headphones at her. "A crazy client who thinks he's Dracula, is going to–pay–for–our box outright." I'd been trying to kiss her in each pause, then I patted the dreaded brown box.

No kisses. Just worried eyes. "What are you listening to?"

"You."

She pointed at me, clearly wanting a serious evening.

I sighed. "Audio I made from a DVD."

"Why?"

"Because... I love you!"

I got a piece of lip.


Tomorrow.

Tad Standing, a lit friend of mine, put me on to all the influences in *Animal Farm*, George Orwell's pig opus. How Napoleon is based on Stalin, and the character Snowball is a mix between Trotsky and shades of Lenin. Though it had been forever since I'd read the book, thinking like this was a good start.

"I want you to read this, I got it off the internet," Celia said, and handed me some printed pages. When the office is dull, I often let her do some of the simple research. I read. Legs on my desk. 3 p.m. The Bangles singing Prince kept things cool.

*Kirby v. Sega of America*, No. B183820 (Calif. 2d Ct. App.). The California 2d District Court of Appeal was in our favor: the appellate court upheld ruling for three video companies who had created a character with very similar traits to a real person—singer "Lady Miss Kier," or Kieren Kirby, from Deee-Lite, a '90s funk band I'd never heard of. Popular? They were in my mp3 collection, but I've got thousands of full albums, millions of songs. Why did they choose her? Anyway, there had been a "similarity test" from prior California Supreme Court cases, and too many dissimilar traits had been found between Kirby and the fictitious 25th-century reporter named Ulala. They even *both* had pink hair, short skirts and platform boots. The vid gamers maintained they had a First Amendment right under right of expression to use her image.

This brought up the key to what I suspected was Vlad's lock on the case: right of publicity. The right to prevent unauthorized use of one's likeness or by a third party for commercial benefit.

Which tied into the other, briefer, case Celia had printed out for me. *Winter v. DC Comics*, 30 Cal. 4th 881 from 2003 was trickier because when it was appealed in Missouri, it reversed itself in favor of one-time St. Louis Blues hockey player Tony Twist who alleged that Spawn, the comic book character, was based on his "name and likeness," I don't know how, it didn't say. It seemed to be a difference of definition between expressed use and commercial use, and once the Missouri Supreme Court got hold of it, Twist picked up $15 million from the jury who thought he *was* somehow the cause of healthy comic book sales.

That's the trouble with Law. It's like the Bible. You can usually find a quote for either side of the justification. We were just going to have to load up with more justifications than Bantam and Universal and wotnot would find.

Of course these internet samples were all *recent*. We still had to work on the time element. 500 years is a long time. Too long, I expected, but the world is a crazy place.

# CHAPTER

While I crunched a cat and let its life wiggle from my hand into the rolling pour down my parched throat, I thought on this Gath, who clearly did not believe. In all the years I had been following him, he had never gone to church, nor spoke of this God who kept building houses. Nor was his family eager for the experience of worship. I will admit, when one bases an entire system of religion upon a book in the public domain, without proof of authenticity, it is only natural that few should want to give up one of two mornings a week they have for late sleeping.

It did not matter that he did not believe. Nor that he smiled when he spoke of me to others, even the other unbelieving colleagues who smiled back at him. He was a hard worker, this Floridian with a penchant for Freddie Mercury and Meat Loaf and a self-confidence against too many Krispy Kream donuts.

He was thorough, and as energetic as a man from the deep South can be. He listened to me, even to my suggestions… I returned all favors. Including my waiting on the repulsive psychoanalyst on the morning of September 20, 2010. The room was…sticky. The woman to my left in the corner furthest from the dim light did nothing but curl her curly hair with her thumb and forefinger and looked at the home decorator magazines on the table from afar. It slightly surprised me how much one doctor's waiting room looks like a dentist's room and so forth.

"Mr. Tepes?" A kindly voice had called me, and I had to control myself. She was 40 and plump, but she had a neck to die for. Her hair was short, just below the ears, just my preference for ease and good grooming.

I followed her, in my own time. She smiled at me while I flashed my eyes at her and she closed the door. She opened up another door, closed it, then another door which led us into the book filled chamber of Mrs. Nusbaum, doctor and proud displayer of university certifications upon her walls.

"Please, sit down," she said in a voice not unlike Anita Loos. She was clearly tired, poor devil, and not attractive enough to be worthy of further description.

"I'm Vicki. Just call me that or Dr. Nusbaum or doctor, I don't care."

"Thank you."

"We're just going to do some talking. Have you ever had a psychiatric evaluation before?"

"My first car was a Ford."

She laughed, as well she should.

"You bought this from Ford himself, I'll bet." She nodded to me as if she wished me to complete her surmise in intellectual fashion.

"That is rather like my living in Oklahoma and asking you if you have been to Universal Studios Florida this past weekend," I said, quite serious. "Since you are a resident of Florida."

That wiped the smile off her face. She wrote something down in blue ink on a Mead composition notebook, not the spiral kind, which must have cost her well over a dollar.

To come clean, and to the point, I said, "As you state, this is mere evaluation, so I do not ask to be mocked or proven wrong on a contest of history. You may head shrink me at your will, but if you are looking for chess of the head, I suggest you are down several pawns, and at least a knight."

After she closed her mouth, she spilled more rapid ink onto her page, as I continued, "Now, shall we prove that I am not crazy, or at least that I firmly believe all that I say?"

Her southern accent was a bit shaken, but she managed to "Y-yeah" before assembling herself heartily. To be truthful, as I have seen it many times before, her questions were more in the guise of a fan rather than someone testing me for professional reasons. Yet, she had doctorial letters behind her name and the appropriate stationary, and I'd given Gath my word not to gather myself into a bat and storm out.

"I take it I was chosen because of my hours."

"Yes, indeed," I agreed.

"You can't go out in the daytime."

"Is that one of your questions?"

"Mmm?"

I shook my head. "I prefer not to choose daylight."

"It does get hot." She laughed. "And humid."

"Why are you open 24 hours? Is that not insane?"

She wasn't offended, but merely gave me the standard, rehearsed answer, though she was constantly agog. "I get asked that a lot? I don't believe that health, mental health, is something that lays itself open to a strictly 9 to 5 regime. If you've got a bad tooth at 9 at night, what are you gonna do? You know? Emergency rooms are open at the hospital. If you've got yourself a *hard* problem, there needs to be a way of solving it, don't you think?"

"I do."

"So, we take turns. I'm not here personally every waking moment of the day."

"That's wise."

"You, you probably sleep during the sun hours, don'tcha?"

I nodded. "It is preferable."

"Yeah, I imagine it is. What's the preference for?"

"You mean… why do I sleep during the daylight time?"

"I mean that."

"I am what society now likes to call a vampire."

"What's *your* favorite word for it?"

"Oh. I think blood sucker is *nice*. Descriptively adherent. But then, people might start to call me a leech. And I wouldn't like that."

"You don't like that."

"No. And if I was a child of 10, say, I would be called nothing but Dracula. And I would not like that either."

"Why not?"

"Well—the man does not exist. He's a fictional character."

"Yeah, he is."

"Based on me."

"You don't look like Dracula."

"When did you see him last?"

"Heh. Can you turn yourself into a bat?"

"Can you?"

She shook her head in the most serious of rattles.

I turned into a bat, and she fainted.

It was humorous, seeing her fall like a stone into the plush carpet she kept from wall to wall of that tiny office. After so many years of watching myself and being careful of who sees what, I must admit it was partially freeing to do such parlor tricks in front of those who dare not tell.

Scooping her up, looking at her and into her eyes and past her eyes into the very soul which she did not know how to hide, I brought her into my world for a few moments. Long enough to calm her breathing with utter relaxation, with no thoughts of losing life and limb but with true peace, perhaps for the first time in her uninteresting life.

When I turned my eyes off and the dim glow sneaked back just below my pupil, she sat up with a weary hand to her head. Then she pointed to something in the corner of the room. I could not find it, so she rose, as if she had just removed herself from a low-speed merry-go-round. Somehow she found a minute bottle in a fake book of Charles Dickens, and she drank.

She offered me a "swig," without reserve nor fear.

"I'm sorry about that."

"About what?" I inquired.

"I just had a spell." She sat. "Whoo!" She crossed her pudgy legs and grabbed the security of her Mead again. "Yeah. You…"

She did not know, so I continued, "You asked if I could turn myself into a bat."

"Yeah, that was it."

I turned myself into a bat, and she fainted.

Eventually, I thought, perhaps she would see this reality and would halt its sublimation to her suppressed dream world. But no, even the second time around, she went for her Mead notebook and refused to discuss the immediate past.

So, we pressed on. "Do you know who the President of the United States is?"

"Today?"

She nodded, so I explained it was, "The black one."

"What's his name?"

"Black Obama."

It seemed good enough, so she wrote that down. "Do you know what year this is?" When I became thoughtful, she said, "I know these are, like, stupid and simple, but I'm not trying to demean your intelligence. This is merely to establish that you can process information, that you know where you are. This could go a long way to establishing that you know where you've been."

"I understand. The year is the easiest of the questions, for when you have lived my length, you see time drag on, and one year stays quite a long time."

"You should have kids and want to be an actress, then look back on your life like me and ask yourself where did the time go!"

A telling remark indeed.

"It is 2010."

"It must cost a lota money to keep yerself for all that time. You gota job? I mean, you can outlive your employer and all that."

"Frankly, Dr. Nusbaum, if I feel myself short, as the cruel expression goes, I merely wisp into a bank and relieve them of as much of what denomination I wish."

"Yeah?"

"It's the truth. It's actual."

"Easy peasies."

"I beg your pardon?"

"You turn yourself into a smoke and all that and get into the safe? Turn yerself into smoke for me."

I did, and she fainted.

This was truly enough. I left her to her natural conclusion, and to her conclusions as to my degree of processing competent information. I ceased to care. Anyone who cannot learn from their own eyes after several lessons must bore anyone. I felt I must seek my solitude. If such was inconclusive, I would try again. But with another doctor. This one did not even ask me about the dead cat in my hand.

# chapter 5

Tallahassee is a city full of rain. They say Florida's rainy season is the summer, but Tally doesn't care, it just rains and rains like Seattle's Best, when it wants. It was doing it right now, and I was in my car for 8 minutes, letting Queen's "The Prophet Song" finish up past the reason you listen to it in the first place—those great echoing harmonies of Freddie's voice only. This son was a perfect reason for keeping my head dry, though my umbrella was somewhere in the backseat.

Time enough to squeeze the daddy's day card out of the USB-sized envelope Doll'd squeezed it into. It was funny how she was always using whatever was at hand for envelopes and boxes and all, and she always made her own cards. She was the artistic type who couldn't draw, maybe like Andy Warhol, and I thought that was just adorable. The thought, you know?

HAPPY APPLE FATHER'S DAY, DADDY. I HOPE YOU WIN LOTS OF CASES AND GET SUED. LOVELY DOLL.

Slipping the note in my jacket pocket, wondering about the "apple," I slid out of the seat and loved the feel of the rain. The umbrella was Medge's. I never liked or used them. I just *loved* the rain.

Holly was on the other side of the door, all excited, and the only one in the waiting room. Celia was super at clearing schedules; I wish she'd been as adept at drumming *up* biz at times, but that wasn't her fault. No complaints those days. The fifties kept coming, so…

"I've got a lead on the birth certificate," she blurted.

"And hello!"

"Hello, can I go to Romania?"

When I didn't answer but made a beeline for my office, she kept tagging along and re-asking in different ways like an annoying teen. "We've got enough in the kitty" and etc.

"Can you feed me constant background, even before and if you don't get it?"

She showed me her phone texting thumb, in good shape, so I shot her a reverse hitchhiker's gesture.

"Go!"

She was gone with a smile, without even a goodbye. There was a page of single-spaced text on my desk with the heading, "Vlad Dracul," typed very close to the paper, as near-sighted people say. I wore glasses, so I had to take them off to read this. It was like in .5 type. What was Holly thinking?

It was all about daddy Drac. A duke (voivode) of Wallachia (again, southern Romania) who was hot stuff in the '30s and '40s of the 1400s. About as boring to read as a Harker journal entry, filled with proper nouns that did nothing for it, but Holly'd her work. All this stuff about the Ottoman Empire, back when people *believed* in things, like God and honor. Good stuff. Just *enlarge the font!!*

Phone. Fred. "Have you seen the 1992 Dracula?"

I shook my head, though I was on the phone. "No. The movie?"

"Rent it. The high-falutin' one, the only flick that's impressed people, according to IMDB and Leonard Maltin's book and all."

"You're supposed to be running the deposition," I reminded. (I hadn't told him Vlad didn't "show up" on the rehearsal. I don't know why.)

"We're almost there." He clicked off, then rang back. "Oh, and get on to amazon. There's a Christopher Lee called *In Search of Dracula* from '75 I think's worth us all seeing."

"A Christopher Lee what?"

"The legend of our boy. See ya!"

He rang off, so I did the deed on amazon, clicking on a few out of print things from other sellers, because **customers who bought this also bought** *Vlad: The Last Confession*, just out, by C.C. Humphreys, and *Vlad Dracula: The Dragon Prince* from iuniverse and Michael Augustyn. I wasn't going to mention these to Vlad as targets. I know *my* Vlad would be just as happy with some millions and recognition from the major players. No use diluting our energy going after *everyone*. *In Search of Dracula* by Raymond T. McNally (from 1972 and updated in '94) looked to be the big deal. I'd have to get Holly to read it to me or read it. 320 pages, I groaned to myself.

Oh yeah, same title as that Lee film, which was also In Stock there for ten bucks. 4 customer reviews, average rating of 3 stars. Well, I'd watch that in the meantime. *Click.*

A thought. I highlighted Raymond McNally's name and did a google on him to see if I could find him. 15 years is a long time. The *Library Journal* review at amazon said he was a historian from Boston College. Good place to start.

No. Damn. He died in 2002. That was the first entry that came up. He would've been a great (character?) witness to have on our side too.

It was then I…felt something. A disturbance in the force. The room grew suddenly colder, and though that was a blessing, it became difficult to concentrate. I put on Enigma, which seemed to fit, but even that did not sharpen me.

Felt like I was being watched.

But there was no one.

Instead, I went into a fog, and then into a dream, filled with horses and shadows and shadows of horses that stood out in a long line from a pie seller at a stall in one of those carnivals you get in small towns. There was a thin, balding man who introduced himself as Armando Iannucci and began talking to me about the origins of various animals while I looked around, if not bored, at least like I was looking for somebody or someone more important.

It was then that the drip of reality slowly came and filtered me into consciousness. I was on the Tally fair grounds, a place I'd not been since I was in high school. Even Doll was uninterested in such things, what with the competition of television (*Princess Makeover* was her favorite) and doggy video games.

There was chocolate covered popcorn in my hand and in my mouth—I felt as if I'd just *eaten* a piece. When clearly I hadn't.

And Vlad was suddenly there, saying, "—for adults, which is why I like it for its novelty. It is always strange to see Fred Astaire in a role in which he does not dance. Even in *The Towering Inferno*, for which he received his only Oscar nomination. He does dance a little, like Russ Tamblyn, in *Peyton Place*, also nominated for an Oscar, who also did not dance, Fred Astaire—and Russ—in *Peyton Place* admitted that he was not good at dancing."

I had stopped and was just looking him. His stash was all caught up in the pink cotton candy which he was somehow inhaling between these insane statements.

"What are you *talking* about?"

As if I had just come into the theatre, he said, "*Ghost Story*. About how it's one of the few horror movies for folks over 50, a trend I wish—"

"Look," I said, somewhat irritably, "what am I *doing* here? *Am* I here? Why can't you leave me to get my work—"

"It is your job to confer with your client. You wanted to see me anyway."

"Did I?"

He'd steered us to a mobile home horror house. His fist was full of tickets, and he shoved them at the local high school girl who tried to give him back his ticket change, but we were aboard and jerkily off before I knew what was going on.

A headache was coming on. As if he knew it, Vlad started rubbing my temples, and before we got to the first plastic scream, it was gone. Which worried me more than the pain.

"You need to talk to me," he said. "What did you think of the deposition?"

We kind of had to shout because this haunted house—it was a fun house, let's be honest—was loud and dark and was as jerky as touring a town with a girlfriend who rides the break.

"Unbelievable," I said honestly. "I've got Fred working on something else. That filmed rehearsal tells me you're not going to be admissible because you don't show up at all."

"And what does that tell you? That's proof itself, isn't it?"

"Proof of what doesn't exist is not proof."

"It proves a supernatural element, does it not?"

"The law requires that you are bound by *content*, not by its lack thereof. What the eye can*not* see does not constitute proof."

"I see." He wasn't any more scary in the dark than he was just walking around with him. "It proves something to *you*, doesn't it?"

I thought he was a mind control freak. Not a 500-year-old asshole. But I didn't want to push him.

"Vlad. Come on. I can't take anymore of these. These..." I meant "mind trips" but I couldn't find my phrase. "Whatever, these vacations. If you have comments or instructions, make an appointment through Celia. Okay?"

I got out as soon as the ride was over, and strode quickly away.

He was there beside me, trying on a dog face that would not fit.

"I'm sorry." After tens of feet more, he repeated, "I'm sorry."

I felt myself softening. By some miracle of the ages, there was a chili dog in my hand. With onions. And I love onioned chili dogs.

I looked at him as I bit in, as if asking him a question. And his face, lip slackered with pizza grease from the large and thin pepperoni he was eating, told me that he knew I liked chilis.

*How* did he know this?

While my heart softened and my pace slowed, we ambled over to the toss rings. Five bucks for a throw of a single light-wood hoop. If you get it over the top of that fat goldfish bowl, you keep it. The goldfish bowl, I assumed, not the hoop. Each flickering bowl reflected the moonlight of a star-filled sky, and I suddenly wondered where the rain had gone, and I suddenly wondered what time it was!

He read me and said, "I phoned Medge and said we'd be a little late."

My shoulders grew cold with this. For the first time since my marriage, I felt I wasn't in control. I began to wonder if, really, the fifty dollar bills were so important.

There were two hoops in my hand. There were two in Vlad's, and a twenty in the paunchy 70-year-old who eyed us like we didn't belong. But, watching the old guy work the thinning crowd, he held the same eye for everyone.

Vlad's first toss went wild, and stuck on a Huckleberry Hound look-alike doll. My keen legal brain, full of copyright yuck, I wondered if the makers of that blue animal, probably made in China for a dime, had any trademark problems keeping them up at night.

Then I looked down, and saw the other hoop was around a goldfish bowl. The two hoops were still in my hands. The paunchy evil-eyed old man was beaming like Gomez Addams, but the begrudement ended in Vlad getting the animal. He then gave it to me.

"A thank you and I'm sorry gift," he said. "I promise I won't annoy you further."

I looked at the fish, bug-eyed and spotty black.

"Thanks."

"But I am keen to know our chances. What do you think?"

"Can I ask you questions without offending you?"

"I hope so," he said with serious cowboy patience.

"No, I mean, there are some things I need from you. And they aren't personal. They're for winning your case."

He nodded.

"I need your fingerprints."

He nodded again. "They're not going to be on file."

"I have an Interpol connection."

He nodded and said, "I will not exist, but that's fine. You don't offend me."

"Oh good."

See, I knew he was a magician and a manipulator, but I didn't want to be the only one who knew.

# CHAPTER

There was a pang in my heart as I watched my friend—dare I call him friend?—leave with his fish and his mouth smelling of meat. I am not a lonely person, nor do I, rarely, feel alone, but his trust was misplaced. I knew that when he looks at the moon, he see a flat yellow thing in the sky. He does not think of green cheese nor rabbits churning butter in it, as they do in Japan, and for that I felt my pang of sorrow for his mind that cannot embrace that which is unproven.

There were many lovely girls this night, several in shorts the length of which would take my mind off this attorney and on to better things. Gath was honest and purposeful, but—

Holly was the student, Celia was the secretary. I said these to myself as I spied the former, in a gaggle of female incredulity, mocking the cheapness of the rides, the potency of the "scary" dummies or what have you, which would suddenly howl or jump or establish their presence to the walkersby.

Each face lovely, every body its own beauty of youth and promise and skin shaved and ready.

They walked at a speed that told of their purpose, yet never did they seem to find anything worthy of riding or payment. No treats, no rolls of the bowling balls, no darts at $10 a throw. They circled once more completely around, merely enjoying their company and lovingly pawing each other as friends do.

Though there were plenty of choice sexes to intrigue and delay me, I felt more alive to keep after this particular group. Dr. Nusbaum might query that having known her, I wanted her *all*, and all of her friends, but truly it was their companionship and vivaciousness and *interest* that was interesting to me. It was as if they had never seen a fair before, and perhaps they had not.

It was not until after midnight when the already lame crowds fell to further nothing that the gaggle split themselves with smiling and laughing goodbyes, and sauntered home, each in shorts and tight shorts. I thought how entrancing an invitation such a wiggle would be to the average horror movie villain who had the patience of a Jason to wait until they were alone, in the dark, and as vulnerable as cake.

Too easy, and rather dull, in my experience, to suck her now. Just as straight sex is to pornography which does not have a story. When there is a little backstory, when you appreciate the character a little more, you fall into the fantasy with greater height, and the sexual intercourse or the feeling of her blood gushing down your throat at climax, this is what gives pleasure its intensity. It is the only way to live after death.

Still, even with three of the five friends peeled away, the one called Holly was still in rapture and laughter with her friend, a thicker brunette who usually had her arm around Holly's waist, more in line with steadying herself than anything more elicit. None had taken a drink as long as I had been stalking, but after hours of walking in circles, it was obvious enough that one of them was still sloshed.

At fifteen minutes to one, the sweepers and money counters began to roam the nearly deserted lanes of dirt between the rides and slushy and taco stands. This was when the duo began to claw their sensible shoes back to the car park where few remaining autos stood. In fact, there were a mere three autos, one of which held the thick brunette as Holly mistakenly put her behind the wheel; this was obviously a girl who should not be behind the wheel. Then my interest, my Holly, made her way back to her own car, and for the first time that night, I did not see a smile on her lovely face.

She looked around, and right at me, but right through me, thoroughly spooked, and wondering… Then she went for her car keys and tried to focus. Eventually she found the right one and tried to put it in a door that seemingly kept moving for her.

"Might I be of service?"

She jumped out of her skin upon hearing me. The nearness of one so tall and beautiful as myself sent her into soberness neatly, I am sure. I fixed her with my royal eyes and bit my lip briefly to counter the full confidence I was exuding, and it surely put her at ease. She smiled broadly.

"No, thanks."

When she found herself awake and behind the wheel, a new gloss covered her holy aura. On her it looked good.

"How—"

I leaned against the car in that way I have, and toyed with the paint job.

"I will drive you home."

"No, thanks—"

"I know where you live."

"Yeah," she laughed. "No, thanks. I appreciate…"

She became drowsy and awoke as we were leaving the confines of fairground parking, I needing directions, she, wide-eyed and scared as if someone dear to her had slapped her.

"Where—!"

"Do not be alarmed," I soothed. "Is it left or right?"

"Is what left or right?"

"You are being driven home, milady. I live to serve." I half-bowed, and she half-laughed. The evening fell away into conversation over the blaring James Blunt who would not leave her confounded radio device.

It was not the most loveliest part of Florida. At night, there is a texture here that could be Lakeland or Tampa. I let the sounds of the smooth, swaying trees guide me up Appalachia Parkway. The road was strangely deserted save the old cruiser containing a 17-year-old male or a constabulary.

"Do you know who I am?"

She nodded and would not remove her smile. I felt like an avuncular nephew. She was fully awake, and kept her hands at the edges of her shirt, else it roll up and expose tummy. I have never been nor will I be a bellybutton man.

"You're very distinctive," she said.

"Thank you."

"Do you know where you're going?"

"Always."

"Where?"

"2763 Dufton Loop."

Her mouth came open, and eventually it would speak, but before that, I said, "You told me. When I got in."

"I *told*—" She stopped, and now eyed me as something rank on the menu, as if I were not really here, but a cartoon effect in a Lucasfilm that would suddenly pop into something grotesque and unbelievable.

"Don't you remember?"

For the rest of our short journey through sudden turns and circles in neighborhoods that looked alike, she struggled with memory and would not win.

By the time we sat in front of her duplex—she did not leave the light on—with the motor humming, I had to remind her we were stopped.

"Oh!"

"May I come in for a nightcap?"

"A *night*cap?" She laughed at this, as well she might.

"A funny and fitting word, is it not?"

"Is it?"

"Not. May I?"

We were at her door when she answered in a bewildered state. It was really quite charming, her state of mental undress and a hazy charm which, body language aside, spoke to me that lack of control was not her bag. Clearly, she had to be charge, or at least on top, as I hoped soon to prove.

"Thank you," I said, as she closed the door behind me. Her tightness on the doorknob screeched against the faux-diamond ring she wore on her index finger.

When she looked in my direction, though not exactly at me, I bowed an inch before I sat on her reclining couch and strutted the handle to elevate my feet. Her dwelling was clean and had a spacious A-frame ceiling that served no immediate purpose, unless she cared for tall Christmas trees during the season. White painted all around, the kitchen ran into the living room which ran into a slight hall of doors, only one of which I could see, and it was closed. Perhaps there was a roommate.

"Mmm. Coffee? Or wine?"

"I never drink…coffee," I said.

"What can I get you?"

There I was, suddenly beside her. As my mother once said, if you don't ask, you don't get. I kissed her on the neck.

"That," I said, and she smiled in a way that I knew would take further effort.

She began to brew a fresh pot of Moose Munch coffee while I teased her next with the tip of my triangular tongue.

From her vague stupor, she smiled and said, "It tickles."

*Of course it tickles, you silly cow*, I thought, and once she had her grounds in place, I moved us to the area before the couch upon which I had placed the bathroom towels.

# chapter 6

Medge had to go into Dr. Hummer's for a new nightguard—she grinds her teeth—so she had the Honda and I took a cab into work, which always makes me feel like I'm important, scribbling on papers in the backseat. It's only slightly marred by the 35 minute wait it takes to put my feet up behind the driver.

Still, there's nothing like that powerless feeling as you weave uncontrollably through dreaded traffic. I couldn't sign a thing, me being the pinball, so I celled (sic) up Celia to set up a 2 o'clock meeting for a general lockdown on where we were. I felt sure we were ready to alert the opposition to the fact that we exist. It was all up to Mark Clock now.

When I called in, Celia was already overly anxious, almost hysterical on the phone. "Oh Gath. Thank Gath. It sounds like…there's a rat or there's…something in your office. Should I call Orkin?"

"Yeah, yeah, call Orkin. Any updates?"

"I can read you Fred's fax, or he wants to talk to you."

"Which is it?"

"I think he wants to talk to you. But he's just going to read from this fax, I'll bet."

That's true, he usually does read from papers. Smart people don't do the same work twice. "I'll call. That it?"

"Barnes & Noble has their own version of *Dracula*, and there's nothing on the copyright page. They used an original piece of art for the cover, but if it was, say, Blue Boy, there's be a notice from whatever art gallery owns it."

"Who's the most creative judge we know?"

"Creative?" I could just hear her shrugging her shoulders. "None."

"Okay, with the best sense of humor."

"Let me work on it."

"Okay," I said, "meantime, work up a tentative list of heads of major companies, connected to entertainment."

"Well, that's what Fred's about, he has an angle on that."

"Good."

The cab stopped, but I didn't feel like getting out.

"Oh! Interpol!" she said.

"Great! What?"

"No records."

"*None*?"

"If our client is wanted for murder or wanted for anything, it's not a matter of public record."

"Well, that's good to know. Thanking God for large favors. Set up another meeting with everyone, please."

Time to get out.


Actually, I didn't. We circled around for me to score a Chic-Fil-a biscuit while Celia worked on all that. I dialed up Mark Clock while we were in the drive-thru. Answering machine. I guess he had the money for one of those now.

Nothing like that Chic chicken coating. Damn, those biscuits are good. Now, whoever said fast food breakfast has to stop after 10:30 in the morning, now there's a crime. I'd sue if I thought…

During my daydream about taking BK to court to open up those hashbrowns for all day consumption, I ambled up to my desk, already tired for some reason. I leafed through the non-mail on my desk and pitched it in the trash. I saw the note that our lockdown was on for 2, with a footnote from Holly that she requested a 7 p.m. start. I thought for a moment, then shook my mind and crumbled the note to join the junkmail. She could come in on her own if she wanted. 7 was too late.

I'd have Celia type up the notes legibly for a change and I'd give Holly the crux when she got in. She was only researching anyway.

By the time 2 rolled around, I was hungry enough to shell a fifty out to land us a pizza party from Papa John's—stuffed garlic crust, pepperoni supreme, with a hint of onion on a fourth of it (I didn't know they could do quarter toppings until Mark Clock mentioned it)—as we began brainstorming the beginning of the end of the prelim.

"Where's Holly?" Fred asked.

"We're going to forego some of this for the moment, so she's coming in later," I said. "Mark Clock, it's all down to you."

"Yeah, well, I haven't had much luck on references deferring much from the samples I've given you before," he said, a bit whinny. "The Dracula name, or to be precise, and we must be precise, *Dracul*, is really down to the father. This is Vlad Dracul, born in 1390, died in 1447, also known as Vlad the Dragon, who I believe was a wrestler in Mexico this century."

"Last century," Fred corrected.

"Last, yes." Mark Clock nodded.

"Have to be precise," Fred said and smiled.

MC nodded and continued, "This is where it gets into *Lord of the Rings*, with all sorts of 'of' stuff that I'd really rather you just read what I wrote on the papers, else I'm going to feel like a lit audio book over here."

I'd re-read it last night. After being enveloped into the Order of the Dragon run by Balkan Slavic noblemen prior to the Battle of Kosovo in 1389, this prince of the House of Basarab, father to our boy and Radu the Handsome, son of Mircea of Batran, half brother of Alexandru I Aldea who took the thrown of Dan II, leader of Wallachia, he and his other son Mircea II were assassinated in 1447 by General John Hunyadi, under the King of Hungary, for the slaughter of the Ottoman Empire.

"A lot of 'of's," I agreed. "Do we want to get a history kid in on this, or a professor? Does history help us?"

"Well, that's the point," MC said, shifting in his seat like the car journey was over, "that's what I was going to say. We're dealing with the *son* of a name, not the name. Granted, a *family* name. The whole point of right of publicity is mainly for the target, not the heir, when dealing with a name and not a specific image. Every person has the right to his own face. Professional publicity seekers, like the President or a Queen, is fair game. That's why you can write and publish a book on the President. But that's separate and below defamation of character; writing a book that the President buggers horses, for instance. You can make profit on a clean book. Even on a controversial one, provided you have truth as your defense.

"Bela Lugosi doesn't look like this…Vlad. Our client. I still want to meet him, Gath.

"The right to prevent unauthorized use of one's likeness or by a third party for commercial benefit is also a state by state issue. In the gray area of personality rights, it's not Federal. So if his main target is the studio system, we should file in California, not here.

"Also. Again. If our client is trying to claim exploitation of name, it's not his name. It's his family's. So. We've got a very senior citizen walking around who has neither his face nor his name exploited, merely a character allegedly based on him.

"Now, in our favor, we've got a slew of contradicting litigation which really *can* be to our benefit, because since all cases aren't going in one direction, it *will* take a court to decide. Only two years ago, Sam Shaw was given his day by a New York judge, a Federal judge, who said he did have the right to sell his photos of Marilyn Monroe, ruling that her rights of publicity ended with her death. Then we've got Tom and Nicole Cruise successfully suing to stop a perfume being touted by—" He held the paper closer to his glasses. "—Sephora, in September, 2002. In March, 2003, *The Sopranos* tell Best Buy they can't put pictures of them in newspaper ads without their permission or paying them something.

"Of course, these are all real people, of this century, nothing literary."

"So what are you saying?" I asked, waiting on my bottom line.

He giggled. "You know. In Indiana, they've been on *our* side for a hundred years, even claiming you have a right to your own signature— exactly like Agatha Christie and Spike Milligan are doing on book series—even your own gestures and mannerisms!"

"Who is Spike Milligan?" Fred asked, but I waved that away.

"What's your recom? Do we move forward?"

He was nodding with cream of gusto. "I say—we have the right to annoy on our side. Anyone can sue anyone. And when you've got things out there like the grandnephew of John Dillinger suing a restaurant in an Indiana Court of Appeals for using Dillinger's *likeness* and *name*, well…I say: forward!"

"How'd that end, by the way, Dillinger?"

He shrugged. "That's all Wikipedia had. Footnote."

"Right." I clapped my hands. The mood was sparking. Smiles all around, sleepy though they were after all that pizza. "Letter of intent in two days' time. I'm just thinking of the wording so we don't give too much away and don't get laughed out before we meet arbitration. Goals?"

"I think our first target should be arbitration with the Academy of Motion Picture Arts and Sciences," Fred timidly suggested.

"The Oscars?" Mark Clock asked.

"They house them, yes. That's their main thing, I guess. But we're looking for... there's not a *union* for movie studios. I know Vlad seems to hate Universal as the end all, since they did the most of the Draculas. But they really didn't. You do IMDB and, even excluding Hammer, there are Drac movies *all* up and down time. Universal has the classics, but let's be fair, let's be honest. These movies are *old*. I say target the newer. We get a big bag of publicity on top of it. The *Twilight* studio or whatever will *love* us, secretly, for all the free pub. And if that's what Vlad's endgame is anyway..."

Good point. "Good point," I said. "What's the most current?"

"*Tru Blood* is popular," Fred said. "I haven't seen it, but it's on HBO, and I'll see some. But I don't think we should target TV. That's cheap, and too spread out."

"I don't necessarily agree about television," I admitted, "because it's all powerful, and their news affiliates are going to be our greatest assets in getting publicity, even if it's that we're repping a crazy man. And whatever we go after should reference 'Dracula,' not just vamps. Vlad's not claiming to have invented the bite on the neck. So, who's our goal?"

No response.

"I know what he'll say, but I'll have another talk with Vlad and see if I can get him to see reason about something larger than attacking one *studio*."

"Gath, what about just multiple letters of intent?"

I'd thought about that for a couple hours I couldn't sleep one night. "I'm afraid of losing our shock value, even if we're simpletons in everyone's eyes. I see this as them seeing this as one big joke, believe me. But I don't want to lose our surprise value on spreading ourselves too thin. The first studio or whatever to take this *seriously* is going straight to the press. They'll see it as ha ha, and especially if it's a tie-in for a new horror movie. They'll time it just right."

MC chimed in. "That's a thought. It's Fall. Why don't we wait a month and chuck it into all the publicity of *Saw 8* coming out, things like that?"

I shook my head. "That's like trying on a Santa Claus suit at Christmas. You think it's wise, but you're really drowned out by all the human interest and the clashing of all those other Santa stories that need to get out there, fighting for air time. No. Best time for a Santa Claus case, if you're trying it in the press, is in January. No question."

"So..." Fred was drawing me out... "...what are you saying, November?"

"I don't know. Trouble with Fall. It's holiday after holiday. I don't know what's fickle enough for an... *individual* case like this. I just say, let's not shoot for Fall or Halloween. Let's grab our goal, look at the pace we're given. If the studio, or whatever, wants to put us on their schedule, to hype whatever they've got, let's use them using us. More publicity, them, more publicity us."

Nods all around. Fred wiped pepperoni grease on his neck, then in the under-knees of his jeans.

"Everyone get an extra gmail email," I said, "and tag Twitter to it. I want to move on this the *moment* I hear from arbitration. I have *no* idea what to expect with keeping the ball in play, and I want to counter any arguments or hang-backs about their not following through. It's ridiculous, I know, but we need them to see *us* as serious."

Nods all around, then Mark Clock slipped out, followed by Holly, to type up her notes. Fred put his still greasy hand on me. "What'd psych say?"

I didn't answer immediately, so he kept going with, "I assumed since it wasn't part of folder..."

Yeah, why put inconclusives in. "She had no opinion, and palmed us off on...I can't remember the name at the moment."

"It's going to have to be done, though," he said, and I grudged to agree with him. "We have to clear him as competent to stand trial. What about the fingerprints?"

I answered, "As he said there would be—no record."

Consternation hit his face hard. "What do you think that means?"

"Well, he was born in another country. So he says."

He nodded at me, and was still nodding as he left the room. I needed some Tin Machine in here. Bowie, like his *Outside* album, was fine for night time, but now was the time to rock and think.

I busied myself with civil law jurisdictions (a boring old case I had to finish sometime) until six ten rolled around, then there was a soft knock on the door. I knew Holly's knock, so I wasn't surprised it was Medge barging in. Still she surprised me. Chilidogs from Woofer's!

"Oh, baby!" I said to the dog. Oh yes. *These* were the ones with the *hot* onions. Just enough bite to make its grey mustard totally redundant. Long and slender dogs with crushed buns, like they'd been steamed and sweated somewhere with the meat. This *was* a dollar chilidog worth 2.50.

I pushed one mostly in my mouth and kissed a wife, and sat down to wolf the rest of it, suddenly hungrier than a Georgian buffet. Once I was 2/3 through the second one, I mumbled, "Thanks…" holding up my hand to keep from spraying.

Medge was eating a small tub of coleslaw, and as usual, she had brought her own pickle relish jar, dabbing into it and mixing as she went.

"How's it going?" she asked, like a lady, nothing spraying.

"It's going." I was into the third dog, that was really all that was on my mind. She knew it.

"Are you busy?"

That made me look up. That question, mixed with her eyes on my eyes, was always code for "Let's make love." As a married man, you take it when you can get it. My smile lit my eyes like the weekend before Christmas, and I began to chew much more slowly.

By the time night came on, it was 8:15 and I had no idea it was so late. The office was a mess, but not from sex. We tried it on the desk, but I like my women petite, and there wasn't enough meat on Medge to cushion the shock, so we moved to my padded chair, her on top. Now we had a problem. I love that chair, but it multi-tasks too much. It goes down flat if you want, or pretty flat, like a dentist's chair, maybe. I never did it down all the way. I like sitting up straight. But the hook that kept it from going from one position to another was broken or close to it, so you never knew when that chair was going to suddenly move to the flat position. That's why I always kept it against the wall these days. But all that bouncing…I had to keep my right arm below the arm rest on the hook all through the ride.

By the time another soft knock came, I was knackered in two ways. Celia had left. I'd told her to go between chilidogs, so who could it be?

I dressed, Medge dressed, like we were doing it in Macy's windows. God, chili on top of sex on top of rushing for someone's uninvited entry, it was enough to give you a heart attack!

"Yes!" I demanded, opening the door to a vaguely smiling Holly who sort of floated in, followed by Vlad himself.

He must've seen my shirt tail out in the open. "Oh, dear. Did we come at a bad time? I thought we were late?"

"For what?"

"I did say 7, Gath." Holly looked tired. But not as worn as Medge who looked like she'd gotten dressed in a Goodwill spin dryer. She put a hand to Holly's check and the two of them sat at the small conference table.

"Yeah," I admitted like a sheep. "You did. It's after 8. We were just...finishing up our hot dogs. I don't get time to eat."

"Eat at home," Medge corrected.

Vlad threw more fifties into the room. His answer for everything. I mean, it was a *good* answer. It was just funny to see crisp bills float and twirl in a windless room.

"We were hoping it had gone on until now," Holly said.

I don't know. Her voice was weak or softer. Drained.

She didn't exactly stare off into space. It was just that she wasn't really using her eyes.

"I think it's time I met the crew," Vlad said, sitting as if someone had just loaded him into a jack-in-the-box. "I should get acquainted. To see what you are fighting for, so to speak."

"Yes," I nodded. "That's on the agenda."

It was stuffy in here. So I took us on the road to this cute after dinner restaurant I know that just specializes in desert. It's one of the best places I know for large or small tables, for any size group, where the light's too dim for reading and just ripe for drinking any exotic recipe on the menu.

Vlad had a Bloody Mary, two straws. Medge had watched her weight with coleslaw, so she was all for splitting a brownie parfait with me.

"Where's Doll?" I whispered.

"Daphne," she whispered back. That was all I needed to know. Daphne was in high school with no friends or boyfriends, so you could get her on literally a moment's notice. She read Jules Verne, was dog ugly and was the safest babysitter around.

I'd collected up the fifties before we left, but I hadn't spent the ones from the last time he did his confetti act, so my wallet was bulging. Between an uncomfortable wallet ass, a sore arm, and the sleepy attitude of a half-lit room, I didn't feel like being here the longer we stayed. But Medge was falling awake on anticipation of the coming parfait, so, I figured I owed it to the enjoyment of all to stay pleasant.

It was Holly I couldn't figure. She was sucking her own personal straw, and looking at Vlad, not like a lover, but almost *through* him, like there was something bland outside. Obviously, the way they were sitting, they were closer. Much closer. But it was…more like an owner and a cat than—

Vlad broke my train of thought with the only business we'd talk that night. "Can we set it up for tomorrow?"

"What?" I was eating my share of nut brownie.

"Everyone," he said. "A team meeting."

I nodded,

and suddenly. Somehow. We were home. In bed. Medge sleeping, snoring minor league beside me. Me, as if I'd just woken up. Not sweating. I didn't have to pee, but in my mind… it was hardly a scary dream. We were just eating a brownie and caramel ice cream, that's all it was.

# CHAPTER

There is nothing more solitary than one's own coffin. Though I have heard of sunlight and still remember its rays, when my skin was a lad's and still growing, the concept of it as a positive concept cannot be sidestepped, even today. To know no woman's love, nor feel these sun streams through something as simple as a window filtering a summer's day, these are what the poet, any poet, tells us are the fruits of life, the goals of a life worth living, the culmination of all that is the best of the best.

As my coffin door creaked closed, without knowing if the night would remain cold or hot from  the coming Fall upon my unfeeling skin, my mind worked on these bits of poetry, these dreams, alone, and not sleepy, but cowardly avoiding the day.

Rested and ravenous, I shook the dirt from my cape and stretched that which did not need stretching. It was these little things, these tedious nuances that I lifted from Paul Muni and his bunch, those purporting to be—and were—great actors.

I needed blood, some simpering college blood to cleanse me of this pompous narrative.

As usual, when in doubt, grace the Taco Bell across from campus, the one next to the Panda Café. I could time my meal just so by entering at 7, just as darkness fell, when all those of a better intelligence would be elsewhere studying sexuality or out working off their loan repayments.

In the corner were two men called George, speaking in whispers and giggles that made them appallingly feminine, regardless of the vast amount of chin and cheek hair that seemed to define cool for them.

I stood before them. I did not like hair. Smooth is a better bite. But as they were the only two losers here, I conversed.

"I have some sod that needs planting," I said. "It is sensitive to sunlight and must be done only in moonlit darkness."

"Look at that…!" said one George, cupping his hand to deflect his spittle, like a funny drunk.

The other sputtered away at me as well, then both launched into full faced laughing, uncaring to my feelings.

I slapped down $300 in twenties which did its usual job of squelching frivolity, and their eyes took on the serious appraisal of my visage.

"Wha—"

"—do you needone," the other soon finished for his friend.

I repeated myself, and both followed me like puppies from this Mexican chain. Their heads were rather bowed before they entered my BMW rental, their legs seemingly stitched up like marionettes caught up in the strings. They were drunk.

Once in the spacious backseat, the motor rumbling, the windshield wipers swishing madly, I instructed, "You're going to get dirty. You do not mind that?"

Their frivolity returned. My apparent lack of contracting *do* and *not* being of sufficient hilarity to envelope their tiny minds for the four miles it took for me to find a dark stretch of land with a theme of solitude.

The motor stopped. I was quick. I was careful to share their first punctures together, so that screams more than seconds did not collectively escape them, and I drank and drank. The loss of intellect was sudden and invigorating and I felt my descriptive powers drain utterly from me.

It was good. Their bodies shook, no longer able, no longer willing. I darted from neck to neck, arm to arm, making new holes, siphoning from every direction, feeling the impulse drive me to spirit every drop, and every crumb of every drop of blood from their weakening blue veins. The heavy rains shook the car as I delighted in the suckle of an under-knee, and the slurp of an earlobe. One tiny dot of ear blood escaping back up through the piercing one had of a cross. How quaint, I thought.

Their eyes bulged, their own shaking, finished. Thunder. Not very much lightning. I relished in the spray of the rain and the lash of the wind against the car, rolling the three of us to nowhere.

How I loved Seattle. But I would not return here.

# chapter 7

The unnamed man who would not shake hands sat his fat ass down in the plastic booth. He opened his paper-thin file folder between the mocha-choco-latte and a half portion of Chopstix Chicken Salad.

"I can only give you ten minutes," he said. "Mr. Dalmonica sends his regrets and wanted me to have a word with you to appraise him of what to expect within his appraisal."

"You said all that on the phone," I said, and he had.

He gave me a half-lip smile and never looked up from the paragraph he studied intently. "You are proposing what, exactly?"

"You have my fax."

He looked at me, so I smoothly sipped from my sweet peach tea.

"You are proposing to sue the world at large for using the name and likeness of Dracula within literature and filmdom," he said without humor, "for the purpose of establishing a right to publicity for an entity over 500 years old."

"My client is suing. I'm merely stating his case."

"Of course." He had some salad. Poured extra dressing on it, and said, "Is your client crazy?"

"I will, naturally, supply Mr. Dalmonica with the appropriate affidavits from our highly specialized doctors in the field of psychiatry. But my client has made it clear from the origin of this case that he is open to any and all tests from any side."

He was still shoveling it in, with some speed, I must say, but he still managed to use these ten minutes. "And why should we care—that is, why should anyone pay for something that is ancient history and viably in public domain?"

No judgment, no laughing at me, just dead serious, and a degree beyond curious.

"Who does Mr. Dalmonica represent, exactly?" I asked.

"A number of interested parties."

"We faxed the Academy of Motion Pictures—"

"It is a group of interest parties," he said vaguely. "But why should anyone care at this late date?"

THE question. I hadn't seen it, the crafty bugger, but he had a silver pen out, spiraled out to write, tip poised for writing *the* answer.

I tried to swallow a sigh and said, "My client has incontrovertible proof that he is, in fact, who he says he is. Documentation, birth certificate, proof of family name. Regardless of the date of the origin of personality rights, and in view of the fact that the name Dracula and vampires in general, which so often culminate from this origin, is in perpetual use by the studio system and the publishing industry, I don't see how one man's claim to be the father of this…multi-billion dollar industry will be so easily ignored when it is ultimately tried not only in court, but on the front pages of every newspaper and in the cameras of every talk show and news program throughout the world."

"Ah." And for the first time he smiled. He'd probably known the answer. Or thought so. He slowly drew a small blue capital N with his pen, outlining it again as he spoke. "That."

Somehow he'd managed to finish the salad while I wasn't looking. He closed the file and stood like a dinosaur.

Smiling, he said, "You'll know that we always settle nuisance cases out of court. And sometimes we get some of our money back with a civil suit for wasting our time, soon but later on."

Smiling, I said, "Oh, no. This is going to court. My client is wealthy. It's not about the money."

That let the air out of his Hindenburg.

The evening was cool as I breezed along to the confines of Meat Loaf shouting "Not a Dry Eye in the House" through my open window out at Tallahassee, this great city of ours, even *greater* tonight. I felt *good*. I'd had myself a few uninterrupted hours with Medge under the sheets, out on the back porch, while Doll busied herself with grandma. A good meal of greens, cornbread and Chicken Marsala, extra wine later, I was stuffed, sleepy, extraordinarily happy, and missed several low-hanging red lights as I drove. But I didn't hear a single siren behind me. The night was *fine*. I'd put the case succinctly and we'd be meeting with Dalmonica *soon*. Good vibes.

The little parking lot we shared with the hairdresser's was only 73% full, and it seemed I was the last to arrive at 8:15. Who cared! They didn't. I was drunk on life, but I'll admit Vlad had his usual Mind Control stare on me when I came in. I thought, a little Enya.

Everyone settled down with the music, jabbering together, and all eyes tried not to look at Vlad staring all the way through the evening.

"Sorry about being late, but there wasn't anything good on the radio, so I had to rifle through my CD case and you know how long that takes me." Titters. Polite, good. "You've all met our client, Mr. Vlad Tepes—"

"Actually, no," our client said. "I have refused to speak until everyone has been assembled."

"O…kay."

He rose. "Gentlemen and persons. I am in love. With the most beautiful creature in the world." More to himself: "Creature is unkind. She is not a creature! Where is she?"

His fist thudded down on the table, leaving an imprint. There was silence.

Fred raised his pencil and asked with innocence, "I'm sorry. Who?"

Dramatically, I mean like a flash of lightning that was as comical as lightning hitting a golfer, Vlad whipped his finger like a pointing dog at an empty seat. We all changed seats often, it wasn't like school where everyone gravitates unspokenly to his/her own desk, but we were only one person short, so we got the gist.

"Holly?"

He nodded curtly. The three of us busied ourselves with trying not to crack up or make that unseemly digesting noise that comes from trying to hold in a laugh. Celia was busy, as always, rushing to take down everything anyone said.

Vlad was livid. Breathing like he'd just run here.

Trying to bite a smile and swallow it down is one of the hardest things a man can do, but I tried, succeeded, and said, "Uh. We can speak of this later. Really. She's doing something for the case. She's…"

"I gave instructions that everyone, everyone should be here! It is time I speak!"

And with that, he sat down and shut up and brooded all the way through nothing much at all. I felt sort of sorry for everyone present, because there was nothing to talk about, just rehashing old stuff. Though I did give my take on the meet with Mr. Arbitrator's arbitrator.

"I've got a good feeling on this," I said, everyone pretty much nodding. It was great news. But with Vlad there calming himself into a seething mire, it was a bit like enjoying a rose in a dog shit factory.

After several moments of this silence, I just put my hands together. "Okay," I said, and reached for the music remote. Handel. Something bright and classical. Exit music.

"I thank you all for coming!"

Mark Clock kept his eyes lowered and just trudged out, followed by a very concerned Fred. He looked at me like I just ate his lottery ticket. Celia was blissfully oblivious, still jotting time wasters as she left.

Vlad was agitated and had another of his mini-earthquakes that did not quite break through to the surface. He was controlled. Again. Like a rollercoaster that slows at the *top* for just a second. He rose.

"Gath, have you seen Holly?"

"She's off to Romania," I said.

"Romania!"

"Didn't she tell you?"

"She is not returning my calls! She did *not* tell me! Romania! Why should she go to that place, of all places!"

"Research."

"Research!" He screamed it like Hitler. His glue was showing. "Research! You can get *everything* off the internet!"

I smiled. "Well, not everyt—"

"She must come back immediately! Immediately!" His eyes grew black. I mean, they really seemed to change from blue to black. "She must come back to me!"

"Are you two…?"

"Are we what?"

"Well… she'll be back in a—"

"She must come back to me now!" He thrust a finger into the void. "Now! You must call her—"

"Well, it's your case. She needs—"

"I shall give you all the proof you desire!"

And with that, he changed into a bat. Then a tiger. Then a goldfish flopping on the floor, then back to an angry man with flashing blue, now, eyes, then a puff of smoke, and then he yelled at me from behind.

"You must—"

At least, I assume that is what happened.

Nothing was very clear for me for the next several days. Medge thought I had stomach flu. I didn't feel like eating. All I felt was terrified. Or, that sense that you feel when you *ought* to be terrified. Because you can't remember.

It was sweet of Doll to climb into bed when it *seemed* like I was reading all sorts of papers about the common law tort of passing off (enforcing unregistered trademarks), but I'm not sure.

I was in a clouded fever.

I remembered Vlad ranting on and on and practicing his magic tricks for me, or whatever I was rationalizing to myself in those early days. I remembered heaps of bed time, watching my baby Doll roll around between us in the sheets as she slept through *Dracula's Daughter* and Medge read up on how to roll chicken and basil into something tasty. Just weird dreams of endless realism. Like trying to memorize ocean waves.

When I awoke from my dead time, I found that a whole lot of work had been accomplished. Some by me, Medge said, and a lot by beautiful Fred. My eyes wouldn't really focus on Celia's notes. I set them aside.

Pissed. Angry. *Really* angry, that's what Vlad had been.

That's when I had that feeling I'd ignored a couple times in the past, and I sat and thought. It didn't take long to decide. It was time to pull in my own personal ace.

Joma (rhymes with "yo mama" if you say it very fast) was a big black guy I went to high school with. Divorced three times, I really believed he stayed a cop to force out all the anger he had for…well, everything. For some reason, the two of us always got on. Maybe because we never talked wives, women, or the state of social reform. With us, it was the occasional lumpy beer down at Biglow's, him watching and loving football, me tolerating it because I just liked being around him. Not much sense of humor, but he had that sheer aggression that was like a magnet to me. And turn a magnet the other way, like he did with most people, and you repel without even trying.

"Don't call me afro- or African-American," he told me a couple years ago between big brandies. "I'm black, you're white, the *rest* of the world is colored."

Have to admire a guy like that, who has arms the size of Sony speakers.

I figured I'd make it easy and relaxed and usual, so I got him to Biglow's about six in the evening, a few days after Vlad's ballistic *pow*, or at least my *memory* of it, and he ordered a few things, like fried zucchini sticks, once I said it was all on me.

I plopped down a fifty, and he stared at it, like people do when you have a fifty, and we moved to a little table just under the sweaty framed FSU shirt from a couple seasons ago when they made it to some Bowl.

Our bowl of sticks came and Joma was planting hot sauce over it all like I wasn't going to eat any of it, so I didn't. He was eating with his right hand, looking at the $50 with his left, eyeing me like a trivia expert.

"Got a client handing these out," I said.

"Uh huh. Is it good?"

"Oh yeah. I'm thinking too good to be true."

"But it's good," he persisted.

I nodded. And I already had my opener ready. "Can you tell if a guy's, like, Armenian, by his blood type?"

"I don't know, man, ax a doctor."

"I'm axing you, in your professional experience. You know, can you solve a case by x-raying some guy to see if he's… you know, like, five hundred years old or something."

"You crazy?"

"Is he crazy, that's the point."

I took out a couple more fifties and just put them in his fist. Luckily that fist wanted to come open or there would've been just no way of getting them in there.

"Is Interpol also Federal, and local? I mean, if you get something clean from Interpol—no record—does that go for the whole world or just non-USA?"

"Whoa, whoa, man, you're jumpin' *all* around." He smoothed out the bills and pocketed them. "Whatchu want from Joma?"

I took out a spoon I'd lifted from the after dinner place the other night, when it was Medge, me, Holly and Vlad. Being careful with the Kleenex around Vlad's fingerprints.

"I swiped this the other night," I confessed.

"You under arrest, man."

"Thank you." I smiled. But it was getting harder to smile. "Can you just run a check on this for me?"

"What for?"

"For fingerprints."

"I mean, what you—" and he "shoot"ed in that way he had without actually saying *shoot* or *shit*. "Yeah, whatever you want."

He took out a Glad sandwich bag and dumped it in.

"You carry those around with you?"

He didn't answer. We drank. He drank, I just had my Dr. Pepper.

"You did it again, man."

"What?"

He sighed, then looked at me. Like that was my sigh.

"Was I sighing?"

"Like you was breathing," Joma said. "Ever since you wheezed in."

"Gettin' worried, man." I put my back up against the padded booth, and it felt good to pretend I was black for another evening. "This case." I must've sighed. I did sigh. I caught myself that time. After a while of pause, I said, "I've been seeing things, man. I don't like to say. But I'm getting scared."

"You don't have to be scared."

I laughed. "Yeah. Well. I'm working hard, and this guy is *weird*. And." Should I say it? I'd been toying with the notion. "You know, the guy came to me because he *says* I'm so honest. Said he'd been scoping me out for a long time?"

"Yeah? How long is long?"

I didn't answer that. Just stared into the dark wet of the Doctor Pep. "If I'm so honest. Why can't I walk away?"

He let me wallow in the emotion for a moment. Then he brought up a bill, ran it between his fingers. "Walk away from *this* shit?"

"I'm scared, Joma. The money's good. But, the things I've been seein'… Feelin.'"

"Like what?"

He wouldn't believe me.

We sat and drank. He was three brandies up on me before he hobbled to his big feet.

"You run a psyche on the guy?"

I nodded.

"Run one on yerself." And he handed me a business card. Which I didn't need.

# CHAPTER

I feasted on the flesh that night in a way I had not drunk for eleven years. I was on some highway coming from Boston, one that I believed had more traffic and fewer missing children placards pasted on rest area bulletin boards.

Women are delicious because they are lovely and never hairy in the correct areas. I found a small red car with three of these beautifully smelling creatures—these *were* creatures—and I tore them apart once they had stopped and peed and laughed into the highway again. First, I smoked to get them to pull the car over, for I did not want an accident. In their drunken state of mind, it was impossible to turn them sexually upon each other, so I merely turned the heater up, melted them into sleep, and quietly stripped their flesh slowly in long, stringy pieces. I felt like taking my time this night, allowing myself the taste of blood on skin, not my usual stick and suck.

Licking their arms as they moaned and their eyes rolled under their dancing eyelids, it was a pleasure to watch their self-hypnotic pleasure from pain. Yet in all of this, I imagined doing this to my Holly, and that was enough.

A fantasy. And a quenching of hunger, no more.

Satisfied.

She would return. She would come back to me.

# chapter 8

Tallahassee is the seat of Florida's gov't, though at times it seems it was created for Florida State University's football season alone. The city is widely spread out. There are a duo of malls in danger from internet sales, and there's plenty to drink and eat here and plenty of traffic to go around.

For some reason, my expert witness wanted to meet in Andrew's Capital Grill & Bar, right across from the erection (what us Tallyers call the tall penis that is the central and main government building downtown). Today the area was sprinkled liberally with politicians, students, and any tame tourist who could make it up the hill from FSU. Noon plus ten minutes, so it was busy. I had the grilled chicken salad, and Dr. Moner had everything greasy on the menu. She had a dog face—and I mean that in the best possible way—with a petite student figure to make up for it. So where all the calories were going, I didn't know. She ate her fried fish pieces with her hands, like it was corn on the cob.

I dug into my salad and smiled. "How would you define a crazy person?"

"The hard one first, huh?"

She kept eating all through our talk, and talked and chewed with her mouth open, making me wonder if this was some kind of test.

"I would define craziness," she said, "as an irrational belief in something that cannot happen."

"Then my client is crazy."

"How's your sex life?"

"Excuse me?"

She kept her eyes on me, but she really didn't know how to smile, so I was never quite sure what to do with her.

Thinking about it—sex in the office, having done it in every room in the house, including Doll's little room, and in every car we've ever had, even while driving a couple times—we both realized I was smiling too broadly for a public restaurant, so I confessed all, and Moner nodded.

"Glad to hear it."

"Really my main…inkling was coming to you to see if you could do me a psych on my client. He thinks he's the inspiration for Dracula, and he's scaring me to pieces."

"Interesting phrase."

The waiter came and asked about wine and desert, just passing the time. The good doctor was still really chowing down.

"Red wine, please. Anything," and she waved him away. Then she smiled at me!

"I work a lot for the police department, doing character profiles. I have a sixth sense when someone is lying to me. Some would call me a witch for that. Seeing the future is using your instinct, as you know. In a way, it's a belief in yourself. So, you could say that having true confidence in yourself, and who you are, doesn't exactly make you crazy, even if you think you're the Pope. Unless you're the Pope."

Red wine was brought, so I figured I'd have a glass too. Why not?

We clinked.

"I know this is a strange question," I said, "but is there any way of…psychologically dating someone?"

"That's what all dates are, I think."

She swished her wine like it was mouth waste. Yuck, her face said. You're supposed to do that with water, I thought.

"No, I mean." How to put this. "Say you were in a locked room with someone, and you're blindfolded. Could you tell the age of the person—okay, let's say it was a voice actor so you won't say you can tell by the sound of their voice—could you tell someone's actual age by the answers they give you?"

She thought about that. Kept eating. And said, "Why does the door have to be locked?"

"What?"

"The door, you said it was locked." I was looking at her blankly, so she just laughed. "Sorry, just one of those Columbo things. Sorry. Well..."

I finished my glass. This, maybe 40 year old woman was making me nervous. Shooting around, subject to subject. She wasn't exactly flippant, but...

"It's an interesting question," she said, maybe finally finished eating. "I think I've seen the question posed in a psych journal. But then again, you're getting into the fine line between belief, I mean, the difference between the truth and what someone believes to be true of himself."

"And there's no way of erasing that line?"

"I can't erase it. Can you?"

She stared me.

"Have you taken this man to a GP?"

I nodded. "Two days ago. He himself wanted to be x-rayed. We didn't dare tell the guy why we were doing it, and it was a good thing. When my associate casually asked the doctor for a date on the bones, just to prove to the court that these x-rays were taken this year, he said there's no way of telling. Vlad is 'undead,' but, the theory is, what he consumes to sustain himself—"

"Blood?"

"Right, that's keeping his DNA from crumbling away. The doctor admitted our guy had no heart beat, no blood pressure, and everyone rationalized that to be faulty equipment. But in comparison to mere mortals' x-rays, he also didn't have 500-year-old bones."

"Or not that your doctor wanted to admit to."

"Who wants to look foolish? The court might have to appoint independent physical exams."

Then, all of a sudden, it was like I was sitting with someone else. Moner suddenly relaxed. She smiled in a regular joe way that I didn't think was possible.

"I'm sorry. Joma's a good friend of mine. He was worried about you."

"I'm worried about me," I said, relaxing a bit. Maybe it was the wine. But it was her. "I've been...seeing things. A lot of things. There have been even whole...days I've been in a haze because I can't remember, specifically, what happened. Days, just, vanished! And every time, *every time*, it comes after a meeting with my client."

"Dracula."

"Vladimir Tepes," I corrected. "The basis of the whole myth. Quote."

"What's the case? Can you say?"

I smiled. "I'd rather not. You'd commit me straight away. But let's just say that there's money in it, from both sides. From my client, and, if they're dumb enough, who we're going after."

She nodded. "Yeah. Money's a good thing."

"It *is* a good thing."

"It's not the only thing."

"It's not."

"Are you taking any drugs?"

I shook my head.

"Addicted to anything?, even Dr. Pepper."

"How did you know that?"

"I asked Joma what to expect, that's all. Asked him the same questions."

Serious, I said, "Well, it's not me. I haven't even had a day's illness in my young life, unless you count getting my tonsils out when I was six. I don't count that, and I think drugs is like gambling, a complete waste of time and money."

"Gambling can *be* a drug."

"What are we talking about here?"

Now *she* was serious. Maybe serious all along, hidden inside that flippancy. Maybe I just couldn't take her seriously, the way she kept eating.

"Perception," she said. "Meaningless questions don't produce meaningless responses. Just because you can't see my point doesn't mean it's not sharp."

"That's clever." I meant it.

"Thank you. What I'm saying is, everything you say to me is wrapped up in your perception. It's like word association, but it's much cleaner, clearer. One word answers don't say much. You then have to define one word answers, based on your, I mean the doctor's, perception. Have you tried a regular conversation with Dracula?"

"Vlad. What is 'regular'?"

"I can do this for you, if you like. In a social setting. It's up to you if you want to instruct him that I'm a doctor or not. I say, tell him. Alert him that it's just for the psych eval, we won't even talk business. No mention of ages or vampirism, just—"

"Then he'll probably talk movies all the way through."

"Horror movies?"

"He likes Charlie Chans, too."

"I've never seen one."

We left it like that. She'd get me, for two thousand dollars, an official eval I could take against the arbitrator, or maybe I'd save it for court. No sense giving all our cards up in the first round, straight flush or not.

When I got back to the car, I pulled into a Mobile convenience store so I could call and check the answering machine. It was true. Holly was officially missing. Fred said she hadn't arrived at the Romanian Hilton, and I have to admit, my first thought wasn't for her safety, which I know is wrong, but I was thinking that I didn't know Hiltons covered the globe *that* well. I put Joma onto it, now that he was half on our team anyway. Actually, I gave Fred Joma's # and heard that Holly's description was all over the wires, or however they spread missing persons reports, in no time. Did I mention before that Joma's a cop? This is my first book, so bare with me.

Trouble was, Vlad wasn't answering his cell, the one I gave him, and I *needed* that psych report before I had my big power play session. It was after dark, so I kept dialing. Ring, ring. I hung up and phoned Celia, who always knew to be on call during the big cases, and had her keep redialing Vlad until something happened. She was smarter than me; she called through her computer, so she could just keep calling even during pizza and things. But when she never called *me* back, I had this Romanian feeling I knew where my star client was.

There was nothing to do but roll my groans and head back home. Medge had some warm skin for me in a hug, and I just kept myself there for minutes while I unwound and got into the family mode again.

My favorite mode. Soon I was soothed and planted in the recliner, slowing erasing the worries of tomorrow with tales of *Home Improvement*, my least favorite show, but a hit with Doll whose laughter never failed to pick my face off the floor. During the commercials she ranted about homework and Dirk, this boy at school and I couldn't believe his name, which was good for more laughs and more work-thought erosion, and soon we were full of called-in Chinese food and good, boring thoughts about what to do this weekend.

"You're getting extra in now," Medge said, "why don't we take a trip somewhere? Just for the weekend."

"Costs more to fly on weekends," I reminded her.

"Road trip?" Doll asked, cocking her head.

"No, let's fly, honey. We could go to San Diego and go to the zoo. Or Chicago? Come on, Gath. We haven't done something spur of the moment since…" She thought. Then she gave a look to our unplanned Doll who didn't get it at all, thank god.

Indulging, I said, "Where then?" I was sleepy. "What's in Chicago?"

"Doll, get on Yahoo," Medge said. "See what's the cheapest round trip from Tally, preferably out of the state."

Our computer expert pounced from the room. Nothing like an online quest to kill her curiosity for the second half of a TV program. God, she could find anything, print out anything. She was 6, right? Hopefully that meant she'd have many, many years geeking for big bucks and taking care of me and mom in Greece or wherever she'd send us.

A wife bounded on my lap and when the chair gave a groan, I looked at her, and she hit me upside the head for that look.

"What's it, a trip?"

"Wha?"

"I said, what's this with a trip."

"Gath, baby, honeybaby, why not?" She kissed me. On the nose. Then a good one elsewhere. "Do you know how much you haven't been around lately?"

Interior groan. "I never even thought about it. I don't think about you two when I'm at work."

That threw her for a speech loss. She laughed with wide eyes, reminding me of someone important (starts with v) I wanted to forget for the night.

"You basket!" she cried.

"You footpump!" I cried.

"Your mama's bra size!"

Oh dear. When she got into the *yo mama* arena, there was no competing. Medge was the poet of the family.

"You're right, you're right. Too much work for me. I think I just got addicted to the fifties."

"The decade?"

"Our vampire pays in the *big* bills, fifty big ones. My eyes just went all sparkly with it. Easy to lose yourself in the hours when you're staring at one of those dream wheels. Round and round…Where do you want to go?"

"I dunno, let's wait to see the short list."

Good idea, but the time it was taking, it was obvious Doll was busy indulging her own addiction. The girl just didn't know how to stop searching and browsing, one idea leading to another, and you can wave homework goodbye, you can be late for school. I talked to Medge about limiting her online hours, but the only thing we're competent to go on that score is unplug the machine. A girl as smart as Doll wouldn't let that stop her.

So, the wife and I smooched a while. I had a feel of the good parts, and finally, we just overheated, and turned the tube off and went to discover Doll asleep at her Elmo desk. At least she'd printed out a few things, with airline price comparison charts, before falling off.

*Orlando.* Well, we said no Florida. We could drive there, though.

*New Orleans.* Promising. But being on the panhandle as we were now, we could drive there too.

*Translyvania?* Surely it didn't still exist? Why had she printed out *that?*

My thoughts ran cold.

# CHAPTER

Through broken glass in an abandoned house, I watched as someone killed a dog, some large dog, and began to gut it. He was like a wild animal who works from smell and instinct, and hunger. It was rather ridiculous to see him strip the hairy flesh from the bones in that way. His strength was impressive, but he wasted so much blood. *That* should be the crime, had there been a policeman around. As it was, from the silence, there was no one. No one but that man.

My hunger had reached an…interesting level. The flight had been long, and being in the baggage area, as usual, there were no snacks served. Not that blood was one of their novelty refreshments, even on the most exotic of airlines.

I followed this man to a bar whose title translated as "The Bear Can" and watched him stagger into a dimly lit square of a place which had rows and rows of bottles sitting somehow on a tall window. I'd passed up the crumb of a dog, though my hunger was great, as it was hardly exciting, and hairy. There is nothing to compare to the taste on your lips as blue blood wants a chance to become red as you suck so hard the jealous oxygen can do nothing.

Beyond the wisp of a door I noticed perhaps 80 men in the warm room, all as if dying. Their eyes drained toward the floor and no one seemed to be drinking at all. Occasionally there was movement, and somehow a glass was drained, but I never saw how it was done. A stillness of time had captured this place, save the barman who merely eyed me like a stork. His hands were small, but he still, through skillful practice, laid one dirty hand on top of two glasses and set them in front of me. I'd been moving away from the bar, but found his arresting sales technique charming and halted.

"The second one's free," he said, not unlike a Hungarian Jimmy Durante, "if you down it without scoffing."

When you feel nothing but the taste of blood, challenges of this sort are old hat. I watched him watch my eyes as I downed the murky liquid like rainwater.

He filled the next glass, and took the first one away. To wash it, I supposed? I laid down a 100 forint coin down as the rag on the seat next to me spoke in sporadic volume.

"You looking for a woman?"

"Actually, yes."

"Only reason people come here."

I looked around, finding it hard to believe that all these statues were sitting around for women or drinks alone, and was about to ask when he pulled out a colorful brochure full of tits and promise and made his pitch.

"This one," he said, pointing to a plump brunette with a duck of a face and poised like Warner Oland, "is my girlfriend. And she will do anything. What do you like? She will do anything. What do you like?"

"I like her."

I showed him the picture of Holly I'd had taken in that little machine at the mall, and he sniffed at it. A deriding sniff, clearly to show that this was not the type of woman for any man.

He merely flashed his favorite on top of my picture and said, "You like fat. There is nothing better than having it fat. What do you like?"

"Have you seen her?" I fixed him with a stare that let the catalogue of women fall from his hairy hands. He looked and he shook his head.

"Who else should I ask?"

He pointed to one man alone at the table nearest the fireplace. I took my careful step closer, aware that my presence was chilling and if not terrorizing, at least a novelty to these jobless excrements who have seen everything in this rotting world.

I sat at what appeared to be more of a desk, a round table desk half full of receipts, papers and a phone. Attached to his left hand always was a bottle. He was a white face hairy man who stupidly wore a round hat indoors seemingly for style. I showed him the picture and repeated my need.

He slowly shook his head.

It caused me great concern to know that nothing had happened to Holly.

# chapter 9

I was unprepared. Vlad was nowhere in sight. And no background, *still*, on my client that I could wave around as instant proof. And, of course, no psyche results or fingerprint results, one way or the other. Celia had improved my speed dial lately, so I pressed 7 and Joma answered right away.

"What's up? I need something."

"Sup, man," he said, "I got nothing. So your boy's clean, at least."

Maybe that was good. "How long do records go back?"

"Shit, I don't know. But he's never been questioned or printed in America, and he's not in the CIA's database. That's something."

"Thanks." I hung up.

Semi-completely unprepared from the start.

In they came. Mr. High Power and a small guy in a dark suit who couldn't wait to sit and take out his dictation pad. He sat next to Celia, sensing his place the scheme of things, I guess. They both took down every word spoken.

The other man stuck out a smooth, fat hand and said, "Call me Dalmonica. Arbitrator and attorney. I represent certain interest groups and a certain conglomerate which will remain nameless at present. It's something to meet you, Mr. Wein."

"Is it? Is it a pleasure?"

He just smiled like Perry Mason would and sat his tall frame down. Fred and Mark Clock were already seated, new age music already playing.

Dalmonica was about 60 years old and never seemed to move much, in whatever he was doing. He had what I'd call "presence," like a President or Telly Savalas—something vaguely intimidating; that way someone has who just doesn't care what you think of him. I wish I had that. And that car-costing suit wrapped around him. Rich, past wealthy. Only man I'd ever seen with a diamond wedding ring, too. I knew they made them but…

"I appreciate you seeing us, gentlemen," he said. "Perhaps we can put a stop to this quickly before too much time is wasted."

I guess I'd been staring at him. "I don't feel—"

He looked at me, then equally at the others, like a true speaker of the house. "Of course this is fantasy, and regardless of what comes from this meeting, it will be my recommendation to my clients, and to the board of trustees of the Academy of Motion Picture Arts and Sciences, and the various guilds who I unofficially report to, that no settlement shall be paid, nor any concessions, nor shall anything so childish have even one day in court. Are we agreed?"

I was speechless. "On *what*?"

"Mr. Wein, you are abusing the American right to sue anyone who feels like suing, and I wish to state now, before we *begin* wasting our time, that I believe you to be below contempt for taking money from any client, regardless of his wealth or state of mind, for such a shocking absurdity."

Talk about a closed mind!

"Now," he said, looking around. "Is your client present? I see no mirrors."

"My client's…attributes are such that we reserve them for our case in court."

Like a judge, he simply stated, "This isn't going to court." A pause for effect. "Mr. Wein, what you are proposing here is nothing beyond science fiction, this is Mel Brooks interviewed by Carl Reiner, and I fail to see the relevancy of anything *you* have to say on this subject as progressing the cause of justice."

"What are you here for then?"

"I am here, sir, to save those I represent time by stating the obvious, my case, in such a way that you understand not our view, but the *fact* that you will be committing professional suicide by allowing your client anywhere near a court of law."

"Oh, yeah?"

"Yes."

"Oh, you don't need to worry about what happens to me," I said with the confidence that only comes out as sarcasm.

"State your case, please, so we may state ours."

I nodded to Celia to switch on the DVD/TV combo and dim the lights. Everyone swiveled their chairs to watch the tube: a simple studio set. A chair, a table, a backdrop with Legal Video Services printed blatantly on it. Fred was there, he held up a hand, then moved off screen. He held up a hand at our table here too, but Dalmonica was only breathing through his mouth and watching the screen.

The lighting flickered, then there was nothing for a few seconds. I assumed Fred left the flickers in to underline the fact that the previous flicker wasn't somehow us tampering with the tape.

Then on walks someone, wearing red shorts, a long sheet covering his upper half and head, *over* which was a nice shirt with a cape attached to it, and pillow cases covering his legs below the shorts. Really weird. It was at this point that I seriously wished I was on the other side of the case. It was embarrassing.

Until the figure flipped his wrists and suddenly turned into a bat. Not a CGI thing Lucas likes or hairy rubber on a string, but a *real*—what looked like to me, real—bat. Then he changed into a tabby cat, which manically smiled at us.

Then he spread his little cat arms so that his cape (yes, a cat in a cape) rose off the ground into a semi-circle, and smoke started appearing. He was just enveloped in smoke, not coming from off-camera or from the back, *just from him*. The kitty kept stepping around, sometimes moving in a circle to show that it was…like the smoke was emanating from his pores. But the cat was wearing clothes. The quality of the broadcast wasn't too good, to be honest, and now I wished I'd checked into digital or HD or whatever was tops, so there'd be no question what was happening. Even though obviously there was *going* to be a question as to what the hell was happening!

He just…morphed into smoke. Nothing but smoke in the picture.

Then, in a blink, there was a tiger in the picture. Not cagey, wiggling around, strutting in anger, but like a posed stuff animal, like Dalmonica, just breathing with its mouth open.

I should point out too that there was a video counter going on all the time, and a second clock affixed in the bottom right corner of the picture, to show that this was all real-time hooey.

The tiger changed into a bat again.

The bat changed into a—something. Something very small on the floor. A slug? It was really small, and, really, what was the point of doing that if you couldn't see it? It was a really good trick.

After a duck and a hippo and something odd that seemed like a fantasy creature out of Narnia, he changed back into dear old Vlad, again will those wacky clothes and shorts on, and he started creeping toward the camera.

White fuzz.

Celia dimmed the lights back up.

After three seconds, Dalmonica whirled his chair around to ask me, "You purport this to be what?"

"Just a little taste of what you can expect to find in court," I said. "It's for real."

"That wasn't real."

"He'll be doing that in court. You can search our client first."

"He can show me now."

"He's not here."

"He's a magician."

"He's eternal."

He nodded. His mind was working. "Why could we not see the man, but we could see the bat and the cat and all that?"

I shrugged. "I don't know."

"When he turned into smoke, and back again. Is he wearing a superhero suit like the Hulk, where whatever happens to him, happens to his clothes?"

I wanted to laugh, but the guy seemed dead serious.

"Are those special red shorts?"

"He'll wear anything you want," I said, "when he does it in court."

"How does he do the trick?"

When in doubt, or you've got no fucking idea, they teach you at lawyer school not to acknowledge the other man's tennis point, but just to go on serving.

"I think the press is going to eat that right up."

"Oh yes," he agreed, and wrote something down with a diamond-gold pen I wish I had.

It was a bit miffing. I expected more ranting. This guy was just—*subdued.*

"Anything else?" he finally asked.

I had Mark Clock in on this one. He was to be my heavy hitter.

He quoted from Florida's statue on Right of Publicity, "Chapter 540, Commercial Discrimination states: 'No person shall publish, print, display or otherwise publicly use for purposes of trade or for any commercial or advertising purpose the name, portrait, photograph, or other likeness of any natural person without the express written or oral consent to such use given by: (a) Such person; or (b) Any other person, firm or corporation authorized in writing by such person to license the commercial use of her or his name or likeness; or (c) If such person is deceased, any person, firm or corporation authorized in writing to license the commercial use of her or his name or likeness, or if no person, firm or corporation is so authorized, then by any one from among a class composed of her or his surviving spouse and surviving children."

"How does the law define 'natural person'?" Dalmonica asked.

"What do you mean?" I said.

"Is it natural to live for centuries?"

"It's natural to our client."

"This sounds like a supernatural being to me."

"Nevertheless, it's his lifetime," I said. "His name, *his* likeness. And he's not deceased. Not yet."

"'Surviving spouse and surviving children' it says."

"Right."

"Surviving 500 years?"

MC said, "The law does not choose define the length of a person's life."

"In California it so states," Dalmonica said, and he read from the top page in his little file: "California's Civil Code s 3344.1 states that a 'deceased personality' shall include, *without* limitation, any such *natural person* who has died within 70 years prior to January 1, 1985."

"That is personality status," I countered, flipping to *my* California printout. "I quote: 'The rights of the deceased personality's children and grandchildren are in all cases divided among them and exercisable in the manner provided in Section 240 of the Probate Code according to the number of the deceased personality's children represented. The share of the children of a dead child of a deceased personality can be exercised only by the action of a majority of them."

"We're talking about only one child here." I nodded yes to him, so he continued, "My issue is not with whether or not Dracula is a viable name, merely in what the law constitutes a *person*. Forget where he came from, that he is not American at all. We won't get into that fight, yet. If this man claims to be more than 500 years old, I think we should be less looking at Right of Publicity and more into the quality of a man."

"Then why did you bring up Chapter 540?"

"*You're* suing *us*," he said, on the verge of showing some emotion.

I looked to Mark Clock. We were veering away from this as a rights question, and it threw me a curve.

"It's clear," he continued, "that you may have an absurd case for infringement against the rights of an unauthorized image, particularly name, usage, but I quote the very first definition of the word *man* in Merriam-Webster's dictionary: 'an individual human.'"

He closed his file and looked at me. No smile, nothing smug. "It goes on to give a statement as to the universal and recognized meaning of the words 'humankind' and 'husband,' both related. So too is the definition of 'person' related as 'human' and 'individual.'

He stood. I didn't know what to say.

"So if you're trying to pass this…person off as a higher ideal, something above ourselves, and someone who is the basis for a book long since written and a book long since in the public domain, I take issue with the fact that this is something supernatural, something alien, he is not a man, and he therefore has no rights under the United States Constitution, nor is he subject to the law books of any *man*."

And he left.

# chapter 10

After two days incommunicado with seemingly everyone—my client, my enemy, even Fred was either aloof or not talking to me (he gave me such a look when he left the office that night)—I was getting scared of being total forgotten. True. Deep down I thought I didn't deserve to be a lawyer, or an attorney, and certainly not a rich either of those, because my killer instinct was distinctly vegetarian. Vegan really, when you come down to it. Just always full of doubt and, like, sleep in my brain, in between the cracks where I suppose all intense electricity happens. The fight's fine when it comes to me, but I was never the fight starter. I was beginning to believe Vlad had come to the wrong door, and I was beginning to think he was beginning to think that.

Still, there was plenty of cash in the kitty, so I thought I'd earn some while waiting…for…what, what were we waiting for? Whoever it was Dalmonica repped was sleeping peacefully or waiting for us to peel the apple. I didn't know. Celia was on the phone ever since 9 a.m. the next morning with this thing, and no replies, no call backs. Nothing in the press, just no information. It was looking like we'd lost before we'd started. Like this wasn't going any further, thanks to Dalmonica's obvious tunnel vision. *How could I blame* him?

Anywhere, there was still cash in the kitty and I had time to waste at the office, with all my calendar now cleared for the Vlad case, so I thought I'd do something with the expense account while I was waiting to hear, from *anyone*, and plug up this new hole quickly before the boat sank.

I'd looked up "what makes a man" on yahoo.com and just got a couple pages of dating advice ("how to make a man happy" and the rest of it), so I had Celia look up the biggest philosophy entry in the (local) Yellow Pages and make me an appointment. Apparently there's not even a section for "philosophy," let alone any doctors to choose from. Which I thought odd because I distinctly remember you being able to major in it in college.

That was it. I mentally snapped some fingers and had C make me the quickest appointment possible with the head of the Philosophy Dept. at FSU, which turned out to be buried in the undergraduate program in the College of Arts and Sciences. Celia kept busy on the phone and Fred I guess was still looking for Holly, with Joma's help, so I had no one to suss out the campus for me. It'd been a couple years since I had to set foot on college green and I got turned around real easy there. I found the library and asked from there.

I'm sorry, but I never *did* understand how arts and sciences were related, why they always seem to share the same "and" but grabbing a curriculum sheet in the lobby of the building I *finally* found, one word lept up at me which *sort* of seemed to glue the two. Perhaps I should've started here first.

Metaphysics.

That was a combo of art and science, right? Well, that was one of the first questions I put to Prof. Bradman, a pudgy little man all in brown, including the face hair. He was sitting, grading papers and never got up, never stop grading or at least looking down at them sometimes as we talked.

"Metaphysics is really the cross breed between the explained and the unexplainable," he said like a good ol' boy. Whoever thinks the southern accent is a mask for stupidity should hear some of the attorneys and professors talk up.

"I really have one question, Professor. And I know it's loaded, and –"

"There are multiple definitions of everything."

"Riiiight." I waited a moment. "You can give me some *clear* answers, right?" He nodded. "I mean, I'm not looking to confuse my case."

"Ah!" and he finally looked at me for more than a couple seconds. "I see! Sorry. Sorry, Mister…."

"Wein."

"Wein, Mr. Wein, sorry, usually the only time...the few times I've had an attorney in here...well, they had a weak case and they are looking to make it more complex for the sake of a hung jury, or something like that."

I nodded. "'Reason and Critical Thinking' is the first part of your outline for your prep class, I noticed."

"Right. Argue, and the whole world argues with you."

"Look. This isn't exactly a legal question. But—this is a weird case, so hear me out. I mean. You don't need to know the case, but..." I was rambling. "Okay. Here: what defines a man?"

His pencil stopped scratching red and he turned thoughtful. "Legally?"

"If you want."

"Do you want?"

I laughed. "A straight answer, actually. That is—I want to know if being a man, or fundamentally, being a *person*, can that be open to interpretation?"

"What does the law say?"

"Well, the Declaration of Independence starts off with 'We hold these truths to be self-evident, that all men are created equal, that they are endowed by their Creator with certain unalienable Rights, that among these are Life, Liberty, and the Pursuit of Happiness.' But it's not part of the law. The Constitution, the *Constitution* also fails to define Man as an idea or...legal prop. I take it you've never been asked to define *man*."

"Not in a court of law." He thought. "I can do crazy."

"No, I've got a man to do crazy."

"Not in control."

"No, thanks, I've got all that covered," I said gently, "and it doesn't really apply here anyway, fundamentally. I'm just... I want to slip into what makes a man, morally, philosophically; does man or human or being equal 'entity' necessarily, which is a general sense of being."

"Wow, you're getting deep."

"I need confirmation that existence equals animation equals abstract object, if a man is a man outside of his skin; in death, if a human being ceases to hold his rights *as* a being if he then becomes that abstract."

"You're an attorney?"

"Yes—is abstract real since it *can* be a real thought, or does the touching of the soul merely reek of mysticism, even though our culture believes in Jesus and Satan, going to a *real* church every Sunday morning in a *real* place to sing to something unseen yet believed to be a part of them?"

He was fanning himself. I was hot too.

"What was the question again?"

I looked at the piece of paper I'd brought in with me. "Symbolic logic, what's that?"

"I…I…only have twenty minutes before my next…"

"Oh, yes, of course," I said. "I'm sorry. This is heavy stuff."

"Yeah."

"Can I put you on retainer? Dr. Efegy says you've got the most cloud, the books you've written—"

"Well…"

I took out my wad of bills and that changed everything. His eyes were alert and his back obviously knew how to straighten.

"What was the question?"

"When?"

"Look…" and he had his hand out for money. It was funny really. "I think you'd do well to read up on ontology if you're really interested. That is the real study of being and existence and how to define what is real. What is existence. Does existence manifest itself. What defines *thing* as opposed to idea."

"Well…"

"It's not that hard, really."

I put four fifties in his hand and his thumb and finger did tiny circles on them.

"*That's* real."

"*That's* real!" he agreed, and we laughed. Suddenly the room relaxed.

He smiled at me. "I'm on call."

"Thanks. I hope it helps."

"—Are you—trying to prove the existence of God?"

I thought. "Maybe. Yeah."


I kicked at the dark orange leaves, wet and old, at my feet, and enjoyed the feeling of the wind at my back pushing me to the crowded parking lot. It wasn't a feeling of elation in my head at the moment, but I *did* feel like I'd just scored a point.

Bradman hadn't said outright than a living man's a man. But he didn't slam the idea either. God works in small favors.

Passing a pay phone, I thought I'd try my client again.

I put my fifty cents in and dialed and got a couple rings in before I remembered what time of day it was—daytime—so I hung up and checked back with Celia who was nearly animated.

"Joma wants you to call!"

So, I hung up on her, called him. "What's up?"

"Your boy's under suspicion," Joma said.

"What's the charge?

"Wanted in questioning with a disappearance. Anonymous tip."

"Do you know who this anonymous tip is?"

"Yeah. It's *anonymous.*"

"I mean, you can trace things and—"

"Look, man. They sent a couple cops over to talk to the man, ain't nobody home."

I thought on this.

"Can you be in on this?"

"I like violent crimes."

"Come on, man."

A pause. "I get to meet Dracula?"

"Yeah."

"When?"

"Let's do it after dark," I said.

# CHAPTER

I was scared for a moment. There were three men outside. One of them was Gath. I wondered what he was doing there, and thought of making myself known. But I was only functioning at 88% lately, my full nights merely resting my eyes all of the time. Sleep was something else.

How I love the Autumn, as it quickly trickles into an ever-expanding Winter, with more hours of darkness. When you cannot sleep, the days seem so long.

Someone knocked. Then someone pounded.

I heard Gath's muffled voice through the weakest part of the house. The window, perhaps.

He couldn't see my like this. I scurried to fling all the pizza boxes in my coffin and started a little heavy straightening up, which clearly made no dent in anything. The ruins were a mess. Flowers had begun their growth through the seedy green carpet, plus the sound of a draining dripping from the last shower we had. My god, how it rains in Tallahassee!

Why was I so embarrassed? I was hazy. Not myself. The dankness was reassuring, calming. Perhaps…just the unexpected spooked me. It was difficult to justify my…panic to myself.

Just one more change I'd felt of myself lately.

I used to be so cool.

The pounding persisted, so I merely smoked myself and left through the pores of this dilapidated dwelling.

The men were in the midst of a mild conversation as I spied all their asses. Gath was utterly against the other men entering by force, something along the lines of unjustified cause; one of them seemed his friend. Both strangers were black, but I did not mind.

"Good evening, gentlemen," I said.

"Vlad!"

I do believe Gath was happy to see me, the way he happy slapped me on the cheek and put his arm around my neck. He may have been putting on the dog, as they say, for the more cynical among the congregation. Though one, the one perhaps his friend, was nothing but half smiles all the way through the proceedings.

"Where have you been?" Gath asked.

I said with force, "I have been searching for Holly, of course. I told you she was missing!"

"Did you tell us?" said one of the black people.

"Indeed, I did. I filed my report online."

"Online?" the other black man said urgently and skeptically.

I nodded to them as a gentleman of virtue would. "There is a website for missing persons, and I added my own. I gave a complete des—"

"You're supposed to tell the cops, man."

"Vladimir Tepes, this is my friend Joma Standly. He helps me out sometimes. It's good to have a man on the inside, you know?"

"The inside of what?" I inquired, to which no further information was forthcoming.

He kidded this Standly person who took it not as a kidding, and never looked upon me as one of noble blood, but as an unfunny joke. I could tell by his eyes. I did not like this person.

"We'll check it out," said the other man. "What's the site?"

"missingpersons.com," I said. "They are very helpful."

"You know you tell the cops first, right?" Standly accused. I merely stood like the cool man I was  and stared at him.

This produced laughter, and Gath had to consult him to change tactics. I did not see the humor when a woman's life was at…hung in the balance.

Standly was trying to contain his battle with the giggles when he asked me, "Would you come with us downtown, please, sir?"

"Why?"

Now he lost his battle and plainly laughed at me. The other officer became infected by his howling and body language and the two of them became hyenas, a pitying sight.

Gath came to me as a serious man. My eyes shot into his, but all he wanted to do was relax me and calm me and out of camaraderie to him, I did nothing untoward.

I nodded curtly and was in their rather drab Ford car before they seemed to realize it, which put the bite on their frivolity.

The drive through the rain-soaked streets was pleasant, I admit that. Downtown was dead and boring anyway you looked but the streets were black and slick and still bustled with those young idiots trying to get from one mall to another. The sidewalks were cool and uncrowded, the one I was on, speckled with shaven grass. The yard just been cut not an hour before. It must have been done after dark. Ah, the habits of Americans.

That I was out of the car, looking at the cut grass before any of them shifted their gazes from amused to incredulous, amazed them. I led the way into the police station. There was no laughter now.

Before the blacks began, Gath exercised his right to pull me into a room containing a large mirror as one of its walls, not unlike something grungy from a *Saw* film, and conferred with me on his progress of the past few days. Now I had to prove that I am legally a "man"? It merely strengthened my resolve that I was certainly doing the right thing.

"When did you last see Holly?" he asked.

"When I reported to you that she had not called."

"No, that's when you first noticed she was missing."

"Then I saw her the evening before. We had gone to the zoo."

He thought a moment and said, "At night?"

I nodded.

"Zoo's closed at night."

I further nodded. He sighed.

"What am I doing here?"

"Answering questions," he said. "About her. An anonymous tip came in that you had something to do with her disappearance."

My eyebrows went up. It was a shocking idea. I said this, and proclaimed my love for this beautiful woman with poetry that would put Wordsworth back in public schools.

My friend was tired, and merely plopped into the one putrefying chair provided. I looked around, and weighed my options.

"I do not want to stay here tonight. Can this happen?"

"Well."

Gath must've had a headache. He seemed to have trouble seeing or some such head injury.

"I just say cooperate with them."

I nodded. "I don't want to hurt my case."

"Right." That broke his pain off a little bit. "Yes. This doesn't come at a good time, does it?"

I agreed, and it set him thinking.

Soon, he merely went out, brought me a Dr. Pepper which I did not ask for, and led the assault in the room. The two policemen who had accosted me outside my house retruned. They brought three chairs, and sat, staring at me as if I were Jack the Ripper. I sat.

Finally this Standly person spoke. "You really Dracula, man?"

I looked at Gath. He closed his eyes and nodded. "You can answer anything, really."

"That I have never claimed to be my father is only one thing in my favor," I said, literally oozing dignity. What an asinine question. "You must turn your accusation around and consider the character as portrayed poorly by this Bela Lugosi fool that it is he who represents the copy."

Standly looked at my friend who merely smiled.

"I went to high school, Mr. Vlad," he said. "Stick to high school words."

I said I would. The other black person in the room merely sat frozen, looking at me, perhaps in a way that epitomized hatred. Certainly he held an intimidation gaze. I recognized that well enough.

"Can you smile for me?" Standly requested.

"Smile?"

"Yeah, can you smile?"

I did so for an instant. Standly strained his eyes and said, "Just a little longer?"

I did so.

He finally said, "Huh."

"Can we just get on with the missing persons—"

"Oh yeah. Yeah." Standly took out a small and cheap notebook from his ass pocket to refer. "You know Ms. Holly Tranberg?"

"No."

"No?" he almost shouted.

"I didn't know her name was Tranberg."

Standley paused a second, then laughed. He couldn't help himself.

"That's good. But you know her."

"We have fucked."

"*Damn*, man!"

I looked from face to face seeking explanation. "What?"

"You *fucked* this baby?"

"Baby?"

"She's 19, man."

"What does this mean?"

"What does *this* mean?" He rose and strutted around a little. "*This* means you got almost close to havin' us do you for a minor, man."

"I'm glad you're calling me a man." I smiled at Gath who did not return it.

Suddenly this Standly was in my face with his bulldog lips flubbing, saying, "I'll call you more than that, Dracula! Yeah! I know who you are, baby."

"I'm glad to hear that," I said, and pointed at the mirror wall.

He looked, and his puffy jaw seemed to fall. He looked back to me, then to the large mirror again. He sat, thunderstruck, and his friend became vocal with expletives which were lively and more imaginative than I would have thought capable of a man of his pay grade.

These angry words only rose in pitch and number when they discovered I was gone. They launched into a full argument, then they launched into poor Gath who had to defend himself at the same time as having his own mouth agog. I'm not sure why he was so surprised at seeing myself not in the mirror, however.

I had not disappeared. I was merely an ant in the corner of the room. Excitement and footsteps filled the arena.

Once the initial shock and "find him!" bravado had been accomplished, Gath was told to "wait here!" while the others scrambled to find me. Gath put his hands in his forehead hair and brushed up and down. I felt sorry for him, really, but I needed to know if I was wasting my time.

At least the officers returned and Standly ushered the one police person out, this other being just too angry and swarming with ideas.

Standly quickly sat in a chair facing Gath. "What just happened today?"

"You probably bored him."

"*Bored* him? That asshole—"

"He probably feels the same way."

"*What?*"

"Look, man, I know. I know. He does this shit to me all the time, too. He's either a really clever magician, or maybe he is…" He left it there. "What are you so excited about? This was questioning."

"In relation to a missing—"

"He was trying to *find* Holly. I think there's real—affection between them. Certainly him for her. You should've seen him the other night when she went missing."

"Now *he's* missing!"

"I doubt that."

Standly tried to calm himself, and perhaps did. "What did I see?"

Gath thought about putting my amazing qualities into words. "What I saw."

"What did you see?"

After another pause, Gath said, "How old do you think he is?"

"What?—I dunno, 50?"

"Suppose…he's right outside the door."

The officer went to have a look. I, of course, was in the corner.

"No, I mean, suppose he just—appears. Suddenly. What will you do?"

The policeman had not obviously thought that far ahead.

"Look. This is wacked. I think we should put some steam on this. This is too freaky for the local department. Mitch is a friend of mine, he's a Fed, and I'm going to ask him about the X-Files."

Gath was suddenly awake. "The TV show?"

The other one shook his head. "If there's a branch of government used to handling… you know, chasing magicians and shit."

"Magicians. Yeah."

They obviously did not want to discuss my omnipotence. The door got knocked and that other officer entered far ahead of the time it would take to ask him to enter. He shook his head to Standly, yet beckoned him over with the same action.

The two spoke for far too long, until Gath stood, stretched and said, "Are you filming in there?" He jerked his head toward the mirror.

Standly absently said, "Nothing runnin'."

Gath went out into the hallway, followed by the officers, followed by me. My legs were so tiny it took quite a while to reach the door's edge, at which point the conversation was already in progress, down at the end by the coffee machine.

I could not hear, so I made myself known in my usual body. The conversation was whispered, but when I have ears, they are sensitive.

*Do you believe he's capable of murder?*

*I don't know what to think. I liked him.*

*Tell me about the mind games.*

Then, they noticed me. The full coffee cup fell from Standly's hand, and splashed everyone.

"Joma!" someone shouted. When there was no response for some seconds, a white police office

raced around the corner.

"She's here!" he said, then all eyes gave their gazes to me, and talking stopped.

At which point my love, my one, my own clicked around the corner in high heels, and there was silence.

# chapter 11

I had a dream that Holly came back to us. Trussed up in a red and white dress, the tight kind, with her hair up and in heels, like she was going to or had just been to some party. So real. And except for the fact that I didn't wake up in my own bed, but groggily found myself in the arms of Barlene—reading the nametag on her shirt—in the police station, I would have believed it to be a dream.

It wasn't that everyone was waking up from sleeping on the floor, but there was the sense that collectively we had all been party to the same hangover. Soon the phones grew a little louder, the lights a little stronger, and the dream lasted a little longer than the couple seconds that mine usually live for.

All I wanted to do was call the wife and kid and make sure they were okay. They were. Though I woke them. It was 2:30 and Medge wanted to know where I was, why didn't I call, the rest of it, and I wanted some answers, too.

Joma found me two seconds after I hung up, or he was waiting for me. He was clearly confused, and for the first time since I'd known him, a little scared. He thrust a piece of paper in front of me.

Confirmation that Vlad had indeed put in his complaint or whatever you want to call it on missingpersons.com, long before the anonymous tip came in, long before any of us were worried.

"How do you know it was him?" I asked. "It's just a webpage form to fill out, right? You can… anyone can do that as someone else, right?"

Joma nodded. "That's not in his favor. But then again, he tells you. He was about it, you said."

"Yeah," I reluctantly agreed. "Did you…?"

"What?"

"Did something happen… tonight…?"

He wanted me to say it. He didn't want to say it. That said it.

It was true.

"You know how to get to Holly's?" he ax.

I did.


It only took ten minutes to get there. We took a regular squad car that Joma borrowed from Division, and he had another patrol car check out Vlad's own place, just in case. Nothing there. At least, no response to the cops' knocks at the door. And with the victim no longer missing—unless it was all a dream—they had no probable cause for forcing their way in.

We rolled up quickly to Wind Gull, a bit of posh avenue on the East side of town. More uptown than my place, but now I knew that the rumor about Holly and her rich parents was true.

Doorbell. Vlad answered with a smile and bade us enter.

I don't know. The inside wasn't what I expected going by the outside. Dim lights. Maybe there weren't cobwebs between the ceiling and the tops of the tall bookcases, but you definitely got that idea.

Holly was sitting on the couch, showing off a better posture than I remembered. She smiled at us. With no pointed teeth.

Still, I just went over and looked all around her neck before I sat on the offered plush chair. Not a single tooth had sunk in that neck.

Vlad chuckled at that. "You think I think I'm a vampire."

"What happened to you?" Joma was all serious.

"When?"

"You left the scene of a policy inquiry." Vlad said nothing. Joma turned to Holly. He was within patting distance of her hand, but he didn't touch her. "You okay, Miss Holly?"

She nodded.

"I'd like to hear you speak."

"I'm fine." Same lyrical voice. Like content sadness. With a smile.

"And I'm so glad," Vlad said. He said it with heart. "I was not myself since she went away. My heart ached. I do like feeling such pain."

"Who does?" I offered. Lame.

"Where you been?" Joma asked.

She stared at him. There was a tiny fire in her eyes.

"We shall find out," Vlad said, and it was his turn to be serious.

"You don't know?" I asked him.

Even the shadow of a smile had left his 500-year-old face. This was the look I took away with me that night. I would never forget it.

He *could* be surprised. He could be moved.

"I needed time… to think," Holly said softly.

We closed the door on them a mere 10 minutes later, getting nowhere. Holly hadn't said where she was, why she was looking so Bride of Frankensteinish, she gave us no clues to the new Holly, and Vlad wasn't asking. He was being worried and charming and a lover and ignored his guests passionately. As we walked to the car, I saw Joma had a fret that crinkled his nose. Maybe I never saw him any other way after that night.

"What's goin' on, man?"

"What do you mean?"

"Don't pull the lawyer line on me. Come on, who is this?"

"Vlad Tepes. He claims his father was Vlad II Dracul, the—"

"We done high school together, man!"

All the way to my place—Joma was driving—he tried to guilt me and argue me and all of it into saying some secret story I must've been keeping to myself. Then he turned stony when he wasn't getting anywhere. I used the cool silence to lift the cell from my friend's shirt pocket and daintily dialed Holly's cell. She picked up like she was waiting for it.

There was a lot of barking in the background so I had to speak up. "Holly?"

"Gath?"

"Can you talk? Are you alone?"

"I can talk."

"But are you alone?"

She laid the phone down, I guess, to do her bit in telling the dogs to shut up and behave. Something hairy kept trampling on the phone which miraculously didn't hang up in the couple minutes it took her to come back on.

"Yeah?"

"It's me. Gath."

"Yeah! Gath. Hi."

"What's with all the dogs? We didn't hear a thing and we were *just* there."

"I know," she laughed, "it's crazy, isn't it?"

"Crazy is a word coming around more and more. Look. You sound more excited than a few minutes ago. More… *alive*."

"What can I say? I like dogs!"

Yeah, she *was* laughing. The first time I'd heard that in *so* long.

"Look. What's going on? Can you talk?"

"Yeah, I can talk!" she shouted. I just closed the phone on a lot of laughter and chaos. Obviously if she was going to talk up that loud on the phone, she wasn't going to be alone. I didn't get it.

"Deceit," Joma said.

"What?"

"Deceit." That's all he'd say.

I got dropped off and Joma's screeching tires were pleasantly drowned out by the little girl laughing as Doll tripped gaily, definitely gaily into my arms.

That's when time stopped. Like you're swimming for laps and laps and you finally get to stop at the edge of the pool and catch your breath and look at the other end of the dancing waves. I found comfort. And there was peace again.

It was just another boring night. The TV ruled us, with my belly as the pillow to two female heads, one after the other. No thoughts of work, no Frankenstein or the Wolf-man, just too much tuna fettuccini and a *Get Smart* for me as Medge zzzz'ed on me, and I fell asleep myself before Max could save the world again.

Little did I know that a good hour before Agent 86 was even zooming his red car into the credits, that Joma had rolled his unit back to Vlad's to have a look around. He told me later. The house was just crawling with dogs, all out back in this huge pen that looked like a pound. None of them barked a word either. Not then. Sure, they paced liked prisoners, but even a nosing spy like big Joma didn't get an sound byte out of these guys. He felt like arresting them all for not being dogs, he told me.

It was pathetic. But it did let him snoop around more.

Really what he wanted was to be caught. Push some lite intimidation into Vlad's face—a way of saying, "You're worth catching, man. I'm watching you." But except for the silent dogs, there was nothing going on. No lights through the windows except maybe this tiny thing in the hallway, a nightlight probably. Nothing stirring.

Even when he learned the following morning that they had gone out, he wasn't vexed. In his line of waiting all day for a 30 second spurt of action, Joma had learned how to be real patient. I would've thought it would make him all moody, but no, he was resigned to the thought of getting nowhere.

I knew better. He had that grimness in his eyes that told me Vlad was getting the full dept. attention now.

I was thankful for that rest of a night, because it was to be the last unbreakable hours I'd have with the family. Starting now.

The phone woke me at 9:30. 6:30 Calif. time, a fact the bright voice on the other end didn't mind sharing with me.

"Derek Draco, Mr. Wein, I'm calling about our friend Vlad."

The grogginess left my voice now. The very sleep from my eyes was gone. "Yeah?"

"Do you like my name?" and he laughed. "That's why he hired me. I've just been taken on as Vlad's PR man, so I'd like to get your bio, if I could."

"My what?"

"Your bio. You and your business. I know you'll want to stress your professionalism, but if you could have Celia, that's her name? Have her come up with something that puts the bite of 'small time' on you and your biz. Tallahassee stationary will help too."

I didn't like his sunshine. "Tallahassee is the capitol of Florida."

"Of course it is! The very idea!"

A straight dandy. That's all my mind could picture, him with his serious Joe Besser voice.

He gave me his e-fax #. "Just anything to do with your company. Everything you can get me. This time you don't have to name-drop, I just want the facts, thanks. What are you doing about proving the age thing?"

"Age—"

"I've got a copy of Vlad's citizenship papers." I didn't even have that! How many *times* had I asked Vlad for papers? *Written proof*? "But it's 1938, and you know what that means in 2010! I'm setting up a gmail account just for you, roots right into my assistant's cell?"

"Yeah?"

"I just want every update in any direction you can pump, don't worry about confidentiality. I have Vlad's written assurance that I have virtual power of attorney when it comes to whatever it takes, and it takes a lot!, to get him on telly. Coincidentally, keep an eye on some channel tonight, you'll see our star! So to be *every* program, E you with more!"

He rang off, and I looked at this…strange thing that was my phone.

Good thing I decided to shave then, because those next ten minutes or less of silence were the last minutes of silence I really remembered until the end.

Then, just as I had a couple inches of toast crust to go, the phone started ringing and didn't stop.

First, it was the *LA Times* wanting to know if I'd comment on the case. Arts & Entertainment section wanted to run a short blurb.

Second, some clear voice named "Mickey" wanted me live as a punchline to some radio show he was doing. He always sounded like he was ready to laugh at any second, but he never did. I gave him the standard—since stupid Draco didn't give me a hint in hell of what the standard *should* be—reply of "I'm not at liberty at this time to discuss my client's case. Suffice it to say, we are confident of a clear and concise victory, and look forward to our day in court."

This I told *Newsday, St. Petersburg Times, The Oregonian, The San Diego Union-Tribune, The Denver Post, The Miami Herald, The Sacramento Bee, The Orange County Register, St. Louis Post-Dispatch, The Kansas City Star, San Jose Mercury News, The Detroit News, The Times-Picayune, The South Florida Sun-Sentinel, The Indianapolis Star, The Orlando Sentinel, The Sun* in Baltimore, *San Antonio Express-News, The Columbus Dispatch, Milwaukee Journal Sentinel, Tampa Tribune, The Boston Herald, Pittsburgh Post-Gazette, Fort Worth Star-Telegram*, and *The Charlotte Observer* when they called before I could start my car.

Thank God I never used a cell phone.

By the time I loathed into the office, yes, a horse's trough of messages from the A to Z of the newspaper world were waiting for me, poor Celia shaking her writing hand like someone'd just kicked it.

"Get on to temp," I said to her, "and get me a phoner to field the press. Specify someone polite and *not* creative and *not* hungry. We don't want her giving out her own PR."

Poor nodding Celia shrank from my office, her worried look prompting me to get Queen's *Jazz* album on my personal airwaves asap. By the time "Fat Bottomed Girls" were rolling, I felt at peace, despite the fact that the phone kept ringing. Most of it was Celia asking what she should say to the *Detroit Free Press* and the like who wanted *her* statement on Dracula and what did she think of Frank Langella and John Carradine and ridiculous questions.

"Use your nut!" I said to her like a cross Britisher, then had to call her back and give her some shh shh to tell her that stress was contagious and I was sorry and we smiled at each other and that was that.

The phone quieted a bit, but only from Celia. Now only two lines were buzzing something pathetic. Not just the *Tallahassee Democrat*, but a few out of the blue callers had wills they needed doing, and a couple friends I hadn't heard from in years called up to share a laugh and say they'd just heard about me on some radio show. I finally had to beg off because I just didn't have the time. Their grunting begrudged goodbyes didn't make me feel good, but neither did the anxiousness I felt that morning before I'd even had time to dive into donuts. Good ol' Celia. Always the crullers, and always a single glazed cream filled. I wondered if it would be my last mouthful—if she would get rattled enough to forget this ritual tomorrow morning. A worrying thought.

Emails were twice as bad. It was like I'd joined 40 google groups for the latest in spam and cult news. I didn't mind the greetings from the Horror Mall and stuff, but really, some of this misspelled keyword shit just didn't make sense. I don't know how you can justify penis tattoos and Dracula wood carvings, but someone had done it in a single email subject, and before I deleted it without reading, I had to applaud his wasted life.

I got up and opened the door to Celia's office to tell her to "Get onto temp again and get me someone to liaison as press officer in a—"

The place was packed. I mean, our waiting room is really just two chairs where people usually sit and stare at Celia, but there must've been fourteen, fifteen people crowded into our little area this fine day. I guess I had Queen up loud enough to disguise it, because they were rumbling when I opened the door, and now they roared into an excited frenzy when I showed myself.

Couldn't quite catch the gist of it, but I had the feeling the waiters were passionate about their various cases. They all started talking at once: sounded like someone wanted to sue a stop sign, someone thought someone's ears were too long, someone thought he was an egg from a book. I don't know, it was all just circus babble, jumbled and swirling at me. I shouted as loud as I could that they should leave their contact info with Celia and I'd get back to them asap, then I squeezed out of the office door.

And faced all the reporters north Florida had on hand, apparently. Again, the senselessness came at a charge, packed into no pauses, no cohesive try to let me *hear* anything so I could pass onto their next question. They merely rolled like rough ocean, sticking their tiny mics into my face, their eyes bulging with importance. The parking lot was a mess. I heard the honking and could see the traffic jam in the street and I knew that soon it was going to be *my* fault for blocking 2nd Avenue.

I stood on the steps and waved hands at them. "Come on, pick a question, one voice, one voice!"

All that did was make everyone rush quicker and louder. Then arguments broke out between them—who had the right to say what. I just used the excuse to get to my car and lock it. They beat at the windows and were probably chipping paint, but I had David Bowie on my side.

Something rang. I looked in my pocket. And took out… a *cell phone*? Hmmm.

"Yeah?"

"Look in your mirror."

I did. Just more frenzy.

"No, your top mirror."

A blonde who had hair like a wig—you couldn't see the join—stood in a brown coat looking dour.

"I know you don't have a cell, so listen. I'm from the *New York Post*. $50,000 for your exclusive, you don't even have to talk about the case. Just talk about yourself. How's that sound? Keep the phone with you."

It was like she knew she didn't have much time to live, because the smarter reporters saw me looking in the little mirror, talking, and they followed my gaze and bunched up on her quick. Ms. *Post* was smarter. She'd been standing by her car, so now she was inside, too, also with the doors locked, and I let her pull out first. Not that I had a choice. She was gone.

I drove to A&W for some chili dog energy, but stayed in the drive-in, with my engine off. My every move was tailed. I was afraid to get out of the car. I'm serious. I was even afraid to keep the windows down—and it was a hot day—in case I got caught by an extra long traffic light, and someone might jump me.

Well, it was ridiculous, I realized. They weren't going to hurt me. I rolled down the windows and let "Let's Dance" spill out. Hot for the top of October. Maybe it was just me.

It was just me. I called the house and Medge had to shout above the TV that wasn't the TV; people were banging on the windows, and we have a lot of windows. They were also banging on the doors and phoning. This was one of the few minutes the house phone wasn't ringing, so she shouted at me. Maybe not scared to death, but scared to worry.

"This was pizza night…" she said and she was half crying. "I have to pick up Doll in two hours!"

"Call her a cab," I suggested.

"In *this*?"

Bad idea. "I'll take care of it."

"What's going *on*, Gath?"

"Looks like Vlad broke the news to the world at large—maybe just the newspaper estate right now—that he's the backbone of Dracula."

"Why are they *here*?"

She didn't give me heck, but I was getting no sympathy from the phone call, so I just tried to reassure her while ignoring the blips of call waiting on this cell I was using, and hung up.

So this is celebrity culture.

Finally I answered the *Post* summons and agreed to a coffee at Rondo's, someplace I'd never heard of in the heart of an area, like my own, where all the houses look alike. I guess she chose it because to get there took so many twists and turns that I lost most all of my then tail (I thought). She was waiting at one of the small, round and outside tables, a cup of joe steaming for me already. She was having sweet tea, sweeter than a bag of sugar, she said. I shook her dainty hand and she didn't smile.

"Thanks for coming so quickly. I know the papa can be rough."

"God, this story broke quickly! My wife is frantic. She said there was a CBN guy interviewing our postman."

"You're on the rocket, Mr. Wein."

"To where?"

"Fame? Lady Gaga has to work hard for this shit."

"What's your name?"

"I'm just Susan."

"Just Susan?"

"My byline's just Susan. Are you ready to start, or do you want to set a better time? I know you're busy."

"When do I get the money? Her eyes opened wide, or they looked wide on her little features. "Wow. You're doing this for the money?"

"Why not?"

"What about professional ethics?"

I thought. "Don't we have this kind of the wrong way?"

She laughed to be polite. And took out her a checkbook. The long, corporate kind, but I couldn't see what she was writing.

"Most conversations," she said, "we have to go through this three-stage denying process where you tell me how unreal this is, but you're doing it for charity, 'might as well let the world get something out of this,' then we find out you pocketed it, and we get to run a nice little mock piece where we catch you."

"My client broke the story. I assume he wants the rollercoaster on."

"You haven't conferred with him?"

"He didn't confer with me."

"Eye for an eye?"

"He'd have both my eyes out if I tried that."

"I'm going to quote every word you say."

"Fine. What tipped you off?"

"You don't watch TV? You're one of those TV snobs, aren't you?" She wrote something before I could reply, so I didn't bother. "Your boy was on *Late Night with Jimmy Fallon* for about two minutes. A real walk-on. *Nearly.* I swear. Jimmy's not that good an actor. I swear he didn't know your boy was coming on."

"Vlad *Tepes*?" She nodded. "Was on an interview show—with that guy—from *Fever Pitch*?"

"Oh…..yeah. I forgot he was a comedian. The security rushing in on him, the shouts, the lack of humor. It was real. And real interesting. *Even though you couldn't see him!* Look it up on youtube.com. One of the highest hits for a day after segment.

I mean, that vid went up in the online ratings *quick*. It made it to number ten on the search engines this morning."

Rather than waste time asking what he said and did, I talked about myself for 35 minutes and collected a check that I could write my own name on.

"Can I proof it before you print?"

"Can I proof your deposit slip?"

Whatever that meant, I let it go. Who wants to shaft a lawyer?

"I know my life is boring—"

"Yeah, it is. But I'd like the option on a secondary story about you and your client. How you met. Your take on him. All the stuff that's going to be common once the suit's in motion."

I stared at her.

"Oh, yeah. Why do you think your client went on Fallon's show?" She gave me time to think. "Can I have first option?"

"I don't know about that."

"You think there's bigger money coming," she said/asked.

"I'm sure of that. But I'll call you to set up a bid."

I guess she thought she was going to be in charge, since she had the money and I agreed to take it. It sort of deflated her high heels a couple inches. I wasn't giving the cash to charity, but she didn't ask about Doll's college fund or paying off the house either. She left me while I was still marveling at the money. If the ink was dry, I didn't care, it was there, in my hand, shinning in the Tallahassee sunlight and I didn't know what I'd done to deserve it.

Hours passed and Doll got home in a friend's car. It was a weeknight, but this friend had a daughter and sometimes Doll would sleep over, so this seemed like a good night for a sequel. I ordered an XL pizza anyway, for delivery, and cruised to Hungry Howie's where I waited inside a minute—I was still being followed, but now at a distance—until I heard which driver got my order, then I followed him in my car like he was an ambulance and I was smart enough to be in a hurry behind it.

It only helped a little when I got there. The tall thin pizza guy was utterly bewildered by the media circus, but having him there was some interference. I leapt into the path he was making through the news crews and suddenly agitated reporters. I stuck a whole $50 in Mr. Pizza's top pocket, and bolted through my front door, bolting it behind me, clutching the box hard enough to bend it in the middle. I'd probably only to get to do that trick once.

Medge ran to me and we hugged until the smell became unbearable, and we lit into that pizza like it was the greatest chicken marsala that ever lived. I swear, it felt like we'd just had sex after we scoffed a few quick pieces.

If you've never turned on the news and saw your own house there as you watch, you don't know what weird is. The commentary was about as riveting and sage as asking a football player how he won the game, but I gleaned a couple more puzzle pieces during their backstory on the local, live Channel 4. I was officially a "buzz word," according to "internet sources," and, switching channels, I saw my yearbook picture on TCN, my wedding photo on BCCN and back on the local channel, I was a "nobody suddenly launched into the limelight of one of the most ridiculous stories ever to hit this decade." Hard to counter that one.

I dialed up Joma but his line was busy. Constantly. Finally I just called the station and left a message.

I showed Medge the 50k check and grinned at her. She was too full to faint, she said. But she stared at it like it was hard to read.

"This pays for Doll," she said.

"You mean she's ours now?"

We spoke vaguely of colleges, but really just fell asleep more than anything. Which was a shame, because we missed all the important TV stuff that followed.

# CHAPTER

Whyever they call it a Green Room is lost on me, but I do understand the theme of tradition. A lady named Grace with headphones she adored woke me from resting my eyes to tell me there were two minutes left. I replaced the rancid glass of vodka and green tea and stood.

I was taken into the wings where I stood and watched a silly stick of a man make attempts at humor, and silently I applauded him for his delayed vim and courage. He had a head like a scarecrow made from onion. But I would be civil.

There was applause, and I was given a nudge to start me in the right direction. There was quite a lot more applause, then quite a bit of laughter as I viewed the audience with, what I thought was, condescension. They did not care. I know of mob rule.

A man Conan shook my hand like a princess, and begged me sit in the chair closest to him. I nodded and did so, and whatever action I made seemed to produce a smattering of mild, sometimes wild, laughter. I looked at all the hundreds of people sitting comfortably under the bright, circular lights. They met my gaze with laughter. Perhaps not the ridiculing kind, but I did tend to wonder.

"*Vlad*," spoke my host. "Vlad Tepes. I can't believe it's you."

"Why?"

"You look good, buddy. Good. A man of your years. How many years is it?"

"You are asking my age."

"Well, yah. If you don't mind giving out."

I stared at him. Clearly, he saw me as this buffoon who would be good for laughs. While I knew this was the purpose of his side of the situation, and I understand the concept of ratings and keeping things light, I was determined to keep the upper hand in all that would occur.

I smiled at him and asked, "Wouldn't you rather this?"

I turned into smoke. This time, I dripped myself away, as if the edges of my form were unreal, and slowly melted into a vision of cloud, always moving and turning into a different shape, but only if you continued to stare…very closely.

Then I turned into a curtain of water vapor, and I rained. Slowly, a sprinkle, clouding myself back into full vapor so I could continue to shower.

The Conan man bolted out of his seat like I was about to physically assault him, which of course wasn't the case. The audience, those not in shock, laughed at his tripping over his desk to get to the safety of a sparkling fake backdrop of Los Angeles. Then he quieted down quite completely when, I assumed, the people fully saw me, as I broke away into fuzz or steam or nothingness or whatever it was they thought they saw.

Silence. I must admit it, it was a peaceful feeling. It felt as if there were a whole moment of it, with everyone's legs made from stone and this…awe of impossibility hanging in the quiet air as the lowly people and the bosses both had no idea who to rant toward. Eventually, it passed like a snap of the fingers, and guards were called and some floor director with a lot of gear on his head stalked on to tell someone to tell someone else to improvise to the audience that "something has gone wrong with the effects." In the process of which I was ushered off to the side curtain by a brave man, and I was almost surrounded by these large, rude men who began to annoy me by their persistent standing. I finally merely made myself into a moth and fluttered from them.

In the studio, chaos. Conan was seeking direction from all directors, achieving nothing at all. There was half-loud talk about the taping and what should be done with it; should they bring "that magician" back on; "is he dangerous?"; and lots of "what's going on?" from anyone with an ego and a mouth.

As a slug on the wall, I heard the important people talking. That short bit of tape became "invaluable." They would want to get a jump on all the free cell vids that would be popping up on youtube before this even airs, they said. I could not see any cell phones in the audience, but then the lights had been so bright.

By the time I flew back as a dove to Derek Draco's neighborhood, I couldn't get even a block from his office. It was marvelous! You would think I had knocked over the President. I had my own little Oscar night, and it felt good. If all of this was from a taste, it was clear that what was to come would only be greater than Michael Jackson's life and death.

I called Derek's number. I had asked for a private number, hoping something like this would happen. A number that *no* one else knows about, I stressed. And as expected, it took him considerable minutes to answer my ring. When he did, it was under hushed breath.

He was excited. His excitement excited me.

"Are you sleepy?"

"No," I stated.

"There's a jerk called Diddy who does a show at 2 in the morning here for the pirates," he explained as if he were racing. "He's famous for being one of the few black guys who loves and plays country and he's always looking for stereotype breakers. Now, I know this isn't major network, not *network*, but if we get you underground, mainstream is going to spike right up."

"Yes, that's true. They call *Star Trek* a cult, but look how many millions of fans. What is cult and what is sheer popular culture?"

His hesitation seemed to suggest I was asking him a rhetorical question. "Yeah? Get to the corner of Wilshire and look for the brown car. He's bumped Ann Margaret off the show for you, he *wants* you tonight!"

"Oh dear god, not poor Ann Margaret."

"Be there!!"

"The corner of Wilshire and what?"

"It doesn't matter!"

I don't know what he was becoming so livid about. I thought I heard *The Muppet Show* theme in the background, and possibly, the sound of him running?

"Just a brown car?"

"The *brown* car!"

He hung up on me. An event I would not forget.

Sure enough, almost immediately upon my stepping foot on Wilshire, a brown limousine found me somehow and pulled silently up, all of its windows open. A strange sight.

There was no one in the car, so I took it upon myself to get in, and I rested my eyes. And daydreamed of success.

Diddy was large and jovial and kindly to me in his stupidly cool way. He had brown paperclips on his ears and wore his A's baseball cap the correct way for some reason, and as he waddled he shook his arms. He wore dark glasses which must have made him legally blind by the fact that this underground chasm of a hovel we were in was already as pitch dark as space. As it was a house, it was filled with people, most of them on hard drugs and nodding their heads or sucking on each other. It was a roomy house. We passed room upon room of these pleasure seekers, and I merely glared at them, though I know they couldn't see me. Could they feel anything, I wondered?

Into the recording room I came, instantly angered. I would not have agreed to this pretense had I known this was *radio*. Who listens to *radio?* It was appalling.

I sat and brooded while this fool prattled on into *a microphone* in the shape of a cow's bottom about me and my claims, judging me like some distant sensationalist object. I *loathed* this man.

Luckily, by the time he found patience to let *me* speak, I had calmed somewhat to the situation. Not to him. But I would use him, of course.

"Vlad," he said. "That's a cool name."

"It is."

"You're the *Man*."

"I am."

He laughed. "I saw the show, man. It's everywhere. I mean, it's, like, *all* over."

"What show?"

"The show!"

"That's good."

"Heard Conan's got himself on drugs and he's at the hospital for stress. You should be proud of that."

"You do what you can."

He laughed. "You funny." And he played a commercial. Baffoon.

He played "Octopus's Garden" and turned back to me as if I'd just walked in. "Hey! We got Vlad the Drac dude here tonight. We're chatting about blood and shit. So, blood. You drink blood?"

"How many listeners do you have?"

"Oh… millions!"

"I drink blood nightly. It keeps me circulating."

"Haha. You mean. You mean, it goes right into your veins? Shouldn't it go in your stomach?"

"Should it?"

"I'm asking you, kid."

"Watch your mouth."

He came out of idiocy for a moment. "What?"

"This flippancy," I said. "Your pretention of confidence and self-importance. Cool either *is*, or you should leave it alone. You don't play with cool, baby."

He laughed, nervously this time. "What's blood taste like?"

"It is an acquired taste."

"I heard that!"

"I said that."

"I mean. *Is* it salty?"

"That depends."

"Come *on*."

"It is not unlike cow pus, from the eye."

"Hmm. Uh huh."

He played "So Long, So Wrong" and looked around with just his eyes. I could see them through his dark lenses.

Confidentially, and in a white man's accent, he pulled closer and said, "You suck, man. Come on. A little more *answers*. Blood and guts, aim at the Jason. I ain't looking for history lessons, come on, bare your teeth an' all." He nodded at me with defiance, and cut Alison Krauss off to say, "I'm back with Vlad. Sorry. He changed into a bat an' I had to catchim!"

He laughed. I laughed with him.

"You know," I said. "I met someone like you in 1907 and I ripped his fucking head off."

"Whoa!"

"Ask your fucking questions."

"*Fucking* ask your fucking questions! Vlad the *Impaler*! My man! I look you up, dudie. You old. And you impale. How do you impale someone, Mr. Impaler?"

"To impale is to run someone through with something sharp and pointed, with an eye towards torture."

He laughed, and I joined him. "That's serious!"

"It *is* serious."

"You like torturing people?"

"It's incredible."

"Yeah?"

"Mmm."

"For a lot of years? How long you been doing that shit?"

"Oh, before you were born."

"Heh. You like the *pain*."

I smiled. "Would you like me to show you?"

He laughed, I laughed. "You want to kill someone? Kill someone live on our little show here?"

"I'd like that."

"Shit, we got a house fulla'em! Go ahead!"

I stood, which clearly threw him.

"Kill someone!"

I nodded, and gave him the back of me.

"Uh… he's getting up. He's walking over. Over to my man Jeff. Jeff is coped out on crack, he don't know. Vlad the Man, he puts his hand on the man's chin and turns him one way and the other. Nah. He passes to Beverly. Oh yeah. He likes Beverly. Oh yeah, he *likes* Beverly. Oh *yeah*! Oh *yeah*! Oh."

Her blood was sweet, like honey. Honey from Berkshire bees. I guessed it was the cocaine or whatever "heavy" she was on. My mouth went to the reverse of her elbow, just letting the suction I made drip down and down my throat as I squeezed each inch of skin from her shoulder to my mouth. The pressure squirted beautiful heaven into my hunger. Delicious.

I heard Taylor Swift singing "Love Story" and thought it fitting. I turned back to see this radio  fool standing, bending slightly at his knees because his headphone cord wouldn't let him up all the way. A tall, belligerent, frightened bastard. And as

I took each step toward him, mentally he regarded me more and more as horrible, opening his mouth slightly to dribble, his eyes beautifully bulging like Mantan Mooreland in a good Chan.

The people in the house did not stir. Did they know anything, even their own names?

I looked into Diddy's eyes. He knew. "You may call the police," I said.

He was a professional, I'll say that for him. Only after he changed the tune to Kellie Pickler's "Don't You Know You're Beautiful" and announced the fact as such to his audience, did he call the constabulary.

# chapter 12

When the call came through, I was wrestling with translator resumes. We had the goods, finally, on Vlad's birthplace and time, thanks mainly to my *NY Post* and now *Newsweek* connections who can blaze info a lot faster than college kids working for credit. But seeing as I had money to throw around and I wanted to be *sure*—this was for the gold, not a story in a weekly—of what I was going to read in court, I wanted at least two other independent translators working on this stuff. I'd give them the originals in Romanian and the English that *Newsweek* was going to press with within 48 hours. Then I'd have accuracy and I would be able to see just what degree of truth would be coursing through the bias and sarcasm of the news reports.

My man was locked up for *murder*.

I hurried down to a different precinct, and wasn't surprised when Vlad himself met me at the entrance to the squalid little police station. He was dressed in brown shorts, La Coste green tee t-shirt and tie, and of course the cape. Really, someone should tell the man he looks ridiculous. I just couldn't do it.

"Did they let you *out*?"

"No."

All the way through the halls, me telling cops who I was, signing things so I could dig further into the building, Vlad kept on about how squalid the little police station really was. Terrible smells and when's the last time they cleaned everything, and every new uniform we passed gave us double surprised looks. I knew one was for Vlad's Halloween costume, and I guessed that the other one was because we were walking back towards the cell he wasn't in.

"You drink blood," I said, "what does it matter the last time they swept up?"

"Oh, it matters," he said rather gutturally.

We were starring at a locked cell containing an empty bed and a toilet without a seat or a lid. Then we looked at each other, and I heard the cop behind me take the gun out of his holster.

To change the subject, if such a thing was possible, I said, "Open it, please."

He looked wacky and in deference to having anyone else around to ask, he opened it and sat our asses on the bed.

Vlad handed me pink paper, on which was written, in olde Englishe words, a list of—something. Hard to read, but as I squinted at it, he spoke.

"You are my mouthpiece."

"Right."

"I was hoping this would be a little like *Stir Crazy*, with huge hulking black men in here I could taunt. Is the jail system crowded or not?"

"I don't know."

"Don't you ever come down here?"

I shrugged. "Not in the cells. Usually they give you a room to talk in."

"Why aren't we in a room with a double mirror and a table and coffee where they'd keep me for hours, talking, like last time?"

He was making me tired. "I think you've got everyone *confused*. They don't know what's going on with you, walking back here." I patted his shoulder. Didn't want to, but lack of fear helps everyone. "They probably think you're probably too dangerous to circulate too much."

He looked around.

"There's a camera in this room, too," I said. "Don't meet me at the door anymore, okay?"

"That depends on you."

"What?"

He nodded gravely, then tapped the list in my hand. "You are my mouthpiece. *Inherit the Wind*, if you will. Be my heir."

"What are you talking about, again?"

"I have an engagement tonight. Holly and I are going out with Fred to see *Boyz in the Hood 3*."

"You're in *jail*."

"Yes. But we'd made plans before this happened. So. You give this to the chief of police, because I think he will be the person who can make such high-powered deals, and we'll strike the bargain."

"You're in *jail*."

He nodded gravely. "This will show my seriousness. My proof of who I am. Locals think television is television. When I'm on the street... it is different..."

Whatever, I thought.

I did it. I took his pink paper to the officer in charge. I felt like a fool, and I did it. Of course the lead on duty laughed at me. Who wouldn't? About the only smart thing he said was asking me, "Is there a *Boyz in the Hood 2*?"

I didn't know. I just went back to my client to pass on what we both knew would happen. No deal. Vlad smiled, I turned around to rattle to be let out, and turned around again, and he was gone.

In the car, I finally had a look at that list.

1.  Bring me dogs for food
2.  I must enjoy the comforts of home
3.  No disturbing during my days
4.  Uncompromising press interviews, at night, in my jail cell

And then at the bottom he wrote, "I shall keep your streets safe on condition of this written and

notarized agreement to the above. Vlad Drac Tepes."

It took a couple goes with Medge and myself both reading it, in bed, to figure out what he meant. We were naked, in each other's arms. There would be no sex that night, but the feeling of skin on skin was fine, and just as far as we had the energy to go.

"How did he get out?" she asked.

"He has the power to hypnotize," I said.

A pause, shrouded in Medge's unsure scowl that I'd known for many years. "You sure he might not be—"

"He's a character!" I'd almost shouted it.

"I mean—"

"What? *Dracula*? A literary, fictional character?" I said. " He's a different and utterly different character. He's... Vlad is crazy rich with wild eyes, that's all. You can't confuse him with..."

What could I say that would convince myself? I just listened to the silence. I forgot to put on the usual Mancini CD. It was too quiet.

I put on Mancini.

"The good news," I said, "is that he *believes* what he is. Dr. Moner signed off on his sanity and his PR guy's already leaked it to *The New York Times* and even *Fangoria* and *Penny Blood*, which are these monster/horror magazines, I guess."

"Is Dr. *Moner* sane?"

I laughed. "There's no irrational thought, at least. And EKG confirms regular brain and heart work, which I'm hoping is going to *also* lay me medical groundwork into what makes a 'man.'"

"A man?"

I spoke philosophy to her, which just about closed her eyes. People were still banging on the outside of the house, day and night, when they got past security, and shouting from across the street, but still Medge almost fell asleep. We'd started closing the couple doors between the front door and our bedroom door, and it muffled the din fine. Also we kept our phone consistently unplugged. I was only using the secret cell these days. Doll was spending more time with friends' kids, and I thought, until the trial was on or over, we'd send her up to Peru, Indiana to spend some time with gramma. She could make up the school time, she was still young. At least, that's the way my brain rehearsed it to sell the plan to Medge whenever I could buy the courage to bring it up.

"I think we got proof today," I told her, but she wasn't listening. She was somewhere between falling asleep and worrying. "We can prove that he's who he says he is, or that this Vlad man existed in what's now Romania. His DNA shows he's hundreds of years old. So that's good."

She perked right up. "What? Huh?"

I laughed. "Just wanted to see if you were still with us."

She hit me and settled her sweaty flesh back into mine.

"Is that true? You can prove it?"

I snuggled her, and worried. Because what I'd just said wasn't quite the truth. I guess that's why undead is a word, and dead is a different word. Vlad's tissue samples were screwed up, but they *were* living, they were organic.

I'd been worrying about that all day.


Front page of the *Tallahassee Democrat* the next morning was Vlad and company coming out of that theatre in the Tallahassee Mall after midnight. He (well, the outline of him) and Holly were in front, she was laughing, Fred and whoever his date was were looking more like driver's licenses. Draco was too good at buzz.

Our front yard looked like Woodstock. Finally, I just had to call a security company to send a man with a strong car over to come get me for work. No way all those cars and trucks would get out of my way in less than an hour. There was even a hot dog stand that sold tacos and soup blocking the drive.

This football player of a bloke ran my interference as I dashed to his car, and I sat in the backseat, huffing like a hot cat. Once I realized the windows wouldn't shattered from all the reporters and activists out there, I settled in and felt kind of important and carefree with a chauffeur. I had nothing to do or work on, but my glazed gaze watched the frenzy. Poor Medge. Living on take out Chinese the past couple weeks. She had to get to the store sometime. We needed to eat something *green*.

"After you drop me off," I told the driver, "would you mind coming back and cleaning my house? I want the pile of shit on the lawn out of there. Tell them by 3 p.m. or I slap them all with invasion of privacy."

The driver didn't talk, or never seemed to, but I did catch him nodding yeah, so I took it as fact that he'd deliver the message. I dialed up Celia on the *Post* phone and told her to call the driver at 2:30 and confirm.

There was a text from Holly. It read: *I'm coming in today after 7. I've got background on the time period and the wars. Have you ever listened to gothic rock? There's a guy called Desar who's really good. I'll bring a cd. Love you. Holly*

Wars? I texted back—and I hate doing it because it takes so long: *Are you a vampire?? Gath*

Never got a response.

There were only about 45 people in the office that morning. I asked the driver to post someone on the office door too, and he nodded, I guess, that he'd take care of it. Sure enough, later, when I poked out to grab some Arby's roast beef burgers, there was no one to keep Celia company.

Wading through the shouters and would-be clients at *this* moment in time, on my way to the front door, Fred found me and tugged at my sleeve.

"Why didn't you go in?" I shouted.

He told me once we got through the door and managed to shut it on the zombies. "I wanted them to think I was one of them."

"Yeah, that's good. Did you hear what they said while they were waiting?"

"They're pretty quiet when they don't have anyone to mob."

"Oh well." Then I thought, "But you were in the paper?"

He pointed at his face. I didn't get it.

"I didn't shave since last night," he said. "Besides, that picture looks like we're in the background."

I peered at him, but there wasn't that much stubble. I shrugged it off. "How was the film?"

"Black drama."

I nodded.

"Vlad laughed a lot, though," he said.

"Really?"

"What are we doing about Holly?"

"She'll be in at 7."

"I'll be back."

He had that determined voice, so I reminded him: "Save the anger for the *other* side. I *need* you clear headed for the case."

My desk was awash with Stick 'Em messages. "Oprah personally called!!!! Not sec.!!" Ah, Celia.

"He's done something to Holly!" Fred said.

I nodded. "I know. I don't think she's been bitten or anything."

"Did you look *all* over her body?"

He was being funny, but serious. I put my hands on his shoulders and sat him down. "Joma's on this. He's been spending every waking off-duty minute outside Vlad's place. He's letting Vlad know that he's being watched—by *our* side. And as much as Vlad wants his court case, he's not going to screw it up by screwing with Holly. I'm sure of that."

I bored into his eyes to make him *quite* certain that I was not kidding. I was not kidding.

He finally relaxed his forehead muscle a little and visibly shrank. "Yeah."

The phone rang, which meant it was very important. I'd had calls re-routed through an Indian service lately. Good thing the money was still coming in.

"What do you think he wants with her?" Fred asked, mostly to himself.

I was already on the phone. It was the D.A.

Figuring out the logistics of being in the middle of a national catastrophe or what felt like was a national catastrophe was nigh impossible, so even though the D.A. wanted to meet, we had to ditch the more pleasant idea of lunch in a public place. We were forced to do just instant chat on a Yahoo program, on a secure line for each of us. Too bad. I missed being able to pop out to Krystal for a sweet tea or just driving to think away a case, looking at the speeding green and yellow leaves through my sun roof. Funny the little things you miss when you're in prison.

Even Celia was finding it hard to get me my daily Krispie Kream. She kept having to hire new boys to nip out and get them, because all the stalking, sulking reporters everywhere—around every bloody bend!—knew her face, knew the face of whatever gopher she'd hired after just one KK run (maybe they paid the runners to talk, I don't know; conspiracy like this was beyond me), knew the temp employment agency she was using to hire kids to fetch the doughnuts, etc., etc. I even found a bug, the electronic kind, of course, in an Original Glazed once! I just *missed* fresh air!

DA: How are you holding up?

Me: Like a support beam. You?

DA: Well, it's not the first time we've been through somethig like this, but it's the biggest. What the hell are you doing over there?

Me: I don't know. I don't know how he's getting on these night shows. He was on CNN the night before last. Wow, he really doesn't like being interrupted by a hurrying host. It might stop soon because he's mentioned a deal about staying in jail if the press comes to him.

DA: That's what I want to talk about.

Me: I've got a note from Oprah, not her secretary, sitting on my desk!

DA: You're kidding!

Me: The money's good, but I swear…

DA: What?

Me: I had to hire protection, like bodyguards. I can't make a *direct* call anymore. I can't -

DA: How far away from trial are we?

Me: That depends on Dalmonica. I haven't even heard from him. He's the hold up.

DA: He's not. His office has been on the phone to me the last two days wanting me to do something about you.

Me: Me? What can you do?

DA: Public nuisance. Fraud. His people are helping my creativity.

Me: Do they want to prove it's me doing all this? I'm the agent not the talent here.

DA: What about the killing?

I paused to stretch my fingers, got up and put on some *Diamond Dogs*, because really, I didn't know how to reply. This was a courtesy call, that's all. Vlad vs. Dalmonica, and I typed so.

DA: We're talking about murder now.

Me: The guy in Diddy's place? What have you got?

DA: Are you his defense attorney?

Me: No! I'm not criminal here. Strictly civil.

DA: I'll tell you. Just so you know. No prints. Holes in the neck. A great loss of blood, but not on the floor. The people right there by the body saw nothing. They were too stoned. And Diddy's just missing. We can't find him anywhere. We haven't got a case.

Me: The radio audience?

DA: Thanks for trying to help US. But you know we can't get your boy for an audio murder.

Me: Even if you try to get him, Vlad's not going to stay underground for the court battle that means something to him. You don't understand this guy. I had a dream, and it was vivid, that he shot himself in the head to prove his…otherworldliness to me. I mean, that seemed very real. Like it happened.

DA: So… he can't be locked up?

Me: That's what I'm saying. That's what he's proving. He saw a movie last night when he should've been in jail!

DA: I know, I know, that's why I "called." What do you think?

Me: I think I'm getting tired, of the whole thing.

DA: Before you pass out, tell me my answer. Am I going to have to worry? I don't want to hand this to Feds, but I'm tempted. I have enough to do, and they want it, Gath. They want you.

Me: I say – yeah, worry. Give him his demands. They're pretty simple. But don't let the press hear that you're giving him dogs to eat or suck on. Vlad can do what he says. I don't know how, but you better watch out.

DA: You think he's Dracula or 500 years old?

Me: Of course not. But I can't explain or control him either. Know what I mean?

DA: What's the deal again?

Me: Hold on.

I went to get Vlad's note out of my working file. Took me a minute to type it in again, then I highlighted and cut what I'd written so I could write:

Me: Are you saving this chat?

DA: I think I'd better. I think we're fine.

Me: About what?

(Took him a moment) DA: Hold the line.

I waited all of twelve minutes, and learned by reading tomorrow morning's paper what the D.A. was probably dealing with in the pause. A crazy group of three students from a medieval studies group from SWC (FSU Southwest Campus) had burst into the capital building, all wearing black, with cat's blood, and they were trying to make some statement. No one had a chance to sling much blood because all the cops knew how to shout louder and had pushed the students to the ground quickly. Once they were captured and tortured with police station coffee, they admitted to doing it all in the name of Vlad, the one true leader. Just an hour later E! Entertainment news and all the rest of them had the story. It made sensational copy, though all you saw were reporters standing outside the capital, but it didn't help my side any.

Eventually our conference continued.

DA: Don't come down here.
Me: Okay.
DA: What's the deal?
Me: How are we "fine"?
DA: What?
Me: From before. Scroll up. "I think we're fine."

He was a slow reader. Anyway, the tone of the chat had changed now.

DA: We're not fine, Gath. What's the deal?

He was going to save the chat. Obviously. I'd do the same. I pasted in Vlad's craziness.

Me: 1. Bring me dogs for food. 2. I must enjoy the comforts of home. 3. No disturbing during my days. 4. Uncompromising press interviews, at night, in my jail cell.

The cursor blinked.

DA: Are you giving this to the press?
Me: I don't need to.
DA: Is he?
Me: I'll ask. He seems pretty honest. And he's going to be asked why he's sitting in jail, especially when some jerk asks him why doesn't he just change into a bat and fly out.

DA: Okay.

Me. Want me to ask him not to?

DA: Do you have pull?

Me: …………………..

DA: You know what's going to happen when Oprah hears he's eating dogs at night. Between interviews with the press. All hell will break loose.

Me: Did you see Jimmy Fallon?

DA: The show? Yeah.

Me: Then you know he could be on Oprah whether she wants him on or not.

I saved the chat, which went out with a whimper. No goodbyes, we were both too busy for those.

"Celia!"

She came in, smiling. She knew it helped.

I laid a hand on her. "Now you know this is nothing to do with you. Right?" She threw me a look. "I want a temp to help you field the messages." She visibly sighed without using breath, and I was quick to take her other hand. "This is nothing to do with you. This is too much *work*. Just someone to field the press messages, call people back. You're a *legal* secretary, not a press secretary."

That was calming enough for her, and she nodded.

As she left, I called out, "Can you send the bodyguard in?"

In a moment a new guy, the short, in-shape, military type, came in. He had his head shaved close to the bone like that *Transporter* guy. He listened carefully with one hand clapped on the hairy wrist of his other.

"Can you give me some celebrity tips?" I asked him.

"—Sorry?"

"You've seen celebs pass through Tallahassee, right?"

"Oh, yeah. I had Ross MacDonald through here once."

"Who's that?"

"And I usually get bagged by some of the rock stars who need some force between the car and curb, if you know what I mean. U2, REM and Right Said Fred and like that."

I was a lawyer, so I could phrase it just so. "If I'm U2 and I want to get away from my fans… like, go out and have a Sonic chili dog or something, how do I accomplish that?"

He parted his feet and ran a thinking man's hand over his barely shaved stubble of a neck.

"Woooo. Today?"

"Soonish."

"Can you give yourself a day or two? Then I can tell you the easiest."

"Tell me now."

He laughed. "Yeah, I'll tell ya now, but we can't implement it on ya until 48 hours, let's say."

"How?"

"Buy some coats," he said.


Celia took off for Target at 3 and just stayed the rest of the day and night at home, after slipping a couple long dark coats into a box which Fedex picked up right at the store. Dark glasses and some sensible and silly scarves were also inside when I opened it.

That evening, making my usual escape from the office, everyone saw me in the new look—which even made the front page of *Mira!* for some reason. Others, like *The Star* and *The Paris Review*, had me on interior pages. Medge started a scrapbook; she had little else to do there for a while. I read the rags nightly with her, on the nights when I could make it home.

My persona was taking off, causing talk. *The Philadelphia Tag* instigated a theory of how I was being corrupted by cash, working for a jailed madman and a murderer, and Medge and I talked long and hard about it, yet again. Should I get out? Was it worth it? *Should* I feel guilty? Should I? Would we be safe if I said *Here, Vlad, I can't do this anymore. You* killed *someone. I can't in all conscience…*

We talked and we talked. Part of me didn't feel guilty about *anything*, because I still didn't believe it. Any of it. Medge was doubtful on the Vlad front, but she trusted me, and she *knew* I wouldn't work for someone I knew was guilty, because I never had, and probably never would. But then—why arrest him at all, if there was no proof in the murder? The DA never really told me anything solid. Was it a publicity stunt from Draco? If not, was I going to have to defend him on that count, too? I wouldn't. Vlad admitted to me early on that he killed people. But weren't those just ravings?

So many questions, so many swirling directions my mind wanted to take. By the time I felt like clearing my head, I could. Because the bodyguard's idea about the coats paid off. I left it all to him.

Buddy Greico was a man with my build, and after a half hour studying me on *Good Morning, America*, he had my walk down well enough to slip on the dark glasses I had started wearing whenever sunlight and flashbulbs hit me. He got into my rental; I got into a special kind of cab my bodyguard—now guarding my double—knew about, and soon I had dropped the cabbie off, hopefully not to tip off the press as to what I was driving, and I felt freedom again. Just a taste of it.

At last.

No place to go. No plans. Just driving. Highway driving, thinking.

# CHAPTER

There was a slight fog to the area which not even the rain could drown out. Gath had called from a cell phone of all things to inquire that we might change our meeting place to somewhere large and open and public, not from lack of trust, but he was feeling so…caged of late, which I could commiserate with. Yet I said no, joking that meeting in his office would keep our number of sets down and the cost of this TV movie down, when they finally made a movie of this. Which they will.

"Who would you like to see you play yourself?" I asked of him that evening.

He thought, and as his answer came readily, I knew it was not the first time he had thought on it. "Harrison Ford is too old, but Harrison Ford."

"Are you a Jones fan?" I asked.

"Indiana Jones?" I nodded. "Who isn't? It's the theme, though. That's where his power lies." We hummed John Williams for a moment. Fred merely glared at me, and he glared at Holly too, as if any of this were her fault.

"Who's going to play you?" Fred asked. "Asshole Billingsly?"

"Who's that?"

"That's *you*!" He slammed his hand down on the table. "I don't like where you're taking this case! I've got Feds knocking on my door at 4 this morning, obviously a ploy. They didn't care what I said. Because *you* broke out!"

"Did they find anything broken?" I asked.

"You know what I'm talking about! You're in jail. You should *be* in jail right *now*."

He came over and took Holly's hand, which I quite understood. Even admired. Which is why I did not kill him at any time.

Very softly, he said, "Are you all right?" He pushed her hair back. It did not need to be back.

"It's true, Vlad," Gath said, "we do need to do something about damage control."

"Taken care of," I admitted, but would say no more when pressed.

"You just did this for publicity, didn't you?, you prick!"

Fred wanted to rush me but he was already far too much of a lawyer to do it. I gave him one of my smiles, which produced a mere mutter.

"For blood," I said.

"How long are you going to keep this up?" Gath asked.

"What?"

"The television! The newspapers, the news—I had a tip off you're in *Time* this week."

I nodded. "In a few days. Not the cover, alas. Print and radio don't matter, but this television is great stuff. I mentioned that I like the diet A&W root beer, which I do, and a case showed up at my house the next day. It's marvelous! I'm tempted to say Toyota on Oprah!"

"Yeah, but you're in jail now, asshole!"

It was Fred, of course. Quite tiring, but every film has to have its internal conflict, and I knew this could only help us. Somehow. Well, vaguely I knew, and I loved him for it. Consider how boring *Night of the Living Dead* might be without the bald man and *only* zombies.

"How long, Vlad?" Gath asked. "I never know what you're going to do, where you're going to be…"

"What do you mean? Publicity is the life's blood of justice."

"Yeah, look at OJ," Fred said.

"We must keep in their minds, my friends," I explained. "That is the important thing."

"It is," said my darling.

Gath took one of her hands. They were sitting next to each other, myself on her right. A fleeting pang of jealousy did erupt, I admit, but that was all. He merely cared. I had viewed firsthand how he fucks his wife and I knew it to be true, this loving emotion, so I was not worried.

"You've been so…different since you've been back, Holly," he whispered. It was quite moving, quite bold. "Are you sure you're okay? You can talk to me about anything."

"I would like to talk to you about Dracula Twins," I said.

"I'm fine," Celia said, patting his hand. She smiled at Gath who remained unconvinced…of anything.

It was left to Fred to ask, "What's Dracula Twins?"

"A new download game from BigFish Games," I explained, "in which Dr. Lifelust has captured Count Dracula so he can distill his blood and live forever. That's a wonderful little proof, but I wonder if we might sue them too."

Gath shook his head and put Holly's hand away. "Dalmonica is our butter and bread and when he goes, we pave the way for supplementary, secondary cases."

He breathed in and seemed recharged today by something. It could not have been from that dreadful Jon Anderson music that he'd announced earlier and which still, damnit, played.

"I think we've got a real chance it," he continued. "It's not like Shakespeare himself is going to pop up and start claiming *Taming of the Shrew* and everything. This is an anomaly, 'the author's life plus 70 years' on copyright, and I see the *silence* we're hearing from Dalmonica as being in our *favor*."

"You don't *see* silence," Fred said automatically. Something else was plaguing his brain.

"Do you know who he represents?"

Gath nodded. "I have confirmation. For myself, at least. Universal, Paramount, Columbia, owned by Japanese owned Sony, a conglomerate plus. NBC Universal controlled by General Electric's NBC and Vivendi Universal Entertainment, part of the French Media Group, and it doesn't matter if any of these names change anytime soon. That's the point of Dalmonica. He services up a wide area of these corporate empires which had a clear stake in all of this, much like BMI providing music to be played in restaurants, theme parks, on the radio. Just like that, the kings pay off Dalmonica based on what their accountants claim is their slice of the cake.

"The Fox Broadcasting Company is a part of Rupert Murdoch's news corp. empire, with affiliates from Argentina to South Korea; Warner Bros. Entertainment, a subsidiary of Time Warner, and from there we slip into the publishing side of interconnection: books, e-books on iPad and Kindle, tie-ins and the rest of it. Warner owns DC Comics, so that's where we slip into gothic graphic novels and the rest of it. And now Disney's bought Marvel Comics, too. Mind you, most times clever writers want—they want to deal with 'vampires' rather than *you*" he pointed at me "so we're not mining as deep in that hole as you might think, but I seriously don't think we have to think about splinter groups at all. Just go after the biggies. Everything connects anyway."

He put his hands together like they were claws. The man appeared absolutely giddy. He was pleased with himself. And I with him.

Holly said, "Vlad has a diary."

Gath looked at me quickly with funny, bulging eyes. "You're kidding!"

"I've kept one off and on since 1810," I said. "I doubt you could read it."

"That's not important! Holly, get it over to Charles at Agency and—"

"He's already got it," she said.

"Did he date it?"

"Yes, and it's in several volumes, and we've got a match on the paper. Definitely two centuries old. But what's good and I mean what's *best* is that the ink is certainly within the time frame and gets progressively *older* as the entries move on."

Gath was nodding like a boy with his first snake.

She continued, "We've got it in the same *hand*writing, for hundreds of years, and let the defense loose on tearing up the science of it, but I don't think there's been a case yet with such far yielding trickery. Whatever holes they try to punch, I can see the judge being impressed with the time element."

"I meant to mention that," Gath said, still shaking his smiling head. "Celia, can we find a judge who doesn't believe in God?"

"Wait a minute, Gath," Fred said. He was finally behaving constructively. "Is that a good idea? Wouldn't an absence of faith mean it's harder for him to believe in the supernatural?"

"On the other hand," I said, "there have been far too many films in which the truly devout believe just as strongly that the devil *cannot* exist."

"Name one."

"The Catholic church."

"That's not a film."

"No," I said, "but I have seen the truly faithful believe in a God, but when pressed upon the chapters of miracles and such, they say that these are myths or allegory in order to illustrate the point of faith and poetry, if you will, for ideology—"

"Who here believes in God?" Gath suddenly asked.

No hands. Eventually, Celia's hand met the air. It was as if she were owning up to doing detestable things. Such a thing, faith. How fervent it had been when I was kid.

"Do you really?" Gath asked.

She nodded, clearly ashamed to admit it.

"Do you believe in Satan?"

She had to think a moment on that, which proved my point.

"You see? And then there is *The Day the Earth Stood Still* and *Mars Needs Women* and such—a time when God-fearing people could not believe in men from other worlds. And if they did, these otherworld creatures were things to be feared and stoned and destroyed!"

"Okay, forget God for now, Celia. I mean the judge, never mind."

Gath was trying to think. His hands were stretching his face skin and his eyes popped out at the notebook he'd been jotting things into. Something was very dark on the top page, underlined so much it must have cut through to the next page.

"The diary!" he expunged. "Why didn't you tell me about it before?"

"A man must have some secrets," I said. He could not tell I was joking, nor did I intend to be clear.

"Are you a man?" he asked. "Turn to page six, please."

Everyone had the same group of papers. It was all sheer tedium.

Gath explained, "This is Professor Bradman's report on what threw me for a loop when Dalmonica walked out of here before. Bradman is head of philosophy at FSU's College of Arts *and* Sciences. That title alone I think is a good sign or omen or useable somehow. Arts and *sciences*. Films and science. Anyway, Bradman is prepared to testify that Mr. Tepes here is a man, because he's active, he speaks, he talks, he…do you breathe? It doesn't matter! On Dalmonica's side, they're going to have a doctor, maybe Harvard, they can afford the best, and this big shot is going to ask you if your hair grows. Does your hair grow?"

I shook my head and yawned.

"I didn't think so, but his very *first* question to you might be that. A sort of shock question to lead with. Or maybe hold up a mirror to your nose and I'll object and he'll give a good answer that'll mean he has the right to hold a mirror up to your nose and see if you're breathing or not. Do you breathe?"

"No, no!"

"All right. Don't get upset. Anyway, their contention will be that this is what makes life. Ours is going to be that you're a functioning member of society. That is, you are visibly moving, communicating, you live."

"What will the judge do with that?" Fred asked.

"It might split down the middle. Who knows. Depends on the judge and his believes. But secretly, deep down I believe it doesn't mean a thing. Both sides will score points. But the fact that you are verbal enough to say to the court, 'Hey, look. I *don't* like what you've done with my name. People change. I've come to set the record straight. I'm *not* a bad man.' It's not like I'm literally dragging a dead body into court. The undead just walks right in."

"'No, I just eat people, drink their blood…'" Fred spoke, boring a stare into me that he thought was frightening.

"Vlad doesn't eat people, Fred," Holly said, and laid her hand on mine. Lovely girl.

Dramatically, the little man should have huffed and laid claim to cursing or at least to roll his eyes, but the rebuke merely cowed him into a sorrowful glance and limited silence.

"This structure of definition," said Gath, "matched with all the national—too much, Vlad, too much—publicity you've been getting, I don't see how Dalmonica can say no to open court time when I press him. We're going to stress it's good, insane publicity for him and his clients' back catalog of horror, too. That's the point to press. And I think as a gesture of good faith, Vlad, we should let him have a *Twilight* or something."

"What's that?" I asked, intrigued.

"Whatever their next vamp flick is coming up, you say the words on national TV. Do a promo where you speak the title. Doesn't matter if it's a 'Dracula' or not, just let me tell them something you're going to do *for* them. I know, I know, don't get angry. It's a trade off. Get them thinking in the target area we want them to think in: this is great publicity for them. This will only work *for* them. You mention how much you love or hate *True Blood* or *Twilight*, whatever. You can say it's *crap* on the promo! Just you doing it is going to be the press's wet dream."

"And what does *he* want out of it?" Fred asked, rudely, vaguely pointing at me. "What's your bottom line figure, Vlad?"

I told them as the phone rang. It was an unbelievable figure, sagging everyone's jaw but Gath's. I'd told him in that theatre alley so many weeks ago. Even Holly was appalled. We never spoke of queer things like money when we were alone. Why should we?

But when laid his phone back in its cradle, even Gath was appalled. She stared straight at me.

# chapter 13

"Um..."

"You don't really expect—"

I cut Fred off. "Umm…that was Joma. He's outside in the parking lot."

"What's going on?" Holly asked. Fred went to the window, but could see nothing.

"I need to have a word with him," I told everyone.

"What's up?" Holly asked. She was squeezing Vlad's hand which I thought was cute and stupid.

"Can you get the diary to a transcriber?" I asked her.

"It's thousands of pages, Gath."

"I know."

I left Holly conferring with Vlad in low notes. Fred wanted to follow me out but I had to keep him at leg's length, like a dog, to keep him in the room.

It was raining. Of course. I never liked umbrellas, or never got in the habit of them, so I was dripping when I stepped into the '70s. I mean, Joma's car. It was full of incense and funk booming from the back like—I don't know what like.

"Tell me the worst."

"That depends on who you are, man."

"Come on."

"For you, man, the best. Ain't no dead body no mo.'"

"What dead body?"

"The one that ain't," he said. "Drac's off the hook. No body. No case."

I thought. "You don't need a body to prove murder. And the DA already told me Diddy went missing."

"Yeah, you need a witness, and they've got a house full of stoned ones. They couldn't do it. They've got no case, and with the pressure from the press connecting your man to *The National Enquirer* and *Hard Copy* and shit, they've dropped it. They want out. All charges dropped."

"What are you telling me?"

He did this decade's equivalent of a double take. "Ain't you been listenin'?"

"All right, Joma. I know you. What do you want?"

His face was serious, but there was lifelessness behind his words. "I want Drac. *I'm* not dropping it. But I've got a missing person's case. You know how many of *those* there are in the world? That's where I think your client's real strength is. He sucks 'em up and stuffs 'em who knows where, and moves on to the next town. Think about it. I've been thinking about it. There can't be that many pedophiles in the world."

"There can," I helped.

"Nah, man, this is Drac and his merry band. He sucks one up and buries it or they become one of him, staying out of the daylight, certainly out of the limelight, and that's where *all* my missing person posters come from."

"People would still see them at night."

"Devil's advocate, huh? Think about it. I been thinkin' about it a lot. You're cold because you're dead. You're scared. You stay away from people. You try to control the hunger. Come on, how many vampire flicks have you see since you started this case?"

"All."

"You seen *Near Dark*?"

"One of the best."

"Yeah, that was aw-ite. Lance Hendrikson is cool. And this picture proves my point. It was hard for that white guy to adapt to being a blood sucker. So, I say: by the time you're a missing person, caught up with yourself, by the time you get a handle on the hunger and learn how to get the food and don't mind being seen, then every time you're seen, you take care of the seer, and by then you're younger than you should be to the people trying to find you. *You* haven't aged, the world has!"

"You're saying that every missing person case is a vampire?"

"Not every, course not. I'm saying you can't bury that many kids. Some of these posters show kids and adults being gone a *long* time. So you look at the poster, you see the kid was born in 1965 and then you see a kid in person that looks just like the missing one, but this kid should be over 40 by now, so you think it's just someone who looks like her. Or him."

I let NPG's *Exodus* wash over me. Prince could be good; he could be funny. But the car music was only on the side of my mind at the moment.

"That's good," I told him.

"Course!"

"That we're not drowning in vampires, I meant."

"I know what you *meant*." He looked at me, and he stopped Prince. "You meant you glad there's no complication now. But you watch it, man. You tell Drac that even though he don't have to, coax him into staying in prison. Safer for everyone. Including your boy."

"He doesn't fear anything."

"I know. I threw that in because it's the right thing to say."

Joma didn't want to come in or want a coffee. To tell the truth, I think he was getting tired of me. Of this case. I know I was.

But I didn't want to think about that. Half of me thought Vlad could really *read* my mind. The other half of me knew that all this thinking wasn't constructive. I was in the case.

Right in it.

I went back inside and we adjourned the meeting. Then we just sat there talking about things. Movies, mostly. Vlad wanted to sue Quantum Entertainment for making *Vlad* (2003) because it was just a bad movie, he said, and it didn't give Brad Dourif, the voice of Chucky, enough screen time.

"*Vlad* makes me look like a one-dimension power crazed bully," he said, "a character I never encouraged within myself. I *wish* I'd known they were doing it at the time."

Fred was for some reason more cordial now that the table was strictly unofficial. His tone was just—I don't know—like a college student again when he asked, "Have you ever tried to convince anyone of your—true nature before?"

Vlad sighed and looked at the floor as if this was important to him. He ended up just saying nothing, and we moved on to talking about how *Seed of Chucky* sucks and how it killed the series, much like a Michael Bay redo kills any series, and that sparked Vlad back into the talk. But by then, it was just me and Holly and him. Celia left her notes on the table, gave me an uncharacteristic kiss on the head—I think she sensed my weariness with it all, even before I did—and got out of there before 10.

I called Medge to tell her I'd be late, but Holly put a hand on my phone hand.

"Why don't the four of us go somewhere?"

"You—could—come over to the house," I said in a way I'd hoped would imply my personal imposition, but they merely accepted, and we took separate cars over, they following me, even though I knew Vlad knew the way. It started me wondering in what year he might say he got his driver's license. 1952? 1916? Driving one of the first black, cranking cars off the market?

The press had a field day with all of us arriving. We woke most of them up upon our arrival and boy were they glad *they* slept in their cars and vans. Seemed like most of them didn't mind being rousted by the cops if the neighbors complained that eight to ten cars were parked around our snaky road. We lived in one of those subdivisions that basically has one way in and out, so the smarter reporters slept closer to Titan St., the large-ish main street from which I had come in from Thomasville Road, which was the first place in the neighborhood where they could ambush us.

For a change, I was invisible and could just walk to the door without fear or comment. I unlocked the door and just stood and watched all the mics and lights and interested freelancers all hopping around and hopeful that Vlad might say something tricky. Instead, he just treated them all to a barrage of pictures. This evening he was dressed in a pretty respectable suit, except that the back of his coat went down like a cape. He liked capes. He grinned his unpointy teeth and glared at them slowly, from right to left, sometimes raising his arms which raised his cape— these were the action poses the cameramen liked best. Holly stood on the side for these and giggled, and joined him for the more "serious" boyfriend/girlfriend shots which the paparazzi clamored for equally.

"How much blood can you drink in one night?"

"Hey, why don't you have a European accent?"

"Do Catholics literally suck?"

"Have you ever been in an Italian restaurant?"

"Are you democratic or plutocratic?"

"Have you ever had a stake through your heart?"

"Are you a football or sumo fan?"

"Why don't you live in Alaska?"

"What's with the cape?"

Watching the press as a group is like watching a living animal that you're feeding. Never gets enough, never gets tired. Their questions were unending. Holly walked over to me and I closed the door. Vlad, I guess, stayed behind, frolicking in questions, and then suddenly—he was there.

Medge gasped. I hadn't realized she was watching. I didn't know what had happened myself until he appeared.

Holly kissed Vlad and we all walked into the hallway a little more.

"Medge, you remember Holly?"

Holly shook my wife's limp hand.

"What just happened?"

Vlad smiled and moved into the room more and said, "We are giving them tomorrow's headlines, Medge."

He was right. If Obama had done something spectacular or there was a million death earthquake in Japan, it wasn't on the first page of any paper you could buy in the morning. It was us. *We* were the front page. And we all just spent the night playing Clue and talking about Tim Curry and what a voice he had. At least Vlad did.


It was the first time I think I'd seen *The Wall Street Journal* carry a picture taken in Tallahassee on their front page. Not even a great photo, which was surprising, since I thought they could afford to buy the best, though I'd never met anyone who ever read that paper. All this I thought over Grape Nuts soaking in Splenda and low-fat milk.

That's when the new phone rang. I kept it in my pocket. Just something I'd asked one of the bodyguards to get and program so I could just receive one number calling me. I didn't know you could do that, but it was smart.

It was Dalmonica.

"We've had enough of this." Not even a Hello. "Will you settle?"

"Settle what?"

He clicked off, then phoned back again in four minutes. I was slurping from the bottom of the bowl. Always been a slow eater.

"Let's talk court date," he said.

I told him Celia would coordinate with his secretary and we'd see. Celia had the structure, she knew our pace. Whatever she decided was fine.

Suddenly Medge rushed in from the living room.

"Vlad's on TV!"

"Isn't he always?"

"He was shot last night!"

The news report was—spooky. That was the best way to describe it. You know how reporters usually talk—in their own singsong way of highs and lows and emphasis. Well, this time it was all lows. Medge happened to have CBS on, though reports were now live on all channels at the moment, even though nothing was happening right now. The cute brunette reporter didn't have any singsong. She was downright dour. Even a little depressed at what she was having to say.

"—hasn't been seen since." She was in front of Vlad's place. "In fact all morning. Police and government officials have been banging on this door since the event occurred, at 3:34 last night, resulting in no responses. Dwight Yolm who reported the shooting has been corroborated as having been the one to have called the paramedics from his cell phone, but when the paramedics arrived, their knocks too went unanswered.

"Police have confirmed the shooting. Multiple bullet wounds. Mr. Ray Parked, 26, a laborer from a nearby tree farm, has broken down in tears with his confession. He has said…"

Here she paused so a picture of a weird white guy hovered above her and his dreary recorded voice said, "I had to stop him. I had to stop him, I was the only one who could stop him. Why doesn't somebody stop him? Don't you know who he is? He tells you, you don't listen. Somebody had to stop him."

It rambled on like that until they ran out of recording and finally the brunette with the finger in her ear looked back up at the camera and, crying a little herself, said, "The fact is that the one calling himself the true Dracula, Vladimire Tepers, once ruler of Transylvania, has not let five bullets slow down his stride. Nor did Dracula falter at the door after he was shot. He even unlocked the door—none of this seemed to matter to him. Nor has he reported the shooting.

"As you see, the Federal agents around me are trying to decide—"

That's what happens when you unplug your phone. The *second* I plugged the one back in the bedroom, it rang.

"Will you hold please for Agent Tol?"

I held and didn't wait long. It was a dark, sleepy voice that said, "Gath Wein?"

"Yes."

"We've got a shooting down here, sir."

"I know, I only just saw it on the news."

"As Mr. Tepes's representative, we'd like your permission, sir, to enter Mr. Tepes residence and attain the truth of the situation."

"You've got probably cause. Why didn't you go in already?"

There was muffled speaking and decision taking on the other side that never rose above a mumble.

"May we gain entry, Mr. Wein?"

"I don't think so."

"He might be hurt, or dying, sir."

"He locked his door, didn't he?"

Same bit of muffled stuff, pretty fast this time. "Yes, sir."

"He doesn't want you in there."

Outside *our* house, it sounded like The Arctic Monkeys were in town. There was beating on the front door, then the back door. The security agency had a free hand to call in extra help if they needed it, but obviously they were being slow about it. By the time there was beating on both back and front doors and on the side of the house, we knew it was time to turn the front yard sprinklers on. That quieted things down to a second-degree roar.

Medge had had remote control steel shutters installed on the main windows, so now she pushed a button for a quick second to slant the outside view into the room. There were protestors sporting signs as far as the eye could see, mostly MURDERER!! and variation on that theme. Some were pathetic, like the little ol' man with a big ol' sign reading STOP WASTING BLOOD!! written in blood. There was the comic sign: HAVE YOU BEEN KILLING OUR CHICKENS?! The guy carrying it looked bored, like some farmer had hired him for the standing work perhaps.

There were even signs in other languages, which I couldn't read, and signs shaken by people who were worked up and ranting, walking slow enough to let anyone *read* their signs.

My secret email to the D.A. didn't bounce back, so eventually we got more cop protection, to move people along. I'm sure Mr. D.A. was receiving enough justifiable complaints from our neighbors—whom I expected to join the picketers against us any day now—to act, and soon things quieted down.

Still, that was the night we slept with our Sony mp3 players in our ears, the kind that required no wires, no player, you just upload the tunes directly into the headphones (mine was lime green, hers was cool white) and as long as you charge it for 90 minutes, it'll last you 12 hours. Medge drifted off quickly to new age and ocean waves, while I kept Survivor's *Eye of the Tiger* album on repeat play and shuffle, hoping sleep would one day find me.

The next morning there was shit on our lawn, compliments of the RSPCA, unofficially, wrapped in notes like "We know about the dogs." There were also broken bottles that had crashed against the steel shutters, probably hauled from a distance, over the cop cars roaming all night. I found out later it was actually just one patrol car that roamed all night, but it still felt good. Unless it was the cop who did the bottles. Or peed in our mailbox. With the flag up.

Since Vlad obviously didn't care, he was going to have to give his address on TV next time. Too many people thought he lived here.

When the car arrived, I urged Medge to come with me. Maybe veer off to the airport and go—somewhere. We could afford it. Get Doll some home-schooling and have the two of them visit Peru or Argentina or somewhere until this blew over, while I slogged on with the case. Medge gave me that good wife smile that I hadn't seen since years back when I was studying full time and she had to work at the foot massage place full time for great tips and no salary.

"It's worth it," she said then, and she said it now, and smiled.

"Why?" I asked. "Why is it worth *this*?"

She caressed my check and gave me a kiss.

"It won't be long now," I said.

She nodded and continued the brave face. "I've got so much cutting to do." She meant the scrapbook.

"You see anything informational, let me see it."

Shaking her head, she just said, "It's mostly the rags today. I've got so many *Private Eyes* to do. It's a British weekly. Now git!"

And I got. A heavy hand was placed on my head as we raced for the back door of the Lincoln Continental. Not many people were crapping on us this morning though. I lowered the partitioning window inside to ask the driver why?

"They're all over at the courthouse this morning, chief."

"Uh oh. Why is that?"

"You ain't the only story in town," he said.

But it couldn't be true. This was Tallahassee.

Sure enough, the big thing on the local channels this morning was that someone said they'd found Dracula's coffin, and the first thing I could think of was: poor *Tallahassee Democrat*. They had to go to press in the wee hours and they missed it. I don't know *why* I thought this, but it made me go to their website rather than watch TV for a change. Sure enough, there were vivid pictures of some idiot on the courthouse steps ranting. To his right there were less than vivid cellphone photos, his, of two coffins, with dirt around their bases. But these were clearly in a street, a well lit street, and then I noticed it was the wee hours of the morning.

Calling Celia, I made sure she got Fred over there with the right papers to get this private property back if it was really Vlad's stuff. Most important—was Vlad and friend *in* the coffins?

God, I hoped it wasn't Holly.

The coffins hadn't been opened yet, mostly due to the fact that this idiot, a 28-year-old history student named Phil Nevins, wasn't strong enough to open them. By the time he got the right crowbar, the fuzz had arrived on the street scene, and moved everyone to the courthouse.

I peered carefully at the coffins. Not that I had seen real ones before. I was fortunate enough at that point in my life never to have had death touch me personally. No coffins, no funerals.

They looked real enough. Needless to say I couldn't really accomplish anything that morning until I heard from Fred. Even the Bangles failed to cheer me up.

There were three messages from Dalmonica waiting for me. Brief "call me" things that came in spurts of once an hour for three hours, then nothing. All sent last night to the secret voicemail only he knew about.

I dialed him and knew right then that I'd have to have a cell phone in my life. The one from the *Post* was just too convenient. Then again, if I could handle this right, maybe after two years, when we've finished the backlog of cases that were piling up—I told Celia, "Don't take *anymore* cases."—Medge and I could retire while Doll spends just a fraction of our reserve funds at FSU and then the three of us can travel the world if we weren't shot.

That was a plan. A daydream.

"Hello?"

"Yeah! Mr. Dalmonica?"

"Dalmonica is my first name."

"Oh. Sorry, this is Gath."

"Which is your first name."

I laughed.

"Are you ready to set a date?" he asked.

"How soon can we set the calendar?"

"I have my connections in Hollywood or New York City. My clients would prefer to set this in your backyard."

"Really?"

"Someone to blame if something goes wrong. You know that we don't need to go to court. My clients are prepared to settle and settle amply. There is absolutely no reason to do this."

"Except for my client. He's set on it. I agree with *you*."

"Then how about Tallahassee?"

"Paperwork's already started here anyway. Easier for me to practice right here."

"Do you have a judge in mind?"

"You don't have Tallahassee connections, Dal?"

"We've got them all over. You'd be surprised."

"I wouldn't. But I can get us a date. When?"

A pause. "You know this is our busy horror season. I know that's why you picked right now, isn't it?"

I shook my head even though he couldn't see it. "I didn't pick a damn thing. It just fell in my lap."

"Well, anyway, we would prefer Halloween week. My clients have a plethora of projects, print and televised and motion pictures coming out between those two weekends. For us to have a shot at pushing the publicity up on these even further, that is ideal."

"I understand. You could go public on who your clients are, too. That would help."

"It would not."

That matter was closed. The exact court *date* was really up to the judge and the court to decide. We spent a few minutes dickering with court procedure and logistics of crew and the really prickly nature of me turning my client off for a few days.

"The man's like Britney Spears now," I said. "Just walking outside his house at night, he's mobbed by the waking press."

"The walking dead. You're a bit of a celebrity yourself, Mr. Wein."

"I assure you, like this morning, if I do nothing but live and breathe, if Vlad is doing *anything* visible, including living and breathing, all the walking dead are after *him* and they leave me alone."

"Jury selection is going to take forever," he complained. "In order to shoot us for the proper calendar date, will you help us out there?"

"What can I do?"

"You know."

And I did. He wanted me to look the other way when it came to calling our prospective jurors on prejudice.

"You can do the same thing," I said.

"I know, I know. What are you asking?"

"What do you mean?"

"The bottom line. I have never gone this far, Mr. Wein, without knowing exactly what the stakes are. The fact that money was not the first thing out of your mouth when this whole thing began filled me with puzzlement more than dread. The bigger the bite, the more often you hook the worm."

"I don't get it."

"Simple," he said. "What does your client want?"

It's funny, but I never asked him.

Except for "setting the record straight" and "suing them," I had no idea.

"I'll get back to you."

"You'll tell me before you get off this phone."

I was panicking now. "It's daylight now. Can I call you this evening?"

"What's that got to do with it?"

"He thinks he's Dracula, so he gets up late."

"Right."

Sudden inspiration came. "You never told me your top settlement."

There was quiet on the line. Nearly a whole half minute long. Then Dal asked, "What time this evening?"

Celia had waited for the sound of my muffled voice to go dead before knocking at the door. She was an expert in hearing through the music, which by now was merely Yes doing their *Talk* album, a pretty loud thing in places.

After the soft knock, I said, "Yeah?"

"Gath, there's a Federal agent to see you, Agent Grante."

She left the door open without even waiting for my response. Grante, a large football player type, one who would be great for getting me from the front door to the car, entered and went immediately to click off Yes. Anyone who says no to Yes I won't like right off.

Still, I smiled and said, "What can I do—"

He showed me his ID and gruffed, "Mr. Gather Wein?"

I went sheepish for a moment, because it sounded like the kind of joke name it was. No one called me that, so you won't find it on any credit card or government form, I make sure of that.

"What can I do—"

"My name is Agent Grante and I have been assigned to you semi-permanently, until the resolution of our investigation."

"What investigation?"

"You have been under surveillance, sir, for the past ten days in light of your association with the United States citizen who calls himself Vladimir Tepes."

"Hmm."

"Sir, are you aware that this Mr. Tepes claims to be over 500 years old and claims the responsibility of the deaths of hundreds of people, not just in the United States but in every country he has ever traveled to?"

"Well. I don't—"

"We are cooperating with the CIA and local law enforcement institutions to ascertain the scope of his abilities and act accordingly."

"I'm not sure—"

"Would you be willing to help us with our inquiries?"

"Well. I'm not sure—"

"I think it advisable to warn you, Mr. Wein, that in the event your personality becomes negative, we do have the legal right to detain you in our office for up to 48 hours pending an injunction—"

"Only in the case of a material witness—"

"Which you are deemed to be by your very association with the accu—"

"What exactly are you asking me—"

"Please come with me, sir."

I felt tired by the time I got up and headed into the outer office. Bongo—I called him Bongo, my "character double"—stood when I entered, but I waved him sit. He had my coat on, ready to go.

"Celia, I'm going with Agent Grante for a little while. If you don't hear from me within the hour, have Fred call Judge Arno and—"

"It'll take us 25 minutes to attain location, Mr. Wein," the guy said, and he wasn't kidding.

"Attain location?" He nodded. "Ninety minutes," I told Celia and widened my eyes to her so she got the picture, and I let the man take my elbow.

As the parking lot was staked out with two round-the-clock surveillance men (paid with fifties, once I alerted Vlad to what was going on with his attorney), the photographers had to sulk across the street at the barber place. The hair cuttery was obviously making good money by renting the standing space, because there they were, about nine gals and guys, agitated and snapping pictures like I was the Queen. I was especially good meat today, with this Fed hand on my arm. "Officially escorted," I could just see on tomorrow's *Atlanta Constitution*.

Grante had a typically overpriced government Ford with lots of comm. gadgets inside, windows that shaded every angle from the moon and *The Sun*, enough rolling room in the back for a family of four. The car started, we rolled, but not toward Thomasville Rd. The other, less busy way, through a thread of schools and short neighborhoods of various economic climate.

Finally, the tall man next to me looked at me with a half smile, like he was pleased to see me. Bemused, that's the official description. Bemused. He rolled the car to a stop in the parking lot of a defunct bar-b-q place, took off his driving shades and his whole self changed.

"Mr. Gather Wein." He laughed. "It's an honor to meet you!"

"Why is that?"

"Isn't it an honor? Wouldn't you be honored to death to meet me if I was a TV star?"

"You're not, are you?"

"You can smell the Federal smell in here, can't you?"

I nodded. "I can smell it. And I've got a lot of work to do."

"You do! You're going to help us nab a mass murderer."

"I'm his *attorney*. Italicized: *attorney*."

"Actually, what I really wanted to ask—"

"I'm sorry, who are you…?"

"Wow." He laughed. "Sorry. I've been out of field work so long. You only know my name, don't you? I work at a computer all day, I've lost more people skills than brain cells. I'm 44. They say after the age 39, you lose a million or so brain cells a day. And I keep rubbing my eyes when I get off the computer screen. I'm getting old…"

That seemed to zap the conversation's strength for a moment. All he did was take a large (I mean inches thick) file of papers out of a plastic zip bag below his seat and he started reading. I couldn't believe it.

After a moment, I tapped him on the shoulder. He looked at me, waiting for a question.

"This is the quietest place I know," he said. "When you want to come and get away for a—"

"I don't want to get away. What do you *want*?"

He slapped the great hulking file that he was reading onto my lap. Charts and data squiggles that meant nothing to me. *Pages* of the stuff. *Hundreds* of pages, and not a word of English that I could spy.

"What?"

"It's been a busy week for me, Mr. Wein. I had to get all this—" he tapped the pages "—out within the week. It's a study of all the places your man has been, with the fingerprints he now has on his person. He's been a lot of places, Mr. Wein, and I mean too many."

"What's too many?"

"Without stamps to his passport, without *tickets*. How can you get from…" He flipped some pages as he spoke. "…Madrid to Hawaii on the same day? Without a flight. Within the *hour*?"

I looked at the stuff in front of me, hoping there were answers there.

"He was using an assumed name?"

Grante shook his head. "He was using assumed fingertips."

"Can you do that?"

"Oh, *I* could do that, I have the connections. I've heard of its being done before, by civilians. But these are retro-hind tips, Mr. Wein."

"What's that?"

He put his head back on the cushion like it was philosophy time. "You know. How the detective in a good mystery. He remembers what happened on page one. Even before he knew there was a mystery. And even though the stuff on page one was ordinary and mundane, he remembered it."

No, I didn't know, but I nodded.

"It's like that. For, oh, a while now, we've been monitoring, randomly, all prints. It's not as godly as you might imagine. A 4 gig mp3 player is tiny enough to go in wireless headphones now. And a fingerprint map—we call them tips—can be read like text these days, so you can put millions of prints in a single megabyte if you compress it, for easy extraction. Okay?"

"I don't know what you're talking about."

"What do you think of Vladimir Tepes, AKA Dracul or Dracula?"

"I'm not at liberty to discuss—"

"The man who thinks he's the original, and we all know Bela Lugosi is—"

"I was saying I'm not at liberty to discuss—"

"Because I think he's just a crazy too, like you. That is, until I mapped him. Now I don't know what to think."

"What were you talking about, all those fingerprints?"

"We can map a print from any moment, any day, from a distance."

"How far?"

"I'm talking about stallilite mapping, Mr. Wein."

"What do…You mean…What do you *mean*?" I know it came out like a bored teen sigh, but I couldn't help it.

"I've studied Mr. Tepes and I deem him worthy of chase, Mr. Wein. This." He tapped the pages, which I threw on the other side of me. "Is Tepes' mapping over the last five years. Five *years!* There shouldn't be that much paper on a couple with two kids—for their entire *lifetimes!*"

He was suddenly upset. Like he was upset with me. I thought he was going to put his sunglasses on and pummel me for a second. What was his problem?

"Have you ever seen him suddenly appear somewhere?"

I choose not to comment. But I was thinking.

"Have you had occasion to visit him one place, and…there he was, somewhere else?"

"What are you saying?"

"What are *you* saying?"

"Mr. Grante—"

"How is he doing it?!"

"Doing what?"

He turned to a page, urgently, with a passion that had just come from nowhere. He almost ripped at the pages, trying to find a speck of code among the thousands of obscure jumbles.

He found it. "There! There! How could he get from Tallahassee to Poland within 23 minutes? Come on, you must know! Come on, *please!*"

I tried to make sense of these—figures. It was giving me a headache.

"I don't know."

"Do you know what kind of transportation problems this could solve if we could—"

"I don't *know*! How do *you* know?"

"What?"

"How can you tell if a man is one moment in one country, and the next moment he's in—"

"*Retro-hind tips!*" he shouted.

"*What's that?!*"

"Once we know what print to look for, we can find it anywhere, anywhen, I told you that!"

Science-fiction. I just laid my head back and waited for the insanity to pass. No wonder he wanted to park at an empty lot. Any other place in the world, we'd've been attracting reporters like moths.

Once he started his cool down, I softly asked, "What do you want from me?"

"It's my job to instruct heads of department: is it worth going after the subject. Full-fledged. Chasing the indictment."

I tried to keep it calm. "I'm his attorney."

"But do you *believe* him?"

"About what?"

"His age. His story. What have you *seen*?"

I closed my eyes.


No arrest. No threats. Just a boring ride home. I was piled out like an unwanted cat, and stalked into my office with an Excedrin headache, so I took two Advil, opted for Journey turned *way* down low, and sifted through the mountain of messages from Mark Clock, Fred and Derek Draco.

I called Celia in, just yelled through the door, without getting up. When she arrived, I suggested, "Why don't we close up shop for a week?"

She knew it was coming and nodded. "Besides, we're going to spend all the time preparing. I've got so much transcription work to take care of."

"So do it at home. Get us all rooms at whatever hotel's closest to court by Friday. We're taking things live by Monday. Fred's working on a judge."

"I thought you were."

I nodded. Forgot. "*I'm* working on a judge. Or you could."

She was shocked. "I have no pull."

"No, just get inside to the chambers, then route the call right to me. Any time. On this." I held up the phone and shook it. "You have the number."

"Yep. All separate rooms?"

"I don't think Medge wants me to sleep with you. Even on the floor."

She laughed. "Will she be with you?"

"She has to be, Celia. I feel like everyone else is *against* me."

She came over and patted my shoulder sympathetically, then rubbed them both for a moment. A woman who writes and types all day has the fingers for massage. *Heaven…*

# chapter 14

A couple days later Medge and I were listening to the hate steaming outside in the cold, pouring rain. Protestors don't mind shit weather, obviously. We turned our David Letterman up and up, trying to hear what Vlad had to say. Since we couldn't see him.

"I understand all the hatred and unbelievers, and that's fine. But I don't go around their churches on Sunday morning telling them that their God doesn't exist and pelting them with animal skins."

Letterman laughed, "Why animal skins?"

"It was a mixed metaphor for hate."

"I see."

"Those who *truly* believe are the most vicious and the most dangerous to be around."

"You're dangerous. You suck people's blood out of their necks. Don't you?"

"I have killed people. Yes."

"Oooo. People might be listening."

"Wouldn't that be nice?"

"But I guess it's nothing they can touch you for. Vlad, baby. That's why you're sitting here now."

"I'm sitting here for two reasons, David. The most important being that you clearly don't believe who or what I am, otherwise you would not keep your gap-tooth grin open as you do. Also, yes. There is a gigantic difference between a missing person and a dead one bleeding at your feet."

"Do you leave any blood in there? Is there enough left to bleed at my, or your, feet?"

"You shall learn."

The audience was alive. It sounded more like a football stadium than a studio. How many people were *there*?

"Oh boy. 'Shall.' I like it. Next question. Now. How are you doing these shows when some clods, like myself, tape when it's still daylight out? Answer me that."

"That's why I requested to be on last."

"Really?"

"It is dark out now."

"So…you just sit in your coffin until sundown and you spring out and you do these national shows."

"That sounds reasonable."

"I know it sounds reasonable!" Letterman laughed. "That's what I'm asking you, is that what happens?"

"I don't need a green room that is not green. Just keep me safe in a private parking lot, or under the stage, that's all I need."

"That… can you come out in daylight or not?"

Vlad probably glared at him. Letterman did his funny "sweating" look.

"Aren't you worried that someone's going to drive a stake through your heart? I mean. You're a *very* public person right now. Vlad. Sir. You don't have the elements of surprise, surprise and fear, to quote the Spanish Inquisition."

I could imagine Vlad looking from one side of the audience to the other, inciting laughs and applause and *cool* sounds. "I choose my consorts wisely."

"Who are some of your favorite consorts?"

"Anyone who won't take my f__king head off."

*Whoops* like monkeys in trees descended. It kept going so long, especially once Vlad stood (you could tell by what the camera was doing) to bow and acknowledge them, that they had to take a commercial.

I turned off the TV to listen to the screamers in the street. Hate. Yelling something. I was glad it was to be our last night in our own bed for a while. Celia was making two sets of reservations, under assumed names, and no one but the two of us would know where we'd be until we stuck the cardkey in the door.

We were naked, again, and snuggling. Some secret papers on retro-hind tips were scattered inches from Medge's pink butt, but they made for hard reading and were easy to put aside.

*I'm a good guy, Vlad said I was a good guy, so why am I defending a self-confessed murderer?*

The question kept coming up and up in me, whenever I allowed myself time to think.

I turned the TV back on. Letterman and his twirling pencil came back. The crowd was outrageous, and I couldn't tell what yelling was inside the TV and what was outside on the street. Letterman kept looking to his right, then half laughed and half had consternation going as he tried to ask for peace. The anarchy was incredible.

Finally, Vlad probably moved back into camera range, smiling wildly. After another eternity, things quieted slightly and David took up his plain blue postcard to read from.

"Okay. We're finally back. I think, with Vlad Tepes, a k a Dracula to a lot of people." His next couple sentences were drowned out by fans. Vlad fans. Vlad probably reached into the air to "catch their love" but David put a hand on one of his arms to politely ask him not to rumble the riot. Vlad gave him such a *look* (I'll bet) that Letterman feared for his life for a moment. It also quieted the room into a steady "ooooooooo," but the host of the show was professional enough to use the silence to assume the lead.

"We've been having a pleasant chat with Dracula, or I should say, the story, the true *man* behind the myth. The man who would not die, has not died. He's been giving us *powerful* insight into what it's like to be God, or a god. Do you, do you fancy yourself a god, Vlad? Vladimir?"

"What is a god?"

"Well, if you're going to be philosophical about it…Or are you really asking me?"

"A god is man in man's image," Vlad said with heaviness. "If you're asking me what it feels like to be immortal…" He shrugged.

"You mean because there's no frame of reference."

Vlad just shrugged again.

"Of course, you could just bite me—and I mean that sincerely. I'm not insulting you, you know."

"I know."

"If I say…'bite me.' And you bit me. I'd be a vampire and I'd have my frame of reference."

"Would you like to be a vampire?"

"Well," and the audience laughed while he thought on it and played up to them. "What's the downside? How often would I have to kill someone for food, for instance?"

"How often do you dine out now?"

Oh yeah. Vlad was getting his laughs. And not just because he wore shorts, the cape and little yellow shades made for a six-year-old girl. The man was cool *in spite* of himself.

"Okay." David flicked to another blue card. "In honor of the solemn or hilarious occasion, you can choose. We've polled our studio audience right here, this afternoon, while it was still daylight, while they stood in line waiting for you, sir. And asked them their Top Ten Things They Would Like to See Vlad, the Drac Man Change Into."

The words appeared on our screen, to great cheers in the audience. Letterman pointed at unseen people and I knew from experience that he was having security push the crowd squelchers into submission. Things calmed quicker than before.

"Well…"

"Can you do it? Is it true you can change into anything under the sun? The moon. Forgive me."

"Well…"

"Come on, Vladimir. You're globally famous for doing it on other shows. I'm prepared to take my tranquilizers, I promise. Whadaya say?"

Cheers. Then a cut, like something had been edited for time. David was laughing when they came back.

"Number Ten. A panda hat stand."

Nothing happened.

Vlad's head could have bowed, I could just imagine his eyes moving to Letterman's in that pause. "I should tell you I only have control over the animate."

"Ah. So no bricks then. No Mexicans. I'm kidding! I'm kidding!"

The booing changed into applause and heavy laughs.

"Number Seven. An inchworm. What is an inchworm, anyway?"

Vlad turned into a worm so quickly, and back again, that David didn't even notice; he was still looking at his card. Funny how you couldn't see Vlad, but we could see what he changed into. I didn't get it.

Vlad was toying with the audience. The silence followed by the applause was *unreal.*

David read down the list silently to himself, then said, "Number Four. Barack Obama."

That's when the TV went out. The electric blanket off. Everything.

Medge was asleep. Don't ask me how she could sleep through something like that. I was *so* angry. With the power company. Or whoever caused it. So angry and exhausted and tired of the tricks and the noise and everyday being so the *same* that I just fell asleep too.

The alarm and XM Satillite Radio woke me up at 5 a.m., just in time, groggily, to catch a few minutes of Vlad, pre-recorded, on Glenn Beck's popular radio show, in which Vlad spent most of his limited time complaining about the state of radio and how he hated the editor who clipped everyone's breath out of everything that was said because it made everything sound so similar and rushed and *rant and rant.* Then I fell back to sleep.

There were eggs all over the house, raw eggs with shells on all four exterior walls, and some balloons filled with—something. Medge was not interested, and I couldn't blame her. We were selling the place anyway. It stank. I was confident we'd get a good price regardless, as we were living in a real, live collectible. Dean Koontz or someone had already submitted feelers through his agent almost the second after I told someone at Latch Realty that we'd had enough, we were leaving the area. They could have it, stinking eggs and all. I knew someday we'd cease to be Lindsay Lohan to the press, but for now, it was just good to get out, get away.

In a big way, I admired Vlad and the way he could step through and into anything. That first shot he took in the back was only the first of many, then came bricks and fire. The people didn't care. If anything, they'd found a real *god* or Frankenstein's Monster they could punish, and it made them feel great. For a little bit. Until they found that the pain they inflicted on him wasn't really pain at all. It was nothing. It wasn't felt. Not by him. Then they probably went home depressed, or, if Vlad gave them "the look," they might go home terrified and wonder if they really should've pelted him with pokers.

Only the shit and the lime soup they threw one week annoyed him, because Vlad fancied himself a fancy dresser, and though he was wealthy enough to buy new clothes for every second of his life, since every second of it was being *filmed*, to walk around in a shit-stained sweater was demeaning and worthy of contempt.

Why they wasted so much time and film when you could never *see* him on film was beyond me.

That's why, just two days before trial, when Cynthia Colequit went missing an hour after spraying Vlad with what she shouted out was cat piss, the Feds were all over him, and me, and it was very hard to get my pre-trials done. Fred helped a lot here, as did Holly, putting all the history in order. Usually there are more depositions to worry about, but in our case, it was basically Vlad and his theatrics against the whole corporate empire he was taking on.

Cynthia was an ugly girl, which I know worked in our favor about the "missing persons case" blowing over as quick as it did, because pretty girls get better national coverage, and there was, again, no proof to link Vlad to the crime, even if they could find a body. Which they couldn't. No suicide note either. Just her shoes at the edge of one of those private fishing holes they always keep stocked with trout and stuff. Cynthia's parents told *Dateline* that she was not a fisherperson, keen or otherwise, and they knew who did it, they said. So I took more slack for fronting for a murderer, etc., etc. Even Fred was giving me those looks like I should know better. But I just told him—he should know *me* better.

That's when *I* decided to do a news show. Not talk about the case, but just to get my side—as an attorney—onto the books, and maybe save Medge and Doll some grief down the road. Just in case this does turn into an OJ where it just never shuts up and remains a bad smelling fruit for the rest of eternity.

First, I made sure it was publicized that, since I was getting a huge fee, (second only to what Vlad was getting for a half hour show these days), the million I was promised for my slice of *60 Minutes* was going directly to the Missing Persons Fund of The Arizona Collective, to print more posters for all their rest stops or whatever they wanted to do. And I defended this choice piece of PR honestly on the show to Steve Kroft:

A: Whatever the anti-Weiners say, I care about truth, and I care about missing person cases. I've handled a few in my time. That's the thing these people seem keen to forget—how many defendants I went to bat for, before anyone knew I existed. Before *60 Minutes* even cared about my life.

Q: Have The Anti-Weiners contacted you?

A: What do you mean?

Q: Did you know there is a group *called* The Anti-Weiners?

A: You're kidding.

Q: You can get their t-shirts on zazzle.com. You can.

A: Are they using my face?

Q: Spoken like a true attorney. (BOTH LAUGH) Now that we're talking about *your rights*, now's your chance.

A: Thanks, Steve. Yes, this is exactly the reason I'm here tonight. I don't have a cent invested in zazzle.com, so don't even go there. I'm here to tell you exactly what I told the man known as Vladimir Tepes, the man so many of you seem to think is Dracula or evil incarnate. (PAUSE) I know he is an accomplished illusionist. But that's all he is. I like him. Personally, I like him, and I think he's a little bit crazy and yes, (LAUGHS) he knows all this, so I don't fear for my life or my neck leaking or whatever. (PAUSE) To say that this man is involved in any way with the disappearance of Cynthia Colequit is just ludicrous. I took this case because it was so damn interesting. And yes, because I needed the money. I'm not a high-powered guy. Now that I'm making the "big bucks" with one solitary client, you're all jealous and you're all looking at me like I'm biting necks myself! I wish you could just set aside prejudice for a moment here and *read* me that…just appreciate that I'm here telling the truth. I'm admitting the money and my belief *not* in the supernatural. I know that's not enough for a lot of you, but can't you at least appreciate that?

Q: Gath. Do you believe he is a 500 year old fictional character?

A: Well… he's real.

Q: So, you believe him.

A: (PAUSE) I told you, Mike, I'm not here to discuss the case.

Q: That's merely the—

A: That's merely the crux of the case, of course, but we're not here to discuss that. I'm wanting to tell everyone at home who thinks they understand—my view. I'm telling you my view. And regardless of yours, I'm asking you to accept it and understand it. It's not—I know of people who will condemn a film without having seen it. They've never seen, I don't know, *Hostel*. That bloody horror movie. But they've got an opinion about it. (PAUSE) I'm not asking you to do that. I'm wanting you to listen to me, base your own opinion on what I'm *saying*. That's all.

Q: If you're not going to talk about the case, what else is there?

A: There's my previous record. My record of cases. Look at that. See if I'm a bloody kind of murderer or murder defender. I'm a small time lawyer looked up by this—this man, who is just a man. Not a vision or a…a piece of Halloween or a mask. He's someone very good at what he does. He's not 500 years old, he's not Dracula, I don't know who he is. But he's a friend of mine. I don't know *why*. We don't have anything in common. That movie I just mentioned. *Hostel*. I'd never seen it before last week. Sometimes Vlad comes over and we watch horror movies. We do. Maybe we're living like celebrities, but that's none of my doing. I don't need this. I don't want to be famous now. Vlad likes it! I don't. Vlad rents us these movies and we watch them until the wee hours. Sometimes I fall asleep and he's gone when I wake up. Sometimes I make it all the way something like *Cujo*, but mostly, no.

Q: He's a big time movie fan.

A: Oh, yeah! That's where all this began. The man has movies in his veins. Not blood. He doesn't drink blood. Whatever you think. (LOOKS AT CAMERA) Have you ever *seen* him drink blood? Anyone? (PAUSE) Anyway.

Q: What's his favorite movie?

A: He likes horror movies. Of course.

Q: A favorite?

A: He likes *All That Jazz* a lot.

Q: Is that…

A: Bob Fosse directs it. The guy from *Jaws* is in it.

Q: You're kidding.

A: He gets deadly serious about these flicks. I wouldn't kid. Doesn't kill anyone, but he's deadly serious about Hollywood. Yeah, he likes musicals too. Favorite movie? I don't know. Why don't you have him on?

Q: His schedule is so…

A: It is.

Q: Why does he like films so much!

A: It's a novelty with him, I think. He's 500 years old, remember? (THEY LAUGH) Oh, and he drinks out of nothing but McDonalds' old *Great Muppet Caper* glasses. If you want trivia.

Q: Really?

A: (NODS) We had to get some for our new house, we didn't have any, and he kept bringing them over, so…

Q: He's a Muppet fan?

A: You know, I didn't ask? I usually use the Happiness Hotel glass when I'm over at his place.

Q: You two socialize a lot.

A: The man is unique. I'm never going to see his kind again. I like spending time with him. Medge too.

Q: Aren't you…aren't you afraid? Don't you fear for your life?

A: (LAUGHS) He's eccentric. And he's lonely. And he watches a lot of movies. He's been good to me—and mine. I just don't see…

Q: Why everyone hates him.

A: Yeah!

Q: If you don't *believe* he's who he says he is…how can you defend him?

A: Represent.

Q: Right.

A: I'm not defending him.

Q: I'm sorry.

A: (PAUSE) My take—is he's not hurting anyone.

Q: It'll hurt Universal and Random House and Pocket Books.

A: (NO COMMENT)

Q: If you don't believe he's who he says he is… how do you explain *all* the television shows? Turning into bats and smoke and…I believe on Howard Stern, he turned into a busty blonde? He won fifty bucks off Howard Stern! (THEY LAUGH)

A: Ah, the fifties… (PAUSE)

Q: Are you going to answer that?

A: I told you. He's good at what he does.

Q: What's he doing?

A: Entertaining!

Between the government calls, which I really couldn't duck, and all the NO I kept giving Derek Draco, I didn't have a moment to myself. Trying to find places to duck all this was my new part-time job. I didn't want to make *60 Minutes* a habit, like Draco kept trying to make me believe was my lot in life. So I was good at the interview format, so what? The arms of Medge and whatever hidden hotel room my secret spies (the few I could *trust* enough not to sell me out) could forage for us were my haven, my heaven. Except for pouring over reports and the pre-trial prep work, *all* I wanted to do was take off all our clothes and spoon with her. Mancini on repeat play. TV and phone unplugged.

The media.

The media.

Sometimes you don't know what side you want to be on until you know what side you don't want to be on. Who wants to be a *famous* millionaire?

# CHAPTER

Holly held my hands and said, "You're cold."

"I'm always cold."

She smiled at me. "Are you nervous?"

"I don't get nervous."

"Why?"

That was a question I'd not been asked, in countless interviews. I wondered then if Charles Chaplin had ever fielded a question that had been so unintentionally original and unique in all his many years of superstardom.

"I suppose I'm so used to it."

"But you've only been in the spotlight, the real spotlight a few months," she said softly.

"I didn't catch that," the line producer said.

I looked at the director. "It isn't always going to be like this, is it?"

The little man did not stop looking at his screen, so I stared at him until he looked at me.

"What? Sorry." He took half his headphones off and I repeated the question. "Like what?"

"This is hardly real."

"It's *hardly* real," he defensively rationalized.

"Therefore, it is not *real*. You do not interrupt her."

And they did not again speak within Holly's lines.

The evening wore on and I did as instructed, totally ignoring all of the crew. Reality filming is quite boring in its actual process. Holly, poor girl, had a severe handicap for it all. I'm always partially shocked when I see a truly gorgeous woman self-conscious, because I always see them as everyone else does. It was not that she was being constantly looked at, however. The filming, the ramifications that everything was in a way "live" and would sponsor the rest of her life, the being followed, perhaps it was overwhelming to a simple Florida girl. But we had talked on it and she knew how important this was. Grudgingly knew, but still, she had agreed to it.

The process was digital and filtered into a hub unit, they said, which processes images in real time which can in turn be edited in almost the same amount of time and dumped onto a Fox affiliate. So, as I drank my half glass of blood at 4 the next morning, getting ready for bed, by the time it was 4:04, my audience was already ecstatic at what they were witnessing, so I was later told. I wish I could have seen it.

Every man and gay man of the unit had been hand-picked by someone whom I had warned should not be squeamish, nor should they allow themselves to be swayed by alternate definitions of decency or easily intimidated by the Law which hung around us like dead veins outside, completely surrounding the house. Gath had move to another dwelling, but I was not moving. This was my new Graceland and Neverland and Buckingham Palace in the same ideal. True, the houses on either side of us were going for large bucks, but I had bought one myself, as an investment, and I *reveled* in the onlookers who grew outside daily, as if I were some zombie mall in Pittsburgh.

Death was *beautiful*.

Of course I understood that daylight hours were somewhat horrendous for the crew, who had the option of sleeping, like myself, or running through countless games and simulations and interviews and other reality television games with Holly, poor girl, who had to sleep sometime. She knew this was limited time, though. And how it important it was, to everything. So she did not sleep much. Besides, she was young. She still is.

When I awoke in the evenings, I watched her footage, as I was shot watching her footage, chuckling to myself over Grape Nuts or biting the head off a rat. I *sincerely* wanted dogs to suckle, but that had been a deal breaker for Fox, which

I thought showed nuts and ill will. For $40,000 more I would have gone to NBC from the beginning. But Fox assured me that it was simply people, cats and dogs that were positive no-nos for on-air murder. There was even an RSPCA rep "on site" who assured her superiors that the dog cages in my backyard, now empty, would remain empty. Fools. They never questioned why the cages were there to begin with.

The true realism began about 7 pm most nights. Those last few, spacious, wonderful days before the trial, as Holly, my cape and shades, and a small entourage that slept in the kitchen cots (not the camera crew, but the others) took to the streets, following me anywhere.

It was always a pleasant jaunt merely "cruising" the streets to bring terror to an otherwise complacent civilization, before deciding on the true entertainment of the evening. Once, all of us walking down a wide street in a quite ordinary neighborhood, there was a wise man watching television who invited us in with his hick accent. He was "jest gladly be-deviled!" to sit and talk to me while merely keeping his eyes glued to the television which now contained his fat figure. Yes, we were live, with a 30-second delay.

Jeff was his name. He particularly was a horndog who loved everyone gladly and equally. He even hugged me. He had bottles of pickled eggs and pickled melon pieces and kept dead insects downstairs in his basement or cellar. Unmarried, one could see why, his living room contained a dreariness since all of his walls were painted black, as were his windows. Yet, there were many of my photos cut from magazines and newspapers scattered about, and Thorne Smith's delightful new mass paperback bio of me from Viking turned down in the middle, laying on an unoccupied Lazyboy opposite Jeff's regular TV chair.

I picked up the Smith and said, "You should really use a bookmark."

He laughed at me as if I had said the wittiest thing in the world which, I suppose, to him was. I got this a lot, this hero-devil worship, so of course he didn't mind when I raided his GE icebox and caught myself a Mr. Pibb. Of late, I'd been influenced by Gath's Dr. Pepper obsession. Jeff laughed at that too, waving his hands to illustrate that my thievery was his honor.

"What do you do for a living, Jeff?" I asked him, taking his Lazy chair.

"Me?"

"You."

"What do I do?"

I looked at the camera. I could imagine the viewer's reactions.

"I'm a data processor."

God, the man's twang.

"So, you're a typist."

"Nah, haha, nah, I just type in data!"

"What's the difference between a typist and a data processor, and please don't joke via comparative pay scales."

"Oh, I wouldn't do that, Mr. Vlad!"

I looked at the camera again, then tried to catch my eyes with Sidney's. I finally spotted him outside, peering in at us from the bushes, along with perhaps 35 other hopefuls, as there was certainly not room enough in this house for all.

"Do you see that man there?"

It was the most important in the world to Jeff right then that he should find the man to which I pointed so that I should not be disappointed.

"Sidney!" I yelled, and the lanky youth who was already losing his hair gave us all a wave. Jeff, the bumpkin that he was, waved back like it was the last airplane in Florida.

"I gathered Sidney there from a home just like yours."

"Oh I know!" Jeff crowed, excitedly, affably, foolishly. "I remember that episode!"

"Two days ago."

"Yeah!"

"That man Sidney is now part of my entourage. Would you like to be so favored?"

"What's that?"

"Favored?"

"Nah, the E word?"

"Walk around with me, be a star for the last few days of your life."

Jeff laughed and laughed more, then used some of his brain and somehow formed the words, "When you say…*last*…"

I took off my shades because I knew it would be the coolest thing I could do, under the circumstances.

"Have you ever thought of being a vampire?"

"Well." He paused. "Sure! Who hasn't!"

"Would you like to be a vampire?"

"You want to suck ma *blood*?"

He began peeling his short sleeve up, but I waved him to desist.

"I have other people to do that for me," I said, and laughed. The crew laughed. Eventually those outside who had heard the joke from the next person, they laughed, too.

I put my arm around Jeff's fat neck a second and gritted my teeth for the camera, like I wanted to take his head off, which I did. But I refrained, and merely patted the man's cheeks. He smiled sweetly and wildly, like the madman he was. Vampire, indeed. Foolish poof!

Jeff joined us, he left with us as the last person, shouting to everyone, as the cameras turned to receive his proclamation: "I ain't ever comin' back here, so the door's open! Take whatever y'all want! I'm gonna die tonight!" He made monkey or baboon sounds and wound his fist like an air siren in WWI to the crowd who fully appreciated his idiocy. Cheers and cries of the most intense pleasure carried through the streets.

Streets that were filled with people, some holding guns at us as we passed, others concerned and far away, and no one, certainly no one misunderstanding nor confused. The power of television is indeed mightier than the pen.

Have you ever walked down the street with a party? Thus was our party, making our way toward Tennessee Street, going towards campus. Everyone spoke and spoke at once, and we laughed and spoke of cult icons and I tried to introduce more of Louise Brooks and Vernon Dent into the conversation and there were interested people on my arms for a change. It was delightful.

We spoke and gathered policemen on our quest to The Q, one of the chic gay clubs in the heart of FSU's main organism. All eyes were watchful and jealous of us. Holly was simply tired, so I guided her upper body on my manly shoulders as she trudged, until finally I had to carry her. She was not able to rest until we were all installed in The Q where the thump of techno was atrocious and we were not the main focus. I soon changed all of that.

First, however, there was a vibration in my shorts that came from Draco. I apologized to the group and went to the Gay Boy's Room, as stated on the door, and took the call. As usual, he was miffed at my opting out of media saturation in favor of a single television show, though I had to keep reminding him that here was a show *created* for me, and in mid-season yet, which was *never* done.

"What?" I shouted.

"Where are you? I can barely—"

"I'm in a club, what is it?"

"The President wants to meet you."

That had been my last thought. No, not even that high on my list.

I made sure: "President of what?"

"Come on, the United States. He's slipping, not accomplishing anything with the banks, and he wants a dinner, he'll settle for a snack, with you. He's looking for pictures."

"I don't appear in pictures."

"I know. But he knows you got a series, and you won't even show up on TV. He doesn't want to miss the fad. The boat. He doesn't want to miss the boat."

"You said fad."

"You know what I mean."

"Okay, okay, what do you think?"

"Should you do it? *Hell* yeah!"

"We both know I could just show up there any day of the week I want. That would cause more publicity. Why go on his terms?"

He thought about what I said, but only for an instant. Draco could simply put things simply sometimes: "He'd *smile*. If he knows you're coming, he'd *smile*."

I smiled, and closed my phone.

Only the heartiest of dancers and partiers could keep up with us regularly. Indeed, Holly herself was not one of these, and often slept through some of the best parts, my affairs and flirting and so forth. Sometimes she would unwillingly join, but only if I did not make the first move, which I never did, and only if the male or female had an ugly aura about them. Not unattractive, but more young Zazu Pitts than delicious Patricia Clarkson. Naturally, my extra sexual appetite and bloodletting was done far from my love's sleepy eyes, and no mention was made of it, by anyone. Even the cameras found themselves with unsolvable problems, poor boys. Huge gaps of space in which the film counter would miss an entire seven minutes. That sort of thing.

*Up with Vlad* (a noose of a name) had no chance of being beaten by anything or any show on television. Not even a devastating quake in China could shake it, especially not the week we went into trial. Someone told me during the second day of our broadcasting, Obama's people had to beg for screen time. Sad really. Thinking on it again, I would do the White House thing, but without RSVP. Merely a scamper over when I had the odd moment. And moments were decidedly odd.

Draco's company had gone international, with his poor, sorry face scoring more screen time than myself during certain days. His blood had gone cold with this fact the first several times it had happened, but I patted his stomach and assured him that such was to be expected. I could not be everywhere. He was representing me, I calmed him. Whenever his face appeared, it was *my* face people were thinking of. This was fine.

But he did have to take on a lot more help. Several more hundred people vetted sponsor requests, the interview requests, opened mail and packages, many of which were exploding, even in the post office. He tells me he had to hire a special liaison to the government's postal authorities to take my surprises directly from JFK's main postal facilities, thereby averting disaster.

I'll admit, it all was pretty exciting. If it wasn't for one glaring omission, I would have been quite content with circumstances, possibly tearing my hair out that I had not gone this route ages ago. But then, as my hair could testify, this route did not exist beyond a mere 15 years ago. Death was sweet.

Sitting down beside my snoring love, letting the few reporters who'd managed to get in crowd my TV crew, and fight their way against all who loved me and wanted a touch, a rip of clothing, a kiss, a suck, I closed my eyes a moment to see if I still enjoyed darkness. Peace. The loneliness inside my head.

When I opened them, the bright lights and screaming and the faces in my face had not gone. Merely they told me that I didn't mind them. It was all right.

Someone shoved a cellular telephone TV in my face so I could watch myself, my outline rather, in a three-minute delay, and I was determined to try something.

"Hold that fucking camera still!" I shouted.

Truly, the worse thing in so-called reality filming is its shakiness. Movies don't subject you to such trashy effects. Even your eyes, the realest things of all, do not shake, but hold steady, if you run or you're being chased. Try it.

"Smooth fucking shot!" I screamed, and was *just* heard above the thump of the trance.

They put the camera down. At last. Once they knew I was serious.

I stared into that man's camera. One half of my left eye was looking a few inches below where I was holding this camera. The man was beside himself with glee. I would get Holly to check its going price on ebay tomorrow. I was sure it would be there, fetching gold.

I stared. For a long time. Then someone stepped between my eyes and the camera, and I marked him for death.

"Clear a path!" I screamed.

No one came between my eyes and the camera again.

I stared.

I continued to stare into the camera.

And after thirty short, glorious seconds, I had my achievement.

I could see myself, staring.

I stared into the stare, into the camera. An ever-going stare which fell further and further into itself. I was a double mirror seeing itself and itself and itself for eternity.

That is, I could *feel* myself doing it.

# chapter 15

The kitchen wasn't as big as I'd hoped, but it did have one of those wooden islands in the middle, good for scrambling eggs while someone else pours cereal, so as far as I was concerned, it was ready to take.

Medge had needed more convincing, and had asked all the right questions about neighbors and garbage pick-up and if it was listed, because if the house is listed historically and you want to, like, put up a shed in the backyard, even if it's *your* backyard, you have to ask someone else's permission. All that stuff.

It was a beautiful old place, five bedrooms. We were renting to own in a way, because we were already living there, but now we were talking about buying it outright. We loved it enough. The realty people had kept on about Vlad and "how hard it must be for you," those realtors who had returned our calls or hadn't shut us out completely.

Two stories, three if you count the attic, yards of room, hard wood floors, generous walk-in closets with double light bulbs, it was a modern refurbishment of some farmhouse style old thing that was built in the 1920s by Quakers who'd given up Pennsylvania and had moved south for Florida rain. Well, it was a farmhouse. We'd always toyed with the idea of living on, not running, a farm. About twenty acres of land surrounded us. It would take twelve extra minutes to get to work—I said *extra*, add that on to the regular traffic time—but I cared not a tot. We had no immediate neighbors here. You know—your mailboxes aren't even touching. And the fallow farm land, along with the dead cross streets and the fallow neighbor's land, gave us a nice long stretch between houses. Unless they were using binoculars, our neighbors wouldn't be bothered by us, or the reporters. Once the press found our new address.

It wouldn't be long. I knew that.

But for now, we popped open the champaign on the evening we paid the place off, and settled in for a lovely and quiet night. Doll was there between us. She'd been smuggled in by some relatives I could trust (they had some money, so they didn't need to tip us off to *The Hollywood Reporter*), and a couple airline rides later, she was here, sleepy as ever, just letting us clink our glasses—ting!—and smile our eyes at each other. It felt right.

No phone. Not yet. No cell. I'd thrown it into the farthest cornfield I could throw into, and the three of us cheered that moment. What with jury selection starting in the morning, nothing was going to be so pressing that it couldn't wait until then.

Just a few more reports to read, burp up a little more chicken pot pie from Boston Chicken, and let my eyelids do the rest.

The alarm rang at 7. Medge tied my tie as she always did, I kissed the two of them, and went off into the fires of hell.

There must be a parade this morning, I thought, as I tried every conceivable avenue to get to the courthouse. Everything was blocked with cars and people. Was there an arts festival or something going on?

It took me 50 minutes just to get from one edge of the street to the other. If it hadn't been for my ID and them putting on more cops to deal with the weirdness, I might be there still.

Defense and plaintiff are allowed two parking spaces each under the Local Access Rule, but even so I had only one choice of parking square in the whole of the building. I'd been going there umpteen years now and have never seen a day when there wasn't a place to park on the sunny top floor. Even that was taken, according to the stationary cop on P2. I decided to go down, then up the stairs, just in case. I didn't know what ambushes to expect.

The courthouse was flooded with crazies and police and statesmen wanting some public time and God knows what else. For a moment I thought nuclear war was upon us, until someone spotted me and then it was all shouts and pleading and anger and frustration and poor cops cramming their elbows between passionate and stolid people who refused to move or let the other person stop shouting first. *Whatever* was being said, to me, at me, I couldn't hear a word of it.

I couldn't move. Police tried to infiltrate my circle, and they made it a little wider. I guess it was wide enough, because Mark Clock slipped in, and he isn't a powerful or young man. He shouted in my ear, and that took me back to years ago, going with my friend Britt to an REM concert right here in town. We were both young fools who couldn't hear a thing afterwards, coming out of the civic center. I was right back there with him today, except that now here I was a member of REM and everyone knew it.

Mark tried to pull me in some direction. At last, us moving, we had a foothold on more room between ourselves and the mob, pushed to a further extent by the cops who were good at crowd control. But this was frenzied mob control, and I knew it was beyond their scope.

We waddled one short hallway down and managed to slip inside the door marked

COUNSEL

PRIVATE

It took a moment before I could hear Mark, so I asked him to repeat whatever.

"How are you?"

I laughed. "You know."

Fred was in there already. "Hey, Gath."

"Hey! Are we set?"

He nodded. "I started in at 5 this morning. I knew it would be like this. There were hoodies waiting outside the building, halfway around the building, by the time I showed up. I hear the court's packed."

"We're going easy on this one," I said.

"I know, you told me."

"I know you don't like this, but we're near the end now."

"Are you sure?" It was Mark Clock who asked. "I've seen these cases drag out for a year. Especially when you're in the service of someone with limitless pockets. In fact..." He beat his little plastic briefcase. "That's what we're pitching, with all these case citations. Nothing's over in six days. Six *months*."

"No," I shook my head. "There's only so far we can go with this one. And I can't see our client being a patient entity. This is what he wants, we're here now."

"You have inside information?" Fred asked. "Dracula said something?"

I sat and had a single laugh. "I just hope no one asks where all these legal funds are coming from."

"He was asked," Fred said. "Oprah already asked that one."

"What'd he say?"

"He's from royal blood. 'Where's your kingdom?' she asked. 'I had a plethora of time to hide the family jewels once it had turned into Romania,' he said."

First I'd heard of it. "He said that? He said plethora?"

We all had a good laugh, interrupted by an abrupt head poking in, no knock.

"Ready for you," it said, and closed the door again.

We all looked at each other. A collective in and out of breath. I know I groaned a little as I got up, but I guess I just wasn't looking forward to it anymore. At first, it'd seemed fun, reckless, a little carefree and fantasy oriented. But now with all the angry people in the world, *my* world, it just didn't feel like…anything anymore. I was tired. The world was strange, me cast right in the middle. All these foolish people leaping about, 1. concerning themselves with someone (Vlad) they just didn't know anything about and 2. actually allowing themselves to believe this—magic. The world didn't make sense at all.

I don't know. Seeing all the frothing reporters and angry moms and tiny cult groups shouting for a strand of my hair, cops all around us, protecting us from everyone except them, it was a world of fools, I saw. A world of *fools.*

"Did you murder Mick Jagger?" Mark Clock joked, but I couldn't hear him. He repeated it later, that's how I knew.

The short walk to Courtroom 3 was the noisiest and the slowest. It was a public building, with  many cases going on, so they couldn't just kick everyone out.

It was a riot. An actual riot. The kind I'd only ever seen on The History Channel. (Vlad was on that channel, by the way, last week). A couple people threw stuff at us, but it mostly hit the cops that were circling us. They had no riot gear on. I guess they didn't expect it either.

Doors opened, and the house was packed. But unlike outside, it was completely quiet in here. It was especially noticeable when the big double doors closed in on us. People were standing at the back. SRO. All heads turned to us when we entered, every eye in the house. It was like my wedding.

Cops showed us to our seat, then left us to run back to the swirling mob outside.

"Mr. Wein," said the Judge. That made me jump. I didn't think we were late. No wonder it was quiet in here. "Where is your client?"

"I'm sorry, Your Honor. Am I late?"

"I'm early," he said, loosely. He was a heavy-set white man who went to church every other Sunday. I knew (mostly) all about Judge Londen G. Staite. "I figured it would be like this."

I laughed, "I didn't."

He raised his eyes. "You didn't? Where's your client?"

Fred handed me the relevant copied pages from the casebooks in which we cited plaintiff incapacitation in preliminary proceedings, and there were many of them and so I quoted them.

"No objection to the plaintiff not being present, Your Honor," Dalmonica interrupted, as he and his group of expensive suits entered the arena. Quieter outside now too. "We understand his condition and stipulate in court as to his aversion to daylight."

"He has a skin complaint, Your Honor," I said, before he could ask.

"He bursts out into flames if he even feels the warmth of it," Dalmonica said, not helping.

There were more than diminutive titters in the room, and Staite banged his gavel.

"Remember what I said ten minutes ago," he told the room. "That happens again, you're all outside waiting for the sketch artist on the news. Hold your hands over your mouths, bite your cheeks, I don't care. But *one* more sound…"

He let it hang. Then added, "And I know this whole situation is rife with sidebars and a… possible political commentary on both sides is so tempting for humor and points, but I don't score points here. You put the facts before me. You don't slur, you don't try on statements that masquerade as facts in order to get your point across to me or this jury selection today. Is that understood on both sides?"

"Yes, Your Honor."

"Yes, Your Honor."

"You want to damage the other side, remember this is the original *Jeopardy*. Everything in the form of a question. Are we clear?"

"Yes, Your Honor."

"Yes, Your Honor."

"Call Lewis Stadlen."

The head that had come to collect us from the room was the bailiff, who now called for Lewis Stadlen, a weedy man who stank of cigarettes from a distance. He wore an untucked in plaid shirt and didn't seem to care about anything.

"Defense," I said, meaning Dalmonica could go first.

The great man stood and walked a little, but no more than he had to. I took it to mean he was showing everyone he wasn't too lazy.

"Mr. Stadlen." The bailiff came over with The Book. "Do you swear that the testimony you so shall give to be the truth, the whole truth and nothing but the truth?"

"I do."

"State your name and address."

"Lewis Stadlen, up on I-90 there."

"Be seated," the Judge said.

"Mr. Stadlen," Dalmonica said while he roved. "You live in the country?"

"Country-ish. A spot of land between pecan trees. I've got a trailer."

"That's good. Stay at home a lot?"

"A lot."

"Watching a lot of TV?"

"I like reality."

"Reality TV, you mean."

"Course."

"Have you ever seen *Up with Vlad*?"

"Course."

"What did you think?"

"It's okay."

"Are you a fan?"

"It's okay."

"Are you a fan of Vlad, the man who claims to be more than 500 years old?"

"Well. He's got a good voice. Never *seen* him. Not until right here."

"Do you *believe* that it's him on TV? Just the voice?"

"…It's an *original* show."

Stadlen was cagey, but I don't think either of us could guess if he was pro or con one side or the other. The important thing was: was he stupid enough to be swayed by fact or the emotional courtroom stuff? At least that would give Dal and I a 50-50 chance each.

I asked our potential witness, "Are you an avid reader, Mr. Stadlen?"

"I read *To Kill a Mockingbird* when I was in high school."

"Did you like it?"

"I don't remember it."

"Ever read *Dracula* by Bram Stoker?"

"Nope."

"Ever saw the movie *Dracula* with Bela Lugosi, or even one of the Christopher Lee Hammer films?"

"I don't think so."

"Any film ever to do with Dracula?"

He thought on it for a full half a minute before asking, "Could you give me some particulars? Like stars and such? Maybe the years they come out."

I gave a couple, but it was like pulling fillings. Eventually I just said I had no objections to the witness, and Dal concurred. My guess was in six months time, this idiot would have himself a real nice Harper Collins book deal, being our first juror. I was going to hold out for St. Martin's Press, myself. Already decided.

We both knew it was going to be impossible to find clear minds on such an insane subject, so Dal and I already knew the types we'd shoot for to make this as fair as possible. Out of 12 definites we'd have: 4 men, 4 women, 4 gay. 6 stay at home, 6 professionals. At least 10 college-educated, 5 could be doctors, but no one in the entertainment industry. Retired is fine, but no one with a tattoo or a pierced nose (Dal was adamant on this point), and any strange hairdos would mean quick nitpicking and a dismissal by one of us. No one with prolonged military service, no drinkers, no true believers, no writers of genre fiction, no computer geeks, no utterly romantic people, no one who hasn't washed in a while.

All final choices would have to say No to these:

**Do you believe in Satan?**

**Have you ever eaten Count Chocula (I know how it sounds)?**

**Have you ever heard of Todd Browning?**

**If I gave you a map of the world, do you think you could point out Romania?**

All our jurors would have to have confusion for the following, and we had to repeat our requests for the Court's patience for the seeming rambling nature of some of it:

**What is the significance of 1931?**

**What do you think of Jonathan Harker?**

**What is Bram short for?**

**Do you like Michael Bay?**

"I don't know" was the typical response we were seeking, to weed out the quick answers from obvious fans that had crept into the selection process, and it really worked. It's just as much how *quickly* someone answers as *what* they say that can give you a clue if they're faking ignorance or not. We got rid of the fanboys and cult weirdoes who managed to squeeze into a regular suit for a change, maybe more for Dal's benefit than for our side, but you never know. Jurors as a group can be bloody minded just for the sake of being arbitrary. Being a fan requires some degree of jealousy—"why is he the celeb when I've got twice as much talent?", etc.—so take all your psyche classes, young lawyers, because you don't have to have a gun to kill a famous person. Look at that *Runaway Jury* movie and you'll see the power of One.

The women were the most fun to talk geek with because generally if they were over 50, they had no idea of Dwight Frye from Tom Waits. Though Dal and I had decided secretly together that we didn't want selection to go over 48 hours, if we could help it, sometimes I just couldn't resist toying with a few of the ones that were obvious keepers.

Jane Kean, a 28-year-old, single, flat-chested, right-handed typist, claimed not to have cable, but liked watching DVDs of TV shows.

"So, you've never even seen *Up with Vlad*," I said.

"It's not on DVD."

"It's not."

"Then I haven't seen it. I've heard of it. It's like the opposite of a silent movie."

"That's a good description. It is. Have you seen many silent movies?"

"Probably a Charlie Chaplin at some point."

"What point is that?"

"You know, in a library when I was a kid. They'd have movies for free in the summer. I first saw *The Great Muppet Caper* like that."

Fred was on internet, checking everything ever said instantly. He put a hand of five fingers up which was our signal for something wrong. Not serious, but questionable, like a series of meaningless color codes at a terrorist-free airport.

I came over and looked at the four-digits he'd written down.

"Ms. Kean. What year would that have been?"

"Oh, I don't know."

"Would it surprise you to learn that *The Great Muppet Caper* came out in 1981?"

She thought. "No. Because I never thought about it before."

"It came out in 1981," I explained, as if to a slow child. "Even if your library got hold of a hot copy that same year to show all you kiddies—if you're 28, if you were born in 1981, how could you remember seeing it at all?"

Courtroom drama tends to get more laughter than gasping, especially when the crowd's bored, as this one was. Only Jane Kean got heated up, turning some shade of red, while she tried to figure out how to explain how she'd lied under oath and was really 44. She could get away with it, though, and nearly did, unattractive though she was. "If she's going to lie about her age, Your Honor…" The Judge got the point and we dismissed the lady.

It helped ease the yawn factor, moments like these. Most Floridians didn't seem to care a hoot about Vlad or his celebrity status, though Dal and I were careful to make *sure* they weren't faking. Tough to do in America.

Twelve jurors in the bag, and the Judge called it a day. He banged his little tan gavel and, as I'd requested before, we all bunged in through the back door to the Judge's Chambers for a chat before everyone went home. A perfect ruse to let all the traffic dissipate anyway.

Judge Londen G. Staite's stately room was very plant-oriented, mainly due to a girlish secretary he called simply "Brow" who loved coming in and out of her private place to water and generally busy herself, no matter what was going on in here.

Right now, it was just us three guys sitting around. Staite kept his robes on and looked hot, puffing like a blowfish at the end of each sentence. He didn't do it at all in court.

"What's up?" he asked me. And when I started to say, he kept on with, "You guys got a lot accomplished today. I'm surprised."

Dalmonica said, "We know what we want."

The Judge nodded and said, "What can I do for you?"

"I'd just like a ruling on—"

"There was a man looking for you earlier today," he told me, with a puff. "He said he had four bags of fan mail for your client down in his van. It all came to the court house for some reason. Don't use the courthouse as an address, Mr. Wein."

"Of course not, Your Honor," and I hurried on, "all I'm really looking for is a positive ruling on a night trial so my client might be here in person."

He huffed.

Dal said, "I would welcome such an arrangement, and not because my fees are higher at night." He smiled maybe for the first time in our life together. "For good or worse, I think it would be a fine thing for people to see this man. This man you can't see on a television show that even bears his name."

"I haven't seen the show," Judge Staite stated. "It's reality, right? I don't care for those. I like something with a plot. So?"

"So," I said, "it's beneficial to both sides that we do this at night when my client's...condition allows him to go out in public."

"What do you get out of it, counselor?"

Dal said, "Dracula is going to take the stand. I can rip him to shreds."

"But you're not going to do that," said the Judge.

"No, that's just figurative."

The Judge sat blustering, as if he'd had several sentences ending at once.

After a moment, I said, "I did petition the court on this point before we started. With deferment from defending counsel factored in—"

He blowfished again so we all waited.

"Sounds like a bid for character recognition, to me," he said eventually.

Dal came right in: "No, I see that, but no, I don't think it's harmful to anything. Not to my case. Anyway, there are cases in which doctors give notes to excuse the defendant for one reason or another, so I say we get him to play *in* the game and don't give Dracula an *excuse* to sit it out."

"From his point," I said, pointing at Learned Colleague, "it's easier to fight a person than a shadow."

Dal nodded, and the Judge said, watching us with tired eyes, "You two have decided on quite a lot. You're not using this court for publicity, I hope."

We looked at each other.

He continued, "I don't care what's worked up. I'll fine all of you for wasting the court's time, and that can add up to whatever I deem appropriate."

"Only up to $250,000 per day," Dalmonica said. "And no jail time, if it's not contempt of court."

"You've looked into it, then," the Judge said, and we were all silent.

Eventually it was set. Being late October, luckily the sun was setting late so we got a 7 p.m. perpetual trial date on us, on towards midnight, with waivers from both of us that we would jointly pay government time if things progressed beyond three weeks. We had the Pomproy room in the main courthouse building, a small room that would wreck a lot of TV plans, but really, neither of us saw any limited seating being a problem. It was all going to happen on the courthouse steps and in the parking lot and the men's rooms and the usual places anyway: the press talking and talking and talking.

After we left and I informed my people of our secured night time and waded through the crowds and gave my moments to Fox and CNN and got good kickback from the *LA Times* for a quote they could run, Dal and I met for a drink in a private limo that just kept looping Tennessee St. Because where could we go, really?

That's when he said, "I left a package in a seat in Judge Staite's room."

"What? Why?"

"Just down the side of the chair. No one way of telling which of us left it. No prints."

"Oh my God. What did you do?"

"Relax, Gath, it's just a bottle of 50-year-old Scotch. And from Scotland, for a change."

He was relaxed and had his stinky shoes off and seemed as drowsy-eyed as the Judge had been.

"Do you think he'll drink it?" I asked.

"Why not?"

"It could be poisoned."

"Why would you think that?"

"*He* could think it. You just…left it there."

He thought a moment and finally said, "No. He'll love it. He should be thanked. Night dates are hard to get."

The car cruised and there was Beach Boys Christmas coming from the front part of the limo. Which I didn't like, because even with the partition up, if we could hear the driver's music preference a bit, didn't that mean he could hear *us*?

Dal was getting drunker and more pious or sanctimonious or just internally comfortable and said ten minutes later, "Did I ever ask you if you think Vladimir's the real thing?"

"Does it matter?"

He laughed one of those vague and one-shot laughs that was somewhere between sarcasm and nothing. At last he said, "I had a strange dream two nights ago…A woman came to my door…It was night time…I had a drink in my hand and there was the smell of toast in the house…And I opened the door and the woman right then turned into a dark-featured man with a coat and a cape and his breath…there was smoke coming out of his mouth like cold breath even though it wasn't cold…"

He was falling asleep, so I asked, "What happened?"

"I fell asleep…" And he did then too, so I did the remote to make the partition go down and had the driver take me to my hotel near the courthouse. I hoped I could trust the driver not to tell *The Paris Review* or *Rue Morgue* where he dropped me.

Medge responded to our secret knock quickly, and all I said was, "We've got 48 hours," before melting into her arms for a nice long sexual vacation. Luckily Doll was already asleep; Medge had given her something light and safe so she could sleep through all the adult stuff.

It didn't last as long as I expected. The next thing I knew, I was in a pretty hot shower, the kind that makes steam on the mirror you can't easily wipe off, and I was drying my legs, and there was Vlad, staring at my hairy legs. I guess we were both surprised when I didn't scream.

My skin felt red and uncomfortable, and Vlad was smiling. "I heard. 7 p.m. court time. You done good, kid."

Angry, I just tossed my towel at him. Behind him, somehow, was Holly, who didn't seem to mind anything. Where she was. Me naked. I minded, so I took my towel back.

"What are you doing here?"

"I wanted to congratulate you," he said, but it was Holly who came forward to give me a little hug. I looked nervously at the door which *had* to open any moment now. Incredibly, Medge *didn't* come in the room just then.

"Gath, this is major," she said.

"What?"

"Now it's Vlad's show."

"Just stand back," he said, "and follow my lead."

"I don't follow."

"You do," and he smiled, and the world went graying and black again.

# CHAPTER

A smaller area than I had expected, but in no sense a coffin. I could understand the compromise of it, trying to best me and fool with my confidence, but it meant very little. As Gath himself warned me, the true story would be taking place outside of this tiny legal room. Since such law things require that you cannot tape or film for posterity, there was a little man clicking on a machine, and another tiny man making sketchy oil paintings which captured my drab side.

It was Gath I felt sorry for, coming around from his daze in the middle of his preliminary remarks concerning something so important as my background and how in the right we plaintiffs are. Still, no matter, such statements do not mean a thing, though from my time with *LA Law* it is obvious the weight of a closing statement is crucial. Even on one *Perry Mason* episode, one of the ones based on a novel, Mason wins his case solely on his summation, the trick of this plot being that he has closed off Ham Burger, the District Attorney, into not being able to give rebuttal evidence or comments, therefore  Mason has the last and dramatic word. Cheap and disposable as television is and was, I was determined that our side should have the last word.

That they were all staring at me was good. It had been that way for half of the first evening. Obviously no one was listening to the summation of either side. I must admit to looking delicious and incredibly tight in my thousand dollar suit and shorts and cape of finest gull silk. It is a little known fact that certain Argentinean silk is processed from the fibers of seagulls, and it was my first mission in this tiny room, staring at all the horrified jurors who dared have the confidence to stare at *me*, that I would make the superiority of my *style* known by mental osmosis.

By the time my attorney was fully cognoscente that he was carefully reading from a paper, all twelve members daring to sit in judgment of *me* knew that here was a man of riches and therefore culture.

Though it was too early to exude straight sex appeal, Holly sat directly behind me and, once every ten minutes, bent herself forward to gently massage my manly temples for forty seconds. Then she would sit back. This demonstrated, quite clearly, how I promoted love, how I could make it prosper in my life, via free will, and that if such a one as lovely and young as her may stroke my head, I am worthy of love.

It caused murmuring among the jurors and the gavel rang to quiet them, but it was worth it.

As I was the start and cause of everything here, of course, I was the first to be called by the prosecution, us, which was my desire.

I flashed my devilish eyes at all who dared watch me glide to the witness protection stand, and glide I did. My mouth toyed with part of a smile as I watched this dreaded *old* Judge remove his glasses and stare in puzzlement at my perfect glide.

I wanted to laugh out loud! Signal my ego to throw open the desire to show everyone, every pitiful one here *clearly* who was in control of this entire room! But it was early yet and only the first day and I contented myself to let my lips play with said smile and simply toss it back out like a bad ball.

Gath had wanted and had scheduled many hours of rehearsal between us for the massive list of questions he was to put to me. But I merely made him realize that life and afterdeath is short and there is no need to waste time on questions that a reasonable mind can put asunder in so a short moment. To keep the mind young, I told him, requires the improvisation of the moment and the capturing of all thoughts and feelings to give the supreme answer.

"I shall always be in control," I had told him.

My attorney was clearly nervous, the dark suit of his choice being a wise choice considering the Florida sweat which ran from his various crevices. I could make the room more chilly to help him, so I did.

"Please state your full name," he said.

"Vlad Tepes."

"Your full name, please."

"I am known by many names."

"What's on your driver's license?"

"In this country? Murray Walker."

"You're kidding."

"No."

Here my Gath stammered and requested some additional time that the fat bean known as Dal at the other table was reluctant to give. So I mentally assured my friend that all was right and well and the falling coolness of the darkly-lit room was sufficient to help his questioning to continue.

"Is your name legally Murray Walker?"

"No."

"What is your legal name in the United States?"

"Vladimir Tepes. I require few, if none, middle names."

"Where were you born?"

"Transylvania."

"When were you born?"

"August."

"What is your full birthdate?"

"Some have said circa, but I say *precisely* in 1431, on August 15, so August 15th, 1431."

"You would have the court believe that you are nearing 600 years of age?"

"Of course not. The court is cold and disbelieving and there is little imagination left in this world and that is why Jesus has not returned."

The blob Dalmonica rose to his feet, reluctantly. "If the court would instruct the witness to answer with proper indications." He sat.

"What is a proper indication?" I asked my friend, in my usual courtroom gaze. I realized I was being intensely theatrical. Really, I was too much. With hand gestures and inflections in my voice that made me rather gay, but I did want to give these good people a show.

"No opinions, please," Gath said, "only those things you know as facts."

"I did not know Jesus," I told everyone.

"Mr. Tepes, how do you account for your science fiction-like longitivity? It seems quite extraordinary."

I looked to the Judge, making these wild rollings with my wrists. "My attorney was giving an opinion."

"So what?" the Judge said. I sank down like a proletariat. He was really quite rude and worse than that, disinterested.

Gath repeated, "How do you account for your longevity?"

"I am immortal."

"You are a god."

I fluttered my indifference. Which I knew they would not take for testimony. So I said, "It is of value for you to define. I merely state that I cannot be killed nor die of old age or the like. You need not have my word."

I set myself on fire, in a gradual grade that burned straight up, though not to the ceiling. For half a moment I did this as I heard the crowd gasping and incredulous, at which point I turned my flame to smoke and seemingly disappeared.

So humorous, really, watching a grown big-gut sheriff waving his hand through me as if I weren't there at all. These humans with their scientific concepts. They will sit for hours of a Sunday morning worshipping and singing to something they cannot even see, and then when a true immortal merely changes to smoke, they wave through him like he has gone from them, like some dead soul.

It was pandemonium in the court that evening. The perfect start to a perfect start. I wanted them grunting and disordered and setting upon themselves. It gave a grating to some of their complacency, especially that of the Judge who quickly woke up. Except for a few of the women, *he* was one of the noisiest conspirators of the chaos. Pounding his little hammer and bellowing his red throat at those who paid no real attention to him. The threat of the moment seemed to be this fire they kept speaking of but which, if they had chosen to use their eyes, they might have seen was gone. There was no fire. Yet the talk of the night was how to get water into this chamber and firemen and saving people and orderly fashion.

Within the half hour, large men in yellow rubber suits and ridiculously wide helmets did enter, traipsing within the small room to find where to do what. It seems they had water to distribute and nothing interesting upon which to throw it. Meantime I had dissipated myself into a roach in the corner, so that they did not even have smoke to contend with.

The Judge got the order! he so blatantly desired, and banged on his hammer for us all to return the following evening at seven for further fun.

No one seemed especially perturbed that I did not show myself during the best of the rigmarole, a point to which I took exception, while in the hall, Gath was being interviewed by someone pretty with a blue microphone.

I let myself appear and startled everyone, including Gath, so I used the silence to start talking.

"I give my word to the people of Florida *and* Tallahassee that of course I will burn nothing down, nor destroy anything in my quest for fairness. Of course, all I seek is the truth, and I don't mind giving it to you. For you will hear conflicting stories about the events this evening, and I, instigator, merely love you all for coming."

I told them of my fire and smoke, but not the roach trick, as it is good to keep some things a secret when one is underfoot. Gath was keeping his bulging eyes in check and I, more than ever that moment, appreciated what a team player he was.

He merely sauntered, did not storm, off when he realized I had the full attention span of these national press people. It allowed him a free passage for a change.

He was still angry when I awoke him at two that morning. There was no heat in his hotel room so I suppose he and his plain wife were spooning for a second reason. Crassly, he shoved his palm in my face and pushed me out of the bed and into the bathroom.

Yet still he was not wide awake when he complained, "What are you doing?"

"I am going to let you handle things, Gath. That no longer goes without saying. But I must shake things up with who I am and with powerful images of the truth. It is the only way to shift rock. One must blast, because the pen is not mightier than the sword."

"Huh?"

"I shall be your slave 78% of the time, this is my promise to you."

I bent over to kiss his neck which he took completely the wrong way. Understandably.

His bony hand was on my shoulder as he asked, "Can you tell me before you *do* anything like that again?"

"This is why I have come here," I said simply.

The second evening at court was completely different. Whereas the previous evening had been something of a football and basketball match combined, with the audience being excited and excitable and full of twigeting, now we came to what can only be described as a pall over the night in which movements were slower, eyes more suspicious, and there was a genuine edginess about the proceedings. Especially when I entered.

I believe in greatness entering last, as I have learned from years of infiltrating stately homes and royal teas. So as I took my seat, the Judge, knowing full well by now who was *in charge* of the reason we were all here, banged his little mallet in a far less oppressive tone and whined that proceedings should proceed.

Continued Gath, "I believe we have established upon your previous testimony that you consider yourself a god, an immortal, because you claim you have been alive for nearly 600 years. Is that right?"

"I am immortal."

"Do you have any proof of this fact?"

"Before I answer that, I would like to ask the Judge if he believes in what happened here last night."

There is nothing like putting The Man on the spot, and on the spot he was then. He had nothing to say, though he was busy opening up his mouth and trying to fill it.

The fat one at the other table rose in order to fill the room with something, but it was truly rhetoric, and all that happened was the Judge instructing me with more gravity that I should answer the question that was, to me, out of order. I simply shook my head.

"You refuse to answer?" the Judge asked.

I looked into his eyes and past them with a darkness that stripped his flesh away and drained his right arm, then his left. I gave him my history of impaling and killing for sheer pleasure and the reverberation of my memories which contained such clear hell. The begging for mercy and the torturous, continuous pleasure of giving another person pain. All these hobbies had long since grown cold for me, but they were all thoroughly stored within me.

The Judge read me, and continued to read. I said nothing, he spoke nothing. A long pause of proof which could never be entered into any spoken testimony, save that which would forever be burned into the Judge's believing , numbing mind. If he could sleep at night with these horrors in his head, good.

It was thought to last an hour, though seconds truly crept by. Long enough for Gath, it seems, to come over and shake my shoulder to break my gaze. The disappointment in me was apparent, I am sure, but he still scolded me like a child. As we all waited for the Judge to say something. He smelled of stale Scotch.

The fat one rose again and asked, "May counsel have a short recess in chambers, Your Honor?"

Trance is a lonely, ugly word, but for the sake of short explanations, I will say that the Judge's thoughts were to be long and without vocals anytime soon, so I did my part and snapped my fingers to release the robed man from his trance. Then the two attorneys and Judge whipped through a little hole in the back of the room.

Feeling neither dedicated nor friendly enough to this room of gawkers, I merely decided to go without and have a yak at whatever press were hanging around. I had a feeling it would be most of them, after those cell phone videos of the smoke and court pandemonium were released to the internet and late night talk shows.

They growled like lions waiting for Christmas, an ebullience of fresh and worn faces, the most people I had ever seen crammed into such a large hallway. Every country's news team, all with their patched logos on their arms, cameras flickering, questions snapping, all in English, as if they expected me to hear any of them. I could hear them *all* of course, but how would these fools know this?

"I-"

And I relished in the power of just *my* word. My *one* word slowing the world down. A silence as immediate and deafening as the worst tractors on earth! The fact that the world needed to hear me. My word was a gang of motorcycles!

God, the *power!*

They rumbled back up again, so I said, to immediate and *total* silence, "Thank you all for coming. Justice will be served here today. The rest of that shit. You don't really want to hear the old shit, do you? Is this live? Shit shit shit fuck fuck fuckkkk fufufufufushisisishisittttt!"

Heads tossed at each other, fugitive looks and rolling eyes given to one another. I simply turned myself into a fruit bat, the sort that looks as if it is hung with wires, and it dispersed the crowd like a hurricane on a cat. Scattering, screaming, only the heartiest of the strong sticking around to continue to film.

"You!" I shouted at a short, fat man holding a camera next to a short, fat, balding Bob Newhart vaguely holding a microphone around his knees.

I fixed them with my eyes, giving each one eye, as they peered nearer. I fixed my full power upon the balding one and gave him my thoughts.

*You shall come to my home tonight. Do you want to live forever?*

At his pause, I read his mind which was lite, James Patterson stuff, learning that this man was what pundits call a lapsed Catholic, though according to the camera friend at his side, he was closer to being a lapsed asshole. Ah, it is a pity that the United States requires survival of the prickest and that it has nothing to do with being fit.

I waved my cape at them, after I had resumed my usual good looks and momentous physique, and I channeled them to follow me in their van to my fantastic domicile. Had I not thought they might need their broadcasting equipment in their vehicle, I surely would have spirited them with me as tiny maggots in my pocket. An unfortunate turn of events, as they kept getting lost while trying to tailgate me. Baffoons.

Eventually, I received them into my home with a squeaky door and cobwebs around the entrance way. They smiled and filmed of course, then I offered them tea from a young student who chose to dress like the maid in *Clue*, and we retired into the inner lounge which was thankfully clean and too boring to film.

Instead, they set up a head shot on me for the entirety of the talk. It was only then that I noticed the logos on their shirts which proclaimed them slaves in the employment of ESPN3. While I could not fathom why Sports should care, and while I inwardly cursed this luck that they were non-network, still, I thought, they were cable or satellite and what did it matter once they sold the footage on the open market?

Before the little red light came on, one of them asked, "What do you want to talk about?"

"I don't know, what do you want to talk about?"

I meant it as a jest, but when the question came around to me again, I merely fixed this idiot with the full force of my face and switched the camera on myself.

"Just ask questions!" I demanded.

"We're here with—"

"I am not mic'd!" I reminded him.

The camera man did not want to come forward, but did. All he did was hand me the other man's microphone, so that the other had to shout his questions at me.

"How's the trial going?"

"It is too early to tell," I said. "But if truth is to win, it will here today."

"Here?"

"In court!" I sighed. "Are you utterly devoid of common sense?"

He brought his voice down to its regular volume and pleaded, "Look, I don't think I'm the right—"

"Then shall I make a statement?"

He nodded.

"I believe in truth. I believe in history. They are the same. One equals the other when enough time has passed. I am in court, where I do not have to be, letting lesser men attempt to judge me. Merely to take my place in the history books. I am far too tired of being a cult sensation of something which is not even me. True, the *Twilight* series is merely myth and does not mention me. But I am the vampire. *The* vampire. Though its meaning has been bastardized too long, I fear."

"What's the offshoot?"

"Please, don't interrupt the interview. There are only two things that the world at large believes in today, and both occur on television. One is a movie, which eventually gets its largeness thrown into the small, cheap screen. The other is the truth, filmed throughout history, but only captured on film these last hundred years. If one is to have any part of reality or a chance at history, he must take his place among the storybooks, on television.

"The only trouble with this choice is that there are too many television channels. Therefore, the dross is incredible. So much will be simply *lost* to history. Because as time goes on, and it goes right now, new programs are being shot and filmed with fucking shaky cameras—which really requires no effort, no script, no talent at all—and all history today is pushed back to the crates of yesterday. And only will yesterday's television be taken out of the box and re-aired if someone on a past episode is killed or becomes 'someone.' The historical moment is passed, and moves on.

"This is why I am in court, asserting my rights. My life shall be *legally* true. And it shall be filmed for television. Without shaking the camera. Double exposure. Double proof."

"But just turning yourself into a bat today… I mean, you're like the first alien or…the invisible man!"

My anger began to *seeth* with this **idiot**. I tried to contain myself! "Did you not hear my previous utterances?"

"What you said?"

"Yes!"

His voice was small. "People like a recap. That's all."

Ah. Yes. I thought. Yes. "Ah. Yes." The average viewer was stupid, I had forgotten as much for a moment. They watch programs such as *Lost* and claim it high pop art. "My apologies."

I needed to speak more simply.

"I knew there was a reason I brought you here this evening," I said, and smiled at my co-host. I smiled at the camera. "Rather than let a select few hear my beliefs in a courtroom, interrupted by countless objections that would lead us no further to legal truth, I've decided to come to you all."

There were rumblings outside the walls. Perhaps this *was* live.

"Go ahead, put that simply."

He said, "Well. You just want to have your say."

"Right."

"Mind if I ask you a few questions?"

"Please."

While he tried to think, I suggested, "Would you like some spider broth?"

He looked sick. "Do you have that?"

I laughed at him, poor fat ass.

He called for the camera to halt and came over to me for a whisper. "I'm sorry about this. I'm used to sports interviews, you know—how'd you feel the game went, what do you think you have to do to win the season and that."

"Ask me about blood?"

"Blood?"

"Ask me what blood tastes like and if I like drinking it and how many vampires there are in the world."

He looked at me. My mouth was *right there*.

He backed away, tried a smile, and acknowledged the cameraman who made the little red light go on again.

"What are your hobbies?"

"Hobbies? You mean, like blowing up stuff?"

"Well…"

"My hobby is living—what's your name?"

"Mervin."

"It's not!"

"It is!

He was becoming edgy. Clearly I had pushed whatever buttons he had. And now I knew my mistake—his presence in the courthouse hall was merely cowardess. Some run away from trouble, and some are frozen to the spot. I had taken his ice for strength.

I asked, "Were you assigned to this story or do you have a sincere interest in the occult?"

He shook it off, professionally. "Do you collect blood?"

"Oh, come on. Tell me. Would you like to live forever?"

He blinked. "Is that possible?"

"It is improbable, but not impossible."

While he worked out my double negative, I moved on, "No one is a collector of blood. In my case, it is sheer necessity."

"What does it taste like?"

"It is salty."

"Like the sea?"

"Are you a moron, Mervin?"

"Come on," he whined, clearly not for broadcast."I'm scared."

"I'm sorry. It is not my intention to scare anyone tonight."

"You won't scare *them*," he said plainly, pointing at the camera. "They won't even *see* you at home. You scare me sitting here, I feel like a bag of shit."

The phone rang, and I drew it to my hand and destroyed it. I looked into the camera. "My purpose is to tell you the truth. I drink. I drink blood for life, not enjoyment. It is not a civilized taste. Yes, the depictions of the addict on camera and television are true. It being an almost sexual conquest at the moment of its easing down the throat. It is only a necessary that I cannot be without. That is all."

"Why is that?"

"Oh, I don't know. The same reason God deemed it necessary for people to ingest food, I suppose. Men to watch sports. Women to want babies before they are 35. There is something natural here."

"Are you going to want my blood?"

I paused. "I don't know."

"Are you going to kill me?"

"Of course not."

He hardly seemed to believe me. But he did not start shouting, nor did his friend stop filming.

"You're saying you're a moralistic creature."

"Creature? *Creature*?!"

"Well.....!"

"I shall let that pass." I said intently to the camera: "Do not shake the camera. Set it down if you have to." I don't know why he had put it on his shoulder. For a hasty retreat? "If there is a more competent person outside my door right now who wishes to continue this interview, then dog whistle me. Then I'll know you're serious. Give me your checkbook through the cat flap so that I might pay myself any amount for this intervi—"

I heard the dog whistle. So fast! So near!

Ushering the fat boys out, I waved all outside fans away, except one lovely brunette, and they obeyed.

She was lovely to look at, and had ripped the top portion of her blouse open to expose more cleavage than the manufacturer had intended, and I took and shook and kissed her hand.

She had what is known in crass society as a winning smile, and did not look unlike Anita Loos in her prime.

"Do come in?"

"Only if I will survive the night," she said in a husky voice which reminded me of A.B. in the original *The Fog*.

"I will not kill you," I promised, "nor sup from your blood."

"Can I get a seat in court tomorrow?"

I looked into her eyes. And oh, she wore beautifully plain, brown-framed glasses. "You will."

She tapped her glasses, and I thought of the end of *Mission: Impossible*, the first Tom Cruise vehicle. Indeed, she admitted that these were her spy glasses, and she was eager in her beaver to get started.

"The man before me was an *idiot*!" she said.

"You are a reporter?"

"*Miami Herald.*"

"Are we live now?"

"We're live, baby."

I liked this woman. Holly clearly did not. She was sullen and sulky from a distance, choosing her Raisinets with careful fingertips, in just the next room. The door was open. She watched us.

"So what happens if you don't drink blood, Vlad?"

"I get very cross."

She giggled like spring water. "Do you consider it murder?"

I thought. "I'll have to answer the boring moralistic ones in court. Why don't you try something fun that won't win me my case."

After a moment's thinking, she said, "How many vampires have you created?"

"*Created?*"

"Bit on the neck and…"

I sat there. And finally said, "No comment."

She lost her complacency for a moment. In fact, briefly, like the fluttering of an eyelid, she seemed completely lost.

"What do you mean?"

I shrugged and admitted, "I'd rather not answer that."

"Wow. That many?"

I shrugged again. "Would you make *me* a vampire?"

"You want to be a vampire?"

"Hell, yeah!"

"Why?"

She was about to gush, and then stopped. I'd seen that reaction before.

She, whoever she was, had no clear idea of her ideals at all. Just… "let's have fun." Typical American. Feel first, think third. Young and beautiful, though.

In a moment, it seemed that she was spouting on about immortality and the literal and figurative coolness of vampirism, when I just spaced out and I lost a moment of my life. For a change, I sat there, and understood how the likes of Gath must feel. I know it is unconscionable to believe, but it was the first time in my life that had happened.

Suddenly I grew bored with the whole situation and sought an early day. I tranced this young and lovely thing to show herself out and crept with Holly to our coffins to await the day. Suddenly I felt very old and tired.

# chapter 16

A Presidential order came for me at three the afternoon of the day after the "fire." The militia was out and I was under something like house arrest for the foreseeable future. Roaming house arrest, with armed Feds walking me to and from everywhere, with someone always in the room with Medge and me, so personal space was filled now.

They were treating Vlad like a monster in a monster movie, but a monster you know is coming and you know where he is. Just reams of people and people, all over, all around. Constant noise, the constant ringing of my phone, of *his* phone, of whoever's phone was close enough, etc. and etc. Imagine being in an international airport *all* the time. The noise just drones on and on until you brain is numb with activity, so much that it makes you inactive.

There was always someone watching a vid of Vlad's coffin. "He" was on a screen within my eyesight at *all* times. I guess they thought I was a vamp or a spider eater myself and they wanted me to know that they knew where my "best friend" was at all times. When in fact, as they knew, the only time I ever saw Vlad anymore was in court, as he sat, surrounded by his own armed Feds.

Fear and jealousy and uncertainty and horror and everything else filled everyone's eyes, including the Judge, Dalmonica, just everyone who came close to him. Vlad was seething because his show was just canceled, though MTV wanted an exclusive on an offshoot, but that Presidential order clapped him in moral irons like a criminal—stating that "until right is established in the United States' own ongoing investigation, for the sake of public safety, the person known as Vladimir Tepes shall be confined to a state of martial law."

Now, we all know the injustice and severity of martial law, that it's just the last act of a desperate government to achieve order, but I'd never heard of a *person* being place under it. Usually it's, like, a tract of land, or the whole country. Martial law against one person looks ridiculous.

Nope, Obama's name and sig was on this very legal paper, and Vlad wasn't going to have any more rights or quality time to himself or free shoes or cars from any companies giving out free samples anymore for a while. He complained to me in whispers just before he was to get back on the stand that they were gutting his fan mail and tossing out whatever they didn't like, including things like razor blades he was sent, and they took his several cell phones, and he even claimed that they had spiked the dirt in his coffin with head lice. He had a weird sense of humor, so it may or may not have been the truth.

Meantime, the Judge was giving him the evil eye big time. Whenever he wasn't directly addressed or had to write something, he was staring at Vlad with such a scowl that it made me write a note to Fred about seeing about a mistrial based on personal bias. Surely it wasn't the first time a case somewhere was thrown out because the judge hated a plaintiff. I hoped.

Whatever was going on, the room was sparse, with just witnesses (I assumed) and police and interested parties now dotting the back seats.

The Judge carefully said, "Mr. Tepes. I believe you were on the stand when we last broke?"

Vlad stood and said, "I was."

"Would you care to continue?"

"I would."

"Would you not burn the place down, nor turn into a wolf or a bat?"

"Who is in charge here?" Vlad asked.

All heads turned to the Judge.

"I'm…sorry?"

"Who's courtroom is this?"

The Judge was bulging eyes for a couple reasons, I gathered. After a pause, he softly spoke. "The *only* reason you're not in contempt of court *yet*, is because—"

"I'd like to see you try it."

A silence.

"May I see counsel in my chambers for—"

"No," said Vlad. "We continue. Just answer the question honestly, and we will continue without incident."

A pause. "Honestly?" the Judge asked.

"Yes, of course."

After another pause, weighed and measured, the man toying with his gavel said, "This is your courtoom, Mr. Tepes."

Vlad beamed like he'd just won a victory. From where I sat, this was the *worst* answer.

"You may continue," Vlad said, as he marched in tiny steps to take the witness seat again.

"Thank you, Mr. Tepes. Mr. Wein?"

Vlad held up a hand to back me off, and he said, clearing his throat, "I want to make a small statement to the court about my sort of outburst yesterday. I do not think you truly understand what I was saying."

"What can you say by fire, Mr. Tepes?" the Judge asked with a forced smile. A forced smile lost on my guy, I could tell.

"I am not a madman. Neither am I an intentional showoff. Yes, I like people to see me. But that is a repressed desire hundreds of years old."

Dalmonica stood to object, but Vlad gave him a left hand that he should take his seat.

He continued, "I don't mean that as proof that I'm that old, don't worry about that. My point is that causing fire. Changing into creatures. For me, this is a way of testimony. We are here for the facts, and one of those facts is that I can change at will. If you truly want justice to take place, even to prove  that I am a disgusting murderer, which I do admit, you have to take the evil with the good. Changing to fire is not that far removed from a yes or no answer. That's all I want to say."

And well said too. I really had to smile. And admire him. Not the murdering part, but the rest. Very clear. Respectful.

Of course I didn't know where to start after this. I was all psyched up with the previous transcript and my list of questions, but for some reason, all the heart went out of me then. Not that I was believing in any of this—not *really*—but all the pent up belief *around* me and the terror in everyone's eyes, including Fred's and, probably Medge's in the hotel, I could see that now in my mind's eye…it made me wonder if I was on the right side after all.

Trouble was…I liked this man. Really liked him. The trouble being that I didn't know why. He didn't give me a lot of loving feeling to work with. "The man you love to hate?" I don't know. Maybe I was still under some spell? I didn't know anymore.

With real force, I made myself step into the room more, and plunged into an abridged list of questions. This time there was quiet, the vibe of frivolity replaced with the vibe of glaring dislike.

But first, before I got to the list, I had to ask, off the cuff, "You've murdered people, you say. How come you haven't been arrested?"

"You have no laws to govern the supernatural. By physical, nature's laws, you can't prove I've done a fucking thing."

I looked at my pages.

"Mr. Tepes, I believe when last you spoke—for the record—you were telling us of your immortality."

He paused. "Is that a question?"

"Yes."

"Yes."

"Have you any proof of this?"

He brought, out of a long pocket on his purple shirt, an ancient document, tri-folded, and handed it to me with a curt bow of the head.

"And what does this purport to be?"

"Purport?" He laughed. "That's my birth certificate. The original, so be careful with it. And I don't want it stamped for identification!"

"May it please the court. Mr. Tepes has just handed me a document which I ask to be handled with care. We ask that the defendant solicit any expert in the world he wishes, but that the test be done *here*, whatever the cost to us, so that nothing untoward happens to this document. In view of the extreme prejudice to my client…"

I handed it to the Judge, and now it was Vlad's turn to watch his every move. Vlad was seething again, damn controlled, just like the first day we met.

The Judge read it while Dalmonica, I guess, silently moved over to look.

Dal said quietly, "Your Honor, I object to this request not being feasible. Unless you want bulky x-ray equipment brought in here, I don't know what else to suggest."

I asked, "Do you think this requires that? You should ask an expert what's required."

"Objection," he repeated.

The Judge looked at the glaring man in the witness seat, and, not *seeming* intimidated, said, "Objection noted. What is the providence?"

"That will become clear with my next witness, Your Honor," I said.

He nodded, and I turned back to Vlad, who kept looking at the Judge.

I said, "You claim this to be a true and accurate birth certificate of yourself, Mr. Tepes?"

"Of course. That's why I brought it in."

"Actually, it was found in a church archive in Romania, was it not?"

He glared at *me*. "Yesss."

"What is your definition of immortal, Mr. Tepes?"

He smiled and said, "Well, Webster, the book, not the man, defines it as 'exempt from death, exempt from oblivion.'"

"Have you ever experienced a near-death situation?"

"To me, yes. To you, I have experienced death itself."

"How's that?"

"I've been shot, hung, poisoned, uh…shot. Again. Of course, these are suppositions because I can't prove what I say. No pictures or anything."

"The truth is, you can't be photographed at all, is that right?"

Dalmonica said, without standing, "Objection. We're leaving reality, Your Honor."

"Have you seen *Up With Vlad*?" I asked him.

"Yes. A radio show on TV."

The Judge looked at Vlad and basically said nothing. He just threw me a small hand gesture to continue.

"I'd like to take a picture of you. Mr. Tepes. Would you care to provide us with a first-hand demonstration?"

"Woah, woah!" and Dal was on his feet.

I crossed over to the table and laid my hand on an ancient machine. A Polaroid. "I have an instant camera right here."

"I have a gun," Vlad said, raising me better than poker.

Dal stood and shouted, "Woah!"

Vlad handed the gun to me, which I took in slow motion.

The Judge leaned forward to say, "Mr. Wein, you're not shooting this man in my court."

"Shoot him, Gath!" Fred cheered.

"Your Honor," I said with mock confidence. "My client assures me that such a demonstration is vital to our case, and assures me that there is no harm to him. Even if I shoot him in the head. After yesterday's demonstration, I don't see any real objection."

"I'd rather you took the picture," the Judge told me.

Vlad smiled, so I took the picture. We waited a couple minutes, then I handed a non-Vlad photo to the Judge. The Judge's jaw dropped, then he dropped the photo. The defense came up to look.

"How do we know that's not a magician's machine?" Dal shakily bluffed.

"Shoot him, Gath!"

The Judge banged his gavel and looked sternly at Fred. "Quiet or contempt!"

"Put the gun to my head, Gath." It was Vlad who spoke. And before I knew it, my arm was outstretched. The gun in my hand, aimed at his half smile.

I looked at Dal who glowered at me. I guess I had him, really.

"Your Honor, this is insane!" he said anyway. "That man should be under arrest for even bringing a weapon into this courtroom!"

The Judge said sternly, "He is. And he is in contempt of this court."

Like a bored man, Vlad merely stated, "I have no contempt for this court. And I do not mind serving time in the course of justice."

There was a titter from the limited audience which didn't go down well with my client, but except for a double take, he let it pass.

"Strenuous objection!" shouted Dal.

"And noted," the Judge said. The truth was, he was dying to see it. They all were.

Me, I didn't care. I was *ceasing* to care, anyway. It was either a trick gun or…some special power he *did* hold over all of us. All I know—in my post-blur knowledge— was that while Dal was jumping to his feet and the Judge was about to pound his gavel and the slight audience was opening its mouth to roar, Vlad took the gun from me, put it to his temple and pulled the trigger.

The blood, the juice of a man, and things splattered. As Vlad expected, a doctor, the court doctor, rushed in by the bailiff, who was the first to check the "body," came to check his pulse. When Vlad raised a hand to hold to his mouth to keep a cough from contaminating the room, the doctor fell on his ass like *he* was shot. Mark Clock in the third row was the one person to laugh. Everyone else was shocked. The doctor got off his ass, and gingerly, in a moment, wiped his finger along the side of the exit wound and peered at it skeptically through thin Lennon-like glasses. He sniffed Vlad's head. Took a handkerchief from his pocket to wipe a blood smear on and carefully folded it in three folds before putting it back in his back pocket.

Both he and the bailiff examined the bloody side of Vlad's face like he wasn't there. At least, they weren't afraid of him anymore. Not even when he yawned his head like he was trying to open his ears, like he was trying to ward off airplane cabin pressure.

I said, "Would the court like to instruct the doctor to give testimony on what he observes?"

Dalmonica was speechless, but he still went through the motions by saying, "Objected to as out of order."

"Just a statement for the court, please, doctor," the Judge said.

Eventually, after using his tongue depressor and his little eye light and taking Vlad's pulse, he stood in the center of the room, trying to ignore Vlad's eyes from the witness stand, and said, "This man has been shot and should be dead."

"Is he dead?" Dalmonica asked.

"Objected to!" I shouted.

"Overruled," the Judge said without thinking.

"Your Honor—!"

"You can make your case soon enough, counselor," the Judge told Dal, then turned to the doctor: "How do you explain this?"

The doctor was looking green. "Explain what?"

"Why is this man still alive?"

"Wh-Idunno."

"Objected to," yelled Dalmonica, "as assuming a fact not in evid—"

"Don't object to the Judge," the Judge warned. "I was not giving testimony. Let us just know why he's still moving after all that."

"He shouldn't be." So, the doctor stood there, as we all did, trying to figure out the mystery of life.

"Your Honor," Dal said, "calling this man 'alive' is prejudicial language."

Admonished slightly, the Judge peered over to the jury and said, "The man in the witness chair is not to be considered anything. Not his name, his consciousness, his temperature…" It was a very poor definition of anything—confusing more than clarifying. I could see he certainly wasn't the man in control of the room.

"Doctor?"

He stared at the Judge.

"Take the witness stand, please."

"I'd like to say something first," said Vlad. There was a hint of echo in his voice. It could have been sound escaping his head from the new hole.

A hole that was dripping fresh blood.

"Proce-"

Vlad proceeded, "I am very much alive. Hardly undead. That is a ridiculous oxymoron that ineffectually means nothing. I suggest you strike *that* from the record. I was never dead, so I am not undead. I live, I don't breathe, though I was shot in the head just now. I can roast myself in fire if you like. According to previous court cases, you have to accept the testimony of the witness himself that he *exists*!"

It was more dramatic than I would have liked, him putting his finger up in the air, his voice raised like Jerry Colonna again, but this was my time for bunging in the ol' facts, citing previous cases in which wrongful deaths were settled cut and dried by the witness stating that heor she were alive. Fred had found these goodies when he was searching for blind alleys to plug. Malpractice cases in which a death certificate was mistakingly signed. Insurance scams to claim lots of cash.

Dalmonica was on his feet, raising ruckus that I was going out of order, but I said, "The witness himself—"

"*Your* witness!"

"Gentlemen," the Judge barged in, "this is getting far and scattered. I suggest we confine our arguments and rules of…evidence to things less…zany…"

Vlad was healed. There wasn't a speck of blood, dried or otherwise, on his person.

I tried to press on. No one was pushing me to continue; the silence in court was so loud. It was hard, finding my place…

"Mr. Tepes, we were on the subject of proof of your birthdate long ago."

"We were."

"I'm going to call historian Albert Davis who has written one of the several books out there on you, or who you claim to be, Vladimir Tepes. But before I do, do you have any other personal testimony you care to give?"

"At your instigation, I was examined by several highly respectable and reasonable doctors who x-rayed my bones for density and age, as well as a dentist who thought he was looking into a living skull."

"Well, aren't all people living skulls?"

"You know what I mean."

"I know, Mr. Tepes, but for the sake of the court, please rephrase your answer."

"He thought I was the buried kind. Hundreds of years old. Since my tissue is not technically living. But don't take my words for it, just call them up. I see the dentist at least sitting there." And he pointed.

I nodded. "In due course. But I'm establishing that you did indeed undergo these scientific tests."

"Sure. I don't have to shit either."

Not the best way to end. Especially since no one felt like laughing at that point. Vlad had a face

like a bad smell, obviously thinking that that joke was going to go over better than it did.

"Your witness," I said.

Dalmonica stood, as if not worried. Vlad glowered at him like he was going to rip his hair off. But

he contained himself.

Dal didn't read from any list of questions. The confidence just steamed off him.

"Sir. I'm not going to call you Vladimir Tepes, as I don't believe this can be proven. I do not even believe you are an entity, since as you claim, if you are immortal, then clearly you are not a person, therefore you are above the laws of mortal men. Therefore you cannot seek judgment in this court. What do you think of that?"

He smiled, and nodded. "I like that. I think it's good."

Dal stopped for a moment. "You do?"

"A nice, clean point. But I'm not a lawyer."

"No. You're a man claiming to be more than 500 years old entitled to royalties to everything brandishing your name."

"Am I a man? How refreshing?"

Dal wobbled a bit in his walk, but continued in confidence. "The definition of a man, is *an individual human*. Essentially, in your supposed case, a male human being. Would you call yourself human?"

"Objection," I said. "Your Honor, counsel is cross-examining his own witness."

"Who is the right person to ask to define if this man is human, Your Honor?"

The Judge thought. "Who have you got lined up? Anyone who has the definition of 'man' at his fingertips…"

"Dr. Emilio Brown from Harvard University, Department of Philosophy. Our first witness, in fact."

"You lay your groundwork later, counsel. Mr. Wein, who do you have?"

"Professor Bradman, Department of Philosophy, FSU."

"Without bandying this court into the realm of fantasy, well, further fantasy, and time wasting, and total philosophy, I am dubious about opening up this argument into 'what is life?' and all this, and 'what is the nature of man?'"

"Understood, Your Honor," Dalmonica stated. "But it is the defense's primary defense."

"Mr. Wein? Is this germane to *your* case?"

"If he's going to call his own witness to make a point of 'man,' I'm not going to slow him down here," I said, and sat.

"Then let's interrupt this witness to call Dr. Brown, as he has flown in for—"

"Your Honor, I rather expected my preliminary examination of this witness to be lengthy and frought with objections. I did not instruct my witness to be here this day."

The Judge sighed. "Continue."

Dal turned to Vlad, who was far from bored, as I thought he would be. "Mr. Tepes. We'll leave your origin of species alone for the moment and turn our attention to your age. I'd say that's pivotal in this case."

"—Was that a question?"

"Your previous testimony—"

"I loathe rhetorical questions, and statements that just end. I won't be answering any of those. I

think it's rather fair of me to be upfront about this. As I say: I'm no lawyer." He smiled the manic smile. "And you can't shoot me or keep me caged. So I just wanted you to know where we stand."

As lawyers, each of us is used to dodging shit, and explaining things away or towards our own view, but there comes a time things get so bad you have to play around with what I call your Break Face. Adopt a posture, a stamina, a face that calmly tries to ease the wreck coming so that you don't get pounded by the ten tons of metal coming at you.

Dal was riding the Break Face now, but you couldn't tell if he was worried or just smug. How could he not be worried?

After the pause, he repeated, "Your previous testimony relates that you were born in the year 1430, is that correct?"

"If I testified, I must think so."

"Your Honor, in deference to this thing's hostility toward the court or perhaps those I represent –"

"Thing! Wooo!"

"—request that I treat him as a hostile witness, subject to objection."

"I would grant that right to Mr. Wein as well," said the Judge. I thought that might get a titter, but I guess it was too intellectual a joke.

"You are 580 years old this year," Dal said.

"It's a special one."

"Why is that?"

"It ends in a zero."

He smiled at people. I tried to sit back and observe the reaction. You can often tell how a jury's going to go based on how the gallery plays. They thought Vlad was cool once. Now the average face was sagging, waiting for something to jump out at them.

"How do you account for your longevity?"

"I'm immortal."

"Yes, you testified to that. I mean. How did this come about? Logically, I wouldn't think… I mean, doesn't it stand to reason that if you can be born, you can die?"

"That depends on what happens in between times."

"What happened?"

"Well. I don't like to say."

"Say what?"

"My origin. Marvel is interested in my story and their stocks are way up now. Now that Disney owns them, we're talking real money. Well, you should know. Have you seen *Iron Man 2*? It's about as good as the first one."

"So… you're suing the conglomerate which actually contains Marvel and several graphic novel publishers, and selling them your own story."

"That was not a question."

"So, you're suing the conglomerate which actually contains Marvel and several graphic novel publishers, and selling them your own story?"

"The truth." Vlad sat up. Not that he ever slouched. "It is *my* life."

"All 580 years of it."

"Don't statement at me, ask me questions!"

"You realize this is implausible, don't you?" No response. "I mean. If you're biting people on the neck and making vampires all over the world, how come *no other one* has ever been seen or captured or wants to sit up in court and turn himself into a bear cub or an insect for the attention? This is the YouTube world! I would think being an immortal would give a person…bags of confidence!"

"Bags?"

"Why haven't we heard of this marvel before?"

Vlad wanted to say something and clearly thought better of it. A weird look was on his face.

"I'm after plausibility, Mr. Tepes." After a pause, "How did you become a vampire or an immortal…what would *like* me to call it?"

Gently, Vlad said, "Well, it's not an affliction." After a moment, he humbly said, "Can't you just call me a god?"

Dal laughed, and Vlad's eyes turned purple. "A god?!"

"Well—"

"Do you really consider yourself a god, Mr. Tepes?"

I stood. "Your Honor—"

"Your Honor," Dal said louder, "I believe this juts perfectly into my next question."

"Go ahead."

"Your Honor—"

But Dal was already talking and the Judge seemed bored. Did he just not care anymore?

Dal did. He was warming up; he *felt* in control again. For some reason. "Mr. Tepes, have you ever been institutionalized?"

"Never."

"I refer you to 1979. Milton, Ohio. Were you ever institutionalized in Milton, Ohio for extreme dementia, violent behavior, and…as cutting corners to serving a prison sentence, were you incarcerated at the Jaimin Doyle Psychiatric Hospital for a period of thirteen months?"

He was silent.

Oh, my, god… he was silent.

I looked at Fred like I hated him. He was supposed to go through *all* of this with Vlad. *Ages ago!* Fred just gave me a shrug, almost like he didn't care either. Yet there was something in that uncaring that seemed to want to scream *let the pig fucker hang!* I hoped it was my imagination, but nothing mattered except

the silence in court.

After a while, a voice was heard. Devoid from ego? No. Apologetic? No. But it was softer, and for the first time since I'd known him, Vlad's eyes seemed to come off caffeine, and almost folded like an Asian man sleeping.

"It was the summer of 1979," Vlad said, coolly, slowly. "That Frank Langella flick came out, and I was so depressed." A long pause. People sat forward a little more. "He's a fat bastard now with no hair, but in the summer of 1979, with that John Williams in the background, *damn* he was fucking cool!!"

He shouted it with such anger, the room shook with fulfilled anticipation. Some of the people wanted to run outside.

But it was a single outburst. It came and went so easily, like shouting at traffic.

"I didn't want it to be like Bela," he said quietly. "That was bad. I just tore up the neighborhood then. 1931. Tearing into throats. It was worse in '79. Drinking myself gluttonous, whether I was hungry or not. I got fat. It made me so depressed. I should say…it added to my depression."

"You entered yourself," Dal helped.

"Don't be crude," Vlad said, not really paying attention to him or anyone.

"I mean, you committed yourself?"

"I checked myself in. Some out of the way place. I didn't know it was Ohio."

"You were there thirteen months and didn't know you were in Ohio?"

"Look. That can happen when you're in Ohio." He laughed with derision. "You people have no sane laws here like China, to take away this overpopulation problem." He laughed with contempt. "It's really stupid in America. It is like smoking. You know you shouldn't be doing it, yet there are no real *laws!* Like eating chili dogs and corn chips. You should warn people about these things!"

"Can we get back to—"

"No! We can't! Overpopulation is the world's greatest and most neglected evil in this world!" Vlad slammed his fist down. It made deep indentions in the solid wood seat in which he sat. "This must be said! And for the record!"

"And so, single-handed, you've attempted to rid this world of as many people—"

"Don't be a fool! I'm talking about *all of you*! Making your babies and having your sex for fun and falling asleep on the *one* second it takes to pull out! Pull out!! It's ridiculous!!!"

"Mr. Tepes, I ask that you—"

"You're all fools to procreate and procreate and never once—"

The Judge said, "Mr. Tepes—"

"—coming to the obvious conclusion that—"

"Mr. Tepes!"

"Mr. Tepes!"

"—all your other problems, every problem you have in the world stems—"

"Your Honor—!"

"—from filling—"

"Mr. Tepes!"

"—the world up with—"

"Your Honor!"

"Your Honor!" I said.

"—people!!!" screamed Vlad, and turned into a puff a smoke that clouded the room like it was on fire.

No flames.

No defendant.

Just a room full of shouting from us and the Judge and a room of screaming from everyone behind us who couldn't see well enough to escape or understand. Just laconic pandemonium…

The bailiff found the doors at the back and aired the place out. Everyone but Dal, the Judge and myself had drifted out like disaster victims, with the odd expert and parts of the jury standing around, dazed, wondering. Guards and regular cops stood in the hall, waiting to take direction.

As the moments wore on, and the room cleared, there was Vlad. Still sitting in the chair. Looking worn. Beaten? He was just this side of depressed. For once, his mustache seemed to have lost its stiffness.

The bailiff asked the Judge something, but no one told the cops what to do so nothing was done. I went over to Vlad and whispered a few questions in his ear. I could've been talking to an ant hill. There was no response.

Lifting gently at his elbow, he responded to the pressure and let me take him back to the long table.

Finally the Judge banged his gavel and dismissed us until seven the next night.

"Can I sit with him?" I asked the bailiff. He nodded at me, while the few stragglers left, all staring at us. Dal's face was all consternation. I don't know how I was going to make this up to him. I felt like we were in this together somehow.

I raised Vlad's chin like he was my son.

"Why didn't you tell me you were institutionalized?"

He found voice soon. "I didn't think it mattered if I committed myself."

"Of course it matters. Fred should've asked—"

He waved a hand. "It is no fault of his. It was just thirteen months out of my life. What is that? I was at peace there. How can you remember a short boring part where you're at peace?"

True. I remember a teacher of mine telling me once that it's the wrong not the right answers you remember from a test. Whether it was true or not...well, it was true to Vlad. He looked...

And he was gone.

All the way to the hotel room I wondered if he would come back. There was some...finality about him that I hadn't witnessed before. Like all the fun had gone out of the thing.

It was strange. It wasn't like Dalmonica had dug very deeply either. It was just a couple questions, and Vlad crumbled like cake. He was a very emotional "man," sure, but... I don't know.

All I wanted was Domino's and some *Bob Newhart Show* and just not to think of any of this. For half a night anyway.

# CHAPTER

As I lay drinking the blood of a runaway, I thought on my life. I remembered its phases. Once, for sixty solid years, I would only drink from girls or women. No one under 15, nor over 55. It had nothing to do with the blood, it was merely sexual. As Stoker and those studying Stoker always claimed it was: an extension or a euphemism for sex. Which it clearly is not.

If you have survived on it and feasted on it, clearly you will know. How could the studiers and the writers know?

The phase of wanting to drown myself. That was only a month, so it seems strange that it would always stick in my mind, during the moments that I always felt self-loathing. Which did not come often. But everything that moves must feel this way, sometime.

It is a strange and difficult feeling to feel that you want to kill yourself when you are dead. You can jump in the river and fill your lungs with water, when you do not have to breathe. You can stand and watch as you fluff out water from your lungs. Until you have ever watched it, you'd never know how much water can fit in the lungs until you are alive to watch it all pour out.

It evokes a feeling of insignificance, that whatever you do, there is unlife.

Wrestling with my doubts now.

Thinking of the farmer phase when I gutted pigs and hid to watch the farmers wail and cry and curse god and wonder toward their wives what the hell was going on. Then I would merely move into their dinners and their TV time and crunch their bones and watch their blood gush. The man first, so the woman could watch and scream. Horrible, I was. Unnecessarily rough and unfeeling and nearly wanting to get caught, now that I think about it. Called monster and pleaded with and begged and never once did I take *any* woman up on it when she would scream, "Please don't hurt me! I'll do anything!" That is a regret.

Even 44 years ago I might have wished for an AIDS or something in the blood of this...runaway, that it might graft into me and take me away to a heaven or a someplace *believed* in that could replace this place, my eternal "heaven" that seems to keep on and on like a desert with the occasional stream to keep me wet.

I threw the body away, uncaring. I marched away as if I were drunk. I wanted to be. How I *envied* the drunk! Able to pay a few low dollars and claim memory loss and the sublime afternoon or evening of slowly getting pissed, feeling yourself grow numb and out of pain and past caring and singularly greedy for only the pleasure of self. Not the chewstick of survival.

I suppose I merely wanted to feel bad. Like those in love with being in love. I wanted to feel something, anything.

Yet obviously it didn't really matter to me. Or, though I threw the runaway away, I wouldn't be here in Salt Lake City.

# chapter 17

W e were in an anteroom of the Superior Court building. Mark Clock, Fred, Holly (who somehow had got away from Vlad and had not a word to say), me and Dalmonica and his team of four high-profilers who only spoke when spoken to.

Using his time wisely, Dal was whispering into my ear about the terms of settling the case, but I was only half-listening, nervous. It was mostly about Universal, how they refused point blank to relent on a settlement for royalties on reruns and older broadcasts; there was just no way.

"The *old* stuff doesn't bring in the cash like the *new* stuff does," he kept saying, in different incarnations. "But I don't think they're believing *anything* I tell them!"

I just nodded and tried to remain passively interested and agreeable. The door opened and in walked three bald men. They seemed to stare at me and only me, as they took seats, though one stood in the corner.

"Mr. Wein," one said, "my name is Wayne. This is Jinks and Magi."

"Are you serious?" Mark Clock asked.

He nodded, at me, and continued talking, to me: "This is unprecedented, so please forgive the abnormality of the situation. I've come directly from the President of the United States."

"You're kidding," I said. He wasn't.

"You've got yourself a singular situation here. Do you know where your client is right now?"

"No."

Wayne nodded. "He's in Salt Lake City. At least he was up until an hour ago."

"How did he get there!"

"Great question."

"How do you know this?"

The three looked at each other, and the one called Magi said, "We've got an entire satellite aimed on your guy right now. 25/7."

None of us knew what to say. Dal tried, "Why are we here?"

"There is no to be no court, Mr. Dalmonica," Wayne said. "I'm sorry. We have been authorized to use any means necessary to contain this man who calls himself Vlad Tepes, and who very well be Vlad Tepes."

"What do you mean, no court?" Dal asked.

"Your case is done. It's going to be dropped," Wayne said. "Any moment now your phone is going to ring and you're going to have your plug pulled. This is a case of national security now. Our President isn't allowing these things to happen in open court."

"What things?" But my voice trembled because I clearly knew what.

"Public endangerment. Public murder. Terrorism. You're harboring a terrorist, Mr. Wein."

What could I say to that? The room was deathly quiet.

"Not to my knowledge. I haven't seen him do anything except magic tricks."

"You admit they're all tricks!" Dal said suddenly.

Then his phone rang. He got up, sat back down, looked at me, looked at everyone while he listened.

Wayne continued, in a softer voice, "The President doesn't *blame* you for anything. Neither does the U.N."

"The U.N.! Oh come on now!"

"You're out of your depth."

"So how are *you* going to handle him?"

Magi said quietly, "Mr. Wein. What did you think was going to happen?"

No one had asked me that before. "I don't know," I finally said.

Dal flipped his phone closed and nodded at me. He rose. Jinks got in his way.

Wayne said, "Would everyone follow us, please?"

We all moved into the huge courtroom where the big, daytime cases are heard. There were soldiers—I'm guessing Generals, they had enough clout on their clothes—and more bald guys and a few anxious men and women in suits, all standing around one of the tables, waiting for us. About 19 people.

Ushered closer, I looked at what was on the table. Obvious non-disclosure agreements. I looked at the date that had my name on it. 2090. I'd be dead by then.

Magi put his long fingers on the papers and lightly fooled with them as he said, "We have no earthly container that can hold this man. Low key was the key, yet now we have a global consensus from world leaders that the criminal known as Vladimir Tepes is the number one threat to this country and this planet at the moment. I know that's a comical statement. I know it is. I am telling you all of this because no one leaves this room without signing the paper with his or her corresponding name."

"This sounds like coercion," Dalmonica said with Break Face.

"No," Magi said. "It would only be coercion if I did this." He drew his gun and aimed it right at Dal's face. "And I'm not going to." He holstered the stubby gun. "You want to know this is real, you tell us who you want to corroborate this, and you'll have your proof. I have direct internet and landline connections to the President, just say the word. We're not here to trick you. We're here to end this case. And move on with possible containment."

"Ours?" I asked.

Wayne shook his head. "It's true we have no way of containing this monster, but we do have reason on our side. And we're going to try every possible—"

"Wait a minute," Fred said, plunking down the paper. He was the only one who, I guess, was reading it. "This is not all one sided, Gath."

"What do you mean?" I asked.

"It's Make a Wish time," Magi explained. "Big time. The United States government does not coerce, but neither do we stand by and let anarchy—"

"What he means," Fred interrupted, "is that basically every person names his price for shutting up and walking away from all of this."

Mark Clock quickly scribbled something on a piece of cardboard he had in his pants pocket. He thrust it into Wayne's face. "Is this unreasonable?"

"We're in a science fiction movie, sir," Wayne said. "Nothing's unreasonable anymore."

"What assurance do I have?"

"See this box?" He pointed to a long, empty box on page 33, the next to last page. "What you want, you write in there. We both initial. You sign, you walk away."

Mark Clock did just that. Initials. Signature. He walked away, and didn't look back. Not even a goodbye.

Not even a goodbye.

I never saw him again.

Dalmonica was the first to find voice. He was looking through his copy. "It's already signed by the President."

"You're kidding!" I said, and picked up mine. The others did likewise, except for Holly who kept strangely quiet and aloof through it all.

"Has anyone seen the President's sig?" Fred asked.

"I told you people we're prepared to corroborate in any—"

"I'm thinking of relocating to New York City," Dal said. "If I asked for my own car and driver and a clear path through Times Square to work *every day of my life*, is that outside the realm of possibility?"

"No, sir," Magi answered instantly.

"You answered that really fast."

"Kid in a candy store, sir. You can even build the city containing it, then the store." Time stood still. "This man… this thing is an alien. The first we've ever encountered. And he's dangerous. If you want to survive as a species, what good is hording the diamonds and the Toyotas?"

"Rolls," Dal said.

"Done."

There was a collective non-sigh in the room. That non-sound you don't hear when you all know the tidal wave will hit in the next second, or your own non-gasp when you realize that horizontal speeder in front of you just rushed the light and you know your car is going to be crushed *now*. That's the moment we all realized this was possible.

It was the moment I started to believe. In *everything*.

"What about a billion dollars?" Fred asked.

"Kid, what do you need a billion for?" one of the usually silent baldies asked.

Another said, "Think of the economy, man."

The starting pages were babbling bullshit, not really saying anything except that here were a group of lawyers—both the ones who wrote the contracts and us—covering their asses. It didn't start getting good until page 14, telling us what we'd have to hand over, and about the monitors to be placed beneath our skins, purely for tracking purposes, and that "anything uncovered that is not directly related to the subject of Vladimir Tepes shall be deemed inappropriate and is not subject to this contract." It went on for pages and pages more about the use of the tracking device/bug, the period of time it would take to "cleanse" our possessions and "media extract" us from the "surroundings for a period of up to 30 months." Though they'd be replaced instantly, we'd have to hand in our phones, computers, toasters, cars, security systems, paperbacks, DVDs & players, condoms, canned goods, shoes, watches, etc., etc.

But that write-in box got me dreaming.

"What about Vlad?" Holly said softly, barely caught above the turning pages.

My neck came up. "What about Vlad?" I echoed to the officers.

"You don't need to worry about him," Wayne said.

I took a step forward. "He's still my—"

"This isn't Hitler," Magi said, "we're not going to bomb the shit out of him. We're going to—and I can *tell* you, because you're going to be wiped—use the man. He's the greatest gift to this country God has ever seen."

"Maybe he's even proof there *is* a God," Wayne said, and not like it was the first time the thought had appeared to him. The other officers mumbled in interested speculation.

"He told us he was a god," Dalmonica admitted.

"What do you think?" I whispered to him.

Glancing at the final pages, he whispered back, "I frankly don't see how something like this can be contained at all. I think they are throwing their money or favors away needlessly."

Fred came over. "What if I did ask for a billion?"

I gave him the *you're not going to ask for a billion* look and his mind sort of crept away to come up with alternates. Holly came to take my wrist.

She looked at me, and I felt bad for her and wondered at her.

"I've done a lot of work for you gratis," she said.

"…Yeah…?"

"I never asked for many favors. I gave you a lot of hours when I could've been out partying or going—"

"You've never been to a party in your *life*," Fred said, eyes still on his contract.

I crouched my shoulders a bit and tried to take the naughty boy out of my voice. "I'm looking at papers!"

She gave me *the look*, the one I hated getting from any woman.

"I think one of us should take up them up on their offer of corroboration," Dal said quietly.

I stared straight at Holly. "I'm looking—at—papers! How could you possibly—"

"They said we're not getting out of here without a conclusion, gentlemen," Fred said. I'd never heard him use that word gentlemen before.

"They have no cause to slow us down," Dal said.

I asked, "Were you really fired?"

He looked at me. "I was taken off the case." He tapped the pages. "This is civil liberty."

"This is Presidential," said Fred, tapping the seal and signature on the 17th page. We all turned to that page. Holly kept staring at me.

"This is where the original ends," Fred said.

Dal muttered, "The rest is amendment. Individual for all of us."

"It's like the fucking Bill of Rights."

"Anti-Bill."

"Look," I said, "come on. What are going to do *now*?"

Holly took hold of my arm and shook her head. She was trying to stare into my head, but if it was the Vlad influence, it wasn't taking.

Magi came over. "Problem?"

"Yeah, there's a problem." It was me. Where the courage came from, I don't know. "The release seems straightforward."

"For a car manual," Fred added.

"But you say we have no option."

"That is correct," Magi said.

"Then what validates my signature at all," asked Dal, "if under duress? How can you hope to hold us to sign something we have no clear choice in signing?"

"A good old-fashioned mind cleaning. Am I not right?"

And there he was. The speaker. Vlad. No open doors. No puff of smoke. Just suddenly in the room with, I guess, the only government agents in the world smart enough to realize that drawing weapons would be as useful as drawing them with pencils.

Wayne checked his watch. "It's after six."

"Am I not right?" Vlad asked.

He was holding his hand out for something. Wayne gave a smirk and nodded for one of the bald guys to do something. One of them went into the next room and wheeled in a cart, the kind usually reserved for projects when giving media evidence. But on this metal cart was a group of bottles, syringes, rubber cord, cotton, and lollipops, the latter being a joke, I guessed.

"There's something you can help us with," Magi said, staring fearlessly into Vlad's bemused eyes.

"You want to learn to do my mind control *tricks* without having to use a drug." And Vlad was a little closer. Into the room.

No response.

And before Vlad finished saying, "Because the real art of war games is that of knowing…your enemy…" he was a little *closer*.

Was he walking?

"Who said anything about war?" Magi asked.

"My apologies for insulting the United States of—"

"Decriminalization," Wayne said, "is an even better reason. Keep these streets safer."

Then, suddenly, Vlad was right on top of the pushcart, I mean, right next to it, even surprising Wayne. The Fed waved a hand in front of his own eyes, like he was checking for drunkenness, while Vlad took up one of the little bottles and looked at its colorless insides.

He crushed it in his hand, and turned to no one in particular. "I used to tire at the epic battle of science versus god."

Magi wasn't spooked. "And now?"

"If you can't beat them—"

Then the room was a whirl. Vlad was right upon Magi, bending his neck over to the left slightly, and he dug his suddenly *sharp teeth* into Magi's tan neck, exploding it like a red sausage. Was this the jugular? Apart from the quick explosion, nothing much was left to splurt. Vlad was on him like a sunbeam in Arizona, sucking up blood like he was famished. Chugging. It was gross.

I had to turn away. Just listening…you could hear the event was something like a…straw…at the bottom of the glass… a parting of the flesh…like he was trying to…suck salt water out of someone's nose that had just drowned. Gulping. Chugging. And then, very much *like* a straw, he came to the end of the drink, and the squooshy, fleshy sound, sort of like a big fish coming up for supper in a tank, echoed the silence that was too loud for me.

No one was moving. All the G-men had their hands on their hips which seemed very gay to me, just standing there, doing nothing. I couldn't understand it.

I looked back at Vlad, hoping I had some control. Maybe…I don't know. Maybe friendship? *Stop this, for me, please?* I don't know what I thought then.

Until he let Magi's body fall to the ground with a bone-crunching *thud*. Then I woke up.

I knew what Vlad Tepes was, and who he was.

# CHAPTER

I was not hungry. But a statement had to be made. No one wanted to draw their weapon, but each face was killing me with his heart. Gath, with his sad eyes and Alicia Silverstone frown, was hurt the worse. His body gait, that of disappointment; the way his hands just flopped there at his sides.

After a silence, one of the bald men said, "We thought of cutting your head off."

"But you do not have such authority," I responded. "*My* authority. What is your name?"

He hesitated, then answered, "Jesse Wayne."

Gath's face turned from disappointed to incredulous. He turned to my woman, body language still full of outrage, and asked her, "This is the man you...do you *love* him? Holly?"

She was in my power. My trance, as they call it. But not of my doing. It was her heart's trance. I don't know if Gath would ever understand that.

Certainly Fred would not. He withdrew a gun from the side of one of these g-men, and started shooting me, yelling all the while. With each shot, he came forward, a shuffle somewhere between a walk and a run, until he ran out of bullets. How I wanted to do the stereotype and clutch his stubby neck and lift him from his feet and utter something James Bondy and pithy. But by the time he was close to me and without protection, I saw into his soul. Where he grew terror and jealousy, and I merely smiled at his whim.

I looked to the terrorists, and chose my words like a gentleman, and a lawyer.

"Now it's my turn for the tables. I mean, it's my turn to turn the tables. Oh gawd…"

I am not perfect. The choice words did not come swiftly to mind. Nevertheless, I retained my cool, while my body healed. "Whoever it was who said that you are not getting out of here without compliance, he is correct. But it is *you*!" I pointed at the G-men. "You want my cooperation?"

"Well…"

"You have this!" I waggled one of the contracts at them, then threw it across the room, a lot harder than I had wished, so it shattered a window. "You have the President's voice to speak! It seems you have the world's!"

"Just the U.N.'s," Wayne said humbly.

"Then speak for them! I will make you a deal!"

One of them withdrew a tape recorder from his pocket and asked, "Do you mind if I digital this?"

"What's that?"

"Record what you say?"

"Yes, of course!"

"What's the deal?" Wayne asked.

I told them: "I will not kill anyone else in this room. And you have my word as royal blood of Transylvania that I shall pass my knowledge along, and I shall cause no more trouble."

"Can you define *trouble*?" the fat attorney asked me.

I came close to his face so that our noses touched. "I shall not seek your death, for a start."

He said no more for the rest of the time I knew him.

I spun back to the others for clarification. "Trouble is what I am causing you, isn't it? Gath. I apologize. You are not meant to be in this room."

He rather shrugged, so that I was not put off, but slightly insulted, but I let it pass and continued, "You have my word that if you grant me two requests, I shall not change my shape. Nor will I drink the blood of *anyone* you know. And I know all of you!"

"Well…" one of them hedged.

"I shall be as humans. Humans who do not kill or wound for sport or need," I further expounded. "How's that?"

"And what do you get?" Gath asked.

"Eh?"

Wayne took a step forward, courage I admired in the face of myself. "What do you *want*?"

Quickly, I threw a finger at the man I had just drained. "Burn this body within the next ten minutes before he catches the disease of eternal life. In front of my eyes!"

No one moved. Perhaps they thought I was joking. I stamped my foot once.

"What else?" Gath said it with a sigh, which hurt me. Deeply. I was wounded. He stood there, still, and let me come over and clutch his arm in a comforting way. Comforting to me.

I turned to the other man, the fatter attorney and said clearly but softer than shouting, "I want this trial to continue."

Not everyone heard, so I flapped onto a table and shouted it! "Give me my time in court! And *all* of this can *end*!"

All eyes were there, at me, full of a fury I can only partially describe as I am a feeble writer. Perhaps they were sending me daggers with their eyes, most assuredly they all wanted me dead. Save Gath. From lifetimes of reading people, I could only feel his pity. I pitied him more than myself. I was focused, as the doctors say, but his mind and heart were full of dirty doubt and conflict.

After a few moments of this, Wayne raised his hands up, his gun still in his hand, nodding to the others behind him to lower their heightened senses. Indeed, there were no more hands on hips. It was only then, when they moved closer to me, and I left the table, that I perceived that they were all breathing hard. Like dogs.

Wayne whispered to me: "My position is: I'm not supposed to let you leave this room."

"I just came in," I said at my normal voice.

The police person shook his head imperceptibly. "No one leaves the room. This is way above my head."

"I have given you an out," I said in slang, and pointed at the dead one. "He must go!"

I pointed pointedly at the heaping dead thing on the floor, giving my most serious of looks. Strangely enough, it was the fat attorney who spoke the first.

"I'm off this case. I'm shut down."

The atmosphere was rank. I sighed. "You'll get a call by tomorrow evening. You'll find yourself back on the job."

"If I agree to this," said the government man, wanting to lay a hand on my arm, but did not, "the agreement is all inclusive. You don't harm anyone between now and the end of your court date."

Now it was my turn to whisper in the man's ear. I did not want miscommunication. Neither did I require further difficulties with Gath and his staff.

"I have to murder a *few* people," I said. "Strictly for food."

He thought about this. He was clearly upset.

"Let's get this man out of here!" he shouted at the others, nodding towards the body.

"What are you going to—"

"Burn him!"

I don't know who asked that half question, but no one seemed outraged at the expected answer. They were all merely judgmental and highly negative.

"Now!"

Wayne turned back to me and asked quietly, "How many people do you need?"

"How many times a day do *you* eat?" I asked back.

"One," he said too quickly.

I mused, and thought of all the places I had been in my recent years. "San Francisco has a lot of homeless souls on Market Street. Or between the area between Macy's and the Chancellor Hotel."

"What are you doing?"

"Trying to help."

"Don't!"

"These homeless people frighten tourists. I have heard them talk."

The body was going out, so I held up my hand and marched after them. Wayne kept to my ear. The others were forcibly detained from following us.

The halls to wherever we were moving were miraculously free of people. This spooked me a bit. However, the men carrying the body before us knew how to go, so we crept down, down, down into the colon of the courthouse, all the time witnessed by no one. Truth be told, I was impressed by such lack of humanity.

"I can't agree to you killing people," Wayne whispered to me eagerly.

"We are speaking of panhandlers."

"Yeah?"

"There is still a law against panhandling, is there not?"

"…Yeah?"

"Then why is this permitted in highly shopworthy areas?"

"Look, you can't just suck the blood out of—"

"Who else is readily available? It's only for a few days or weeks, until this wretched verdict is obtained."

"Can't you suck on cats?"

"When did you last have a cat for lunch, smart man?"

Even though I had him there, he was neither impressed nor satiated.

We quietly entered a tiny room that had no exits save our entrance. The body was placed in a dark corner, and the door was pushed shut with a creaking thud behind us. At which point all four police persons, Wayne included, drew their weapons and aimed them at me. From another dark corner—well, everything was dark, there were no windows—one of the bald men brought forward something like a scythe. Two scythes, in fact. One of which went to his partner who were now attempting to circle me.

Strangely, though I should have been appalled, I suppose some dark recess of my superego knew this had to happen. These humans cannot give up without a fight. No matter how many films they make of these situations, the people who need to watch them the most never seem to be able to afford to view them. In a way, it was laughable. I did not want to kill any more. Truth. That's what I desired.

Yet the "cops" were not cagey or overconfidence. They carried worry and horror and uncertainty in the stale, uncirculating air. They were forcing themselves to do this. I suppose the FBI pay is that good.

Firstly, with a look and a flick, for their sake, of my finger, I set Magi's body on fire. Not as much for the fact that I would forget to do it later, as for the psychological impact it would have on the others. Rather than rush to stomp it out, they merely became more agitated in their lack of confidence to move close enough to do me harm. No doubt they would fight like a kung fu film, one at a time, when coming at me in bunches was the intelligent way to go.

Yet they did nothing. They were choking on my second reason for blazing the fire: smoke. These people and their need for air! Wayne, gun still in hand, moved to open the door and waved it in short flaps.

I smiled and asked, "If we had not brought the body down here, what was going to be your context for bringing me to this place?"

No response, merely action. Each man lunged, while I turned into a slug on the wall. With all of the smoke and their vehemence and passion for the kill, it's a wonder they didn't harm one another. Well, one man did have another man's arm off with a scythe, but that was it really.

Between the screams of "where is he??" and what not, I decided my time would be better served if I made my way back to Gath to explain. Wayne had slammed the door closed instantly after my disappearance, but some of these roughian types certainly can't think "outside the box." I made myself into smoke to join the other smoke and was out in the hall before anyone said Jack Robinson.

The lawyers were pacing in their own ways. Fred was languid and bemused with a paper that held his eyes, though his mind was so far away. Perhaps in the Bahamas.

I was at Gath's side before he knew it, so he tottered at my voice and I caught him. He recoiled from my catch so his ass hit the ground anyway. Bending to help him up, he scampered. He literally scampered from my touch. I was devastated!

Fred stood and angrily defied me with his face. "What happened?"

"They carried out the first part of your bargain?" Gath asked.

"You really want to see this trial through?" the fat one queried me, like a child.

I was supremely miffed. I gave my arm out to Gath, my thoughts boring directly into his brain. *You've better take it.* And he did—with attitude!

Holly was strangely quiet. I turned to read her thoughts. Her thoughts were of *love.* And concern…

"I can't…" Gath was searching for his words, when the door bolted open. Wayne was there, gun drawn, bleary, weary of spirit. He wanted to cry but was using the smoke as a smokescreen, coughing, dramatically overcompensating for his doltish *stupidity!!*

Later in the evening, around two of the clock, I haunted the head of Universal and urged him to reconsider my case. It doesn't matter how this was achieved, but it was without many tricks or horses, and so the fat lawyer was back in court the following night.

Gath was a further complication. One cannot have a puppet if one wishes originality. I said as much to my attorney early on, and I tried to make him aware that nothing has changed. Nothing *could* change. Not with me. It must only change with others.

The three of us, their child strangely missing, sat in a nice-ish hotel room, the sort that has a living room between two wings of bedrooms, not that they were using both sides. The one he calls Medge sat with her hand in his, willing him power and might and good things, yet archaically blocking herself from using the true *power* that she might. The power—*influence*—that I would not use on my friend.

"Friend!" Gath scoffed.

"Friend," I repeated with my touch of realism. Perhaps I did feel it. Certainly the aura of respect was there. "Why else would I choose such a lowly and un-high powered attorney?"

"Wait. What?" the female asked.

"My apologies. You cannot read my mind. I have a glob of respect for your husband. I viewed him from afar, these many years during which the thoughts of this case grew like watery seeds in my mind."

"…Yeah?"

"Yes. I trust this man." I took his other hand. The flinch of needing to pull away was there from the first trite second, but I deemed to tell myself that he let me touch him to re-establish our friendship.

He shook his head like he could read my thoughts. "It's out of fear," he said.

I slipped back into the couch-like chair and considered. "Fear comes out of respect. I have killed many men to know this."

The woman's eyes began their glistening, tears were coming, so I merely made my point.

"Death is inevitable. But not in the way you might think it for me. No. Gath. You gave me your promise. I have seen you are a man who takes promises and keeps them in a safe place. You have a good heart."

The female tightened her grip on the husband hand. Mushing his plain, ordinary ring deeper into his third finger. Commitment. Shallow life, lived to the fullest. How I sort of envied them.

Gath kept his eyes low and said nothing for a moment. When he spoke, it was with a choked accent, and still his eyes rested on the bedspread. How drab these tired rooms are.

"I'll keep going with you," he said.

I waited. "Well?"

"What?"

"What's the condition?"

"What condition?"

"'On one condition?' Or something?"

He shook his head. Emotionally drained, that's what he was. Hardly the person I hired ages ago. "I can't control you."

"Of course not!" I proclaimed. "When someone…goes to the movies and smells the popcorn, he can hardly contain *himself*. How is it possible to contain *me*?"

"Hmmm. So. Let's just get through this."

He stood and held out his hand for me to shake then leave. Yet I was not satisfied. I shook the offered right hand but did not take leave.

I looked in his head, in his eyes. And he gave me back tired Sly Stallone eyes. His woman got to her sock feet to stand beside her man. Quaintly appropriate. I wanted to be moved.

"Any instructions?" he asked.

I did not think this over carefully. But in the wake of an apology, or some sort, you must make the other party feel that they have something to contribute or that you are interested in their answers or their direction.

I made to consider it, and said, "Do your best."

# chapter last

7:07 p.m.
   Dal put a garlic bulb, a crucifix and a mirror down before Vlad , seated boldly in the witness stand. The entity purporting himself to be the origin of Dracula merely sniffed at these objects. Then he picked up the garlic and *actually* sniffed it, in a curious way. He put it back down again and looked at defending counsel.

"Doesn't bother you?"

"Garlic?"

"Yes."

Vlad shook his head, so Dal said, "For the record, please."

My client turned to the jury and spoke suddenly, loudly, "No!"

"How do you explain that?"

"I like garlic. It's good for the heart." He laughed. "It's also one of the tastiest herbs you can cook with."

"You can taste it?"

"Assuredly!"

"Isn't Dracula supposed to be terrified of or allergic to garlic?"

"That's a myth."

"Myth!"

"Have you ever *read Dracula*?" Vlad held up the garlic, put in his mouth, then spat it on the floor. "Or did someone read it to you? A researcher and Cliff Notes, perhaps?"

"I read the book."

"Then you'll realize it *does* say that Dracula hates garlic in the text. I love it! But Abraham Stoker *had* to change it so *didn't* look too much like me, don't you see? I could've sued his ass back *then*. *He* knew it! You're only proving my case for me!"

"There are myths about everything. There's probably a myth about yo' mama somewhere in the world. Time crawls on and history becomes bastardized. As Dan Brown has proven."

"Okay…"

"But sometimes Stoker gets it right. It's so fucking dramatic, he can't resist putting it in, he can't! I can turn myself into smoke and bats and geese, as I have proven here on several occasions. I *can* only move at night. I *don't* cast a reflection. These are things he stole from *me*! My life!"

The heart was out of Dal now. You could tell. But he pressed on. "Would you consider yourself to be alive?"

"I thought this was gone through. I exist. I *am*! Definitions do not matter in this case."

"You're so right," Dal agreed, sweeping around the floor with his big feet. "You go to the movies often."

"Are you asking me?"

"Do you go to the movies often?"

"Yes."

"You buy popcorn."

He looked at *me*, accusingly. I don't know why. But that's the way he always looked at me.

"Of course."

"Do you get butter?"

"Of course. In Japan and England they have caramel kinds of corn too, so you can get yourself a half and half bucket."

"You—"

"Don't ask me how I digest it."

"No, no, not at all. But you taste it. You get the popcorn because it's good, you like it."

"Some chains are better than others. AMC sucks. Hoyt's is overpriced. The ones where you have to pump your own butter after you have your bucket and you've paid are *atrocious*, but still—"

"And you like Italian food."

"*Excuse me!!*" It was quiet already, but this clinched the fact. Vlad's eyes were wildly regarding the far wall. Could this be his way of controlling himself? "You must have courtesy! This is what is wrong with the 21st century! Impatience, sarcasm, haveseenitallness…the—the lack of respect! I believe in not asking a question unless one is prepared to hear the answer!!" We all waited. "Popcorn can be heaven in certain locales."

"And you like garlic. Does that mean you like Italian food?"

"It does."

"But you are aware of the vampire legends."

He smiled. He and I knew where this had always been going. "There are many, many stories. The vampire myth is an old myth. Stretching, in its way, long before the advent of Edison's motion pictures and Stoker's *Dracula*."

"Yet we are really only concerned with Stoker's vision. Isn't that right? As you claim to be its savoir."

"Savoir! I *am* Dracula!"

And with that, Vlad turned into a bat, then back again. Not *too* fast. Still, none of us was sure it had happened…

It took Dal a moment to recover. Me, too. Even both of us expecting something like this, it was difficult to take when it *happens.*

Hand on his forehead, Dal read from a paper. He had a headache or was stalling for recoup time. Either way, I felt for him. The sympathy of the room—who knows which way it was running.

"I read from the third chapter of Bram Stoker's *Dracula* novel which is in the public domain," he said, "entitled Jonathan Harker's Journal Continued.

"'I had hardly come to this conclusion when I heard the great door below shut, and knew that the Count had returned. He did not come at once into the library, so I went cautiously to my own room and found him making the bed. This was odd, but only confirmed what I had all along thought, that there are no servants in the house. When later I saw him through the chink of the hinges of the door laying the table in the dining room, I was assured of it. For if he does himself all these menial offices, surely it is proof that there is no one else in the castle, it must have been the Count himself who was the driver of the coach that brought me here. This is a terrible thought, for if so, what does it mean that he could control the wolves, as he did, by only holding up his hand for silence? How was it that all the people at Bistritz and on the coach had some terrible fear for me? What meant the giving of the crucifix, of the garlic, of the wild rose, of the mountain ash?'

"That is the first mention of garlic in the novel. Are you familiar with Stoker's *Dracula*?"

Vlad laughed, and laughed and laughed.

Not amused with how long it was taking, Dal merely mumbled, "Let the record show the witness is laughing."

So far there was nothing to object to. Half of me hoped this murdering person......... half of me wanted to see justice done. Not for the murders. Not for any of the *horrors* Vlad had perpetrated. But for him. This man was alive! They *did* steal his life.

"*Dracula* is a story about a count. A vampire. Who seduces. Kills. Drinks blood. He is, to be correct, a monster. A monster against humanity."

"He's a Universal monster," Vlad said, hardly helping his case.

"Objection," I said, standing. "Objected to as prejudicial. This is in essence an identity theft and copyright case, and the personality of the witness or his alleged personality in the form of 'Dracula' from which the book is allegedly based is not under moral fire here, except in direct relation to matching up similarities."

"Sustained," said the Judge.

Dalmonica took the crucifix in his hand and tossed it to Vlad who caught and admired it.

"From that self-same, previous passage that I read," Dal said, "you should be scared to death of that as well. Put it to your face, if you would."

Vlad smiled and obliged. He put the cross against his cheek and made a sizzling noise with his mouth, and hollered and shook in his chair. Finished, he merely smiled and tossed it back to the attorney.

"The sign of the cross doesn't bother you at all."

"Nah. It's not made of silver."

"Does a silver cross have some power over you?"

"Nah, I'm just kidding." He giggled. Yes, giggled. "A vamp's gotta have some fun, right, judgy?"

Was he getting giddy? I just didn't get it. But I couldn't object to my own asshole.

Dal didn't seem delighted one way or the other. "Would you mind putting the cross in your mouth, Mr. Tepes?"

Even the Judge said, "Counsellor, is this really necessary?"

Vlad didn't wait, he just popped the small Christian symbol in his mouth and tried to grin at the jury. Then he spit it onto the back of his hand, and did that child's trick of catching it in his same hand. Several times. He was good at it. He even flipped it off his arm muscle a couple times, and it sprung back onto the back of his hand. What a juggler. Yet he didn't seem to be concentrating much. He was more interested in the reactions of everyone. The jury, especially. Even Dalmonica was impressed beyond what he wanted to appear.

Finally Vlad bounced the cross into his hand and in one fluid motion, threw it across the room where it stuck deep into the wall, just below a light. His face was potent, serious. This was the face of Dracula.

After a dramatic pause or Dalmonica collecting himself sufficiently, Dal laid his hand on the mirror.

"Ah, now this one…" Vlad said, laying his hand on Dal's hand. The attorney removed himself with a speed I didn't think him capable of. Vlad didn't care. He was smiling and admiring himself in the mirror.

"Look," he said, handing it to the Judge.

The Judge looked at himself in the mirror. Unimpressed with what he got. "Yeah?"

Vlad moved up beside him. He was so fast doing this, none of saw him move. Like one of those ghosts in a Japanese horror flick, he was just instantly there. It spooked the Judge. So did having a monster at his shoulder.

"Now look…" he said.

The Judge's eyes were wide with horror, with surprise. Vlad was angling around, like he was looking for something. At last, in a small voice, the Judge said, "I think you should…"

"Yes, yes," Vlad said—

and *wham*, he was there. Back in his seat. Then, he was behind Valerie, the foreman of the jury. She was statuesque and usually undeterred; maybe even bored. But even she had the shakes by being suddenly challenged by the whisperer at her ear. She melted like she *had* feelings, when Vlad breathed behind her, holding up the mirror in front of their two faces. He smiled. She did not. Her hand, in his hand, shook when she looked. She wanted the mirror out of her hand, that much was clear, even from my distance.

Vlad moved from one juror to another, always smiling into the mirror, always seeming to delight in the same reaction that came every time: puzzlement, then wide eyes at seeing what was there. What *wasn't* there. He moved from one juror to another with mortal pace this time, not suddenly. They knew he was coming for them, one at a time. It must be *so* enjoyable to be Dracula.

Dalmonica tried to sum up his emotions, but he was starting to crumble. Just goes to show you that even fantasy can defeat a high-powered paycheck. "Your Honor, what this proves is that *some* of the descriptions from Bram Stoker's book, *Dracula*, are true, and some are not. Stoker researched for years and based his character on folk tales and half-truths, even, as we see now, those dipped in supernatural forces that *are* true."

"Counsellor, this is not summation—"

"Viola!" Vlad said, having reached the end of the line. Now all the jurors were thoroughly spooked. What that would mean for his case, I had no idea. Do you vote for or against Satan's copyright infringement rights? Do you blacklist God for the nearest tornado or Haiti earthquake, if you can catch Him? Who are we to say? We lowly people. These philosophical notions just flooded through my brain as I watched Dal and the Judge saying things, whatever they were. I didn't know. I wasn't listening. I didn't even care if Vlad won or not at this point. Why would Vlad care *what* twelve non-supermen think? Who are *they* to pass judgment on a supreme being? Even if that being is evil. Kills people—

The Judge cleared his throat. "For the record, members of the jury, do you understand this… evidence?"

Valerie stood, or tried to stand. It was like she had on liquid heels. "Your Honor, we have witnessed the fact that the plaintiff casts no reflection." She sat.

"*Casts!*" Vlad shouted, then laughed. He jumped around, flapping his black cape, like he was crazy. It was sweet, in a way. I don't know why the word "sweet" came to mind. "Casts! Yes, it doesn't *cast.*"

He laughed, and sat back down.

Dal reluctantly waddled back over. "Mr. Tepes, why don't you…emit a reflection?"

"Why don't *you*? So there!"

"Uh…"

"I could kill every one of you in here," he answered, brooding. Very manic person.

Dal tried to plow through. "Mr. Tepes, do you claim to be a vampire?"

"No."

"No?"

"That's right."

"How do you acknowledge or explain the fact that you c—emit no reflection in a mirror?"

"In any mirror." He was still seemed half-depressed by something.

"You are aware that the absence of reflection in a mirror or indeed any reflective surface is one of the oldest parts of the legend of vampirism?"

This perked him up a bit. Like it woke him. "What are you trying to say?"

"You claim you are not a vampire."

"I prefer my own definition."

"Let's not haggle semantics, Mr. Tepes. What would you prefer? Murderer? Blood sucker?"

I stood, but I found it hard to defend the indefensible. Whether Vlad knew my thoughts or not, he eventually waved me to sit. "It is true I drink blood for nourishment."

"Isn't that what a vampire does?"

He looked at Dal. "How many vampires have you met?"

"We're speaking in a literary fashion right now."

"Are we? I thought you were asking of my diet."

"I'm trying to label you, Mr. Tepes."

"Label, label, Americans are always on about labeling! I suck the blood out of a man's neck, it makes me gay. I destroy someone's neck, it doesn't matter the sex, I am called killer. Two movies come out at the same time on Truman Capote, and one copies the other, yet the first one there gets the Oscar for Best Impression. Labels are for *jeans*, and even then you tear the outer label off! The label on the inside is the one you can't see!"

Dal paused to try to figure it out, and how to climb back inside the argument. "You don't mind labeling yourself as the origin of Dracula."

"Dracula is *my* family's name, unjustly exploited by Hollywood!"

"You suck blood for food, like a vampire—so it's not the act of murder that appalls you, but the act of theft?"

"Unjustly, in that I have not been fairly or even at *all* compensated."

"No moral claim. This is just about money."

"Damn straight! How much did Francis Ford Coppola make from *Stoker's Dracula*? Millions. Give me my money or give me my name back!"

"Surely the book is in public domain by now."

"So is Shakespeare, done *all* the fucking time, and if he came right back, you'd either pay him, *constantly*, or never do *The Tempest* again! Puccini, same thing. *The Nutcracker*? All those poor little kids, nothing to dance to at Christmas? Then who's the monster?"

The Judge moved forward, clearly worried in his curiosity. "Is that likely to happen, Mr. Tepes?"

Vlad just smiled straight ahead like he was the only one worthy of knowing.

"Let's get back to the rights of studios to use your Dracula name," Dal said. "Your alleged family's name."

"Nothing *alleged*. My attorney has all the documents." He pointed at my table. "This is the age of the digital editor. I'm looking for royalties on everything that ever mentioned my family name, or you can edit it out. It's not going to be easy, I know this. But I've watched enough Hong Kong fight crap to know that you can simply go through a film and redub. You can take the word Dracula out of every point-of-sale display, every character's voice. It can be done."

"You're mostly concerned about film."

"Nobody reads fucking *books*!" He paused to let that sink in. Then, more quietly: "Let Dean Frankenstein Koontz do whatever the hell he wants."

"Isn't that—"

"But when Paramount is sniffing around, that advance nets me a percentage, baby!"

"Isn't that—"

"Even between Koontz and his publisher, *before* the book's written, when he's signing the contracts for all rights! Film rights and *whatever* fucking else!"

It was obvious to all that Vlad was seething. Pure and simple hatred was being contained within every supernatural pore.

Dal waited, then he looked at the jury. They were just as concerned. Personally, I just wanted to leave this place, and never return. I had this raw feeling that this was the last act and everything was going to turn to blood.

But Vlad was so *moody*. Maybe he'd always been crazy and I was just too close to him or too under his spell or whatever to see. He sort of giggled. It *could've* been that since he was finally getting his way, he was enjoying every second of it. He *was* known as an Impaler, so he must've had some cruel streak, even if most of the mass murdering part of it had been dormant these 500 years. I've heard that humor is cruel, so…

The Judge cleared his throat again. "Mr. Dalmonica, it would seem that your questioning is all over the place. I would've expected the witness's attorney to put in some formal objection, or some little squeak."

I stood. "Your Honor, my client wants to state his case, and I think he's doing a fine job of it."

I sat, meaning what I said, though not agreeing with anything Vlad was pumping out.

Vlad. He'd lost his anger and seemed to be drunk. It was all up to Dal now.

His voice was soft. "It seems the key question we must ask ourselves is, what is you, and what is the legend." He was quiet. "Do we acknowledge a classic author's outright theft of a life? Do we—"

"Before we get into a 'do we' list, counselor," Vlad said, his rolling eyes lucid again, "let me ask your legal opinion. If this was 1820 or whatever and Frankenstein was on the bestseller list and in walks the Monster to complain, what's going to happen?"

"Copyright laws of the 19th century were noto—"

"All right then, suppose Luke Skywalker is real and came from outer space and proved who he was and that he'd burned his dad Darth Vader on a funeral pyre and got real specific like that, what would happen to the Skywalker Ranch Empire?"

Dal thought. "Good question."

"Oh I have loads of those. Consider…Zion. This is a planet that Neo and his friends are supposed to love and cherish, when the real glorious reality seems to be their own inner consciousness, not their garbage bag Zion, which I'm sure any three out of four people here would not choose to live in."

"—To what do you refer?"

"I'm talking about *The Matrix*, of course. That is a film about perception, and I don't happen to agree with it. You say killing is what should be our main concern; I happen to kill for food and in a different, highly cool way. Why is your perception of 'most important' greater than mine? If anything, mine should take precedent, since I am a better person."

"You think so?"

"I'm *Herculian* strong. I live forever. Can't you see who is the better person?"

"Murder is not a prerequisite of—"

"Your Honor," I said, standing, "we're getting into a moral issue here—"

"Susta—"

"You're quite right, councelor," Dal said, turning back to the witness. "Have you ever met a man name Van Helsing?"

"No."

"Do you sleep in a coffin?"

"Yes."

"Is there dirt from your homeland on the bottom of this coffin?"

"I can't sleep without it."

"Security blanket, or live or die?"

"I'm always dead."

"I mean—"

"I can't survive without that dirt on my back, right."

"Can you survive in sunlight?"

"No."

"I'm employing the shotgun method here, Mr. Tepes. I'm sure you see why. Some of this is old-school creepiness, based on legend. Some comes from the book *Dracula* itself. Some is a composite. Do you know which questions of mine go with which answers?"

"Let's stick with the word Dracula, then. That's my name."

"Suppose we sue Disney for using the character name of John Smith in their film *Pocahontas*. Would that be alright, if John Smith wants to do it?"

"We're not talking about John Q. Chucklehead, we're talking about *my* family name."

"Do you agree—"

"Do you agree that Dracula is about like Sherlock Holmes? *Sherlock*! Just think about it a minute. Have you ever heard of *anyone else* called Sherlock? Unless you stand there like a dummy and just think of all the countless times someone compares thee to a smart prick and calls him Sherlock, or says 'no shit, Sherlock,' in that crass way *every one* of Stephen fucking King's characters might do!"

Dal considered the point. "We're not talking about Sherlock Holmes." He smiled. "Do you not agree—"

"No, let's *take* Mr. Sherlock Holmes here a moment! And consider the Arthur Conan Doyle estate and how they've been pissed on for a solid year of rain in the United States. This prick Andrew Lloyd Jr. or whatever the fuck his name is—"

"...You mean Robert Down—"

"Yeah, that's the bastard, Robert Downey, Jr., getting himself a fucking Golden Globe for playing a 'public domain' figure and what does the estate get out of it?"

Quickly Dal said, "The Copyright Act of 1976 allows heirs a—"

"Doyle died in 1930 and I only wish I could've been there to get his autograph, I really enjoy the stories. He handed the rights to the stories/characters down to his three children and second wife, Jean, and on and on until everyone dies, but not before the wife, Nina, of a Doyle son establishes Baskervilles Investments, Limited, which also doesn't survive, so the Bank of Scotland picks up rights in 1976 and sells them to—"

"I don't see that—"

"—which comes under the thumb of American producer, Sheldon Reynolds, who makes a 1954 TV series out of—"

"Your Honor—"

"Shut your fucking mouth and *learn*—in 1980 no-shit Sherlock finds he's homeless in the UK because guess what? He's fucking in public domain. *Now* we get to your precious Copyright Act of 1976 by which poor Doyle daughter Jean gets the name back to herself in 1981. And she's a good sport. Like me. She gives her permission for a few decent films that tickle her fancy, like the one where...oh, that one where Watson is the brilliant one. What was that...? *Come on!!*" he *shouted* at the audience. Wow. It was really a production.

Everything settled down a moment, but there were rumblings from the onlookers. Finally a hand gingerly raised itself up and not waiting for official permission, the voice attached said, "*Without a—*?"

"That's it!" yelled Vlad and pointed to the person. He stood, triumphant. "*Without a Clue!* Like *that*. And these films have *official* permission, just like I would do…" He shook his head; I guess thinking we wouldn't ever believe he'd give his permission. "But! In 1997 she dies, and she leaves her great 'namesake' to the Royal…National Institute of Blind People, and they sold the rights back to the Doyle family, who then form a company, and there we are into the present.

"*Now*. Consider aaaaallll that, and the subplot I'm not even getting into about producer Reynolds' wife who says the Sherlock name is hers and has tried to trademark 'Sherlock' and all this, and *still* the Lloyd, Jr. film gets made!" He was counting angrily on his whitey-white fingers. "*Still* there's a Red Bull commercial featuring Holmes and no one even knows they have to license new contracts through the Doyle estate! And still you ask me what the fuck any of this has to do with *me*, and *my* family name, and *still* I wonder how you manage to wipe your own ass and *mouth* with the same hand, you're so **stupid!!!**"

His wild eyes were wide, and wilder than usual. He was *thoroughly* pissed. I mean… I'd never seen him like *this*.

I didn't even notice that it was considerably darker in the room. It was like a raincloud had come in and parked over the overhead, circular lights on the high ceiling. There would've been silence, except for Vlad's seething. Which I wanted to ask him about: why did he need to breath if he was dead? I'd often wondered about that.

At that moment, I felt ashamed. I should've been thinking heavier thoughts. Fearing for my life, or for others, or feeling sorry for Vlad's personal turmoil (which I did). But really, I guess… when you see drama too *much*, you become immune to it. Like those shaky camera action scenes, which Vlad finds appalling, but I don't even notice anymore. And I should. He's right. Shakiness always *sucks,* because you're not given a clear view.

I was doing it again.

I couldn't help myself.

I felt bad.

The Judge cleared his throat. "Can I see opposing counselors in my chambers, please." He banged his gavel once. "Court adjorned ten minutes."

I looked at my watch.

"Your Honor—"

I didn't get to finish, not with that look he gave me. It was the same malady everyone was suffering from. Though the bailiff called everyone to Rise and called out what the Judge just said, no one rose. It was old-man-like time, and no one officially cared. The Judge shuffled off, and we followed.

He was weary when he plopped down in his massive chair. So were we.

"Gentlemen," he sighed… "How long does this go on? Where are we going with this?"

Dal spoke through a gravelly throat. He'd been sweating and even through a *dark* brown suit I could tell he was a marathon runner. "Your Honor, it's after eleven o—"

"And we're not getting out of here until we finish this thing up. I'm tired of it. Aren't you *tired*?"

Dal nodded. "I'm tired…"

"I'm tired," the Judge repeated. "I don't know when this night started. Are we getting anywhere? Where are we going, Mr. Wein?"

Dal said, "Looks like, wherever Dracula says we're going."

"Are we prepared to make a settlement—I mean, rest our case?" I said. "Come on. You can't argue with a madman. He's very…"

"He is," Dal agreed.

"Your Honor," I continued. "It's very possible that we are not alone in this room. Every ant crawling through a crack in the door could be him."

"Can he do that?"

I mused, lost in more thought than I should've been at that moment. "I've been thinking about Godzilla a lot lately. How eventually the monster is destroyed. Or contained…"

That was all I had to say, though my colleagues were expecting more.

"Well," the Judge finally said. "Mr. Dalmonica, I see it's down to you. Do you have the authority to put an end to this?"

"Does he want an end to it?" I asked.

"You're his attorney," the Judge scolded.

"What does *that* mean? That doesn't mean anything!"

All our faces conceded the point. But the others weren't above being hopeful.

"I don't feel that it's up to me," Dal said quietly. "This isn't a case. It's a dictatorship. And I don't see any of us ruling *ourselves* again as long as that entity is alive. Or that man is alive."

"But do you have the authority to make a deal?" the Judge persisted.

He considered the point, and whether he should state it. Cagily, he admitted, "Something has been put on the table."

"What?"

"An offer."

"Oh, come on, man," the Judge barked. "We're not in court now. Can you end this?"

Dal shook his head. "I can only offer fifteen million."

We all took our places in the courtroom, gloomily. There was no way a man *that* passionate was going to go for fifteen mil. We all knew it. That's like…I didn't even *have* anything to compare it to. It was too stupid.

Funnily enough, Vlad was significantly calmer. He and Holly were in chairs in the audience, with the chairs all around them empty. The asses once in their seats were still in the room, spread out and teetering on their feet like anxious cattle. Unable to dare to stay close enough to this mad man and his mate, yet definitely unable to leave such a drama.

That was when I noticed Joma. Just sitting there. I came over, still watching Vlad and his girl quietly conversing.

"Hey, boyfriend."

"You watch what you say," he admonished.

Joma didn't take his eyes off the couple either. They were a fridge, we were the magnets. All of us.

"How long have you been here?"

"Today?" He looked at his watch. "Does it usually go this late?"

I shook my head. Which he didn't see, of course. "I can't place the word 'usually.' What language is that?"

"Yeah, I hear there's some scary shit in here. You know how much the scalpers want for a SOR to this room?"

I just shrugged. "You can't buy a ticket into court. They don't have tickets."

He pointed at the bailiff. "That man's brother is making a fortune."

"Oh."

We sat and watched for a while. The Judge was afraid to interrupt. Vlad was just holding Holly's hand. His head was bent, he looked beat. She was saying something. She did her fingers through his hair. It was strong looking hair. I wondered if you could take a strand out of his head, would it hold up a jackhammer worker or some muscle guy like those Superglue commercials, if you could somehow attach him to it?

Then I wondered how much a strand of his hair would go for on auction. And *who* would win it—a *massively* rich fan, or an LA daddy who would quickly resell it, or some gov't agency with all oriental scientists...

I shook my head.

Joma asked, "What's wrong?"

"My head. My head is full of these..."

"I know, man. It's fucked."

"No. It's—"

"I know, man." He tried to pat my hand in that manly way that is impossible between two men. Shoulders. I guess he should've tried my shoulder. Pat it twice or something. No one was looking at us anyway.

Suddenly. Vlad lifted his head. Not a broken man. No tearful or overcome face, it was just a smile. Not even a thin "resigned to my fate" smile, but a big ol' cheek to cheek one that spooked the hell out of *all* of us.

"...the artists there are in this city," Joma was saying.

"What?"

"Every news station in the world is outside that door, and as soon as these lottery holders pile out, they sell their stories to *every* one. They get fat, and every artist in Tallahassee is recreating it on the news of the world. Did you see the last cover of *The New Yorker*?"

"Oh come on, when was the last time you read—"

"When your face and lanky frame were on it," he said. "That's the last time I picked up a copy."

I looked at him. He looked at me. For the first time in a long time.

"My frame is not lanky."

"It's also not tall as one of the Twin Towers, but there you are, beside your Count friend, he's casting you as his shadow. It's pretty clever. You're both out in the sun..."

Joma's words rolled to a stop, like a giant boulder at the bottom of the hill. Vlad had taken Holly's arm. Her lower arm. Her hand. I felt Joma instinctively shift his weight.

I wanted to say how long I thought she had been under his influence. But I also didn't want to talk about my own missing nights and days and some hours. Somehow it felt like giving up, or admitting that you're not in control. I'm no control freak, but who likes to do that?

I also couldn't betray the silence. It was the loudest noise I'd ever heard, and I hated it.

Finally it was broken by the sound of sucking.

At the place on her arm where a girl might kill herself, Vlad supped from Holly's wrist with all the care and beauty and majesty that I never thought him capable of. When they say the bite and the breaking of the skin and robbing of one blood into another is sensual, they are dead on. You wouldn't believe it.

It was like he loved her.

It had always been a possibility. A highly unlikely one.

And it didn't last a moment. She patted his head, and he drew it back.

But not before kissing her red spot, licking it once, then kissing it—to heal?

Holly nodded, and seemed to say something. No one was anywhere near them, so it was never known what she said to him. A few "witnesses" claimed later that they'd heard snatches of their previous conversation, but that wasn't possible. They were further away than Joma and I and we didn't hear a thing.

Holly stood. Then Vlad flopped himself up a little, like he was Rocky or someone. He twirled his neck. Just a little. He was psyching himself up.

Holly moved closer. Vlad leaned over to his right, just ever so slightly. Giving her room. Letting her come closer.

Joma removed an ass cheek from his chair, then realized he had no gun. No one's allowed them in court. Of course.

Holly bit into Vlad's neck. And stayed there. We all heard the sucking. It was like sucking on a nipple, amplified, because it was the only noise in the room. Who was breathing? I wasn't. Occasionally there might be a "fuck me…" from someone but it was rare.

She stayed at his neck. Vlad made a sound, only once, and it was a sort of release or relief or ecstasy, who knew.

He drew away from her, but Holly stayed in place a long time. She was *so still*. Then she swayed, pausing once only to breathe, twice to catch her breath away from the intake of blood.

There had been a lot of blood. None spilled.

The people on the other side of her, the ones standing, could see *really* well and later gave more graphic descriptions of the sucking. Aliae Johnstonshire in her best-selling *A Red Neck* claimed that "she clutched his throat like water passing through timeless rock. The red of blood bubbled past her two thorny front teeth, her nose smeared with his tainted, evil blood. There were flicks of whiteness in his blood, as if it was diseased, which ran triumphantly down her tiny chin. She held his cheek bones like a kiss. Forever and eternal." But nothing had gone down her tiny chin.

Eventually, everything stopped. Holly kissed her lover—I assumed they were lovers—and she looked at him, a long time. He was staring at her, surprised. Frankly, he looked like a man defeated. Still, there was a twinkle in his eye. The left eye. The first time I had ever seen life or something like it in his stare.

Suddenly, she was holding him by the cheeks, like she was keeping him up. She yelled, "Can we get the air mattress in here?"

The bailiff was startled into speech. "What?"

"Now! Outside!" she screamed. "Right outside those doors there's a—"

She was spitting blood on folks who were venturing too close, and she realized it. Holly held her mouth while she apologized, to keep the blood inside her.

"Now!"

The bailiff went to the door and unlocked it. The immediate hallway was clear; it had to be, it was policy. The bailiff looked. He strained his shoulders further out the door to the left and yelled, "Hey!"

In a moment, a few heavy guys bustled into the room carrying a blown-up air bed. Not the simple pump-up job, this was top of the line. I'd seen it at Target.

These guys sprinted into the room like they knew they were lucky. It was like being present at the death of Jimi Hendrix. They raced over to Holly who was giving mimed orders, so she didn't have to use her mouth. But it was hard. She was still clutching Vlad's shaky form by his head, refusing to let it fall. Chairs were moved. The huge padded thing wearing a large pink-flowered sheet was spread flat out—

And she could release him now. His weak frame eased onto the mattress. He was still smiling, seemingly at peace.

Holly sat next to him, sliding herself up a little, resting on her arm. Now she finally had the chance to do what she'd been dying to do. She wiped her mouth on her sleeve, and almost gagged.

Vlad laughed, "It's horrible, isn't it?"

She just smiled at him. And wiped her hand on his face. The hand with some blood on it. They were staring into each other's eyes like Romeo and Juliet and really, I was moved.

It is so interesting—the *power* of a moment. In that moment, I didn't feel there was a lick of animosity towards Vlad Tepes in the room. And certainly nothing but compassion or pity for his killer or champion or whatever posterity was going to call her.

All faces either streamed with silent tears or there were sniffles. One guy snorted largely, and I thought that was very insensitive.

The couple in love didn't care. They were fondling their hands together, their faces. Holly bent to whisper something in his ear, and Vlad laughed like it was the best dirty joke he'd heard in a while.

The laughter seemed to kill him. He grew weaker, and didn't seem to know how to cope. Holly was there to help. She held his hand.

"Gath," she whispered.

I could hear her, as quiet as it was. I stepped forward, then forward more. I even sat on the bed because nobody stopped me.

To my surprise, Vlad took my hand with his left. It was still like steal. Perhaps nickel. Strong, but,  you know. Dead…

"It's done."

"What's done?" I asked.

"I'm satisfied with the result," he struggled to say. His voice was like a parrot's, I'm afraid. I'm sorry to say it was funny and remained funny and there *were* giggles from the others at this inopportune moment.

"Case isn't over yet," I said.

"I'm over," he countered. Always in control. "The truth is a matter of record now. I've had my say. There's nothing else to do."

"Uh…"

"In your office is 34 million dollars," he said. He looked at Holly: "Right?" She nodded solemnly. "Right. You've done an outstanding job. I got exactly what I came for."

"Uh…"

"You don't need to understand."

"Uh… What am I going to tell the press?"

"That's true," he croaked like a parrot. But he couldn't go on. He just leaned his head down, and to the side.

"What's going on…?" I tried to whisper.

Holly just held a finger to her lips, and looked at Vlad. She kissed him. And almost gagged again.

So, she kissed him again, and kept it down.

She kissed him, again. Softly. On an eyebrow.

She stroked the hair on his ear and said, to me or to him, "You're only immortal if you leave something behind."

"What do I leave?" Vlad asked, not quite unundead yet. Everything he said was slow and like he was coming to the top of a hill. "What do I leave? Dead people? There's no such thing as a zombie. I know. They are popular now."

"I don't understand," I said simply. I looked around. It was like the three of us were trying to keep secrets. Everyone was looking at us. It seemed like there were hundreds of people here, though the door to the hall was still closed.

"He gave me his gift," she whispered.

Vlad put a hand on her cheek.

"I'm not…" Others were crowding around us; sensing Vlad wasn't at his best now. "*You* bit *him*, didn't you?"

She nodded. "That's how it works. Don't believe everything in public domain." And she smiled, at the room. And stroked Vlad's cheek. All the color was coming back into his face. He'd been white for so long. It made no sense. Was this blood, circulating again, now that he was dead? Or re-undead? If two wrongs make a right, if you die and you're undead, does that make you alive again?

So many questions swirling through my mind.

She kissed him on the lips. It seemed to last so *long*.

When she removed herself from his face, Vlad's lips were full, strong, so red. Years beyond lipstick. It was creepy.

She put his head down. Gently. And it broke. In half, like heavy ice. Then it shifted, and broke again, and again like Teutonic plates, which then began sifting like concentrated sand. And his…skin-sand just moved further down, though where it went, I didn't know, because his head was on the mattress. He was just…

going. Particle by particle, he was edging down, but not like liquid. Like… a big block of red pepper paper, sheet by sheet.

And he was gone.

Nothing but clothes.

It would be poetic to say that everything was quiet for a long time after, but even while Vlad was literally breaking up, there were all kinds of ooos and cussings and musings about who would get the cape, and just a wealth of sounds from those who had seen the miracle.

The door got thrown open once he was… after he left, and the room became even more swirling with maniacs. How they got so far into the building, I don't know. Unless they bribed some security. All the press in the world descended on us.

They shoved right in. Too close. And someone was trying to take Vlad's clothes from the bed. With all this stress, Holly just bared her teeth at everyone. Sharp teeth that made them all step back and film from afar.

I looked at her, and she smiled gently at me. No trace of sharp teeth. So I wondered if I was seeing things.

She shook her head.

*Can you read my mind?*

She shrugged a little. How do you take that?

A hand laid on mine and I looked at her. "He really liked you," she said.

When I spoke, it was like a cracked 13-year-old, but eventually my voice changed. "Did he? I don't know anything anymore."

"You don't need to."

"Will you explain it to me?" I asked.

We were sitting in a pub restaurant called The Ack, some Scottish place on the west side, way past the university. A part of town where you could actually buy old buildings. If you like rundown areas.

I'd never been in here. I wasn't sure if I was in here now. My head felt—funny, ha ha. And it seemed like we were in the middle of a conversation, though I wasn't sure.

There were four others around us, in a sort of semi-circle. If those other people were at other tables or part of our group, I couldn't say.

"—box," she finished.

"The what?"

"Check my p o box."

"I'm sorry, I didn't catch that. You want me to check it."

She took my hand, and opened the palm. There was a key in it.

"You're going away?" I asked.

"That was the plan."

"What plan?"

She smiled. "Didn't you hear a word I said?"

"Please tell me he left a note."

"Who? Vlad?" She chuckled. I was startled. For so long, I'd forgotten what even the remnants of laughter sounded like. "Alive hundreds of years and thought writing and reading was boring. Saw too many films, I told him that." She was behaving like a widow on the second day. Which reminded me to ask what day or hour this was. "9:19," she helped, looking at her watch.

"P.M.?" She nodded. "So, it's the next evening?"

"The next evening from what?"

"The last thing I remember is Vlad *dying*!"

She nodded.

"What's going on?!"

I was getting hysterical. She patted my hand, like she didn't *really* hear me, she was just continuing her thoughts.

There was a ring on her ring finger. Great hulking diamond that would build up the muscles in just one arm. "What the f—?"

She looked at the ring, and laughed. "Yeah. That's what I said. But *I* went for the whole 'fuck.' Isn't it nice?"

"It's…"

And it was. But whatever came after "it's" was clutched behind a yawning headache that just wouldn't close its mouth.

"When did…?"

She looked at me with wide eyes. "You didn't hear *anything*! Wow… It works." More to herself: "I need to practice more…"

"You slipped me a mental mickey, didn't you? Just like Vlad used to…"

She nodded. "He taught me. But not well. He was impatient. That's why the court case just… *ended*. Living for the moment. Making love and sucking blood like there was no tomorrow. I guess philosophically, there wasn't."

There was disappointment in my voice. I looked at her with pity. "I don't understand you. Such a…"

"Good girl?"

"Nice person!" I yelled. "You marry—or get involved with—a *murderer*? A blood-sucking killer! That diamond doesn't even look *real*, it's so big! What happened to you?"

She was just looking at the ring. "I fell in love."

That was unanswerable.

Nothing was said for a while. The barmaid kept clear of us, but the truth was, I was *starving*. I didn't notice until the long pause here. But I—I didn't know when I'd eaten last.

And there was blood on Holly's upper lip. So maybe she wasn't hungry.

It was disgusting.

Yet, here she was. *My friend*. What was I supposed to do?

"Just listen," she said. "And no, I can't read minds. But when you're alone in the world. Like Vlad was. Like I was. Poor, and putting myself through…college. Well, we had a lot in common." A long pause, then she said, "So he left me all he had. His soul."

I mulled this over a long while before speaking.

"Couldn't you have kids?" I asked her.

She shook her head. "I'm undead."

"Yeah, but—"

"I never really wanted kids. My career. That's my kid. Now I'll have a lot of time to set the law straight. Make laws. Right injustice. Do some *good*."

"Kill some people, Holly," I said.

She shrugged and said, "Eggs and omelets." Whatever *that* meant.

"The world knows me now, Gath. I can pick and choose. Get some *good* cases. Maybe wheedle myself into Congress. Who knows."

Maybe.

Yeah, maybe.

Even if she's a monster, she could do some good, though. The old Holly. I knew her.

"You're a… vampire?"

"The only one. Tigger."

"What—" I tried to work it out. "What do you…"

She was shaking her head. "There's just one vampire. That's how it works. Forget 80 years of film and TV. You can't just bite someone and become something that superhuman and complex and changed, that's just ridiculous, isn't it?"

"Well…" I wanted to shake my head, but…

"I mean, that's *fantasy*," she said, getting heated up. "There is only one god. Some of the religions got it right. Now, she's a goddess."

My headache was turning massive now. The more I thought, the more burning it became, right over my eyebrows.

"He had no one else," she was saying to the table. Picking at the brown paper coaster. "You're dead, you're shooting the ultimate blanks. Dead people can't have kids, can they? You have to give your eternal life to *someone*.

"I'd wanted power. Money. That's why I went into law. That's why it's done. Yes, and now I *can* make the world a better place. Good from evil, right?" She was trying to convince herself? "Like the ultimate revenge movie. Oh, Vlad loved those. That *Gran* something by Clint Eastwood. And *Sudden Impact*. God, he loved those.

"Strange, though. You know what the *last* thing he ever said to me was? 'Don't let Eastwood direct it.' Funny, isn't it?

"And he couldn't even leave a picture of himself, you know? All that footage of his TV show. Nothing. Nothing to leave. Just a big outline of where he was. Just a huge batch of radio interviews on TV. What good is that? God, he hated radio…

"No one to know you're here. *Me…*"

It was like she was drunk.

I held her hand, and soon, soon she looked into my eyes. Eyes that softened, as she was seeing me again. Me.

"He loved you," she said. "All he wanted was the recognition. Before the end. *You* did it. Now whenever someone hears the name Dracula… I love you for that. Too."

She leaned towards me, and I edged back. My wooden seat creaked, and she puffed a semi-laugh at me. Kissing her finger, she laid it on my lips. And smooched it around in a little circle.

I took her hand in mine, and squeezed three of her fingers. Trying to get her back to reality.

"You're going to have to kill people. Holly. Do you understand?"

She just looked at me.

"Holly? Have you sucked blood before? Do you know what you're doing?"

She took my hand and kissed it, like I was a lady.

"Survival, man," she said. "What do you think passing on a bloodline is?"

She turned my hand over. There were two marks there. Between two of my knuckles.

I was petrified.

She laughed at me. "Don't worry!" And she rubbed them off my hand in two quick movements.

There was a black magic marker on the table.

I laughed.

She was gone.

www.ingramcontent.com/pod-product-compliance
Lightning Source LLC
Chambersburg PA
CBHW051144030726

47504CB00004B/1029